W9-BWI-255

# the eternal ones

WHAT IF LOVE REFUSED TO DIE?

KIRSTEN MILLER

An Imprint of Penguin Group (USA) Inc.

The Eternal Ones

RAZORBILL

Published by the Penguin Group
Penguin Young Readers Group
345 Hudson Street, New York, New York 10014, U.S.A.
Penguin Group (USA) Inc., 375 Hudson Street,
New York, New York 10014, U.S.A.
Penguin Group (Canada), 90 Eglinton Avenue East,
Suite 700, Toronto, Ontario, Canada M4P 2Y3 (a division of Pearson Penguin Canada Inc.)
Penguin Books Ltd, 80 Strand, London WC2R 0RL,
England
Penguin Ireland, 25 St Stephen's Green, Dublin 2,
Ireland (a division of Penguin Books Ltd)
Penguin Group (Australia), 250 Camberwell Road,
Camberwell, Victoria 3124, Australia (a division of
Pearson Australia Group Pty Ltd)
Penguin Books India Pvt Ltd, 11 Community Centre,
Panchsheel Park, New Delhi – 110 017, India
Penguin Group (NZ), 67 Apollo Drive, Mairangi Bay,
Auckland 1311, New Zealand (a division of Pearson
New Zealand Ltd)
Penguin Books (South Africa) (Pty) Ltd, 24 Sturdee
Avenue, Rosebank, Johannesburg 2196, South Africa

Penguin Books Ltd, Registered Offices: 80 Strand,
London WC2R 0RL, England

10 9 8 7 6 5 4 3 2



ISBN 978-1-59514-308-2

Library of Congress Cataloging-in-Publication Data
is available

Printed in the United States of America

FOR MY PARENTS—*if not my first, then certainly the best.*

# PART ONE:
# THE POSSESSION OF HAVEN MOORE

## CHAPTER ONE

*Haven was back. She glanced across the familiar little room. Silver clouds hovered over the skylight high above a rumpled bed. A candle sat on the edge of the vanity, waiting for the sun's weak rays to finally fade. Her gaze returned to the mirror in front of her. She smoothed a strand of her blonde bob and tucked it behind one ear. The reflection in the mirror wasn't hers, but she knew it as well as her own. The big brown eyes rimmed with kohl. The smiling lips shaped into a red cupid's bow. Once again, she watched a slim hand bearing a glowing garnet smooth a robe embroidered with gold. Haven could feel the silk passing beneath her fingertips.*

*The girl in the mirror was waiting. A clock on the mantel over the fireplace was frozen at five minutes to six. Time had slowed to a trickle.*

*Outside, the fall wind wailed. The trees groaned in the park she somehow knew was less than a block away. The crackling fire had banished the evening chill. But the girl felt no need for its warmth.*

*She heard the sound of ladies' heels on the cobblestones below. Her heart fluttering, she scurried across the rough wooden floorboards to the window, careful not to let the heels of her slippers slide into the cracks. She peeked between the velvet curtains. One story below her, on a quaint narrow lane, two women in fur coats walked past, arm in arm. The shape of their hats and the style of their shoes hadn't been in fashion for almost a hundred years. The women didn't stop, and the girl sighed with relief when they finally disappeared from view. The last thing she needed was a visit from her mother on this, their first night alone together.*

*Her eyes darted up to the skeleton of a skyscraper being built in the distance and quickly returned to the street below. A dark figure had appeared outside in the lane. The girl's breathing quickened when the figure stopped at her door and stealthily checked both sides of the street. She heard a key enter the lock downstairs, then heavy steps bounding up to the second floor.*

*In an instant, he was inside her room, his coat and hat in his hands. Auburn hair tousled. Green eyes flashing. Old-fashioned tweed suit slightly ragged about the cuffs. She met him at the door and threw her arms around his neck. He let his coat drop to the floor so his cold hands could find the small of her back. Then his wet lips found hers. She pressed herself against him, feeling the warmth building under his layers of cotton and wool.*

*"I've been waiting forever," she told him.*

*"I'm here now," he whispered as his hands passed over her body.*

*"Ethan," she murmured as the room turned blindingly bright.*

# CHAPTER TWO

Haven Moore stood on top of a footstool, gazing out the open window in front of her and willing herself not to fidget. Over the winter, the anticipation had been building inside of her. Once the weather turned warm, she found herself unable to sleep or stay still. It felt as if every cell in her body were dancing.

Beyond the tall mountains that surrounded Snope City, something was waiting for her, and her impatience had grown almost too much to bear. Haven felt the urge to leap out the window, certain that the wind would carry her over the trees and deposit her exactly where she needed to be. The only thing keeping her tethered to earth was Beau's hand on the hem of the dress she was modeling.

"Haven, get in here and find me that remote control!"

Her grandmother's squawk shattered Haven's concentration. She teetered for a moment, then stumbled from her stool.

"Damn, Haven! When'd you get so clumsy?"

Haven heard a needle hit the floor and saw Beau dip a wounded finger into his mouth.

"Aw, poor thing." She mussed the boy's shaggy blond hair. "I'll be right back. Imogene always sits on the remote. It's probably wedged between her butt cheeks."

"Should I go get a crowbar?" Beau joked. He rose to his full six foot four and offered Haven a wicked grin, unaware he was only inches away from getting scalped by the ceiling fan.

"Keep your voice down." Haven snickered as she threw open the bedroom door. "You want to get banned for life?"

Haven's bare soles pounded against the floorboards. She liked to put her whole weight into the unladylike display. As she bounded down the stairs and toward the kitchen, her mother stepped out into the hallway, wiping her hands on her apron. She shook her head in a silent plea and held up four fingers still sticky with biscuit batter. Haven slowed her stride and let her feet land lightly. Goading her grandmother was a pleasure she'd have to forgo for now. Four months of good behavior was a small price to pay for her freedom. Come September, she'd be a student at the Fashion Institute of Technology in New York City, with six hundred miles and an entire mountain range between her and East Tennessee.

THE CURTAINS IN the sitting room were pulled tight, and even the floral wallpaper looked gray in the gloom. Imogene Snively sat in a silk-covered chair, her spine rigid and her legs crossed at the ankles. Just back from the hairdresser, she sported a silver bouffant that floated several inches above her scalp. Haven stopped in the doorway and let her eyes roam the room, searching for something out of place. A wilted flower snuck into the bouquet of summer roses, or a run that had started in the old lady's hose. She spotted the smudge she'd left on the mirror above the fireplace—a perfect thumbprint in the right-hand corner—and giggled softly. It was a game they played, and today Haven was ahead.

"Something funny?" her grandmother asked in the sugary voice she used to bait her traps.

"No, ma'am."

"That boy still here?"

"Beau," Haven corrected her.

"Excuse me?" Her grandmother's dainty hand reached for the eyeglasses on the table beside her.

"His *name* is Beau."

"I *know* his name. . . . " With her glasses on, she looked the girl over. "Haven, what on earth are you wearing?"

Haven spun around in the low-cut black gown. "Like my new dress? Thought I might wear it to church tomorrow."

Imogene Snively's eyes bulged with indignation. "No granddaughter of *mine* will stand before the Lord with her—"

"Don't have a stroke, Imogene, I'm only kidding. We're making this for Bethany Greene." Haven sighed as she reached beneath the cushion that supported the prim little woman. She fished out the remote control and switched the television on. "Now, what channel do you want?"

"Smart aleck," her grandmother snapped. "Put it on the five o'clock news."

Haven punched a few buttons, and the host of a well-known gossip show popped up on the screen. "I think you're a little early for the news," Haven said. "This all right for now?"

"When did everything get to be such trash?" her grandmother clucked. "Well, if that's all there is, go on then and turn up the sound."

Haven watched the volume bar expand at the bottom of the screen.

"*. . . the nineteen-year-old playboy returned to New York late last night, only a few short hours before his father's funeral was scheduled to begin. Though their relationship had been strained in recent years, inside sources have informed us that . . .*"

Haven's eyes glanced up at the action. A tan, handsome young man slid out of a black Mercedes as camera flashes sparkled in the car's windshield. For a moment, he stared back at the paparazzi, his face dark and unreadable. Then, unexpectedly, a corner of his mouth curled into a grin.

"Ethan," Haven whispered. A blaze ignited at the tips of her toes. As it began to burn its way upward, Haven felt her knees buckle beneath her.

A BARRAGE OF images faded as Haven woke. Her eyes were still closed, and one leg was twisted uncomfortably beneath her. She could hear her mother and grandmother whispering nearby.

"We can't let your girl leave town," her grandmother insisted.

"But it hasn't happened in years." Her mother sounded frightened.

"You weren't here, Mae. You didn't hear what she said. It's starting all over again."

## CHAPTER THREE

The Snively house sat on a wide grassy shelf carved out of a mountainside. Two stories tall, with a fanciful turret that might have held a princess or two, it was the landmark every child searched for when driven into town. In the mornings, the house's white walls glowed in the sunlight and the crimson azalea bushes that circled the first floor seemed to burn like a bed of live embers. By late afternoon, as the shadow of the mountains crept over the valley, the magic of the Snively house turned dark. Even in the gloaming, with lights blazing from its windows, it couldn't have appeared less inviting.

Shortly after ten A.M., Haven lugged an Adirondack chair to the edge of the lawn. She adjusted her large, round sunglasses and loosened the sash of her kimono. The silk billowed in the late-morning breeze, almost exposing Haven's naked backside. Sometimes on Sundays she preferred to go without clothes. As far as she was concerned, that was just as the Lord had intended it.

At the base of the hill, far below her grandmother's grand house, lay all of Snope City. Two hundred years after Haven's ancestors had founded it, the "city" remained little more than a short stretch of shops that sold nothing worth buying. But delusions of grandeur still ran in the family. For Imogene Snively, who refused to travel past the Tennessee line, Snope City was nothing less than the center of the universe. That and casual nudity were two of the many subjects on which she and her granddaughter would never see eye to eye.

With the church bells pealing in the valley, Haven plopped down in the chair and flipped open a large sketchbook. She gnawed on the tip of her pencil, trying to focus on the image propped against her knees—a headless, busty body in an emerald green dress. Prom season was the busiest time for the little business she'd started with Beau. There wasn't a single decent dress to be scavenged for a hundred miles in any direction, and that meant for three months every year, Haven and Beau were the most sought-after duo at Blue Mountain High School. The rest of the time, the other students kept their distance. They were rarely unpleasant, but always wary.

Haven studied the sketch she'd drawn the day before. The green flapper dress appeared familiar. The dresses she designed always did. She wrestled with a sense of déjà vu, trying to recall where she might have seen the gown before. But when she closed her eyes and tried to concentrate, all she could see was the boy on TV. She couldn't understand how, but she was certain she knew him. When he had looked into the camera, it felt as if he had been looking for *her*.

Haven's stomach fluttered, and she slid a hand under her robe to steady it. She still had no idea how much trouble her collapse had caused. Afterward, she'd been too exhausted for excuses. Beau had carried her to bed, where she'd woken sixteen hours later, embarrassed that she'd lost control and frightened by the look she remembered seeing in her grandmother's eyes. When she'd found the house empty, its other occupants already at church, she knew she should prepare herself for the worst.

"I guess they decided not to send you to the funny farm just yet."

Haven pushed her glasses on top of her unruly thicket of black hair and squinted into the sunlight. Beau Decker was ambling across the yard. With his body still toned from football season, he moved with a grace uncommon in boys his size. He flashed the smile that made half the females in town curse fate. "Cover yourself up, girl. You can't go around exposing yourself to every man who stops by for a visit."

"Like *you* care." Haven grinned and pulled her robe together. "And it's not as if the rest of them are lining up to see what I got. Why aren't you in church?"

Beau squatted down beside her chair and surveyed the town. "Decided to let them take a week off from trying to save me. D'you know there are camps out there that can turn kids like me around? Train us to be productive members of society?"

"Productive as in knocking up some Snope City girl and pushing out pups till the day you keel over?" Haven asked, making Beau snort with laughter. "Yeah, well, don't stick around too long. Imogene's probably gonna drag Dr. Tidmore up here after the service is over. What do you say I give him an eyeful? That ought to teach her."

Somehow Beau always knew when to stop laughing. "You think she'll bring the preacher back here? Things that bad?"

Haven nodded gravely. "They haven't let me skip church since I had pneumonia in the eighth grade. God knows what must have happened while I was out cold yesterday."

"What did you see this time? Do you remember?"

Haven let her body fall back in the chair. "I couldn't forget if I tried. I was sitting in a room, waiting for Ethan. Then he got there, and . . . oh God, I hope I didn't say anything I shouldn't have in front of Imogene."

Beau reached up and squeezed Haven's hand. "I thought you

figured out how to keep from fainting years ago. How long has it been since something like this happened?"

"Since Tuesday?" Haven offered weakly.

"What? Jesus, Haven! Why didn't you tell me?"

"I didn't say anything because I was trying to get it under control. I've been seeing the same thing off and on for a few weeks now. I can't seem to stop the visions anymore. And to be perfectly honest, I'm not even sure that I want to." She paused as the memory of the kiss passed through her mind, followed by a wave of anxiety. "It felt *real*, Beau. Like I was *there*. I really think I might be losing it this time."

"You're not losing it," Beau insisted, like a doctor comforting a hysterical patient. "Let's try to think this through. Do you have any idea what brings on the visions? What were you doing yesterday when you passed out?"

"Nothing much. There was some gossip show on TV. They were talking about a rich guy in New York whose father just died. He must have reminded me of Ethan."

"Let me guess. Dark and brooding. So good-looking it makes your eyes ache?"

"How'd you know?" Haven sputtered.

Beau's smile was anything but wholesome. "After all these years of showing no interest in the male species, who'd have thought your taste would turn out so wild? Your mystery boy's name is Iain Morrow."

"How *do* you know?"

"The Internet's only good for two things, Haven. Gossip's one of them. The person you're talking about's been all over the tabloids for the past few months."

## CHAPTER FOUR

Haven dropped the stack of celebrity magazines on the coffee table. Beau picked one off the top of the pile and began to thumb through it.

"You mean to say that your mother keeps treasure like this hidden under her bed and you've never bothered to plunder it?" he asked.

"And risk Imogene's wrath?" Haven scoffed. "She says those magazines are Satan's newsletters. Even my mom won't read them in front of her. If Imogene caught *me* with a copy of the *National Enquirer*, none of us would ever hear the end of it."

"Well, Miss Moore, you have *no* idea what you've been missing. Here we go." Beau turned his magazine around to face Haven. "Let's see if this does the trick."

"Is this really necessary?" Haven groaned, refusing to let her eyes drop toward the page. As much pleasure as the visions could bring her, it wasn't worth the embarrassment of fainting for an audience.

"We're trying to make a diagnosis here," Beau intoned with mock seriousness. "Either you have hormone poisoning or you're hopelessly insane. Don't you want to know which it is?"

"You know what Imogene's going to say about it." As much as Haven hated to bring up her grandmother's theory about the visions, they couldn't afford to avoid the topic forever.

Beau wouldn't entertain the suggestion. "I've already diagnosed your grandmother. I'm afraid she's got a terminal case of evil old bitch disease. Now look at the damn picture!" He shook the magazine at her.

Haven leaned in to study the photo. Iain Morrow had the sort of face that is usually discovered sculpted in marble, staring back at explorers from ancient ruins or shipwrecks. Straight nose, square jaw, wavy brown hair, and lips set in a permanent pout. It might have been a little too perfect if not for the green eyes that glared back at the photographer. Haven realized she had seen Iain Morrow before. His face was on all the magazines at the supermarket that week.

"What do you think?" Beau asked eagerly.

"He's gorgeous."

Haven looked up from the page and was startled to catch sight of her own reflection in the mirror across the room. For a moment, she almost failed to recognize the face, with its pug nose, dark gray eyes, and smattering of freckles. She wasn't stunning, but she was pretty enough. An acquired taste, Beau liked to say, and there were already a few boys who'd acquired it. Haven might have been pleased with her looks if it hadn't been for her curly black hair, which seemed to sprout in every direction.

"Okay," said Beau, rolling his eyes. "Why don't we move beyond the obvious? You feel anything when you look at the picture?"

"No," Haven admitted with a mixture of relief and disappointment. "Not a thing."

"Really? Boy, you *are* a cold fish. That photo's got me feeling all warm and fuzzy inside. All right, then. Let's see what I can tell you about Mr. Morrow. Just let me refresh my memory."

Beau scanned the article, tracing the text with a work-calloused fingertip. He cleared his throat. "Okay. Says here his father was heir to some kind of toothpaste fortune. Iain got all of it when his dad died a little while ago. Nobody knows how much. His parents were separated, and his mother lives in Italy. They don't get along. From what I can tell, Iain was a bit of a bad seed. Got kicked out of a bunch of schools."

"You're getting all of this from a gossip magazine?" Haven felt as if she had parachuted right into a stranger's life. She already knew far more about Iain Morrow than she knew about anyone outside of Snope City.

"Yeah, it's *terrible*, isn't it? So hold on, this is where it starts to get weird—remember a few months back when that musician disappeared?"

"What musician?" Haven asked. "I just told you I don't read all that gossip crap."

Beau glanced up from his magazine, amused by Haven's self-righteousness. He was well acquainted with each of Haven's faults, and he knew gossip would have been the least of them. "It was in the *newspaper*, Haven. Don't be so judgmental. Anyway, this is the musician guy. His name was Jeremy Johns." He handed Haven a picture of a skinny kid with stringy brown hair and a lost expression. His forearm bore a tattoo that resembled a serpent consuming its own tail. "He was a singer. Supposed to be pretty good. He disappeared right after a concert in Los Angeles. That was a few months ago. No one's seen him since."

"What does that have to do with Iain Morrow?"

"He was the last person spotted with Jeremy."

"So?"

"So nothing," Beau said. "But the thing is, Iain and Jeremy weren't all that friendly. And Iain's known to be something of a ladies' man. There were rumors that he and Jeremy had been fighting over the same girl. People started to wonder why they were seen together the night Jeremy disappeared."

"They think this Iain guy murdered Jeremy Johns?"

"Naw. Nobody really believes that. It's just a coincidence. But it makes a great story for the gossip columnists." Beau paused. "Is *any* of this doing anything for you?"

Haven flipped past dozens of pictures, each showing Iain Morrow with a different girl. There was nothing familiar about the boy's beautiful face or his strange story. Yet every time she recalled the way he had smiled on TV, her heart seemed to stumble.

"I don't know," she said.

Beau opened his mouth as if to speak, but all that emerged was a weary sigh. As much as he tried to make light of it, both he and Haven knew just how dangerous the situation had become. Imogene Snively would be back from church soon, and she'd had plenty of time to draw her own conclusions.

## CHAPTER FIVE

Haven and Beau had been trawling the gossip pages for over an hour when her grandmother's car rolled into the driveway. Magazines still littered the living room floor, and as the Cadillac's engine died, Haven scrambled to return them to her mother's room.

Two car doors slammed, and they heard the clicking of high heels on asphalt.

"Why's *he* always here?" When Imogene Snively didn't bother to whisper, Haven knew the pastor had stayed behind at the church. Certain less admirable sides of her grandmother's personality were reserved for those closest to her.

"*Please*!" Haven's mother tried to keep her voice low. "He'll *hear* you."

"We're on *my* property, Mae," Imogene pointed out at top volume. "I'll say what I like."

"Don't go just yet," Haven pleaded with Beau, who'd started to gather his things. "We haven't done any work, and we've got Morgan's fitting tomorrow."

"Then maybe we should work at my house tonight." The boy straightened his posture and plastered a pleasant smile on his face. "Mrs. Snively. Mrs. Moore," he said as he opened the front door and let the two women pass, the younger trailing the older like a shadow.

"Hey there, Beau." Haven's mother couldn't hide her embarrassment, and her forced smile looked more like a grimace. "You have to leave so soon? I was just fixing to make some supper."

Imogene turned a hard eye on her daughter. "Let the boy go, Mae. We've got things to discuss as a family."

"I appreciate the invitation, ma'am," Beau said, gracefully pretending he hadn't heard the old lady. "But I do need to leave. My dad's probably wanting his lunch by now. Six o'clock suit you, Haven?"

"Sure." Haven managed a weak smile, already dreading what she knew would come next.

As soon as the door shut, Haven's grandmother wheeled around to face her. "Haven, you want to come with me to my sitting room? Mae, would you excuse us?"

Neither sentence was a question. Haven looked to her mother, who stood frozen with indecision, trying to determine whether this was a battle she should choose to fight. Haven knew there was no point waiting for her mother to come to her rescue. Mae Moore could stay frozen for weeks at a time.

HAVEN AND HER grandmother assumed their usual positions in the sitting room. In her high, wingback chair Imogene Snively sat with the pinched nose and perfect posture of a meerkat. Haven sank into the center of the overstuffed sofa. On the table between them, a lush bouquet of wildflowers that Mae Moore had gathered slowly suffocated Haven with its cloying scent.

"Do you really think it's a good idea for someone in your condition to keep spending time with that Decker boy?"

Haven snorted and shook her head, half relieved that they were still on familiar ground. "He's gay, Imogene. It's hardly contagious. And what *condition* are you talking about? So I fainted. Big deal. You know I forget to eat when I'm working. Or who knows, maybe I'm pregnant."

Imogene's eyes narrowed. "You're not well, Haven."

"I feel perfectly fine."

"You know that's not what I mean. You remember what you said during your fit?"

She didn't.

"You said, 'Ethan.'"

Haven tried not to panic, but she felt herself beginning to flush, and she knew the telltale crimson blotches would soon follow. There was no way her grandmother would miss them.

"When did you start having the visions again?"

"I haven't had any visions. I just passed out, that's all."

"You're lying, Haven. I can always tell. And I won't let you go off to college if you're seeing and hearing—"

"But *Grandma*—"

"Don't interrupt me. Dr. Tidmore and I had a talk after church today. I want him to see if he can stop all this before it gets out of control again. I'm afraid you're going to have to stay here with us a while longer."

"But Grandma," Haven pleaded, her desperation growing. As she scooted forward to the edge of her seat, her knees knocked the coffee table and the flower vase nearly toppled. "I swear there's nothing wrong. It's been forever since I fainted. This was just a freak accident. You can't stop me from going to school in the fall."

"I can't let you go, Haven. You're not strong enough to resist. The sins of the flesh are a constant temptation."

Haven pinned her hands beneath her thighs before they could throw Imogene's vase across the room. "So they say," she muttered under her breath. Over the years, she had heard stories about her grandmother's wild ways in the years before she found the Lord. The six-month span between her grandparents' wedding and the birth of their daughter seemed to confirm at least one of the rumors. But Haven had never summoned the courage to confront Imogene with the facts.

"Excuse me?"

"Nothing," Haven said miserably.

"I thought so," Imogene said. "You *are* your father's child, Haven. And you saw what happened to your daddy when he couldn't resist the demon of lust. I'm sorry, but it's my job to protect you."

She wasn't sorry. That much was clear. Haven stood up and glared down at the old woman. "You sure this isn't just an excuse to keep me here?" she asked in a slow, steady voice.

"Look at yourself in the mirror, Haven, and tell me if I need an excuse."

Haven reluctantly turned toward the mirror over the fireplace. The flush had scaled her neck, and she watched in horror as it crept over her cheeks.

"I'm calling that Fashion Institute in the morning. They'll refund our payment when I tell them you're ill. And may I remind you, Haven, I am your legal guardian. Until you are eighteen, you're my responsibility."

Haven's eighteenth birthday was ten months away.

## CHAPTER SIX

In the town below, a half dozen cars and twice as many pickup trucks had converged on a gas station. Kids still dressed in their church clothes milled about the parking lot, sipping well-disguised beers and smoking hand-rolled cigarettes. It was a Sunday tradition in Snope City. Later, after the sun sank behind the mountains, the same vehicles would be seen cruising downtown in endless loops that could leave an observer feeling dizzy and disoriented. Though she could see it all from her bedroom window, Haven had never taken part in the rituals. She pretended she didn't care, but the truth was, she'd never been invited.

Somewhere in that crowd was Morgan Murphy, the girl responsible for making Haven an outcast eight years earlier. The two had been best friends until the day Haven had fainted in front of the entire fourth grade. When she had woken, she'd told Morgan about the boy named Ethan whom she missed more than anything and the visions that could overpower her at the very worst moments. Haven watched the confusion creeping across Morgan's pretty face, and she knew she should have heeded Imogene's warnings and never mentioned the things that she saw. But Haven didn't stop. Angry and hurt, she kept on talking until Morgan knew the whole story.

No one said a thing to her face. She was Imogene Snively's granddaughter, after all. But the sleepover invitations stopped coming. Other kids whispered that she was crazy. That she'd said dirty things. Even grown-ups who might have known better looked at her with fear in their eyes.

At Imogene's insistence, Haven was forced to spend two afternoons each week in Dr. Tidmore's office. Her father resisted, but her mother agreed, hoping the new pastor might help them make sense of the things Haven said. Eager to fit into his adopted community, Dr. Tidmore had quickly won the hearts and minds of Snope City. His fiery sermons reminded the town's old folks of the ones they had heard in their youths, and it was a testament to Tidmore's popularity that only a few months after his arrival, no one seemed to mind that he was a Yankee.

Tall and gangly, with a thinning patch of red hair and a face that made up in nose what it lacked in chin, Dr. Tidmore sat at his desk, quietly scribbling notes as Haven talked. Away from the pulpit, he was soft-spoken and kind, and it wasn't long before he had coaxed Haven into repeating the words that had caused so much trouble.

When she did, he didn't seem shocked. Haven had expected the preacher to gasp or grimace or launch into prayer. Instead, he calmly rose from his chair and came around his big oak desk to give Haven's shoulder a reassuring squeeze. And when Haven had dissolved into tears of relief and embarrassment, the squeeze had become a hug.

"I'm sorry you're having such a hard time," Dr. Tidmore had told Haven once her tears had dried. "From what I've heard about you, I can tell you're a very special girl. And special people aren't always appreciated in small towns like Snope City. But mark my words, Haven. One day you're going to find a place where you'll be admired for being different. I know for a fact that you have a great life ahead of you—as long as we can get these visions to stop."

"Why do I see these things?" Haven had asked.

"I don't know," Dr. Tidmore admitted. "Your visions aren't good or wholesome—that much is certain. But we're not going to let anything like a little fainting stand in the way of your wonderful future. Are we, Haven?"

"I guess not," Haven murmured halfheartedly as she stared at the floor.

"Oh, come now," the preacher had said, taking her chin and lifting it until her eyes met his. "What's with all the doom and gloom? I'm here to help you! So what do you say? Can I help you, Haven?"

"Yes, you can help me," Haven had told him, feeling more hopeful than she had in ages.

HAVEN'S GRANDMOTHER WASN'T satisfied with Dr. Tidmore's tenderhearted approach to the problem. It was only a few days later that she delivered her own verdict. Haven was the victim of a demon, she announced to anyone who would listen—and the affliction was a sign. An innocent child should never have drawn such a powerful fiend. The sins of her father were being visited upon her. Imogene instructed the town to pray for Haven. But she warned there would be no salvation until her son-in-law examined his own soul. Ernest Moore, she said, had given Satan access to his own daughter's heart.

That's when Haven began to hear the rumors about Veronica Cabe. The woman was the cashier at her father's hardware store—a buxom redhead who snuck Haven chocolates whenever her parents weren't watching. During the hours Haven had spent hanging out in the shop, she'd seen Veronica laugh a little too loudly at her father's corny jokes. And she'd watched Veronica's eyes trail Ernest from the paint aisle to the nail bins and back again. Everyone in Snope City could see that Veronica Cabe had a crush on her father.

"Veronica likes you," Haven had once teased him as he drove her to school.

"Oh yeah?" Ernest Moore responded in utter surprise. "What makes you think that?"

"She looks at you like she wants to eat you."

"Does she now?" Haven's father had said after a hearty laugh. "Well, I'm pretty sure you're imagining things, Missy. Besides, Veronica's smarter than that. Everyone knows I'm a happily married man."

NOW, IN THE EVENINGS, after she'd been put to bed, Haven listened to the muffled sounds of her father arguing and her mother weeping. She knew people were saying that something had happened between her father and Veronica. Though her father swore he was innocent, the town had turned against him. The scandal led Veronica to flee Snope City in shame, and few people shopped at the Moores' store anymore. They'd travel all the way to Unicoi for a pack of nails or a can of paint. Money was scarce and bills couldn't be paid. And thanks to Imogene Snively, the whole town believed that Ernest Moore's sins had brought Satan to Tennessee.

Once the house was dark and silent, Haven practiced controlling her visions. The very first night she heard her parents arguing, she had whispered one last goodbye to Ethan and then set to locking him out of her head. She learned to empty her thoughts the moment she felt the hot flush begin to creep up her legs. She battled the visions whenever they appeared and prayed on her knees that they wouldn't return.

Haven worked hard, rushing to cure herself before the devil could destroy her family. Eventually her other world grew fainter and fainter until it disappeared altogether. She'd almost managed to forget Ethan's face when she came home from school one afternoon to find Imogene packing her things in a suitcase. Ernest Moore was dead, and her mother was missing. Imogene had been given custody of Haven, and the girl was moving to her grandmother's house.

## CHAPTER SEVEN

For several months after her father's death and her mother's disappearance, Haven developed the curious habit of spying on the citizens of Snope City. She'd hide behind a hedge while Mr. McGuinness mowed his lawn or perch on a tree branch outside Ms. Buncombe's living room while the old lady watched her stories on an ancient TV. She knew that Mrs. Dietz, who claimed to have a glandular problem, hid her Milky Ways in an empty box of laundry detergent. And she'd seen Mr. Melton visiting his sister-in-law's house in the middle of the afternoon when his brother was still at work. But it wasn't just people's secrets that Haven was after. She suspected they changed when she wasn't watching—that the face they wore in public was peeled off when no one else was around—and Haven wanted nothing more than to witness the moment when their true natures were revealed.

She had to give up her new hobby when her mother returned to Snope City. There was simply too much work to be done taking care of Mae Moore. Haven knew that her mother had been rushed to the hospital after she heard her husband had been killed in a car crash. While Mae was missing, Haven was told that her mother was sick in the heart. Imogene said it quickly and quietly, as if eager to get the subject out of the way. Haven knew without asking that she wouldn't be allowed to visit. She imagined her mother lying in a hospital bed, hooked up to wires and IVs as she recovered from a heart attack. But when Mae had finally stepped through the door of Imogene's house, Haven could see that her body worked perfectly. It was somewhere inside that Mae Moore had broken.

Haven made her mother's meals twice a day and sat with her as she stared blankly at her oatmeal or scrambled eggs. Eventually Mae began to pick up her own fork. Later she started to talk again. But the real Mae—the one who laughed and danced and sang as she cooked—never really came back. She accepted her wealthy mother's financial support and even agreed to let Imogene keep custody of Haven. Without a husband, responsibilities, or even a job to keep her busy, Mae Moore became little more than a ghost, condemned to wander the house she'd once escaped by eloping with Ernest Moore.

Practically an orphan, Haven turned to the only person left to trust—Dr. Tidmore. Though it was no longer mandatory, Haven continued to visit the preacher in his office after school. She often brought a few of her latest drawings to show him, which he dutifully examined before announcing that Haven was bound for great things. Sometimes he asked if she'd had any visions, but she always assured him they had stopped. Instead, the two of them talked about the world beyond Snope City. Dr. Tidmore had grown up just north of New York, and he enjoyed recounting his days at college in the city. Haven was astonished to find that she knew when the preacher mixed up his Greenwich Village streets or got his subway stops wrong, but she was very careful not to correct him.

After each visit, Haven would leave Dr. Tidmore's office with the feeling that there was a life waiting for her outside of the mountains.

Once the preacher even gave her a postcard—an aerial view of Manhattan with its dazzling forest of concrete and steel. Haven pinned it to her bedroom wall and studied the picture every night before she went to sleep. As she examined all the buildings and followed all the streets, her sense of certainty grew. Behind one of the windows—or inside one of those cars—was someone or something she needed to find. At times the urge to begin the search was almost impossible to resist, and she prayed that whatever it was would still be waiting when she finally escaped from Snope City. At the age of ten, Haven started counting down the days. When she turned eighteen—when no one could stop her—she would find what was waiting for her among the skyscrapers.

## CHAPTER EIGHT

Even with the town preacher as Haven's confidant, it would have been a lonely eight years if Beau Decker hadn't shown up in the school cafeteria with a Barbie lunch box. Back then he was one of the popular kids—so good-looking, even at that age, that girls blushed and giggled when he glanced in their direction. Everyone knew that his family had fallen on hard times. His clothes were a few years out of date—patched-up hand-me-downs from older cousins. But the pink lunch box with Barbie astride a glittering unicorn was a pristine treasure. Some of the girls watched with envy as Beau proudly opened it and pulled out a sandwich. The rest of the kids knew something was wrong, even if most of them couldn't have named it. Remarks were made. Haven heard the word *faggot*. Someone got pushed. Then a melee of epic proportions broke out.

Beau took down three older boys with perfectly aimed punches before a group of seventh graders overwhelmed him. Teachers dragged them off Beau, whose face was bloody and eyes wild. As the combatants were escorted to the principal's office, Haven crawled through the slurry of spilled milk and trampled food to retrieve the Barbie lunch box from beneath a table. She rinsed it out in the bathroom sink, carefully dried it, and fixed the dents as best she could.

When Beau's father arrived to collect his son from the principal's office, Haven was waiting. She held out the lunch box to the tall boy with two black eyes and blood caked in the corner of his mouth. He smiled at her as he took it, and Haven's heart started beating for the first time in months. Whatever he'd done, (and Haven couldn't figure it out), Beau Decker was not ashamed.

AFTER THAT, HAVEN and Beau became inseparable, and her friendship with Dr. Tidmore slowly faded away. The preacher counseled Haven to keep her distance from Beau. He wasn't a good influence, Dr. Tidmore insisted, and he shared his opinion with Imogene Snively, who lectured Haven on rotten apples and bad seeds. But Haven refused to be swayed. Once she'd found Beau, she wasn't about to let him go. And she spent the next eight years trying to convince herself that one loyal friend was all she needed.

But there was still something missing. Something that nagged at her—an emptiness she couldn't explain. There were mornings she woke with her heart pounding wildly and the sensation of arms wrapped around her. But the feeling slipped away the moment she opened her eyes, and no matter how quickly she squeezed them shut, she couldn't recapture the contentment she'd felt.

In the ninth grade, she watched her classmates begin to pair off, until she and Beau seemed the only ones left. Not that Haven didn't have her share of admirers. Throughout their sophomore year, Bradley Sutton had pursued her with a passion that was evident to all but his girlfriend, Haven's former friend Morgan Murphy. Had Haven accepted his affection, it would have ensured her a place among their school's most popular students. But Haven turned him down. She knew there was someone out there for her, but whoever he was, he certainly wasn't a student at Blue Mountain High School.

With no social life to speak of, Haven was free to throw herself into the business she'd launched with Beau freshman year. To their surprise and relief, it had flourished immediately. Having promised his ailing mother that he'd attend Vanderbilt University, Beau needed money for school. Haven had her own reasons for working. She told Imogene she wanted to help pay for college in New York. But in truth, Haven had always suspected she'd need ready money for the day her destiny finally revealed itself.

When the visions had returned, Haven had known it was almost time. She pored over her savings account statements when they arrived in the mail, ensuring that the twelve-thousand-dollar escape fund she'd stashed away was still safe in the coffers of the First Citizen's Bank. Now, thanks to Imogene, it would stay there just a little bit longer.

## CHAPTER NINE

The bedroom door creaked opened, and timid footsteps crossed the room.

"I've got something for you, Haven." Splayed across her bed with her eyes squeezed shut, Haven refused to acknowledge her guest. She didn't need to look to see her mother's stooped figure and anxious smile. It was a posture that made the best people want to protect her and the worst want to kick her.

"I know you're upset about school and all. But I think you might want a look at this," said Mae Moore, this time in a whisper. Haven opened a single eye and saw her mother clutching a shoe box to her chest.

"What is that?" Haven threw her legs over the side of the bed and drew herself upright.

Her mother sat down beside her. Her gaunt cheeks were flushed and her eyes flashed. For the first time in years, she almost looked alive. Her hands caressed the box as if it were human skin.

"Something Ernest did a long time ago. I brought it with us when we moved here. Mother doesn't know about it. But I thought it was time you took a look."

Goose bumps sprouted on Haven's arms. Mae Moore had mentioned her husband only a handful of times since the accident. Hearing his name spoken aloud was like hearing someone summon a spirit.

When Haven was younger, while her father was at work, her mother had told her countless stories. How she'd met Haven's father on his very first day in town. How they'd eloped three weeks later, young and poor and crazy in love. How he'd slaved fifteen hours a day to earn the money to open his store. Haven hadn't found it hard to believe that the hero of all of Mae's stories was the man with a crooked nose and an unruly thatch of curly hair who shared their home. When seen through her mother's eyes, Ernest Moore was the very picture of perfection—the fairy-tale prince who had rescued Mae from a wicked witch and with whom she was fated to live happily ever after.

The stories had stopped after Ernest Moore's death. But Haven sometimes wondered if Mae Moore still told them to herself late at night when she didn't think anyone could hear her crying.

MAE MOORE SLID the box onto Haven's lap. Afraid at first to touch it, the girl let it sit there for a moment, heavy as granite slab. Its exterior was warped and stained, and when Haven looked inside, she found it stuffed with paper. Scraps torn from notebooks. Pieces of copy paper folded into tiny squares. Words scribbled on gas station receipts. Haven reached into the box and pulled out a propane bill. Her father had used the other side to print out the draft of a letter he'd written. Haven skimmed across the paper and landed on a line halfway down the first page. "*Ethan's not a doll. He's* real."

"Oh my God." Haven's eyes met her mother's. She knew in an instant how much Mae Moore was risking.

"He wrote it down," Mae whispered. "Every word you ever said. He never believed there was anything wrong with you."

"What about you?" Haven pressed her mother. "Do you think there's something wrong with me?"

Mae Moore studied her hands, which lay clenched together in her lap. "No," she admitted. "I don't. And after you take a look at all that, you might not, either."

Haven watched silently as her mother rose and prepared to leave the room.

"I'm sorry, Haven," Mae said before she left. "I shouldn't have kept it hidden so long."

The door closed. Haven's eyes returned to the box that lay in her lap, and she picked out another scoop of paper. Soon the things Haven had tried to forget began coming back to her.

## CHAPTER TEN

[Draft letter dated December 7, 2001]

*The Ouroboros Society*
*17 Gramercy Park South*
*New York, NY 10003*

*To Whom It May Concern:*

*Let me start by saying I was raised Christian, and I spent the first twenty-eight years of my life without thinking much on the subject of past lives. But I'm not the sort of man who refuses to see something that's staring him right in the face.*

*Ever since she was a tiny little thing, my nine-year-old daughter's been talking about someone named Ethan. The first time I caught her, I was walking past her bedroom. The door was open a crack and I heard her whispering. I remember she was sitting on the floor with her dolls around her talking to someone I couldn't see. Her eyes looked all glassy, like she was in some kind of trance. She said:*

*"Remember that time you kissed me by the fountain?"*

*"What was that?" I asked, and Haven jumped like I'd caught her in the middle of something. "Who are you talking to?"*

*"Ethan."*

*"Which one is Ethan?" I thought she was talking about one of the dolls, which made her laugh.*

*"Ethan's not a doll. He's real."*

*"Well then, if he's real, where is he?"*

*"Dead," she said.*

*As you might imagine, that answer of hers sort of threw me for a loop. But Haven's always been a little eccentric, and I figured she just had an imaginary friend until I finally got around to asking a few questions. The first thing she told me was that she needed to find this boy named Ethan. When I asked her where she thought she might find him, she was sure he'd be in New York. She said he'd be waiting for her. She kept on talking, and I realized she knew all sorts of things she shouldn't have known, like the names of different parts of Manhattan. Nobody in our family has ever been anywhere near your city, but when I looked up the neighborhoods on the Internet, I found out she was right. I wondered if she might have been watching too much TV. But some of the stores and restaurants she mentioned hadn't been around since the 1920s. There's no way she could have seen them on any of the shows she watches.*

*That's when I began to think that Haven might be remembering another life. I've been trying to write down the conversations I have with her. There haven't been too many so far. Haven's always been a little pigheaded, and she won't always answer my questions. But I've started . . .*

The page ran out, and the rest of the letter was lost.

[Written on the back of a receipt for $9.00 from Cope's Gas and Mini Mart]

*"When did you meet your friend Ethan?"*

*"A long time ago when I was big."*

*"You mean an adult?"*

*"Yep."*

*"And where did you meet Ethan?"*

*"In the Piazza Navona."*

*"Is that somewhere in Italy?"*

*"It's in Rome. I got lost. My mother and I were looking at the fountains and then she was gone and I couldn't find my way back to the hotel."*

*"Your mama Mae?"*

*"No, silly! My other mama. The one from before."*

*"What was her name?"*

*"Elizabeth."*

*"Elizabeth what?"*

Haven looked all frustrated, and I was afraid she'd stop talking. *"I don't remember right now."*

*"What's* your *name?*

*"Constance."*

*"Okay, Constance. So you met Ethan in Italy?"*

*"He found me in the piazza. He said he'd been looking for me."*

*"But I thought you were talking about the first time you met."*

*"I am."*

*"So you met him for the first time, and he said he'd been looking for you?"*

*"Yep."*

*"Were you scared?"*

*"A little bit."*

*"What did you think?"*

*She smiled and turned bright red like she does. "I thought he was the most beautiful person I'd ever seen."*

[Written on the bottom of a spelling test. Date at the top: September 15, 2001]

*"You told me that you met your friend Ethan in Italy. Is that where you used to live?"*

*"No. I lived in New York by the big lake in the park. We used to row boats there."*

*"You mean you and Ethan?"*

*"Yep."*

*"So Ethan was from New York too?"*

*"No, Dr. Strickland brought him to New York. That's where I met him when I got back from Rome. At Dr. Strickland's house."*

*"Dr. Strickland? Why did Ethan need a doctor? Was he sick?"*

*"No, Daddy! Dr. Strickland had a club for people who remembered things."*

*"People who remembered things? What sort of stuff did they remember?"*

*"Who they'd been. How they'd died. That kind of thing."*

*"The sort of stuff you remember now?"*

*"Mmhumm."*

*"What about Ethan. What did he remember?"*

*"Ethan remembered everything."*

*"What do you mean, everything?"*

"Everything, *Daddy."*

[Spiral notebook paper]

*Just got up at four A.M. and found Haven with a suitcase packed full of dolls.*

*"Where are you fixing to go?"*

*"We're going back to Rome."*

*"In the middle of the night?"*

*"Tomorrow. Right after we're married."*

*"You and Ethan?"*

*"Yes."*

*"I thought your parents didn't like him. Did your father finally give you his permission?"*

*"He doesn't know."*

*"So you're going to elope?"*

*"Well, we can't stay here!"*

*"Why not?"*

*"You've heard what everyone's saying about Ethan."*

*"No, I don't think I have."*

*"Well, if you don't know, I'm not going to tell you!"*

*And that was all I could get out of her. Once her suitcase was filled with dolls, she lay down on her bed and went right back to sleep.*

[Draft e-mail dated October 8, 2001. Not addressed. Second page not found]

*I took Haven up to Mae's mother's house this afternoon. The boy who rakes Imogene's leaves broke his leg, so I was volunteered for the job. Haven helped for a little while before she set to jumping around and making a mess. When I had all the leaves in a pile, I got a couple of sticks and some marshmallows. I figured me and Haven could roast them while the leaves burned.*

*I put a match on the pile and it went up in flames. Haven was a little too close, and I told her to step back, but she didn't move. She was just standing there with her eyes fixed on the fire and a look on her face that scared the hell out of me. I was about to grab her when an ember landed on her dress. It hardly even made a mark, but she started screaming like she was being burned alive. Later that night, I woke up to find Haven poking me.*

*"Do you smell smoke?"*

*"Smoke?"*

*I thought there might be a fire in the house until I saw the glazed look in her eyes. She ran to the window and looked down at the yard. . . .*

## CHAPTER ELEVEN

Haven lay on her bed with the last scrap of paper still clutched in her hand and her brain filled with little but static. Each of her father's notes had been a small bomb. Together they had blown away Haven's reality. Suddenly she was no longer just Haven Jane Moore, daughter of Ernest and Mae. If the notes were to be believed, she had once been someone else. A girl named Constance. And her visions weren't fantasies or hallucinations. They were scenes from a past that was every bit as real as the present.

The whole notion was going to take some getting used to. Haven was almost certain that the word *reincarnation* had never been spoken in her presence—by her father or anyone else. She had come across the idea in books, of course, and she knew it played a role in any number of faiths. And she knew hers wasn't one of them. Still, she had to admit, reincarnation was far more appealing than the alternatives. Deep down, Haven had always worried that she might be insane or possesed by a demon. It was a relief to finally have a third option on the table.

As Haven listened to the chorus of crickets and frogs outside her window, a thought drifted through her mind. If her visions were showing her real events—then Ethan must have been real too. Haven dug back through her father's notes until she found the letter he'd written.

*The first thing she told me was that she needed to find this boy named Ethan. When I asked her where she thought she might find him, she was sure he'd be in New York. She said he'd be waiting for her.*

The idea jolted Haven to her feet. If Constance had died and returned to earth as someone new, then Ethan must have come back as well. And Haven was supposed to look for him. She stood electrified in the center of her bedroom, her heart pounding and hands shaking. She thought of the boy she'd seen on television just moments before she had fainted. Could Iain Morrow be the person she was meant to find? She couldn't deny that there had been something about his smile that had recalled Ethan's lopsided grin. And he *did* live in New York. . . .

And yet Haven refused to believe it. The idea was all too strange to take seriously. The Ethan that Constance had loved would never have returned to earth as a billionaire murder suspect. Haven dropped down on the mattress and squeezed her eyes shut, hoping she could summon a vision. Another visit to Constance's life might provide a clue that could lead her to the real Ethan. But the visions refused to arrive on cue. Finally, after tears of frustration, Haven fell asleep next to the box filled with her father's notes.

EARLY IN THE MORNING, she began to smell smoke. Choking and wheezing, she tried to force her eyes open, but she found herself pulled further and further into the darkness, until she emerged on the other side.

* * *

*She was in the familiar room again. The flames were getting closer, and she could smell her hair beginning to singe. She crashed through the room, knocking over furniture, searching through the smoke. She caught a glimpse of movement out of the corner of her eye. It took her a second to recognize the blonde girl with a soot-covered face as her own reflection in the vanity mirror.*

*"Ethan!" she heard herself scream. The panic took over. She couldn't get enough air. "Ethan!"*

*She felt his arms envelop her just as a terrible cracking noise came from above. Something hit her. And then it was over.*

## CHAPTER TWELVE

"Oooh. You don't look so good," Morgan Murphy informed her. "You aren't coming down with something are you?"

Haven had been staring at the wall of the home economics classroom, waiting for Beau to finish pinning Morgan's prom dress. The girl must have heard about her latest fainting spell, Haven realized without surprise. Few secrets survived the Snope City gossip mill, and Imogene loved to talk.

"Don't move, Morgan," Beau ordered gruffly. "Unless you want a dozen pins sticking out of your pretty little back."

"I'm fine," Haven insisted, refusing to let eight years of resentment bubble up to the surface. "Never felt better. What do you think?"

She yanked the sheet off the full-length mirror and let the voluptuous blonde admire her new dress. Emerald green wasn't the color Haven would have chosen for her, but Morgan always got her way. She'd also insisted on a neckline that showed a little more cleavage than was customary at a Blue Mountain prom. But for the four hundred dollars Morgan was paying, Haven would have designed her a sequined bikini.

Ignoring Morgan's *oohs* and *ahhs*, Haven gazed at her own ghostly reflection. She hadn't bothered to tame her black curls that morning. The circles under her eyes were the color of eggplant, and the freckles sprinkled across her nose resembled some exotic strain of skin disease. The face had never really felt like her own, and now Haven knew why. She turned to the window, trying to forget the fire still raging in her head. Outside the classroom the kids from the neighboring elementary school were at recess. Haven watched them kick up little orange clouds of dust as they zigged and zagged across the dry dirt field.

"You know, Beau, Bradley says there's a guy over in Unicoi who's like you," she heard Morgan remark.

"Like what?" Beau responded, adding a few pins to the back of the dress.

"*You know*." Morgan giggled. "Homo*sex*ual. Maybe you two could go out on a date. Ouch! Was that a pin?"

"Yeah, sorry. I slipped," Beau said. "I'm not looking for love right now, Morgan. And even if I was, I doubt I'd go looking in Unicoi. I like men with a full set of teeth."

"Is that some sorta sex thing?" Morgan asked coyly just as Mrs. Buchanan entered the classroom with a cake tray balanced on one meaty hand.

In the past, Blue Mountain High School's domestic diva hadn't had much time for Haven and Beau, and they were both surprised when Mrs. Buchanan had offered to lend them her room for fittings at the end of the school day. Her change of heart had coincided with her husband's brief stay at the Johnson City Regional Hospital. She had riddled his backside with BB pellets after catching him slipping the sausage to her cousin Cheryl. Charges were never pressed, but Mrs. Buchanan's unfortunate brush with small-town infamy left her a little more gracious toward the likes of Beau and Haven—though neither expected the goodwill to last.

"Don't you think that dress is a little revealing, Morgan?" Seated at her desk, Mrs. Buchanan began decorating her cake with dainty frosting rosettes. "You know what they say about giving the milk away for free."

Morgan smiled serenely at the large, prissy woman. "Oh, you're just old-fashioned, Mrs. Buchanan. This is what you got to do to *keep* a man these days."

"We designed it to be practical," Haven added hastily before Mrs. Buchanan had a chance to catch the girl's gist. "So Morgan can wear it to work after she graduates."

Beau snickered and Morgan looked confused. "I don't get it," she said. "I'm marrying Bradley. Why would I want a *job*?"

"You're all done, Morgan!" Beau announced, abruptly putting a stop to the conversation. "We'll finish up the alterations tonight and have the dress to you first thing in the morning."

"*Thanks*, y'all," Morgan chirped as she disappeared behind the changing screen. "You know, I'm so glad you guys go to school here! Everybody else is so darn *normal*." She emerged wearing a pair of tight jeans, a tank top, and an earnest expression. Like most Southern girls, Morgan was an expert when it came to killing with kindness, and she was about to deliver the death knell. "Anyways, you take good care of yourself, Haven Moore. Blue Mountain *needs* people like you!"

"Thanks," Haven managed, snatching the dress from the busty blonde and wishing she could strangle her with it.

AFTER MORGAN WAS GONE, Haven and Beau carried their supplies out to the parking lot without a word passing between them. Once they had climbed into the Deckers' ancient truck, Beau put his key into the ignition but didn't fire up the engine.

"There something you want to talk about, Haven?" he asked. "You've been kinda quiet all day."

"I'm just thinking," she said. Haven didn't know how to tell Beau what she'd learned when it still didn't make any sense to her.

"Does this have something to do with your imaginary boyfriend?"

"Maybe."

"You planning to let me in on the secret?"

"Eventually," Haven said with a halfhearted smile.

"I'll let you keep thinking until we get up to the house," Beau informed her. "Then I'll get it out of you one way or another. You know my dad taught me a few of the interrogation techniques he picked up in the Army. I've been looking for a chance to test them out."

Gazing out the passenger window at the mountains in the distance, Haven didn't bother to laugh at the joke.

THE GRAVEL ROAD to the Decker house was pitted with craters, and Haven bounced in the seat of Beau's truck. The fields surrounding the old Decker farmhouse had been sold off long ago, and now it sat at the edge of an enormous trailer park. A squad of little boys on mud-splattered dirt bikes patrolled the narrow roads, a few mangy hunting dogs chasing behind them.

Beau parked the truck by the Deckers' listing tobacco shed and Haven pulled the cardboard box filled with fabric from the back.

"That you, Haven Moore?" a voice called out from inside as Haven climbed the stairs to the front porch.

"Hey there Mr. Decker," Haven replied. An older, more weathered version of Beau strode out onto the porch. One sleeve of the man's work shirt was pinned up and out of the way. "We've come to fit you for your gown."

Ben Decker laughed as he held the screen door open for Haven. "I'm afraid I don't have the figure to do justice to one of y'all's dresses."

"Aw, you don't have to act all modest for us," Beau said. "I've heard the ladies down at the fabric shop talking about you. From what I gather, they're great admirers of your figure."

Beau was joking but he wasn't exaggerating. Ben Decker might have left an arm behind in Kuwait, but most women in Snope City still considered him the handsomest man in town. His only competition would have been his son, had Beau not been disqualified from the running.

Beau's father clicked his tongue in mock exasperation as he gave Haven a warm hug. "You going to let him tease an old man like that? It's downright cruel."

"I'm not teasing you," Beau insisted. "And a couple of them ladies ain't too bad looking, either."

"I'll be the judge of that." Ben Decker's ears turned bright red. "You two best mind your own damn business."

"Just a suggestion," Beau said, chuckling as he led the way to the kitchen at the back of the house. Cozy and warm, it was Haven's favorite place in the world. She loved the old porcelain stove, the wooden table decorated with a century's worth of knife marks and water stains, and the pool-blue curtains they'd sewn for the windows. Beau had assumed housekeeping duties after his mother had died of cancer three years earlier, and Haven always marveled at how well he'd done on so little money. The boy had a talent for making things beautiful.

"So. What's been eating at you?" Beau said as he slid their box of supplies onto the table.

"Imogene's not letting me go to school in the fall."

"You're kidding." Beau paused as if waiting for a punch line.

"Nope."

Beau leaned back against the sink and watched his friend. "What are you going to do?"

Haven shrugged. "Listen—you remember any of the stuff I used to talk about when I was little?"

"Not really," Beau said, thrown by the sudden change of subject. "Your visions had pretty much stopped by the time we became friends.

But you told me all about Ethan and Constance, of course."

"D'you remember if I ever mentioned a fire?"

Beau thought for a moment. "No. Don't remember anything about a fire. What's this all about, anyway?"

"My dad wrote down everything I said when I was little. Mom gave me a box filled with his notes, right after Imogene decided to ruin my life."

Beau stood bolt upright. "She had something like that all this time, and she never showed you?"

"She didn't think I was ready to see it."

"Well, what'd you find out?"

Haven reached into her back pocket, pulled out a folded sheet of paper, and began to read.

*"Haven's always been a little eccentric, and I figured Ethan was just an imaginary friend until I finally got around to asking a few questions. . . . That's when I began to think that Haven might be remembering another life."*

"Whoa." Beau looked as though Haven had just announced that aliens had landed on the front lawn.

"That's what I thought," Haven said, her confidence fading a little. "I told my dad that my name used to be Constance. And that I lived in New York. Ethan was my boyfriend."

"Let me see that." Beau took Ernest Moore's letter from Haven's hands. He sat down at the table, and Haven watched as his eyes tracked the words to the bottom of the page and then started all over again. "Do you really believe in this reincarnation stuff?" he asked when he looked up at last.

"What do *you* think?"

Beau ran a hand through his blond curls. "I don't know, Haven. I guess I just need a little time to wrap my head around all this. I mean,

I don't think you're crazy—and I'm *pretty sure* you're not in league with the devil. But I was brought up to believe that God judges each of us. And I have faith there's a heaven, even if most people in this town wouldn't want to see me there."

"Me, too!" Haven exclaimed. "But you got to admit it kinda makes sense. How else would I know about places I've never been? And . . ." She paused.

"What?"

"Well, I think I might be having the visions for a reason. I'm pretty sure I'm supposed to find Ethan. That's what I told my dad when I was little."

"Ethan? You think he's still around? Wouldn't he be awfully old for you by now? I mean, even if he is real, at the very least he'd be pushing a hundred and ten—"

Haven cut him off. "I had another vision last night. There was a fire. That's how Constance died. I think it killed Ethan, too. And I think he's been reborn, just like me. I have to find him, Beau. And you have to help me. I can't explain how, but I know he's out there."

"Right." Beau's blue eyes locked on Haven's. "So you're telling me that Ethan's your *soul mate* or something?"

Haven frowned and looked away. "Well, it does sound kind of cheesy when you put it that way."

"I'm not trying to make it sound cheesy," Beau said softly. He folded Ernest Moore's letter and slid it across the table to Haven. "I think it's kind of a nice idea. Totally insane—but nice. But where do you suppose we should start looking for Mr. Right? Johnson City? Unicoi?"

"Funny. He's in New York. You read my dad's letter. He said I told him that Ethan would be waiting for me in New York."

"Wait a second. *Now* I get it." Beau looked as smug as a TV detective who's just solved a crime. "You forget I can read your mind, Haven Moore. You think Ethan's come back as Iain Morrow, don't you?"

"I do not!" It seemed even more ridiculous when Beau said it.

"Oh, yes, you do," Beau teased her. "But don't worry. You don't have to admit it yet. I just hope *my* soul mate turns out to have a billion dollars and the face of a Greek god."

"Be serious for a moment," Haven pleaded. "You don't think this whole thing is crazy, do you?"

"No crazier than demonic possession, I guess," Beau said with a shrug. "At least you didn't claim you were Cleopatra in your past life. But how does reincarnation work, anyway? Why would God keep sending us all back to this screwed-up planet?"

"I have no idea. Maybe God sends people back if they still have something to figure out," Haven mused. "You know, maybe that's why you're gay. Maybe you were a woman in your last life and you were terrible to lots of guys, so God sent you back so you can see what it's like on the other side."

"I was *not* a woman," Beau snarled. For someone so good-natured, he could be surprisingly quick to quarrel. "Are you saying being gay is some kind of punishment? You sound just like Tidmore! Do you want me to help you find your damn soul mate or not?"

Haven winced. "Sorry, Beau. That didn't come out right, did it? It's just that this all makes me wonder if *I'm* being punished. Why else would I have been born into Imogene's family? I must have murdered a whole town."

Beau grinned, his anger gone. "So who do you suppose Imogene was last time around?"

"Oh, that's easy." Haven laughed. "Attila the Hun."

## CHAPTER THIRTEEN

"*Haven*, what in G—O—D's name are you doing?"

"Going up to the attic, Grandma." Haven paused halfway up the ladder and looked down at the old woman who was twisting her pearls into a garrote.

"For *what*?" She had been following Haven around since Sunday, sniffing for signs of demons. Haven was prepared.

"I'm blocked. . . ." she started to say.

Imogene's face wrinkled with disgust. "Well, how is going up to the attic going to help with *that*?"

Haven rolled her eyes and let loose a theatrical sigh. "I'm *creatively* blocked. I can't come up with any new ideas for dresses, and one of the juniors wants something '80s style. So I thought I'd look at some of Mama's old stuff."

"You aren't planning to rip anything up are you?"

"No, Imogene!" Haven insisted. "I'm not gonna destroy any of your priceless heirlooms. I'm just looking for a little inspiration."

"Well . . ." Imogene paused, still suspicious. "Well, go on then."

As her grandmother's heels clicked down the hall, Haven pushed open the trapdoor and climbed into the attic. There were no cobwebs in the corners or dust bunnies roaming the floor—Imogene's maid saw to that. Just boxes stacked neatly along the walls, entire decades relegated to obscurity. Most were filled with Imogene's things, but one short stack bore labels scrawled in Mae Moore's handwriting. Two of the labels read HAVEN.

Haven hauled the top box off the pile and tore off the lid. Inside was a pile of papers. Her first-grade report card. *Too chatty. Forgets to wear underwear.* A note from the principal dated 1999. *Haven saw fit today to educate some of her classmates about the birds and the bees. Please let her know that this is not appropriate behavior. . . .* Dentist bills. Handmade Christmas ornaments. A children's Bible.

Disappointed, Haven shoved the box to one side. She'd come up to the attic looking for something—*anything* that might bring about a vision. Her desire to see Ethan had grown too powerful to control. Though she'd never tried drugs, for the first time in her life Haven knew exactly how it felt to be an addict.

She found what she was after inside the second box, nestled beneath a few books and a neatly folded baby blanket. A stack of drawings, each done in colored pencil on white typing paper. Though they were crude and clearly crafted by a child's unsteady hand, the illustrations showed evidence of real talent. Haven pulled the pile from the box and knelt on the rough wooden floor. She was surprised to discover that she could identify several of the people and places in the pictures. A haughty blonde woman with her nose in the air and the trace of a sneer on her lips was Constance's mother. The stern older man with glasses was Constance's father, whose name was Bernard or Bertrand or Benjamin. He and his wife lived in the twin-towered building she had drawn that looked out over Central Park.

But most of the drawings featured a young man with auburn hair. Ethan. Haven paused with one in her hand and found herself trapped by the green eyes that seemed to stare back at her. Something about it left her breathless. The air in the attic grew thick, and Haven felt her scalp tingle. She braced for the vision to come just as the walls dissolved into darkness and a warm wind whipped around her.

*The breeze lifted her hat from her head. It tumbled across the plaza and came to a rest at the feet of a young man standing nearby. She had noticed him a few minutes earlier, staring at her from an outdoor café. As she started toward him, she scanned the dusty plaza for her mother's blue dress. They had become separated on their tour of Rome's fountains, and though she had tried to return to her mother's suite at the Ritz, the narrow streets had led her here instead, as if she were following a familiar path. Once in the Piazza Navona, she was overcome by the sense that she'd been there before. It was a feeling that had tantalized her since her first day in Rome. Her mind was playing tricks on her again.*

*Now she approached the young man, hoping he couldn't hear her heart pounding in her chest. No more than twenty years old, he was uncommonly handsome, with auburn hair and a face that reminded her of the statue of Apollo she'd discovered in the Vatican Museum. She'd stood so spellbound in front of the nude marble god that her mother had found it unseemly.*

"Buon giorno," *the man said, holding out her hat.*

*"Hello." Her throat was dry and her voice cracked.*

*"You're American. What luck."*

*"I'm from New York." She knew him, she thought. "Have we met somewhere before?"*

*His smile was a little lopsided, she noted, a tiny flaw that rendered him perfect.*

*"Not in this lifetime. My name is Ethan Evans."*

*"Constance Whitman."*

*"What do you think of Rome, Constance?" Ethan asked. He had barely looked away from her face since she'd arrived in the piazza.*

*"It's lovely." She could feel herself blushing.*

*"Yes. I feel oddly at home here," the man remarked. "Sometimes I can't help but think that I've lived here before. Do you ever feel that way?"*

*"A little," she admitted.*

*"And the Piazza Navona. Perhaps you've seen it before. Perhaps you've dreamed about it?"*

*"Who are you?" Constance asked. "How do you know these things?"*

*"I've been looking for you," he said. Suddenly his face was close, his lips brushing hers. She closed her eyes.*

*"Constance!" A voice screeched across the piazza. "Get away from her at once!" Her mother was rushing toward them, wielding her Japanese parasol like a sword.*

*"Now it's your turn to find me," Ethan whispered, slipping a card into Constance's hand.*

*She looked down. Printed on the back of the card was an illustration of a silver snake swallowing its tail.*

FOR A FEW BRIEF seconds after Haven woke on the floor, she felt happier than she ever had. With the taste of Ethan's lips still on hers, Haven closed her eyes before the attic could come into focus and desperately tried to reenter the vision. When she found herself stuck in the dreary present, she reluctantly rose and began to sift through the pile of drawings that had fallen from her hand and now lay scattered around her. An ivy-covered mansion. A beautiful girl with dark hair. Her eyes briefly rested on a picture of a row of little houses that lined a cobblestone street. Colossal apartment towers rose behind them in the distance.

Mixed in among the drawings was a scrap of newspaper. Haven

turned it over to find a short article, accompanied by separate pictures of Ernest Moore and Veronica Cabe.

*Two people were killed when a truck driven by Ernest Moore of Snope City crashed on Route 36 just outside of Johnson City. Moore died instantly, and his passenger, Veronica Cabe, was pronounced dead at Johnson City Regional Hospital early yesterday evening. The cause of the crash has not been determined.*

With the article in hand, Haven snatched the drawings and rushed for the ladder that led down from the attic. She took two stairs at a time on her way to the kitchen, charging past her grandmother who didn't have a chance to chide her. Haven arrived at her destination out of breath. Her mother dropped her spoon into the pan of gravy she was stirring and took a step back, one hand raised as if to ward off an assault.

"What is this?" Haven thrust the paper at her mother. Mae Moore gazed at it as the blood drained from her face. "What is it?" the girl insisted. She was furious and she didn't know why.

"A bit of newspaper?" her mother muttered.

"Technically, it's a crash report. You know which one?"

"Can I see it?" Mae asked softly.

"What's going on in here?" Haven's grandmother stood in the kitchen door.

"Go away, Imogene," Haven growled. "This isn't any of your damn business."

"How *dare* you curse at me in my own house!" Imogene barked back.

"She's right, Mother—this isn't your business." When Mae lifted her eyes from the newspaper, they were clear and determined. "Leave us be."

Imogene was taken aback. It was the first time in years that her daughter had dared contradict her.

"*Please*," Mae repeated. "Let me talk to Haven in private."

"If you insist, but tell your girl she'd better watch her mouth," the old lady said before stomping off toward the parlor.

"Sit down, Haven." Mae pointed to the breakfast table that sat beneath the kitchen window. "I suppose you're old enough now. I'll tell you whatever you want to know."

Unable to look her mother in the face, Haven stared out the window at the mountains speckled with dogwoods in bloom and the setting sun balanced atop a purple peak. "Why was he with that woman when he died?"

Mae Moore tried to smile and failed. "I've been looking for the answer to that question for a long time now," she admitted. "And I've never managed to come up with anything other than the obvious."

Haven felt pressure building, as if a large weight had been placed on her chest. "So they *were* having an affair?"

Mae Moore nodded. "People had been talking for a while, but I didn't want to hear it. You know, sometimes when you're too close to someone, it's hard to see who they really are. Your father swore to me that he'd been faithful, and I believed him. But it turned out he'd been lying all along."

"I don't understand," Haven sputtered. "How could he do such a thing? All those stories you used to tell me about how you met and got married. You really believed the two of you were meant to be together."

"Those stories . . ." The wrinkles on Mae's forehead deepened, and she seemed to crumple a little as though the grief might crush her. But she somehow managed to maintain her composure. "I was half hoping you'd have forgotten about them. I feel so silly now. I let myself get carried away."

"What do you mean, you got carried away?" The edge had returned to Haven's voice. "You made them up? You lied?"

Mae Moore took the blow without flinching. Haven could see she'd been preparing for this conversation for years. "I didn't lie.

Sometimes when we're in love, we take the facts and spin them into pretty stories. But it's a dangerous thing to do—because one day, like it or not, you're going to see the world as it really is. You find out people aren't always who you want them to be. And if you're not ready for the truth . . . well, let's just say it can come as a bit of a shock."

"Is that why you went to the hospital?" Haven asked.

"It wasn't really a *hospital*, Haven," Mae said.

"I know," Haven said, scratching at a stain on the tabletop.

"I'm sorry. It must have been hard for you. But please try to understand. Every dream I ever had died with your father. Everything I'd believed in my heart to be true turned out to be false. Your grandmother tried her best to warn me, but I chose not to listen. I was young and I was stupid, and I paid dearly for it. If it hadn't been for you, Haven—"

"So Imogene was right about Daddy all along," Haven muttered.

Mae Moore lowered her voice and leaned toward Haven across the table. "Your grandmother hasn't been around all these years without learning a thing or two. She sees the world for what it is. Now, I guess I do, too."

"You mean you don't believe that people are ever destined to be together?"

Mae sat back and studied her daughter. Haven felt her face burning. "Would your question have something to do with Ethan and that box I gave you?" she asked.

Haven didn't answer.

"I'd *like* to believe that people can be meant for each other." Mae Moore seemed to have saved her one last scrap of hope to give to her daughter. "Who knows? Maybe there was someone out there for me—I just didn't happen to find him. But you shouldn't let my bad luck stop you from looking. You've been talking about Ethan since you were a little girl, Haven. If he's really out there, I think you owe it to yourself to look for him one day."

## CHAPTER FOURTEEN

Haven sat down on the floor and leaned back against her locked bedroom door. With her head in her hands, she thought not of her mother or Ethan Evans. Instead, her mind somehow made its way to Morgan Murphy's house. She could see ten-year-old Morgan prancing through her family's den in the frilly white dress she'd worn as flower girl in a cousin's wedding. Whenever they had played dress-up, Morgan always insisted that she be a bride. By the fourth grade, she already knew she wanted pink peonies in her bridal bouquet, a dress with a ten-foot train, and a handsome husband who would devote himself to paying for whatever her heart desired.

Over the years, Haven had come to look down on girls like Morgan—girls whose imaginations seemed stuck in a romance novel. There were plenty of them at Blue Mountain High School. They practiced signing their future married names on the backs of their spiral notebooks and registered for imaginary bridal showers on the computers in the library. Love was a harmless game to them—a pretty story they told to amuse themselves. Haven had always thought such girls were silly. Now, after the conversation with her mother, Haven saw just how dangerous their behavior could be.

Haven had always imagined that the secret to finding love was following one's heart. She'd never realized a heart could lead its owner astray. Mae Moore had truly believed she'd discovered her soul mate. Her error in judgment had almost destroyed her. Now Haven was in jeopardy of making the same mistakes her mother had made. She knew she needed to take things a little more slowly—and look carefully before she leaped into anyone's arms.

"Haven!" her grandmother shouted from the bottom of the stairs. "Haven!"

Haven opened her door and yelled through the crack. "What?"

"Come back down here! Dr. Tidmore's on the phone. He wants a word with you."

HAVEN GRABBED THE cordless phone from its cradle on the kitchen wall. The drawings Haven had gathered in the attic were still sitting where she'd abandoned them on the counter.

"Hello?"

"Hello, Haven," Dr. Tidmore said, sounding a little too familiar for a man of God. "I hope I'm not interrupting anything. I just wanted to check in on my special girl."

Haven shuddered. As a child, she had liked it when he called her that. At seventeen, she felt it was more than a little bit creepy. "No, you're not interrupting anything," she said.

"Something wrong, Haven?" Dr. Tidmore asked. "You don't sound like yourself."

"I'm fine," Haven assured him, adding some phony cheer to her voice.

"Well I'm glad to hear that. I was just calling to make sure I'll be seeing you after school tomorrow afternoon."

"Tomorrow afternoon?" Haven said, casually shuffling through the drawings from the attic. She stopped at a picture that showed a row of little houses, and her pulse began to quicken. In the center of the drawing was a white cottage with a red door. Green velvet curtains were hanging in its second-floor windows.

"Your grandmother arranged for you to see me on Wednesdays. Our first meeting is scheduled for tomorrow at four," Tidmore reminded her. "We're going to talk about your visions."

"Four," Haven mumbled mindlessly as she bent forward and studied the image she'd found. She was certain it was the house where Constance had kissed Ethan. The house where they both had died. Haven knew she had seen it before. And not in another lifetime.

"Haven, are you still there?" Dr. Tidmore asked.

"Sorry, sir," Haven said. "What was the question?"

"You'll need to learn how to listen before you get to New York," Dr. Tidmore snapped. Then his tone softened again. "Never mind. We'll talk about all of this tomorrow. So can I expect to see you at four o'clock in my office?"

"Yes, sir," Haven said. "I'll see you tomorrow." She hung up the phone before the preacher had a chance to say any more and sprinted up to her mother's bedroom.

AN HOUR LATER, Haven's bedroom door opened.

"Dammit, Imogene, I told you to knock!" she shouted before she saw Beau's handsome face peeking through the crack at her. "What are you doing here?" she demanded, still frazzled by the scare.

"Your mom let me in." Beau stood in the doorway, his eyes wide. The floor of Haven's bedroom was covered with celebrity magazines in various stages of dissection. "What the hell is going on?"

"Get in here!" Haven hissed. "And close the door!"

"What's all this? Have you finally cracked?" Beau joked.

"I found something. Sit down." When Beau dropped to the floor beside her, Haven put the drawing of the little white cottage down in front of him and tapped the paper with her finger. "I drew that when I was *eight years old*," she told him.

"It's beautiful," Beau said. "What's it got to do with all of these magazines?"

"I'll show you." Haven reached behind her and found a *National Enquirer* she'd set aside. "I remembered seeing it the other day when we were going through the tabloids. But I guess I was paying so much attention to the guy in the pictures that I barely noticed where he was." She pointed to a picture on the page. It was a shot of Iain Morrow unlocking a red door. Haven held her drawing of the row of little houses next to the photo. The door, the cobblestones, the surrounding buildings were all strikingly similar. "That's the house where Constance used to live. Iain Morrow lives in *my* house."

"How do you know he lives there?" Beau asked skeptically.

"Either he lives in the house, or he just likes to pose for photographs outside it," Haven said, passing Beau six more pictures that showed Iain Morrow exiting or entering the same building. In each photo, he was wearing a different outfit and the same bemused expression.

"Okay. That's weird," Beau agreed. "Possibly even weirder than what I came to show you."

"You have something to show me?" Haven asked.

Beau leaned to one side and pulled a rolled-up copy of *Star* out of his back pocket. The cover featured a photo of Iain Morrow and a headline that screamed, MURDERER?

"I stopped by the supermarket this evening," Beau said. "The latest batch of magazines had just arrived, so I figured I'd do a little research for you." He flipped through the pages until he reached the cover story. "I guess the intrepid reporters at *Star* hunted down some model that Iain Morrow used to date. She said they never got serious 'cause she was sure he was in love with someone else. She said that no matter where they went, it felt like he was always searching for the other girl." Beau tried to hand Haven the magazine, but she wouldn't take it. She wanted to, but she couldn't allow herself.

"Maybe he was in love with that musician's girlfriend," Haven suggested. "Isn't that what the gossip people say? That he murdered Jeremy Whatshisname to get to his girlfriend?"

"Maybe. Or maybe Iain Morrow's been looking for *you*."

Haven tried to tame the emotions that the comment had set loose inside of her. "That interview isn't evidence of anything," she pointed out. "There may be some connection between us, but there's absolutely no proof whatsoever that Iain Morrow and I are *soul mates*."

Beau eyed Haven as if he suspected she'd been replaced by an impostor. "Have I missed something? I thought you were convinced that Iain Morrow was the person you were meant to find."

"I just have to be careful, that's all," Haven explained, stacking magazines in an attempt to look busy. "I can't run around falling in love with fantasies."

"But what about the house you drew? How do you explain that and all the other crazy shit that's happened?" Beau demanded.

"And how would you explain *this*?" Haven asked, handing him another pile of photos. Each of the pictures showed Iain Morrow with a different girl on his arm.

"I don't understand."

"If Iain Morrow was really looking for me, do you think he'd go around diddling every model in New York City?"

Beau laughed. "You expect a nineteen-year-old guy to live like a monk until he finds you? That's kinda sweet, Haven, but you don't know the first thing about men. Besides, how do you know Iain Morrow 'diddled' all these girls?"

"I don't care what Iain Morrow did with them," Haven insisted. "I just don't want to waste my time chasing after the wrong guy. Unless I find some solid proof that we're meant to be together, I'm not taking any risks."

"What's this about not taking any risks?" Beau barked. "You somehow manage to talk me into believing that you've lived other lives, but now that I think we've found your old boyfriend, you suddenly get cold feet? Well, I'm not going to stand for it. I'm going to find a way for you to talk to him."

"Some rich guy who could be a murderer? Are you *insane*?"

"Are you *scared*?" Beau taunted her.

"Of course not! But how am I going to get in touch with this Iain guy, anyway? It's not like I can call him up on the phone. Plus, Imogene's got me trapped here in Snope City for the foreseeable future. How the hell am I supposed to go to New York? I'm not even sure if I can control my visions anymore. What if I passed out in the street somewhere?"

"I already figured everything out."

"*Sure* you have." Haven wished Beau would just give in. He wasn't making it any easier for her to keep her expectations under control.

"I'm not going anywhere till you hear me out."

Haven could see it wasn't an idle threat. "Fine. Let's hear it," she huffed.

"Okay, remember that letter you showed me—the one your father wrote—the one that said he thought you'd been reincarnated?"

"Yeah . . ." Haven said warily. "I remember it."

"Well, it was addressed to something called the Ouroboros Society. I thought that it sounded a little strange, so I did some research online. Turns out it's a group that helps people who think they may have lived other lives. And guess what—they're in New York! I bet if you sent them an e-mail and told them your story—told them you'd found someone you may have known in the past—they'd probably invite you up and find you a place to stay. Can't be every day they come across something like this. And while you're up there, what would it hurt to pay a little visit to Mr. Morrow?"

"Right. I'm supposed to tell the Ouroboros Society that the guy I knew in my last life is now a famous billionaire delinquent? That should go over *real* well. They'll think I'm crazier than hell. Why don't I just tell them I'm best friends with Bill Gates, too?"

"Damn, Haven, don't be so boneheaded. So you leave that part out. Just tell the Ouroboros Society that you might know someone in New York who could back up your story."

"Okay, but even if that works, how d'you figure I'll be able to hop on a plane to New York when Imogene's got me under maximum surveillance? She'd have the cops all over me before I made it to Maryland."

"Explain to me again why Imogene needs to be informed? Tell her we're going camping for a couple of days. She'll never know the difference. It's not like you can't afford a short trip to New York. I bet you've still got every cent we've ever made sitting in a vault in the First Citizen's bank. And you know as well as I do that we're set to make upward of five grand off the dresses this year. I'll even loan you my half of the proceeds if you promise to give it a try."

"Don't even think about it. You need that money for college."

When Beau sighed, Haven knew she'd successfully changed the subject. "I don't think I'll ever be able to pay for Vanderbilt."

"Are you saying you might not go to college?"

"I'm saying that if I take classes at East Tennessee, I can drive back and forth every day and save on living expenses," Beau explained. "And it'll keep me out of trouble if I live at home a while longer. Look, we're getting off topic here. We can talk about this later. In the meantime, you can borrow my dress money if you need it. So e-mail the reincarnation people already!"

Haven couldn't come up with another excuse. "I'll think about it," she promised.

## CHAPTER FIFTEEN

Haven was staring out the window when Miss Henderson brought the blinds down with a crash and the classroom went dark.

"I know it's a gorgeous day outside, but you guys have to keep your eyes on me for the next fifteen minutes."

Even after nine months on the job, the perky little brunette was still bursting with enthusiasm for English literature. Haven had seen her type before. Fresh out of UT Chattanooga and dying to make a difference. They didn't last long.

Bradley Sutton raised a meaty paw. "No offense, Miss Henderson, but what's the point? I mean, there're only a few weeks left of school. Nothing we learn now's gonna change anything."

Bradley liked to brag that the only book he'd ever read was *Green Eggs and Ham*, and he wasn't about to have some pansy play like *Othello* ruining his spotless record.

"For the right person, a few weeks can change *everything*," Miss

Henderson snipped. She'd come to despise Bradley, who divided his time in class between causing trouble and ogling her chest. "So unless you want to spend this period in the principal's office, I suggest you let the rest of us get back to work."

The teacher swiveled and addressed the students on the other side of the aisle. "Iago sets out to ruin Othello's life. He convinces Othello that his wife has been having an affair with Cassio, and he manipulates the other characters by playing on their weaknesses. But why? What's his motivation?"

"Gay," grunted Dewey Jones from the back of the room, and half the class tittered.

Miss Henderson barely blinked. "That is one theory. Some people have speculated that Iago's actions are driven by homosexual jealousy. I'm not sure I buy that argument. The poet Samuel Coleridge once called Iago a 'motiveless malignity.' Anyone know what that means?"

The class was silent except for the sound of two dozen pencils doodling. Haven couldn't bear the growing defeat on Miss Henderson's face.

"It means that there was no reason for his actions. That all he wanted to do was create chaos."

"Thank you, Haven. Can the rest of you think of another character like that? One who plants evil thoughts in people's minds? Who pretends to help while he's secretly undermining them?" She waited. "Oh, come on, you guys, none of you have ever heard of Satan? Is Iago the devil?"

"Ask Haven," Bradley quipped. He'd had it in for her since she'd spurned his advances. "She's probably got the devil somewhere deep inside her right now." The class howled with laughter. Miss Henderson slammed her book closed and dropped down in her desk chair. There was no taking back control. When Haven turned around to give Bradley the finger, she saw there was at least one other person who wasn't laughing—a smart, mousey girl named Leah Frizzell.

* * *

BLUE MOUNTAIN WAS a relatively peaceful school. With fewer than a hundred people in each graduating class, it was too small for the typical cliques and tribes. There was really only one clear way to divide the students: There were those who would stay in Snope City for the rest of their lives and those who would run as far and as fast as possible. In each class, there were no more than a dozen students who fell into the latter group. Among them were the kids from Snope City's tiny African-American community, who tended to vanish the day after graduation and were rarely seen again. Until that blessed day arrived, they and their fellow outsiders tried their best to blend into the background.

For the most part, the strategy worked. In Haven's four years of high school, she'd heard tale of only a few troubling incidents. One of Blue Mountain's three goth kids once let down his guard and drank too much beer at a party held deep in the woods. As soon as he passed out, four football players tied him to a tree, wrapped him in toilet paper, and set it on fire. The kid survived with all of his skin, though it took a full year for his eyebrows to grow back. Then there was the time the captain of the girls' basketball team called one of her black teammates the unforgivable word and received a broken nose in return. And Dewey Jones went through a phase freshman year when nothing delighted him more than imitating the school's half-dozen Pentecostal students by rolling around on the cafeteria floor and screaming gibberish. Leah Frizzell had put an end to the displays.

Leah had always been a little unusual. Her body appeared emaciated, though she never seemed to stop eating, and thin red hair clung to her narrow skull. She rarely spoke, and when she did, her drawl couldn't have been cut with a chain saw. Beginning in the fourth grade, whenever Haven got the feeling that something wasn't quite right, she would often discover Leah's light green eyes watching her. It made Haven nervous at first. She'd heard kids gossip about the things Leah carried around in the beaten-up backpack that Haven had never seen her open. Those fears seemed justified when, one afternoon while Dewey Jones writhed around on the floor, Leah stuck a scrawny hand into her bag and yanked out a snake.

"You know, we don't just talk in tongues—we're snake handlers, too," she'd said as she shoved the serpent down the front of Dewey's football jersey. Unaware that it was nothing but a harmless blacksnake, Dewey had soiled his pants in front of the entire school. Leah was suspended for three days, and when she returned, she went right back to lurking in the shadows.

By senior year, Haven barely noticed Leah Frizzell. When the girl was named the school's valedictorian, Haven had to think for a minute to place the name. It seemed likely that they'd finish high school without exchanging a word—until that day in Miss Henderson's class, when Haven turned around to see the girl glaring at Bradley Sutton.

"Shut your mouth and leave her alone," Leah warned Bradley Sutton and the snickering stopped. "Or you'll *wish* you had the devil to deal with."

## CHAPTER SIXTEEN

After the last bell rang, Haven pushed through the doors of Blue Mountain High School and set out to walk the half mile to church for her appointment with Dr. Tidmore. Snope City's sidewalks, usually quiet, were momentarily jammed with giddy students set free into the warm May afternoon. A couple of freshmen on skateboards raced recklessly around Haven. A group of girls giggled behind her. A junior in a baseball uniform scurried out of the sporting goods store, grasping a new athletic cup in one hand. One by one, the kids disappeared into shops or up driveways until the only other student left on the sidewalks was Leah Frizzell. She was walking on the opposite side of the street, a physics book clutched to her chest and her eyes fixed on the path ahead. Not once did she glance in Haven's direction. Haven quickened her stride, but Leah kept pace. Haven stopped to gaze in the window of the town pharmacy, but when she turned around, Leah was no more than a few steps ahead of her. It wasn't until Haven had reached the front door of the church that the strange redheaded girl turned down a side road and vanished from sight.

HAVEN'S NERVES WERE still jangled when she dropped down into one of the hard leather chairs in the preacher's elegantly appointed office. Every decorative touch had been paid for by donations from Snope City's finest citizens. Imogene Snively had personally commissioned the stained-glass window behind his desk.

"I'm glad you made it," the preacher said warmly. "It's been a while since we had a heart-to-heart." Dr. Tidmore beamed at Haven from across his enormous oak desk. In the years since they'd last sat in these same spots, the preacher's hair had started to silver and a pair of wire-rimmed glasses now rested on his nose. His harsh Yankee accent had even softened into a subtle drawl. "It seems like yesterday that you were just a little bitty thing. And now here you are, a stunning young woman."

Haven managed a smile but said nothing.

"Your grandmother seems to think that you're in a bit of trouble."

"Did she tell you she's not going to let me go to school in the fall?" Haven's temper flared. "That evil old lady wants to trap me here for the rest of my natural life."

"Now, now." Dr. Tidmore chuckled. "I know you and your grandmother don't get along, but let's not go overboard. There are some things even Imogene Snively can't control. As soon as we take care of your little problem, I'm sure she'll let you go off to New York City for college."

"I'm glad *you're* sure," Haven said with a huff.

"Well, I'm going to try my best to see that she does. Do you think you can tell me what happened over the weekend?"

Haven folded her arms against her chest. "Imogene's told you everything there is to tell. I fainted."

"You had another vision?"

Haven hesitated. "Yes."

Tidmore nodded. "Did you see the same girl? The one called Constance?"

"Yes," Haven said, surprised that he remembered.

"And the boy, too?"

"Yes."

Dr. Tidmore's mood darkened, as if his worst suspicions had been confirmed. "There's something I should tell you, Haven. Your grandmother stopped by to see me this afternoon. She brought something with her." He slid open a desk drawer and pulled out a shoe box. Haven could see a slip of paper peeking out from under the lid, and she gasped when she recognized the handwriting that covered one side of it.

"That stuff is *mine*. Imogene must have gone through my room. She had *no* right to give you that!"

Tidmore placed one long, thin hand on the box. "Your grandmother is only trying to help you, Haven. She thought I needed to see this."

"I want it back!" Haven insisted.

"In time, Haven," Dr. Tidmore said more firmly. "But I think we should talk about what's inside here. I'm afraid it's proof that Ernest Moore was not a well man."

"All it proves is that my father believed I'd been reincarnated."

"Reincarnation is not a Christian concept, Haven. Christians believe that God judges us all when we die and sends us to either heaven or hell."

"And I'd say that the Lord works in mysterious ways," Haven shot back.

Tidmore frowned. "This is not a conversation I ever hoped to have," he told her. "But now that it's come to this, it's time you knew the truth. Your father was spiritually ill, Haven. Toward the end of his life, his behavior became impulsive and he began to imagine things.

He must have taken innocent comments of yours—ones that any young girl might have made—and turned them into proof of a previous life.

"Ernest came to see me right after I moved here. He was rambling about reincarnation and devils and all sorts of crazy things. He wasn't even making sense. I tried my best to help him, but I could see he was already lost. I spoke with your grandmother about it. I was worried that he would lead you down the wrong path as well. I'm afraid that's what ended up happening. Ernest was your father, and you wanted to please him, so you went along with the story he'd concocted. Even added to it and began to believe it. Think about it, Haven. Haven't you ever wondered why the visions stopped after your father died?"

She refused to see the preacher's point. "If that's all true, then why have the visions come back? My father has been dead for eight years."

Dr. Tidmore removed his glasses and rubbed the lenses with a scrap of red silk. "*That* is what worries me most," he said. "The possibility that you might have inherited your father's affliction—that the same evil forces may now be acting on *your* mind."

Haven turned the statement over in her head. It was ridiculous from every angle. "You're not saying I inherited a *demon* from my father, are you?" she scoffed.

"Demons take many forms," Tidmore said scientifically, like an entomologist describing different species of cockroach. "Sometimes they manifest as physical and mental illnesses."

Haven stood up. "Give me my box."

"Sit down, Haven," the preacher commanded, placing the box back in his desk drawer.

"Fine. Keep all the stuff. There's plenty more back at the house," Haven lied as she headed for the door. "Imogene only found part of it."

"You're free to go," Dr. Tidmore informed her. "But if you do, you may find yourself stuck in this town for longer than you can possibly imagine."

Haven froze.

"Good. Now sit back down," Tidmore added gently. "Remember, I'm here to help you." Once Haven had returned to her seat across from him, he picked up a pen and prepared to take notes. "Let's talk about this boy from your visions. Ethan, wasn't it?"

"Yes." Haven's head was bowed in defeat.

"Tell me. What do you remember about Ethan?"

"Not very much. I don't know." There was no way she could tell a preacher the things she remembered.

"When you were younger, you said that you loved him. You used to talk about how he was young and handsome and brilliant. Do you remember that?"

"No," Haven muttered. She felt her scalp begin to tingle and the sensation of flames creeping up her legs. A vision was on its way.

"But you didn't trust him. You questioned his faithfulness. You know, Haven, sometimes Satan disguises himself as an angel of light."

Dr. Tidmore's voice was growing fainter. Haven struggled to empty her mind, repeating the Lord's Prayer over and over again in her head. But the fire kept burning. There was nothing she could do to stop it.

*She was approaching a mansion with an engraved invitation clenched in one hand. To the left of the mansion's door, just below the bell, a small plaque read* THE OUROBOROS SOCIETY. *The words were encircled by the image of a snake swallowing its tail. There was no need to be nervous, Constance thought. The new president was meeting with everyone. She hadn't been singled out.*

*Inside, she nearly bumped into a desk that now sat in the foyer, blocking access to the rest of the mansion. The young man behind it greeted her with a humorless smile.*

*"Constance Whitman?" he inquired. "The president will see you in the parlor."*

*"Thank you."*

*Constance stepped around the desk and hurried down the hallway. She had almost reached the room at the end when she spotted the two of them standing only inches apart. Ethan's back was to the door, but she could see the female face gazing up at him. It belonged to a girl named Rebecca Underwood.*

*Every suspicion Constance had ever entertained returned at that moment. Rebecca Underwood was one of the Society's first members. She had spent months with Ethan before he left for Rome. Constance often wondered if anything had happened between them. Ethan and Rebecca shared so much in common. Both were orphans rescued by Strickland. Both claimed to recall details of multiple lives. And both were uncommonly beautiful. Particularly Rebecca, with the ebony hair that she still wore long and the voluptuous figure she refused to disguise. Ethan had always insisted they were only friends, but seeing the two of them together, Constance had to admit they made a stunning pair.*

*"You don't need her anymore," Rebecca said, her voice a little too loud for a whisper. "We both know you only cared for her money. Now that Strickland's made you his heir, we can finally be together. That's how it's meant to be!"*

*Struggling for air, Constance rushed for the exit. She couldn't allow herself to faint until she'd made her escape. In the foyer, she collided with someone coming down the stairs. The man caught her in his arms before she could fall.*

*"My dear," said a voice both soothing and concerned. "Are you ill?"*

HAVEN'S EYES OPENED and she found herself staring at the ceiling of the pastor's office. Dr. Tidmore was still sitting behind his desk, looking past her out the door. All around him were flapping papers, fragments of a porcelain vase, and shards of glass. Haven's chair had been hurled through the cabinet at the far end of the room, and the stained-glass window behind Dr. Tidmore's desk had been shattered. Haven turned her head toward the sound of prayer and saw the cleaning woman, Eula Duncan, standing in the hallway.

"That girl ought to be locked up!" Eula exclaimed with one hand pressed to her heart.

Haven groaned and dropped the paperweight that was clenched in her fingers, ready to be thrown.

## CHAPTER SEVENTEEN

Thursday morning Haven didn't get out of bed. She knew word would already be spreading that she had succumbed to a demon in front of the pastor. Soon the knowledge would infect the entire town. When her mother urged her to dress for breakfast, Haven refused, too anxious to face her grandmother across the dining room table. Instead, Haven locked her door and spent the morning studying the postcard Dr. Tidmore had once given her. For eight years, the aerial view of Manhattan had stayed pinned to the wall above her desk. It was faded and crumpled, but the feeling it gave her remained the same. Haven traced the streets with her eyes, and no matter where they started on the map, they always arrived at the same tiny patch of green toward the bottom of the island. She had always known there was something waiting for her there. Beau was right, Haven thought—she had to find a way to get to New York City.

At last she set the postcard aside and pondered Dr. Tidmore's suggestion. As much as it frightened her, Haven knew in her heart he was wrong. The only thing she had inherited from Ernest Moore was her unfortunate head of hair. A demon or a mental illness might explain the visions. But it couldn't account for her talent for drawing, her skill with a needle—or her knowledge of a city in which she had never set foot. Haven knew she'd inherited these gifts from someone with whom she shared no blood. She had inherited them from Constance Whitman.

The visions, however, remained a mystery. Constance wanted Haven to find Ethan. But Haven no longer knew *why*. She had always assumed that love was drawing her back to New York. Now, after the vision in Dr. Tidmore's office, Haven was no longer so certain. Constance had made the same mistake as Mae Moore. She'd fallen for the wrong man, and he'd broken her heart.

So why did Haven still feel the irresistible urge to make her way to Manhattan? The desire was so strong at times that she knew if she started walking, she wouldn't stop until she crossed the George Washington Bridge. Was she doomed to fall in love with someone who would hurt her? Or was there another reason she had to find Ethan Evans? Haven needed answers. And as far as she knew, she only had one lead to follow.

Shortly before three o'clock, Haven crawled out of bed, cracked open her laptop, and typed in the address of the Ouroboros Society: www.OuroborosSociety.com. She remembered seeing Constance visit the club in her most recent vision, and she was sure the girl had been a member.

As the Website loaded, the silver snake swallowing its tail spun on the black screen, creating a mesmerizing effect. Haven felt dizzy as she clicked on the snake and read the list of options that appeared on the page.

*Reincarnation and the Ouroboros Society*
*A Message from Our President*
*Our Headquarters*

*Share Your Story*
*Members Only*

Haven chose *Reincarnation and the Ouroboros Society*. The snake began to spin again before it dissolved, leaving behind a page of silver letters.

*Do you long for a place you've never been?*
*Do you often experience the sensation of déjà vu?*
*Have you ever fallen in love at first sight?*
*Do you possess skills or talents that defy explanation?*
*Are you haunted by fears or anxieties that make little sense?*
*Do you feel unusually close to certain people in your life?*

*If you answered yes to any of these questions, you may have experienced a previous life.*

*Reincarnation explains many of the mysteries of human existence. Why some of us are born with remarkable gifts. Why we love the people we love. Why we fear the things we fear. We return to earth time and time again, driven by love, vengeance, passion, or greed. And each life leaves its mark on us, even if we lose most of our memories as our souls are transferred from one living body to the next.*

*Since 1923, the Ouroboros Society has been devoted to the scientific study of reincarnation. We provide financial assistance so that members with exceptional talents can live up to their potential. We help other members reunite with lost loved ones or solve mysteries from their pasts. Those with recollections of previous lives will discover more about the people they've been. Those without memories can learn more about the hidden role that reincarnation has played in their lives.*

*If you believe that you may have lived before—or if you're interested in learning more about reincarnation—we urge you to contact the Ouroboros Society today.*

Intrigued, Haven returned to the previous page and clicked on *A Message from Our President*. The picture that accompanied the text showed a beautiful Indian woman with violet eyes and a regal nose.

*I was born in Suriname in 1978 to parents of Indian descent. When I was barely two years old, I began to utter strange words and phrases. My parents, who spoke only Dutch and Hindi, believed I was just another babbling baby until a family friend came for a visit. He had lived for some time in the United States, and he instantly recognized the language I was speaking. It was English. He says the first thing I told him was that I wanted to go home.*

*Throughout my childhood, I spoke of a city by the water where it snowed every winter. I described giant buildings, crowded streets, and trains that ran under the sidewalks. And I told anyone who would listen about a beautiful mansion across from a park. That was where I belonged. I also began to display an unusual gift. Though I had never had any lessons, I found I could play almost any instrument set in front of me. It wasn't until years later that I discovered the names of the musical pieces I had played as a child. They were the works of a little-known composer who lived in Austria at the end of the seventeenth century.*

*My parents, both Hindus, were no strangers to the idea of reincarnation. However, despite their support, my teenage years were troubled. I had come to believe that New York was the city I remembered, and I begged my parents to take me there. When they explained that we didn't have enough money to go, I repeatedly tried to run away. I felt that my destiny could only be fulfilled in Manhattan.*

*At last, my old family friend contacted the Ouroboros Society, and the OS arranged for me to visit New York for an interview. When I finally laid eyes on our headquarters on Gramercy Park, I knew I had found my true home. It was the same mansion I had explored in my dreams. Later I discovered that I had been a member of the Society in one of my previous incarnations. To this day, I am the only OS member who has returned for a second term.*

*Thanks to educational grants from the Society, I have been able to continue broadening my skills as a musician. Today, as president of the organization, I am devoted to helping people like myself. Our senior members include some of the most talented and successful individuals in the world, and each year we welcome hundreds of junior members into the fold. If you believe that we may be able to assist you in reaching your full potential, please do not hesitate to share your story.*

*Padma Singh, President, the Ouroboros Society*

# CHAPTER EIGHTEEN

That night Haven was watching the fireflies dart about the yard when a small object flew through the window, landed on the braided rug, and rolled under her desk. She slid off the bed and crawled on all fours to retrieve it. It was a piece of paper wrapped around a small, round stone.

*Meet me in the yard,* it read.

After stepping carefully over the creaky floorboard outside her room, Haven tiptoed barefoot to the stairs and slid silently down the banister. On the first floor, she crept past the parlor where her grandmother stared blankly at the television. Each action was performed to perfection, like a gymnast executing a familiar routine. Within seconds Haven had escaped out the back door.

She found Beau at the edge of the forest. He was leaning against a tree, his blond hair gleaming in the moonlight.

"What's up with the secret notes?" Haven asked. "Why didn't you just knock on the door?"

"You weren't at school today. I thought Imogene had you under house arrest."

"Maybe she does," Haven said with a shrug. "I've been avoiding her all day."

"So what happened with Tidmore?" Beau asked.

"You haven't heard? I figured everybody would be talking about it by now."

"I'm sure they are. But do you really think they want to talk about it with *me*? Besides—why would I listen to gossip when I can get the goods straight from the source?"

Haven sighed. "Imogene gave Dr. Tidmore all the notes my dad took. I got worked up about it and fainted right there in his office. While I was out, I saw something I'd never seen in any of my other visions. It was Ethan with another girl. I guess I was so mad that I destroyed Tidmore's office."

Beau's eyebrow shot toward the stars. "You mean you saw—"

"No!" Haven interrupted before he could spell it out. "They were just talking. But it was pretty clear they'd been together."

"Wait—hold on a second. I don't know what you saw, but Constance must have forgiven Ethan. Remember—you told your dad they eloped! You showed me the notes!"

"Let's just drop it, okay," Haven pleaded. "Whatever happened between them, it's pretty clear their relationship wasn't exactly 'soul mate' material. I'm not interested in hooking up with some guy who cheated on Constance. But I'm still supposed to find Ethan. I can't explain why, but I know I'll go completely insane if I don't." It was the only conclusion Haven had managed to reach.

"So what's your plan?"

"I'm going to go to New York like you said I should. You were right about the Ouroboros Society. I need to pay them a visit. I saw Constance there in my last vision, and I think she may have been a member. Plus, their Website said they help people solve 'mysteries from the past.' I guess this qualifies, right? And maybe—just maybe—I'll try to say hello to Iain Morrow. So. What do you think? Want to take a trip? You think your truck can make it up to New York in one piece?"

"You're saying you want *me* to go?" Beau looked away into the woods, as though searching for an excuse among the trees. "I'd love to, Haven, but we've got school."

Haven's spirits sank to new depths. "But it would only be for a few days. Come on, Beau! You were the one who told me I needed to go!"

"I still think you should. But I can't," Beau replied stubbornly. "Who'd take care of my dad while I was gone?"

The ridiculousness of the question pushed Haven over the edge. "Your dad's forty years old! What's going on here?" Haven demanded. "Why have you suddenly turned into some sort of wuss?"

Before Beau could answer, they heard a shriek from the house.

"Never mind. I gotta go," Haven said, shaking her head in disgust. "Imogene must have caught sight of her own reflection."

"Will I see you at school tomorrow?" Beau asked as Haven stormed off.

"Of course," Haven said without turning around, unable to give any other answer to someone she'd just called a coward.

INSIDE, HAVEN RAN straight into her grandmother, who was hurrying toward the phone in the kitchen. The old lady's hairdo was tucked under a protective net and her robe tied too tight to offer even the briefest glimpse of her nightgown. It was hard to believe that Imogene had once been the beauty who, according to Mae, favored ruby-red lipstick and tight sweaters and drove all the Snope City boys crazy.

"Where'd you come from?" Imogene yelped. "Were you outside?"

"Had to get some fresh air," Haven said. "What were you screeching about just now?"

"Did you see anything when you were out there?" Imogene asked breathlessly. "I was looking out the sitting room window, and I could have sworn I saw a man sneaking across the lawn. I was fixing to wake up your mama and call the police when you came through the door."

"It was Beau."

"I don't think so, Haven."

"Take my word for it. I was just out there. You saw Beau."

At last, Imogene appeared convinced. "And what exactly were you two doing outside on the lawn at nine P.M.?"

"Oh, hell, Imogene, you might as well know. We were out there summoning Satan."

The old lady's eyes bulged as if she were being strangled. "That is *not* funny, Haven Moore."

"Who said I was joking?" Haven left Imogene standing in the hall and started for the stairs to her room. She could hear her grandmother's slippers sliding across the floor behind her.

"Just where do you think you're going, Haven?" Imogene demanded. "You better start taking this situation seriously, young lady. You have no idea what kind of trouble you're in. Do you even remember what you said to Dr. Tidmore?"

Haven spun around at the base of the stairs. "Why don't you go ahead and tell me?"

"They say you called him a . . ." Imogene put her hand over her mouth and whispered prissily. "Bastard."

Haven rolled her eyes. "That all?"

"You accused him of having relations with someone named Rebecca Underwood."

Haven felt herself blushing. Hearing Imogene Snively refer to sex was like hearing the queen of England make a fart joke. "Wait a minute. How do 'they' know all this?"

"Eula Duncan told everyone you were yelling something awful. And Dr. Tidmore called this morning to cancel all your appointments with him. He said he needs to spend more time in prayer before he can confront your demon again. He told me I'll have to watch you like hawk in the meantime. He's convinced you might try to run away. And he thinks that if you have any more visions we should consider having you put away for your own good."

"Put away? You mean in a *mental institution*? Like Mama? You'd really do that?"

Even Imogene seemed to know she'd taken things too far. "It would only be temporary. I just don't know what else to do after everything that's happened. I never expected much of you, Haven. But this . . ."

"Well, whatever I've done, it's all *your* fault," Haven declared. "How dare you go through my things and give my personal possessions away?"

"Are you saying *I'm* responsible for this? I'm *trying* to save your soul, you ungrateful child. I saw the look in your eyes after you fainted in the sitting room. It was *lust*. I saw the same look in your mama's eyes after she met that no-good philanderer she married. You want to end up like her, Haven? Is that what you want?"

"You mean end up like *you*, Grandma?" Haven had finally said it.

Imogene gasped.

"Yeah, I've done the math. Either Mama was three months premature or you suffered from a little lust yourself."

The slap caught Haven unprepared. She glared at the old woman, then brushed past her and started climbing the stairs.

"You get back here this instant!" Imogene snarled.

"I have to get ready for bed," Haven told her through clenched teeth. "There's school in the morning." She would have loved nothing better than to stay and fight—to have it out with her grandmother once and for all. But she knew she had to resist. Imogene was looking for any excuse to lock her away, and Haven wasn't about to give one to her.

"School?" The idea seemed to strike Imogene as ludicrous. "You don't really plan to go to *school* tomorrow, do you?"

"Why shouldn't I?" Haven snapped back. "Who's gonna stop me?"

SAFE IN HER BEDROOM with the door locked, Haven stared at the silver snake spinning on the computer screen. Imogene would be breathing down her neck for weeks to come. She might be able to keep Haven trapped in Snope City, but she couldn't stop her from searching for answers. Haven clicked the *Our Headquarters* link on the Ouroboros Society Website and found herself gazing at a photograph of an old, ivy-covered mansion. Somehow it was as familiar to her as the Snively house. As Haven studied it, the sky behind the building darkened and lights appeared in its windows.

*She was climbing the stairs to the mansion. The silver snake near the front door was the first clue that she had found the right address. Before she had a chance to knock, the door opened as if her arrival had been anticipated. As a servant led her toward the parlor, an arm whisked her out of the hall and into a dark closet filled with winter furs.*

*"I saw you on the stoop." It was his voice. "We have a few moments before anyone finds us."*

*He pushed her against the wall, a mink coat serving as a cushion. His hands traced the outline of her figure, and she felt his lips on hers as he bent to kiss her. For three weeks, she had thought of nothing but this moment. She forced herself not to faint, refusing to let her legs collapse beneath her. Still, it was over too soon.*

*The way Ethan took her hand, she knew she was already his. He steered her though the mansion to the parlor, where a group of people stood chatting by the fire. She hadn't seen Ethan since Rome, and she wished she could study him for just a few minutes. When he caught her peering up at him, he offered the same devilish grin that had made her heart pound in the Piazza Navona.*

*"Here she is," Ethan said, presenting her to a white-haired gentleman in an old-fashioned suit. "This is Constance. Constance, I'd like you to meet Dr. August Strickland, the founder of the Ouroboros Society, the club so exclusive that no one can pronounce its name."*

*Dr. Strickland laughed. "It's a pleasure, Miss Whitman. I have heard a great deal about you. Ethan says you'll make a wonderful addition to our Society."*

*She looked up at Ethan in surprise and his grin grew broader.*

*"And this," he said, gesturing to a stunning young woman standing by the doctor's side. "This is Rebecca Underwood."*

*"Your lipstick is smudged," the girl pointed out. Rebecca's voice was friendly, her expression deadly. Constance couldn't remember meeting anyone else who'd taken such an instant dislike to her.*

## CHAPTER NINETEEN

As soon as Mae dropped her off outside Blue Mountain, Haven saw the faces staring at her through the bank of glass doors that led into the lobby. But it wasn't until she was inside the school that she realized what a terrible mistake she'd made. At least twenty people had gathered near the entrance, waiting for Haven to make an appearance. Led by Bradley Sutton, they followed her as she made her way down the hall toward her locker, some walking so close behind her that she could smell the bacon on their breath. Many of the students Haven passed looked on helplessly. A few slunk back into their classrooms. When she reached her locker, Haven discovered it had been decorated with dozens of images torn from books. Satan leered at her from each of them. There was even a hand-drawn picture of Haven and the devil cavorting naked in a graveyard. The artist had taken liberties with Haven's anatomy that might have made her laugh under other circumstances.

Instead, she felt herself struggling to breathe. She ripped down the pictures and opened her locker. A pile of fabric tumbled to the floor, and she reached down to pick up an emerald rag that had been ripped in a dozen places. She barely recognized Morgan Murphy's prom dress. The dress that hadn't been paid for.

"We always took you for a freak." Haven tried to ignore Morgan's hate-filled voice as she searched for her math book at the bottom of the locker. "I mean, who goes into trances and says perverted crap in the fourth grade? But we never figured you'd turn out to be dangerous. What do you do with the money you make off of us, anyway? Spend it on black candles and goats to slaughter?"

"Hey, how'd that demon get up inside you, Haven?" one of the boys called.

Haven felt the tap of a finger on her back, and she let out a screech. Leah Frizzell was standing behind her.

"You okay?" the scrawny girl asked. Haven gulped and said nothing, afraid she might pass out at any moment. While the invisible flames began to climb Haven's legs, Leah released her fury on the crowd. "Who do y'all think you are?" she yelled. "What right do you have to torture this girl? You think this is how Christians are meant to act? You think your preacher's going to be happy when he hears about this?"

Bradley Sutton started to laugh. "How about that? The Holy Roller's sticking up for the devil. You got any snakes on you today, Leah?"

"I've got something for you, Bradley." Beau had arrived on the scene. "You wanna see what it is?"

"Look, now we've got a Holy Roller, a demon, and a big ol' homo." Dewey Jones snickered.

"It's better than a bunch of damn hypocrites!" Leah yelled, working herself into a lather. "You go around drinking and gossiping and having sex with anything that moves, and you think you're so righteous?"

"All right, everybody." It was Principal Cogdill—a notorious disciplinarian who'd been promoted to the job from PE instructor in Haven's freshman year. "Mr. Decker, don't even *think* about starting a fight. The rest of you, get to class. Miss Moore, maybe you'd like to come with me?"

Haven took a single step before her knees buckled, and she crumpled into a lump at the principal's feet.

*As they strolled past the restaurant's window, she checked her reflection. The golden dress she'd designed herself sparkled under the streetlamp.*

*"You're lovelier than you've ever been," Ethan whispered in her ear. She laughed and released her grip on his arm as he opened the door for her. It was their first night out since the funeral—the first night either of them had felt up for an evening on the town.*

*Inside the restaurant, the crowd roared, their spirits lifted by homemade gin served in crystal water glasses. A suave man in a tuxedo was singing "Yes, Sir! That's My Baby."*

*"Look!" a female voice called out over the music. A tipsy woman stood up and pointed toward the front of the restaurant where they were waiting to be seated. The woman's long strands of pearls swayed from side to side. One by one, every last head swiveled in their direction. Silently, with eyebrows raised and jaws slack, the diners waited to see what would happen next.*

*"Miss Whitman, Mr. Evans!" The maître d' was rushing toward them. "What are you doing here?"*

*"Is something the matter?" Ethan inquired, and for a moment the man was struck dumb.*

*"You must leave," he whispered at last. "Come back in a few weeks when the talk has died down."*

*"What talk?" she insisted.*

*"Murderer!" a man's voice shouted from the back of the room.*

*"Please!" urged the maître d'.*

*A blinding flash of light greeted them as they returned to the sidewalk outside the restaurant. Ethan grabbed the man with the camera by his collar.*

*"Who are you?" he demanded.*

*"Take your hands off me! I'm with the* New York Daily Mirror*!"*

THE ENTIRE SCHOOL seemed to be watching the spot where Haven woke. As Principal Cogdill helped her to her feet and guided her down the hall, the school erupted with chatter that only got louder as the two disappeared into the principal's office. Even his secretary stopped typing and watched them walk past as if the principal were leading a herd of elephants. Haven knew the woman would be on the phone the second the door was closed.

"I think it's best if you finish the school year from home," the principal informed Haven without giving her time to sit down.

Haven nodded, but the man continued as though she had chosen to argue. "We can't have this kind of distraction every day. And to be perfectly honest, I'm not sure I can guarantee your safety anymore. You do understand, don't you, Haven?"

He didn't bother to disguise the fact that he would be pleased to see her go.

## CHAPTER TWENTY

*To Whom It May Concern:*

*My name is Haven Moore. I'm seventeen years old, and I live in a town called Snope City in eastern Tennessee. As long as I can remember, I've had visions of another life in New York, a city I've never visited.*

*My name then was Constance, and I was friends with some members of your Society. I believe I was around twenty years old when I died in a fire in the mid-1920s.*

*The person I remember most is a young man named Ethan Evans. He was a member of the Ouroboros Society, so you may be familiar with the name. I was in love with him then, and as strange as it sounds, I think I still might be. He's back again, and I think I know who he might be in this life. I want to find him, but I'm not sure if I should. Some of the things I've seen in my visions have frightened me, and the person Ethan's become makes me wonder if I ever really knew him.*

*But none of this seems to make any difference. I'm still being drawn to Ethan, and I don't know why. There's something I'm supposed to do. Unless I figure out what it is, I'll never have any peace. I'm hoping you can help me. . . .*

Haven stopped and imagined the response her e-mail would receive. Even she found her own story hard to believe. She saved the document and closed her computer. There was no use troubling the Ouroboros Society with what most people would see as the heartsick ravings of a seventeen-year-old girl.

## CHAPTER TWENTY-ONE

Haven's business had gone belly-up. Fourteen prom dresses had been returned—though most were in better condition than Morgan Murphy's. Fitting appointments were canceled one by one, and Haven and Beau found themselves saddled with fifteen hundred dollars' worth of silk, satin, and sequins. They saved one pretty pale-blue chiffon dress as a thank-you gift for Leah Frizzell, and the rest they packed away in the Decker attic. The profits that Beau and Haven had been counting on disappeared overnight. The thought that she was responsible for losing Beau's tuition money made Haven feel sick to her stomach.

With Imogene Snively monitoring her every move, Haven stayed home. And she had no desire to leave. She couldn't face the hatred and anger that had been simmering in the souls of people she'd known her entire life. Even Dr. Tidmore had turned against her. Haven's teachers sent homework assignments, which she dutifully finished. Exams were completed under her grandmother's eye while

Mae Moore puttered around the house, trying to act as if her daughter had been afflicted with nothing more than a bad cold.

Prom night passed with a never-ending round of honks and *yee-has* from the town below. Then the students of Blue Mountain began preparing for graduation while Haven watched summer arrive from her bedroom window. The mountains shed their delicate blooms and transformed into impenetrable jungles. Kudzu vines swallowed a telephone pole at the edge of town. Thunderstorms blitzed the valley most evenings, sending the gas station kids scuttling for shelter.

Haven tried her best to push the past aside. Whatever Constance's mystery was, it could wait until she was out from under her grandmother's thumb. Solving it wasn't worth spending ten months in a mental institution. But this time the past couldn't be forgotten. Every night when Haven fell asleep, Ethan came to her. It was as if he refused to let her go. Haven dreamed of his nights with Constance in the little white cottage on the cobblestone lane, and it was like some missing part of herself had been restored. She woke each morning with the feeling of his hands on her body. The smell of his skin lingered, and she burned with desire until the dreams finally faded.

Terrified that another vision might arrive in front of her grandmother, Haven spent her days in bed with the boy who was haunting her. She began waking only to eat, and her mother started to fret. So when Beau finally arrived to lure Haven out of the house, Mae was happy to lead him straight up the stairs to her daughter's bedroom.

"What are *you* doing here?" Haven asked sleepily as her mother stepped aside to let Beau in. "Skipping school?"

"Let's go. We're taking a little field trip," Beau announced. "I've got my dad's truck, and your grandmother's spending the day at the beauty parlor."

"I'm not going anywhere." Haven pulled the sheet up over her head. "I'm still half naked, and I have a paper to finish for Miss Henderson."

"Your paper can wait," Beau insisted. "You gotta get a little exercise, or you're going to turn into a big blob of saggy flesh."

"Gee, thanks." Haven knew she'd gained a little weight. Her mother baked as though home-cooked meals might be the answer to all her daughter's problems.

"And make sure you bring your bathing suit."

She pulled the sheet down to her neck and scowled at the boy. "After you just called me 'a blob of saggy flesh'?"

"I'm not taking no for an answer." Beau waited with his arms crossed for Haven to move and stomped one foot when she didn't. "Go on, get cracking! We're going up to Eden Falls. It's noon on a Tuesday. We aren't going to run into anybody you know. Besides, everybody in Snope City's forgotten you exist."

"No they haven't. They give me the evil eye every Sunday. In *church*. It's like they expect the altar to melt or a million locusts to fly out of my butt."

"You're exaggerating. Quit feeling so sorry for yourself."

"Why *shouldn't* I feel sorry for myself?" Haven moaned, fighting to keep the tears from her eyes. "I think I have some pretty good reasons."

Mae, who'd been waiting in the hall, took the opportunity to jump in. "Haven Moore! You stop giving this young man a hard time and get your bathing suit on. I'm tired of watching you mope around the house all day."

"I'm not leaving this room without you," Beau announced, dropping down on the side of her bed.

Haven knew there was no way she could win. "All right." She groaned. "Give me a second."

Mae marched off in victory while Beau grinned like a dim-witted kid at a carnival. "Meet you outside," he said.

THE DECKERS' OLD TRUCK struggled to climb the mountain roads, sputtering and backfiring at every hairpin turn. The air was cooler and sweet with the scent of honeysuckle. As soon as they had left Snope City behind, Haven had felt her tension ease. She closed her eyes and let the wind tousle her hair, twisting it into knots she knew she'd suffer for later.

Twenty miles out of town, the road narrowed and turned to dirt. Only a few ramshackle houses peeked out of the woods. They looked forlorn and neglected, but the mountain people who lived there didn't care about appearances. In the past, Haven had spotted a few of the men walking along the road's shoulder, dressed plainly in overalls or work clothes. They'd nod, but it was clear they didn't much fancy outsiders.

Near the top of the mountain, a church appeared on the side of the road—a simple wooden structure with pristine white walls and a short, squat steeple. Beau pulled the truck into the tiny gravel parking lot and turned off the engine. Had there been another car in the lot, they wouldn't have stopped. Though the building bore no sign, everyone in Snope City knew it belonged to the snake handlers. None of the Pentecostal kids who attended Blue Mountain had ever struck Haven as particularly frightening. But the thought of coming upon a group of Leah Frizzell's uncles and brothers waving deadly snakes and speaking in tongues was enough to convince her to maintain a respectful distance.

Haven and Beau had been ten years old when Beau's dad first showed them the way to Eden Falls, and they'd returned there countless times once they were old enough to drive. Yet it took the two of them a frustrating five minutes to locate the start of the steep path that led from the church parking lot and wound down the mountain toward the falls. At the end of the trail, they followed a wild, rocky stream until they reached an opening in the forest. In the center was a massive granite pool that had been carved out of the hills. Even with the bright sunlight sparkling on its surface, the water looked dark, and no one they knew had ever touched bottom.

Haven whipped off her sundress and dove into the pool. Her body shivered violently as she swam toward a shallow shelf at the far end. There, the water emptied out, plunging a hundred feet before reassembling itself in the form of a stream at the bottom of the waterfall. Haven stood on the mossy ledge, the water flowing around her toes, and peered down at the mist rising up from below.

"Damn!" She barely heard Beau over the roar of the water. "I'll be right back."

"Where you going?" she called.

"Forgot the cooler in the back of the truck!"

"Stay here, I'm not even hungry," she shouted, but he'd already disappeared up the path.

HAVEN SPREAD OUT a towel and lay down in the dappled sunshine with her eyes closed. A pleasant heat rose from the rock beneath her, and she felt drops of water slide across her skin in the breeze. It was the first time in weeks that she'd been really alone, and somehow she felt cleaner, as if an invisible film of pollution had been washed away. She was drifting toward sleep when she heard the sound of leaves rustling. She sat up, expecting to spot a black bear or one of the feral hogs that roamed the mountains. Then an old man and his dog appeared at the edge of the woods. Haven grabbed the towel beneath her and wrapped it around her body as he stood silently and watched. The man's white hair was slicked back and shiny. He carried a large wooden box in one hand. Even in the summer heat, he wore a flannel shirt and well-worn work pants held up by suspenders. To Haven, the outfit looked oddly formal, and it reminded her where she had seen him before. He and a younger man delivered firewood to Imogene's house every winter. Haven doubted she could overpower him if she needed to.

"Who are you?" the man demanded as if he'd caught her trespassing in his own backyard.

"My name's Haven Moore."

The man nodded. His pale eyes were a milky blue, clouded by cataracts. "What's a young girl like you doing up here by yourself? You know these woods are full of rattlers and copperheads, doncha?" He gave the wooden box a shake, and Haven heard the reply of several angry snakes.

"I'm not alone," Haven told him, trying to keep the quiver out of her voice. "My friend Beau just went up to his truck to get our lunch. He'll be right back."

"Who're you talking to, Earl?" Leah Frizzell stepped out of woods, wearing a faded blue smock that might once have been a pillowcase and a pair of black work boots. Her hair was pulled back in a ponytail, and her ears stuck out from her long, thin face.

"This that girl you told me about?" Earl asked, pointing at Haven with a gnarled finger. "The one who gave you that dress?"

Leah's face showed no sign of surprise. "Hey!" she called out to Haven as if they were old friends. "I was hoping I'd see you here. Haven Moore, this is my uncle, Earl Frizzell."

"Pleased to meet you," Haven told the old man. "How did you know I'd be here, Leah?"

"Sometimes I just know things," the girl responded matter-of-factly.

"Leah?" Haven asked nervously. "Have you been following me?"

"Not following—*observing*," Leah corrected. "And I ain't the only one."

"Them people down there think you got a demon, that right?" Earl butted in as he rested his load on a boulder by the pool.

For a moment, Haven was too shocked to speak. She looked to Leah, who seemed amused by her uncle's boldness. "I wouldn't know, sir," Haven finally said.

"Leah says you see things."

Haven squirmed. The man was strangely insistent. "It's not

something I like to talk about, if you don't mind, Mr. Frizzell."

Leah took over. "What Earl's trying to get at is, we don't think you have a demon."

Unexpectedly, a flicker of hope began to dance in Haven's brain. "You don't?"

"You know our church?" Leah pointed up to the hilltop where the little white building lay hidden by trees. "Our faith tells us that the Lord gives some people gifts. Lets us see things that others can't. I'm one of the lucky ones. I got a hunch you are, too. If so, we might be able to help you out."

Haven felt her eyes being drawn to the box at Earl's feet.

The man slapped his knee and let loose a high-pitched cackle. "No, we ain't gonna make you touch any snakes if you don't want to. And we don't roll around on the floor the whole time, neither."

"Haven?" Beau had heard the sound of voices, and he barreled into the opening in the woods. "You okay?"

"I'm fine. Leah and her uncle were just talking about their church."

The old man stood and picked up his box. Though he was six inches shorter than Beau, he managed to give the boy a good looking over. "You Ben Decker's son?"

"I am." Beau bristled. In Snope City, where everyone knew he was gay, the question was usually followed by a snicker or a scowl.

"Tell your daddy I said hello." Earl glanced back at Haven. "Service starts at ten in the morning. Six o'clock on Wednesday evenings."

"We'll see you there," Leah said, as if she already knew what Haven would do.

BACK IN SNOPE CITY, Beau pulled into Cope's Gas and Mini Mart, switched off the engine, and turned to face Haven.

"You *can't* be serious." He groaned. They'd been arguing the whole drive into town.

"Why do you keep saying that?" Haven asked. "Where's the harm in stopping by the Frizzells' church tomorrow? I told you, Leah says she sees things, too."

"Anybody would 'see things' if they chugged jars of strychnine and juggled snakes in church twice a week," Beau argued, opening the door of his truck and setting one foot outside on the ground. "That whole family is crazier than hell."

"Who cares if they're nuts as long as they can help me."

"Help you do *what*, exactly?"

"I'm not sure," Haven admitted. "I guess I'll find out tomorrow. Hey, what are you doing?" Haven asked as Beau slid out of the truck.

"What's it look like? Getting some gas!"

"I'll pay," Haven insisted, eager for a chance to escape from Beau if only for a minute or two. She didn't want to hear any more of his opinions about the Frizzells. Crazy or not, at least they were on her side. That one little fact made Haven feel better than she had in weeks.

The Mini Mart was empty but for Nikki Coggins and Trisha McDonald, two Blue Mountain juniors who worked the registers in the afternoons, and a customer comparing toothpastes. The girls started tittering the second Haven opened the door, and the man fumbled a tube of Aquafresh as she passed. Haven grabbed a package of gumballs and a jumbo-size Snickers for Beau. As she breezed past the fidgety man in the hygiene aisle, she took note of his clothing. White button-down shirt, pleatless black pants, and black leather shoes that could have been purchased at any store on earth. It was an outfit so bland that its owner would have blended into a crowd. The man finally settled on a package of Crest and came to stand behind Haven at the counter.

"Hey Haven, how's Satan?" Trisha snickered, too stupid to come up with anything clever. A couple of days earlier, Haven might have cowered. But now her strength had returned.

"He's doing good," Haven said, mimicking the girl's thick accent. "Fact, I was hoping to find him a virgin tonight. Too bad *you* haven't qualified since the sixth grade."

Nikki Coggins, who'd been pretending to stack cigarette boxes, doubled over laughing.

"You're hilarious, Haven," Trisha snapped. "What the hell are *you* laughing at, Nikki? You lost yours in *fifth*."

"I don't have time for this, Trisha. Just ring me up, would you? I'm getting Beau's gas, too." Haven thrust a wad of bills across the counter and waited for her change.

"Excuse me," she heard the man with the toothpaste deadpan as she went out the door. "Did I hear you girls say you know Satan?"

## CHAPTER TWENTY-TWO

The next afternoon, Haven climbed into the attic of her grandmother's house. At the top of the ladder, she wiped a bead of sweat from her brow. The heat had been steadily building outside, and with no air-conditioning to cool it, the room was sweltering. On the floor lay the boxes Haven had opened weeks earlier, their contents still strewn across the room. Imogene's maid had discovered the damage the previous evening, but Haven's grandmother had waited until the hottest hour of the day to insist that Haven return the things to their proper places.

Kneeling on the floor, Haven began her task, carefully wrapping the Christmas tree ornaments and tucking them next to the photo albums and keepsakes. When she reached for her baby blanket, now covered with a fine layer of dust, a book slipped out of the folds and fell open to where a sheet of paper had been tucked inside. As Haven began to gather them, her eyes landed on a familiar name.

*August Strickland*, her father had written. *Professor of Theology, Columbia University. Founder of the Ouroboros Society. Born January 21, 1860. Died June 10, 1925. Murdered?*

In an instant it all came back to her—the visions of Constance at the Ouroboros Society. She had known August Strickland. He was Ethan's mentor—the kind old man with a mane of white hair who had died and left Ethan his heir. Haven drew in a breath and closed her eyes. She knew she should put the book back in its box. She couldn't afford to let the clue drag her back into the past. One little slip—one badly timed vision—and she'd find herself even more at the mercy of her grandmother. But the spark of life that had returned to Haven at Eden Falls had grown into a raging fire that couldn't be stopped.

With her finger holding the page where the book had opened, Haven examined the cover: *A History of Gramercy Park*. The black-and-white photo below the title showed the open gate of a wrought-iron fence. Beyond lay a park in the full bloom of spring, its walkways carpeted with tiny, bright petals. The upper floors of a row of mansions were visible above the trees. One of the buildings was the home of the Ouroboros Society.

Haven opened the book and read a passage that had been underlined in pencil.

*The Strickland mansion was built in 1850 by shipping tycoon Samuel Strickland, and his family lived on the southern border of Gramercy Park for the next seven decades. In 1918, most of the Stricklands fell prey to the infamous influenza epidemic. The sole survivor was August Strickland, Samuel's grandson. With his wife and children dead from the flu, August Strickland became obsessed with the notion of reincarnation. In 1923, he formed the Ouroboros Society, an organization devoted to working with individuals who had lived multiple lives. The OS welcomed people from all walks of life and was one of the few private clubs of its kind to accept women as members.*

*One of the beneficiaries of August Strickland's charity was an enigmatic young man named Ethan Evans, whom the doctor had rescued from humble origins. Members of the OS believed Evans possessed extraordinary talents, and Strickland went out of his way to encourage such reverence. His family gone, Strickland made his protégé heir to his considerable fortune. August Strickland died unexpectedly in June of 1925, and Ethan Evans inherited the Gramercy mansion, briefly becoming the tenth-richest man in New York.*

*The gossip began almost immediately. It was rumored that Ethan Evans had been responsible for the death of his mentor. Evans vigorously denied the charges, going so far as to donate the Strickland mansion and fortune to the Ouroboros Society. Evans died in a house fire before he could fully clear his name.*

*Today, the mansion remains the headquarters of the organization that August Strickland founded more than eighty years ago.*

Haven's eyes returned to the photo on the cover. An ivy-covered mansion in the distance seemed to grow until it towered over her. She could feel the slick marble stairs beneath her feet as she climbed up the stoop to the front door and then the cold brass knob in her hand.

*She was weaving through a crowd. The men were all in somber black suits. The women wore black hats and dresses with low-slung sashes and hems that brushed their knees. Everyone she passed was red-eyed, and a few were still sniffling. Dr. Strickland was dead.*

*She was searching for Ethan. The guests were waiting for Strickland's heir to say a few words. But Ethan had disappeared. She heard voices coming from Dr. Strickland's office. A small group of people had gathered inside to pay their final respects.*

*"It's true that Evans stands to inherit the entire fortune?" a man said.*

*Constance stopped short of the door and stepped back out of view.*

*"Yes, lucky bastard," a second man replied.*

*"I've heard luck had little to do with it," another jested.*

*"I don't know what you're suggesting," a woman snapped. The voice belonged to Rebecca Underwood. "Ethan and Dr. Strickland were like father and son."*

*"She's right, James," said the second man with a snicker. "One shouldn't listen to rumors. So who's this new fellow Strickland named to take over the Society?"*

*"Some foreigner, I recall. The name slips my mind."*

*"What makes you think he's a foreigner?" Rebecca asked. "He doesn't speak like a foreigner."*

*"You've spoken with him, then?"*

*"I have," Rebecca confirmed. "He's been meeting with some of the more important members."*

*"Important members?" A man laughed.*

*Constance crept forward. Peeking through the doorway, she saw Rebecca sitting on Strickland's desk, her legs dangling over the side. The lack of respect made Constance bristle.*

*"He told me all about his plans for the Society," Rebecca boasted. "He's devised a system that will allow members to help each other get ahead."*

*"Isn't that what we do now? I just donated a heap of money to help one of Strickland's charity cases—some ten-year-old physics genius in New Jersey."*

*"And the new system will ensure that your favor is repaid," Rebecca said.*

*"You're talking about an accounting system? Didn't Strickland believe that doing good should be its own reward?"*

*"Strickland was an idealist," Rebecca said. "The new system will take human nature into consideration."*

*"Certainly, Miss Underwood," one of the men said, laughing. "But*

*I doubt if paying people to be good will ever do much to improve human nature."*

A LOUD BEEP BROKE the silence, and Haven woke with a start. The noise was coming from the back pocket of her jeans. She grabbed her phone and saw an appointment reminder flashing on its screen. She didn't have time to ponder the latest vision. She'd almost forgotten it was Wednesday.

SHE FOUND HER MOTHER and grandmother in the sitting room. Mae was studying a cookbook while Imogene watched a television preacher heal a woman with a wounded arm. Once the preacher had delivered his blessing, the woman stood up and triumphantly threw off her sling. Haven was pretty sure that she saw the woman wince.

"Now *that's* amazing," Imogene marveled.

"Can I please borrow the Civic? I need to run up to Beau's house," Haven interrupted. "Miss Henderson gave him a book and an English assignment for me."

"*May* I," Imogene corrected her. "Did you finish in the attic?"

"Yes, ma'am," Haven told her.

"Then sure, honey," Mae said without lifting her eyes from her cookbook. "The keys are on the table in the hall."

"Be sure you're back here in time for church," Imogene added.

"I'll try," Haven told her.

"Do more than *try*," Imogene warned.

Haven left her grandmother glued to the television. She guided the car down the long, steep driveway, through town, and took the turn to Eden Falls.

## CHAPTER TWENTY-THREE

For the first time, Haven noticed that the church had no windows. The only signs of activity were the four trucks parked outside. As she walked up to the double doors, she heard the discordant twangs of an electric guitar being tuned. She paused, wondering if she should knock. Then she took hold of the rough wooden handle and stepped inside.

The interior of the church was as plain and unpretentious as its exterior. Five wooden pews lined either side of a wide aisle that led up to a plywood platform at the front of the room, and ceiling fans circulated hot, humid air. On the wall behind the platform, a large cross was the church's only decoration.

Haven spotted Earl Frizzell bending down to plug in an electric amplifier while three men dressed in identical shirts and trousers readied their instruments—a guitar, banjo, and bass. The women of the congregation wore long, flowery dresses with the ruffles and frills of another era. There were no more than fifteen people in total, yet somehow the church seemed full.

"Haven!" Leah waved from the first pew and motioned for Haven to join her. "I want you to meet my mother. Mama, this is Haven Moore."

Haven gazed down at a plump woman with long red hair that hung down her back in a single braid. "It's a pleasure to meet you, Mrs. Frizzell."

The woman returned the greeting with a lovely smile. She might once have been beautiful, but life was hard for women in the hills. "Thank you, Haven. That prom dress you gave Leah was real pretty."

"I owed her one, ma'am. She saved my behind at school the other day. And I'm awful grateful to y'all for letting me visit your church."

"Oh, it's our pleasure," Mrs. Frizzell insisted. "We don't get all that many visitors up here. I sure hope we'll be able to help you today."

"Well, we're gonna give it a shot." It was Earl Frizzell. He reached out a hand that was gnarled and scarred. "I'm glad to see you here, Haven. We're just about to get started. Are you ready?"

"I'm not sure what I'm supposed to do."

Leah laughed. "You ain't supposed to *do* nothing. If you feel the spirit coming on, just let it carry you. We'll do the rest."

The congregation rose as Earl Frizzell stepped up to one of the microphones on the platform and addressed the crowd.

"We're going to do something a little different this evening," he told his people. "As y'all probably noticed, we've got a visitor here with us. Her name's Haven, and they've been saying in town that she's got a demon. That's what they call it down there when somebody starts having visions and speaking in strange tongues. Any of that sound familiar?" The congregation chuckled. "Since those people down there weren't blessed with the gift of interpretation, the good Lord's sent Haven here. We'll see if we can understand what He's trying to tell us. And if it turns out the girl does have a demon, then we'll just go right ahead and root the sucker out."

"Amen!" cried the women as the band started to play.

It was a familiar gospel tune, played faster and louder than Haven had ever heard. The congregation began to sway and a few members started to dance. Leah had her eyes closed, and her shoes shuffled to the rhythm of the song. One by one, people's lips began to move in prayer. A hum of voices rose as the dancing turned passionate. Then the sound of unfamiliar languages spoken in unison broke through the music. Haven watched with growing horror and discomfort, forcing her feet to move and wishing she were anywhere but there.

"Relax." Leah Frizzell laid a sympathetic hand on her shoulder. "This isn't something you can think your way through, Haven. You gotta let go. You gotta try to *feel* it."

Haven closed her eyes and ignored her own embarrassment. She let the music fill her mind and focused on a tingling in her toes as they danced. The tingle began to burn, climbing up her legs, engulfing her stomach, and then finally exploding inside her head.

*"I've loved you for centuries," whispered a familiar, soothing voice. She could feel her nervousness drifting away. "Whatever you want, you can have it if you'll only agree to be mine."*

THE MUSIC HADN'T stopped. She opened her eyes and saw three members of the congregation dancing around her while Earl Frizzell and his niece knelt by her side.

"What's going on?" Haven asked, pulling herself up on her elbows.

"You were talking," the preacher said. "Leah interpreted for you."

"It wasn't a demon talking. It was prophecy. The Lord's trying to tell you you're in danger," Leah said, her face pale and frightened. "You have to leave town. I think there's going to be a fire."

"No," Haven tried to assure her. "The fire already happened. A long time ago."

"Someone's going to start another one."

"But I didn't see a fire, Leah. I heard someone talking—a man with a wonderful voice."

"You can't trust him," Leah warned. "Listen to me and get out of town while you can."

## CHAPTER TWENTY-FOUR

After the church service, Haven drove for hours. Up hills and down hills. Over gravel and asphalt. She passed no more than five or six cars throughout the journey. With the windows rolled down, the hum and crackle of her wheels on the rough country roads helped calm Haven's mind.

Haven knew Leah was right. She had to leave Snope City. It was ridiculous to think she could hide from the past. The visions would never end unless she figured out what was behind them. The only way to do that was to get to New York before anyone could stop her. Yet the prospect terrified Haven. Who was the man she'd heard whispering? Was he the one who would start the fire?

Haven wished she remembered more of Constance's life. She had a hunch that the name of the man who couldn't be trusted was hidden somewhere in the dark gaps of her memory. Logic told her it might be Ethan. The very person she needed to find. If so, her trip to New York might wind up a trap.

Haven's car came to a halt at a stop sign at the intersection of two deserted roads. The crickets' song drowned out the sound of the car's motor, and Haven sat and listened to them as the leaves rustled overhead. Finally she stepped on the gas and took the turn toward Snope City. Her decision was made. She'd call Beau and start packing as soon as she got home. By the time her family woke in the morning, Haven would already be gone.

IT WAS JUST past ten o'clock when the Civic rolled to a stop in the driveway and Haven cut the engine. She wouldn't have been surprised to find the front door open and an angry old lady standing on the threshold. But the Cadillac wasn't there and the house looked dark and still. Even the porch lamp, which Imogene believed to be all that stood between her and the world's criminal community, had not been switched on. Haven wondered where her mother and grandmother could be. Imogene often liked to stay at church after services to talk to Dr. Tidmore, but she was usually home by eight and in bed by nine thirty.

"Hello?" Haven called out as she entered the house. There was no answer, just a muffled creak from a loose floorboard on the second floor. Haven held her breath and set her senses on full alert. She recognized the sound. The creaky board lay just outside her room. She flipped the switch in the foyer. The light was unusually dim—barely powerful enough to illuminate the stairs. The second floor of the building remained in the shadows. Haven stayed frozen, listening for sounds of movement over the pounding of her own heart. She heard nothing.

Looking back at the car in the driveway, Haven wondered if she should leave. But there was nowhere else to go. The town was asleep—even the gas stations were closed. She thought about calling the police, but she couldn't bear to face their scorn when they discovered they'd been summoned to investigate a loose floorboard.

With her courage slowly growing, Haven moved cautiously around the first floor, turning on lights in all of the rooms. In the kitchen she grabbed a butcher's knife. Then she headed back to the stairs and began to climb toward the darkness on the second floor. She took one step at a time, waiting and listening before climbing another. At the top of the stairs, she fumbled for the switch to the hallway light.

Room by room, she quietly nudged the doors open, then hastily turned on the lights. The bathroom and the guest room proved empty. But when she reached her own bedroom door, it didn't budge. After a moment's pause, she stepped forward and twisted the handle. She took a deep breath and held it as she threw open the door. She was reaching for the light switch when she saw a figure illuminated by an orange glow that was emanating from her bed.

She knew at once that she'd seen the man somewhere before. His face was bland, his clothes unremarkable. Even his dark hair, parted on the side, seemed oddly average. He stayed frozen for only a second before he bolted past Haven, pushing her out of his path and knocking her knife to the floor as he ran for the stairs.

Haven slammed against the door frame and lost her footing. She felt her head hit the doorknob as she fell, and then she felt nothing at all.

SHE WAS CALLING for Ethan. She felt the heat on her face and the pain in her lungs. Suddenly Haven was awake, half her face mashed against the wooden floor. The other half was hot. Her handbag and the butcher's knife were lodged beneath her, and when she rolled onto her back, she noticed that the room looked cloudy. She couldn't even see the ceiling. Something bright flickered in the corner of her eye. Haven let her head flop to the side. Flames were consuming her bed and scaling the wall behind it. She watched, still woozy, as a line of fire inched across the braided rug and climbed the legs of her desk. She knew she was going to die but felt no panic.

Her eyes drooped and she drifted to sleep. She found herself back in the familiar room. Ethan's lips were on hers, his arms encircled her, and the smell of smoke grew stronger. When he pulled back, there was something different about the look in his eye. He reached out and tenderly brushed a strand of hair from her face.

"We'll be together soon," he promised, and she believed him.

The next time she woke, the entire room was ablaze. Haven knew that she needed to move quickly, but her limbs felt as heavy as marble pillars. She made it to the hallway on her hands and knees. As she pulled herself upright, she heard a single cough. It had come from Imogene's bedroom.

She found her grandmother in bed, asleep. A pill bottle on the nightstand suggested she'd had some help counting sheep.

"Get up! Where's Mama?" Haven yelled, shaking the old woman awake.

"Have you lost your mind? She's out looking for you!" Imogene managed to croak before she succumbed to a fit of coughing. "What have you done, Haven Moore?" she demanded when she realized the room was filled with smoke.

Haven didn't take the time to answer. She grabbed her grandmother and dragged her into the hallway and down the stairs. The old woman was surprisingly light, as if she were made of nothing but spite and bitterness.

When they were both safely out the front door, Haven dug into her pocketbook and pulled out her cell phone. She punched 911. "Fire. Snively house," she gasped and passed out in the azalea bushes.

"LOOKS LIKE THE girl carried the old lady down."

Haven felt herself being lifted and heard the sound of sirens and men shouting around her.

"Oh, thank Jesus. Are they hurt? Are they burnt?" Mae Moore was hysterical.

"Doesn't look like they're burnt. Probably suffering from smoke inhalation. We'll need to get them to the hospital."

"It was your girl, Mae," Haven heard her grandmother wheezing. "You can't tell me it wasn't."

Haven swooned as she was loaded into the back of the ambulance. Her mother climbed in beside her, crying as she held Haven's hand. Before the doors closed, Haven caught a glimpse of a crowd that had gathered in the nighttime. Past them lay the house. The attic and half of the second floor were black and smoldering.

## CHAPTER TWENTY-FIVE

"Haven, honey," Mae Moore said. "Sheriff Lambert's stopped by, and he wants to ask you some questions about the fire." The curtain that had shielded her bed was suddenly yanked back. There stood a short, stocky lawman with a bushy red moustache. The kids at Blue Mountain called him Yosemite Sam. He took a seat at Haven's bedside and flipped through a small notepad until he found a clean page.

"How you feeling, Miss Moore?" The question appeared to be more scientific than sociable.

"Fine, I guess." Her lungs still felt as if she'd inhaled drain cleaner, but at least she'd had a good night's sleep.

"You want to tell me where you were last night? You told your mother you were going to see a friend. Then she found out you weren't with him when the boy called your house. Scared the tar out of her and your grandma. Your mama went out looking to see if you'd driven into a ditch somewhere."

"And Imogene went to bed," Haven mumbled. "Figures."

"I'm sorry?" the sheriff asked. "What was that?"

"Nothing. I was at the church near Eden Falls."

"You were *where*?" Mae Moore blurted.

Even the sheriff struggled not to look surprised. "What were you doing up there?"

"The preacher invited me to visit. You can check with him. His name's Earl Frizzell."

"I know Mr. Frizzell. Don't think he wants me coming up to his church, though. Some of the things they do up there aren't exactly smiled on by Tennessee law. So what time did you get home?"

"Around ten."

"Earl Frizzell preaches till ten?"

"No, I took a long drive after the service."

Sheriff Lambert scribbled a quick note. "And where were you when the fire started?"

"I'd just gotten home. I went up to my bedroom, and there was a man setting my bed on fire. He threw me against the door when he ran out of the house, and I hit my head on the doorknob."

The Sheriff looked up from his notepad. "Can you describe the intruder?"

"Sure," Haven said, but when she tried to conjure the man in her mind, he was already an anonymous blur. "He was a few inches taller than me, and he had brown hair and brown eyes. He was wearing a white shirt and black pants."

"You just described around two billion people," the sheriff said. "Can you tell me anything else?"

"I think I may have seen the guy at Cope's on Tuesday afternoon," Haven said. "He was wearing the same outfit."

"We'll come back to the man you saw in a moment. Do you have any idea who might want to break into your house or do you any harm?"

"Not unless you want to count the half of Snope City that thinks I'm possessed by Satan."

"Any names you care to give me?" He'd taken the suggestion seriously.

Haven sighed. "No." The kids at Blue Mountain might enjoy making her suffer, but even Bradley Sutton didn't have it in him to hurt her family. "Besides, I don't think the guy was from around here."

The sheriff made another note. "Now, I've been told that you've had some trouble lately. Is it true you've been seeing things? Fainting?"

"Yes." Haven squirmed.

"Are you taking any medication for these problems?"

Haven suddenly realized that no one had ever mentioned medicine. She hadn't even seen a doctor. "No."

"I see. Well, we found the cause of the fire pretty easily, Miss Moore. Looks like somebody dropped a lit candle on your bedcovers. One of those fancy types that smell like perfume. Did you have anything like that in your room?"

Haven thought of the strawberry-scented candle that had been sitting unlit on the side of her desk for more than two years. "My mom gave it to me."

"I did," Mae confirmed. "I won it as a prize at the library raffle."

"Any chance you might have knocked it over while it was lit?" the sheriff asked Haven.

"No, sir," Haven said, her frustration growing. "I already told you what happened. I got home and found someone setting fire to the room."

Sheriff Lambert spent a long, silent minute studying Haven's face. She suspected it was a tactic that he'd picked up from police shows. "You say there was a man in the house, but nothing seems to be missing, and you can't think of anyone who'd want to harm you. That doesn't leave us with too many clues." He closed his notebook. "I gotta level with you, Miss Moore. Your grandmother spent the morning trying to convince me that you're responsible for the fire."

"Oh, yeah?" The machine monitoring Haven's pulse was now beeping double time. "Why am I not surprised? Did she tell you that she thinks I have a demon?"

"She might have said something like that. Now, I don't believe in demons, Miss Moore, but I think there must be something wrong with a girl who'd do what you did to the preacher's office. Way I see it, you're lucky Dr. Tidmore didn't press charges."

"You really think I'd burn down my grandmother's house?"

"Angry teenagers have been known to do worse things than that. Your grandmother says you're upset she's not letting you go off to school this fall. She thinks you're troubled, and she recommended I call Dr. Tidmore for a second opinion. He agrees with your grandmother, Miss Moore. They both think I need to find a place to put you until you're no longer a danger to others."

"So why don't you?" Haven challenged the sheriff.

"Oh, Lord," Mae muttered in embarrassment.

"I would," the man assured Haven, "if it weren't for one thing. Call came in last night after the fire had been put out. A lady driving by claims she saw a man snooping around your house after dark. Said he was wearing a white shirt and dark pants, but she couldn't tell us much more than that."

"That's the man I was talking about! So why are you here giving me the third degree? Why aren't you out looking for *him*?"

"I'm afraid the description doesn't give us all that much to work on. There are a whole lot of white shirts and dark pants out there. Is there anything else you can tell me that might help us focus our search? Something you might have left out of your account of the incident? Arson is a serious crime, Miss Moore. Someone could have been killed last night."

"Well, I can give you one clue, Sheriff," Haven said with her best phony smile. "You aren't going to find the arsonist sitting here in the emergency room."

"Haven!" Mae Moore yelped.

"That's all right, Mrs. Moore. I was just about done here anyway. If your daughter remembers anything else, have her give me a call."

As soon as Sheriff Lambert rose from his seat, Haven reached over and pulled the curtain closed. "Someone saw a man by our house, and the Sheriff *still* thinks I'm the one who set the fire," she whispered fiercely to her mother. "How could you let Imogene tell him that?"

"You know I can't control your grandmother," Mae said. "She's real upset about the house right now. She might have said a few things she didn't mean."

"How bad is it?" Haven remembered the charred second floor and felt a little nauseous waiting for the answer. The house on the hill had been in her family for a hundred and fifty years.

"It can be fixed. . . ." Mae started, trying to sound optimistic before she gave up. "The second floor is pretty bad. The attic and your room are totally gone. The roof caved in after they put the fire out. And there's a lot of water damage downstairs. Insurance will cover it, but it's going to take a month or more before we can move back in."

"You said my room is gone?"

"Yeah, honey," Mae reported sadly.

"Everything? My clothes and my computer and everything?"

"I'm afraid so."

"Where are we going to go? What are we going to do?"

"I don't know. Beau and his daddy said you could stay with them for as long as need be."

Haven drew back the curtain, fully expecting to find her friend on the other side. "Where *is* Beau? Why isn't he here?"

"How should *I* know?" Mae asked, handing her daughter a cell phone. "I have enough trouble keeping track of my *own* child."

Haven punched in the familiar digits.

"Haven?" Beau answered immediately.

"Where are you?"

"I'm here in the waiting room. They won't let me see you. They said only family is allowed in the ER."

"Then I'm coming out *there*." Before her mother could stop her, Haven slid the IV needle out of her arm and sprang from the bed.

"GOOD GOD, HAVEN," Beau whispered as he stood up to greet her. "That hospital gown doesn't leave much to the imagination, does it?"

"Who cares?" Haven asked. She had bigger problems to deal with.

"I do! Here. Put this on." He took off his button-down shirt and handed it to Haven. The black T-shirt he was wearing underneath had faded from a thousand washings.

"Someone tried to kill me," she told him.

Beau's attention suddenly shifted to a middle-aged man who was angling to get a look at Haven's backside. "Hey, buddy. You better turn around before I come over there and *turn* you around."

A second man, dressed in a white shirt and gray slacks, kept a straight face as he tapped away at a BlackBerry.

"You sure?" Beau asked as the first man picked up a copy of *Field & Stream* and pretended to read.

"There was a man in my bedroom when I got home last night. He knocked me out and set fire to the house."

"What should we do?" The absence of doubt on Beau's face kept Haven's own doubts from growing. She'd started to wonder if Sheriff Lambert might be right. After what she'd done in Dr. Tidmore's office, setting a house on fire didn't seem like much of a stretch.

"I don't know about you," Haven said, "but I'm not sticking around to find out what happens next. I've gotta get to New York."

## CHAPTER TWENTY-SIX

Haven left the hospital on Friday and took up residence in the Decker guest room. On Saturday morning, Mae Moore arrived at the farmhouse to beg a favor from her daughter. She wanted Haven to come to church on Sunday and make peace with her grandmother. The old lady had finally admitted that Haven might not be an arsonist—but she hadn't forgiven the girl for seeking help from the snake handlers. It was Imogene's personal request that her granddaughter make amends by attending Dr. Tidmore's latest sermon. It was the least Haven could do, Mae had told her. If Haven hadn't felt a little guilty about her secret plan to skip town, she never would have agreed.

Still, she knew from the beginning that she shouldn't have given in to Imogene's demand. It wasn't as if she and Beau had two spare hours to spend listening to Dr. Tidmore. They had worked every second of the weekend, trying to improvise a wardrobe that wouldn't mark Haven as the homeless hillbilly she was. Unwanted prom gowns were ripped apart and refashioned into breezy summer sundresses.

The leftover black silk from Bethany Greene's dress became a daring evening dress. ("You never know!" Beau had insisted.) Haven planned to buy T-shirts, jeans, and sneakers before she left, but she'd wait until she got to New York City to purchase a decent pair of heels. When she thought of visiting Manhattan's fabled boutiques and wandering among the racks of beautiful clothes, Haven could barely contain her excitement. Once her decision to leave had been made—and staying in Snope City no longer seemed like the safer option—some of the fear she had felt had vanished. Now Haven could focus on one simple thought. After almost a century, she was finally going home.

WHEN SUNDAY ROLLED AROUND, Haven realized that despite all their dressmaking, she still had nothing suitable to wear to church. Imogene would keel over in her pew if Haven arrived in anything with a hem that came to a halt above the knee. And the last thing Haven needed was to give the old lady a heart attack in front of Snope City's finest citizens. When Beau's father got word of Haven's dilemma, he disappeared into his bedroom and returned holding a lovely blue dress covered with tiny white flowers.

"I can't wear that, Mr. Decker," Haven whispered. It had belonged to his wife. For three years, it had been sitting in her closet, just waiting for Emily Decker to come back from the grave to claim it. Beau had once shown Haven the closet, which was kept as perfectly preserved as a shrine.

"Course you can. I'm no expert in ladies' clothing, but I reckon it should fit you."

"It's not that—"

"I know. But Emily would want you to have it, after all you've done for this family."

"After all *I've* done?"

Ben motioned to his son and winked. "You and me both know he'd have turned to a life of crime without you. Probably would have been in jail for assault by the eighth grade. Now he's going off to Vanderbilt like his mama wanted."

Haven winced. Ben Decker was going to be crushed if Beau abandoned his college plans.

"Just put the dress on, Haven," Beau snapped. "We gotta get going."

Haven shot her friend an evil look as she took the dress from his father. "Thank you, Mr. Decker. I really appreciate it."

"Ain't nothing at all," Ben Decker insisted, trying not to sound too proud of himself.

RIGHT IN THE center of Snope City stood Imogene Snively's church, a grand brick structure with a white steeple that rose high enough to puncture heaven. The doors stood open, and the church was awash with light. Flowers overflowed from marble pots, and the mahogany surfaces gleamed with lemon-scented polish. Haven and Beau trod across thick burgundy carpet toward the Snively family pew. All around them, people whispered, but Haven smiled serenely as she and Beau took their seats next to Mae Moore.

"I didn't know if you were going to make it," Imogene said in a starchy tone.

"Wouldn't miss it for the world," Haven trilled as the congregation rose and Dr. Tidmore took the podium.

The pastor examined the crowd as the choir stood behind him, as straight-faced and serious as a squad of professional bodyguards.

"Please be seated," Dr. Tidmore said quietly as he shuffled through his notes, which were written on a deck of index cards. He did the same thing every Sunday, though he never seemed to use them. When at last he gripped the sides of the podium and began his sermon, his gentle manner had disappeared. The voice that came booming down from the pulpit was powerful and authoritative.

"Devil's Chimney. Devil's Courthouse. Devil's Stomping Ground."

He paused briefly as the names echoed in Haven's head. "Have you ever stopped to wonder why so many places around here are named in some way for the devil? Maybe you thought it was just a *coincidence*. Or maybe you thought your ancestors enjoyed a good joke. Well, you thought wrong. See, your ancestors understood something that many of us today find hard to imagine. They knew that Satan isn't just an *idea*. He's not a *metaphor*. Satan is as real as the person sitting next to you. Fact is, Satan just might *be* the person sitting next to you."

Everyone in the church saw him look directly at Haven. Mae Moore fidgeted in her seat, and Haven knew she'd been set up.

"But most of you would never know if you met the devil face-to-face. You'd probably expect to see cloven hooves and goat horns and a forked tail. The *Bible* never describes Satan that way. The Bible calls him a trickster, a tempter, the father of lies. But the Book of Job makes one thing *very* clear—Satan is a flesh-and-blood being—a flesh-and-blood being that's right here with us on God's green earth."

Dr. Tidmore opened his Bible to a carefully marked page and began to read.

"*Now there was a day when the sons of God came to present themselves before the LORD, and Satan came also among them. And the LORD said unto Satan, 'Whence comest thou?' Then Satan answered the LORD, and said, 'From going to and fro in the earth, and from walking up and down in it.'* Book of Job. Chapter one. Verses six and seven."

When Dr. Tidmore raised his head to face the congregation, his glasses caught the light, and for a moment, the lenses blazed like two tiny suns. How could he do it? Haven marveled. How could the man who'd once been so kind decide to turn on her so completely?

"Your ancestors gave names to the places they believed the devil had visited," Dr. Tidmore continued. "And don't fool yourselves into thinking he doesn't still visit us. It's just that we can't see him like they used to. But he's here, sure enough, working day and night to keep us from reaching salvation. He tempts us with earthly delights and taunts us with the pleasures of the flesh until we're so covered in the muck of this wicked world that we're unable to gain passage to heaven.

"But there's no need to worry, for we have the Bible to guide us, and the good book tells us exactly how to keep the devil at bay. Chapter six of Ephesians, verses eleven to thirteen:

*"Put on the full armor of God so that you can take your stand against the devil's schemes. For our struggle is not against flesh and blood, but against the rulers, against the authorities, against the powers of this dark world and against the spiritual forces of evil in the heavenly realms. Therefore put on the full armor of God, so that when the day of evil comes, you may be able to stand your ground."*

Dr. Tidmore closed his Bible and took a slow sip from a glass of water that had been left inside the podium, a gesture he often used to keep the congregation on the edge of their seats.

"Now, some of you might ask why I chose this subject for our sermon today. Why I felt compelled to issue a warning. It's because I believe that the devil has been *right here* in Snope City. That's right. He's fooled you, he's fooled me, he's fooled *all* of us. Fact is, he's been here for years, weaseling his way into our hearts, trying to convince us to let down our guard. Getting us to relax our standards. Conning us into believing that we may not require Jesus's help to reach salvation. And that we need not live as the Bible instructs us.

"And we haven't fought back! We've come to accept things we *know* the Bible calls abominations. Ideas that Christ *himself* would call heresies. Homosexuality. Clairvoyance. Reincarnation. Don't let yourself be deceived. These are the devil's work. And it's time for us to put on the armor of the Lord and do battle with the forces of evil once and for all. We must show Satan no mercy. We must punish those who have spread his lies and send the devil where he can do no more harm."

Haven looked over at Mae, whose face was buried in her hands.

Imogene stared straight ahead at the pulpit, basking in the pastor's wisdom.

"I know exactly where the devil is," Haven hissed at her grandmother. "Let's go, Beau." Together they marched out of the church, the pastor's booming voice barely drowning out the whispered outrage that came from the pews.

HAVEN BROKE THE stunned silence just before she and Beau pulled into the Decker driveway.

"You should come with me."

"To New York?" Beau asked, as if the issue had never been broached.

Haven still couldn't understand his reluctance. "Why not? You want to stay in Snope City and listen to that crap for the rest of your life? Come with me, or join the circus, or enlist in the damn Navy if that's what you want. Just do *something*. They don't want you here, and there's no reason for you to stay."

Beau's jaw was set and his expression stoic. "I told you, Haven. I can't just leave my dad. He needs me."

"Why? The man isn't missing *all* his limbs. You gotta live your own life."

"We all have our crosses to bear," he said.

"Sure, but there's no point hauling one around just for sport. I know you find it hard to believe, but your presence isn't necessary for your father's survival. He needs to move on. Get a girlfriend. Cook himself dinner every once in a while. He can't do all that if you treat him like a cripple."

"Have you gone blind?" Beau lost his composure, and his voice inched toward a shout. "He *is* a cripple."

"Look at my dress. Look at it!" Haven insisted. "A year ago he would never have loaned me one of your mama's things. He probably would have shot us if he'd found us in that closet. Your dad is ready to move on, Beau."

"Why do I have to listen to this? First I get accused of working with Satan to pervert Snope City, and now I hear that I'm ruining my dad's life. All this tough love is starting to seem a little sadistic."

"I think you're scared."

"I think you need to mind your own business," Beau barked back.

"I think you're using your dad as an excuse to do nothing with your life. And I don't think that's fair to him."

"I think you need to shut the hell up, Haven." Beau turned off the ignition and slid out of the driver's seat. He started to stomp away and made it halfway to the porch before he returned and thrust his head through the truck's open window. "You got a lot of nerve handing out advice left and right, Haven Moore. Just 'cause your life is a mess doesn't mean mine is, too. Maybe you should figure out your own problems before you start trying to solve mine."

"I'm not trying . . ." Haven began to argue, but Beau had already walked away.

"HOW COME Y'ALL are back so soon?" Ben Decker asked, emerging from his bedroom as Haven stepped inside the house. Before she could answer, they both turned to stare at Beau, who'd already changed out of his church clothes and was heading out the back door. "Where you going?" Ben called out to his son.

"For a walk." Beau let the screen door slam behind him and vanished into the woods behind the farmhouse.

"Boy's got a temper on him," Ben muttered. "Something happen at church?"

"The usual. Got accused of being in league with the devil."

Ben Decker shook his head. He was disappointed but not surprised. "I imagine that must be getting a little old by now. It's a good thing you two won't have to put up with that sort of thing much longer."

Haven bit her lip, but she couldn't keep the words from slipping out. "Mr. Decker, have you talked to Beau about college lately?"

Ben's eyes narrowed. "What's to talk about? He's been planning to go to Vanderbilt since he was ten years old."

"It's not my place to say, but I think those plans may have changed." As she headed toward the guest bedroom, Haven wished she'd never spoken.

Too nervous to risk running into Beau, Haven spent the next hour hiding in her room, packing and repacking her suitcase three times. As eager as she was to leave Imogene, Dr. Tidmore, and Snope City behind, she hated the thought of what she'd done to her only friend. She knew she would never have told Ben Decker about his son's college plans if she had to stick around to deal with the consequences. Haven wanted what was best for Beau, and she had been certain she knew what that was. If Beau didn't escape from Snope City, the town was sure to smother him. But Haven regretted betraying his confidence. She should have taken the time to look for a better solution.

HAVEN JUMPED AT the sound of wheels on gravel and looked out the bedroom window to see a truck pulling up near the tobacco shed. The doors opened and a girl stepped out. The hem of her old-fashioned dress brushed the ground as she walked.

Haven met Leah Frizzell on the front porch. The girl pointed at Haven's outfit. "Looks like you've been to church this morning."

"For all of ten minutes. Just long enough to hear that I'm responsible for Satan's hold on Snope City."

Leah's laugh was short and harsh. "Those people down there wouldn't know the devil if he came up and goosed 'em. Lord knows they keep looking for him in all the wrong places."

"Well, they sure think they've found him this time," Haven said. "Pretty much everyone in town thinks I tried to kill my grandmother and burn down her house."

"I heard. I tried to come see you in the hospital after the fire, but they told me you weren't allowed to have visitors."

"Thanks for thinking of me," Haven said. "I just wish I'd listened to your warning. I might have saved my family's house."

"Don't worry about that. They'll fix it soon enough," Leah stated matter-of-factly, tucking a strand of lank red hair behind one ear. "Listen. You mind if we sit down for a minute? There's something I want to tell you."

"You didn't have to drive out all this way if you wanted to talk to me." Haven led Leah to a pair of wicker chairs Beau had found at a garage sale and fixed up for the porch. "You could have just used the phone."

"I'd rather not," the girl said. The wicker crunched when she sat. "You never know who might be eavesdropping."

"Eavesdropping?" Haven laughed. "You really think someone's listening in on my calls?"

"They've been watching you for years," Leah said bluntly. "Why wouldn't they be listening, too?"

Haven suddenly felt cold. "What do you mean?"

"When we were about nine years old, I saw you in the park one day. You'd come by yourself, and you were playing on the swings. There was a man taking pictures of you, and I knew he wasn't your father. I pointed him out to Earl, and Earl went and chased him off. Then another time, I saw you in town. You were eating ice cream while you crossed the road, and you weren't paying attention. You would've stepped right out in front of a truck, but a man grabbed your arm and pulled you back. It wasn't the man with the camera, but it looked a lot like him. There were other times, too. There always seemed to be somebody watching you."

"I don't remember any of that," Haven said. "Who were they? Why didn't you warn me?"

"They weren't a danger to you then, but they are now. I gave prophecy this morning in church. Mamma did the interpreting. I know you're not one of us, Haven, but you got to listen to what I'm going to tell you." Leah paused as if searching for a way to continue. "You have to leave before they can stop you."

"Don't worry—I'm leaving soon," Haven assured her. "I'm not going to ignore your advice again."

"Good. But you have to be careful when you get where you're going. It'll be dangerous. There's a man . . . I don't know which name he uses," Leah said. "But he knows who you are. And he'll be looking for you. You're going to have to take your faith with you, Haven. It'll be your only protection."

"I don't understand."

"Haven," Leah said, "I know this is going to sound crazy. But I think the person who's looking for you is evil. He's . . ."

"Yeah?" prompted Haven.

"I think it could be the devil himself."

## CHAPTER TWENTY-SEVEN

Haven flung her suitcase into the back of Ben Decker's truck. It was early in the morning, and the sun was just rising over the mountains.

"Nine P.M. tomorrow," a voice announced. "The Apollo Theater."

"What?" Haven looked up to see Beau standing on the Deckers' porch, dressed only in a pair of boxer shorts. She'd heard him arguing with his father the night before. Ben had demanded to know what had changed his son's mind about Vanderbilt. Beau had refused to explain himself. The yelling had gone on and on until Haven heard Beau stomp down the hall, barricade himself in his bedroom, and turn his TV up to full volume.

"I saw it on television last night. There's some stupid music awards show being held at the Apollo. Iain Morrow is supposed to be in the audience." Beau spun around and headed into the house.

"Don't go, Beau. . . ." Haven pleaded.

"Good luck in New York," he told her without looking back.

"Beau, I'm sorry," Haven pleaded. "I need your help. I can't do this without you."

"It's too bad you didn't think of that earlier or you might've kept your damn mouth shut." He slammed the front door, leaving Haven in tears.

ON THEIR WAY to the train station in Johnson City, Haven and Ben Decker passed by the Snively house. Even in the cheerful morning sunlight, the place looked like a desolate ruin. Blue plastic tarps covered the roof, and the second-story windows were hidden behind plywood. The blazing azaleas, untouched by the fire, seemed cruelly out of place. Gazing out the truck's window at her old house, Haven thought she saw a figure pass the picture window in Imogene's sitting room.

"There's somebody in there," she told Ben.

"Probably insurance people," he responded. "Don't know who else would be up there. They've moved out all the furniture. There ain't nothing in the house left to take."

"I sure hope Imogene gets it all fixed," Haven said.

"Oh, she will. It'll be as good as new by the time you get back."

*If I ever come back,* Haven thought to herself as they reached the freeway entrance at the edge of town. There was nothing left for her in Snope City. Her future and fate lay in New York City, and for better or worse, she planned to find what was waiting for her.

When they reached the train station, Haven gave Ben Decker a long hug.

"Remember, you always got us if you need us," he told her. "And don't worry about Beau, either. I didn't spend ten years in the Army learning how to be a nice guy. That boy's in for a world of pain if he decides to live at home."

They were interrupted by the announcement. Haven's train was ready to board. She managed to choke back the tears until she was in her seat. They were still flowing when the train rolled out of the station and onto tracks that snaked through the mountains. Haven closed her eyes. As hard as it was to say goodbye to the Deckers, she had no interest in taking one last look at a town that had never wanted her in the first place.

# PART TWO:

# THE ONE WHO WAS WAITING

## CHAPTER TWENTY-EIGHT

The sun had set and the train car was dark. The shadowy landscape outside the window offered no clues as to her location. They were passing through a rundown town, and isolated streetlights illuminated odd scenes. Three teenagers dunking each other in an aboveground swimming pool in a seedy backyard. A barking pit bull straining at its flimsy chain. A little kid in a nightgown aiming a plastic pistol at the train that sped by less than twenty feet from her window.

Haven shuddered and rubbed the goose bumps that had sprouted on her arms. This world felt different, more dangerous than the one she had left. Snope City had been a cocoon—smothering but safe. She was beginning to sense that freedom came with a new set of perils. Yet she could still feel New York drawing her toward it. The pull of the city was stronger than it had ever been.

"Excuse me, sir," Haven called out. The man with the Amtrak badge slowed long enough to grab the ticket stub from the seat in front of her. "Where are we?"

"New Jersey. Next stop Penn Station," he replied, picking up speed as the words left his mouth and disappearing through the sliding door at the back of the car.

Haven stood up and looked to see if the bathroom was occupied. Its door was open, and the car was empty but for a man sitting three rows behind her. He wore a bland navy suit and sported a thirty-dollar haircut, and though his eyes were closed, Haven was certain that he wasn't asleep. Haven slid back down into her seat and stared out the window. The buildings were smaller and closer together now. Streetlamps bathed the roads in pale yellow light. In the distance, she could see the first suggestions of a city rising into the sky.

OUTSIDE PENN STATION, the taxi line snaked around the block. A hot wind whipped through the streets, and the scent of ozone in the air told her a storm was on the way. The man from the train was behind her, seemingly oblivious to her presence as he tapped away at his BlackBerry. She kept one eye on him and felt for the cell phone in her pocket, wishing she could call Beau for advice. Just as the first fat drops of rain began to splatter the sidewalks, Haven reached the taxi dispatcher.

"Where you headed?" he asked without looking up. Behind her, the sound of typing paused.

"Twenty-eighth Street," Haven whispered.

"Twenty-eighth Street?" the dispatcher repeated at top volume. "Here you go," he said, thrusting a yellow sheet of paper at her. "Enjoy your time in the city."

While the driver loaded her luggage into the trunk, Haven ducked into the taxi and slammed the door. Looking back at the crowd, she saw the man in the suit standing at the head of the line. He wasn't pretending anymore. He stared straight at her.

"Where to?" asked the driver.

"The Windemere Hotel," Haven murmured, hoping the man outside couldn't read lips.

"Which way you wanna go?" the driver asked, leering at her in the rearview mirror.

Haven sensed it was a test and that the wrong answer would cost her an extra ten dollars. "Fifth Avenue to Twenty-eighth Street and take a left," Haven heard herself say.

"No problem," the cabbie replied with a hint of disappointment in his voice.

As the taxi tore south through the city, Haven watched the skyscrapers pass as if they were part of a movie that she'd seen before. But new scenes had been added and others removed. The effect was baffling, at times disturbing. Everything was taller, shinier, brighter than she'd expected. She was relieved when the cab stopped in front of the gilded entrance of the Windemere. Curtains of rain cascaded from the hotel's awning as streaks of lightning wove between nearby buildings. The driver dumped her suitcase on the curb, and Haven watched passengers disembark from another cab that had pulled up in front of the hotel. The man from the train was not among them.

"May I?" The doorman reached for Haven's bag, and she jumped. "You are a guest, are you not?"

"Yes," Haven sputtered.

"Right this way," the man told her, leading Haven through the lobby. When Haven reached the reception desk, a haughty woman in a stiff gray suit looked her up and down.

"May I help you?" she droned.

"I have a reservation under Haven Moore."

"Let me check," the woman said suspiciously. She typed in the name. "Yes. Here it is."

"Good evening, sir." The clerk at the next desk was a little too chipper. "How may I help you this evening?"

"I don't have a reservation, but I'd like a room."

Haven looked over and saw the man from the train sliding an ID across the counter.

"Excuse me," she said, suddenly feeling emboldened. "Weren't you just on the train with me?"

The man's face remained expressionless. "I don't know. Was I?" he asked.

"I saw you on the train," Haven insisted. "The train from Tennessee."

"That may be true," said the man. "But I didn't see *you*."

"Miss?" Haven heard the clerk say. "Your key." There was something about the woman's smug smile that made Haven want to punch her.

## CHAPTER TWENTY-NINE

Haven checked under the bed and inside the closet before climbing between the sheets. She left the curtains open and watched the lights in the office buildings across the street extinguish one by one. She dreamed of Ethan. She felt him beside her, his chest rising and falling, each breath expelled with a soft, purring snore. When the bright summer sun finally woke her, Haven found herself wrapped around a pillow, clinging to it like a life preserver.

She splurged on room service coffee and called her mother. Mae was troubled to learn that her daughter had skipped town, though after Dr. Tidmore's sermon, she was hardly surprised.

"Why *now*?" she whispered in case Imogene was listening. "Why couldn't you wait?"

Haven searched for a reasonable explanation but didn't find one. There was no point in telling her mother that she was in New York to find out what had happened to a girl who'd been dead for ninety years. Or that later that night she'd be standing outside the Apollo

Theater, hoping to catch a glimpse of a rich boy who was suspected of murder. And even if she'd tried, she couldn't have described the forces that had compelled her to act when she did.

Once the dreaded call was out of the way, Haven dressed and hopped a number 6 subway downtown. When she climbed up the stairs and emerged onto Spring Street, she felt, for the first time in her life, that she was where she needed to be. As she walked east, a woman in a pleated skirt and T-strap heels hurried past her. A green ribbon wound around the bottom of her bell-shaped hat. At the curb, a man waited behind the wheel of a fancy car with whitewall tires and a rumble seat in back. It was in remarkable condition for a vehicle that had to be almost one hundred years old. The newspaper the man held bore the headline British Explorer Feared Lost in the Amazon. A nearby store offered the latest in "Victrola Talking Machines," and a movie poster plastered to the side of a building advertised a Charlie Chaplin film.

Haven blinked and the scene disappeared. Though the buildings around her remained the same, the cars and pedestrians belonged to the present day. She turned down Elizabeth Street and found the neighborhood stores had been converted into cafés and boutiques. She chose some overpriced jeans and two T-shirts from one of the shops she visited, making the first real dent in the money she'd been hoarding since the fourth grade.

At the next boutique, she selected a pair of heels to match the black dress Beau had insisted on making. As she waited for a gum-cracking salesgirl to return from the storeroom with a pair of size eights, Haven wondered what she was doing. She had come to New York to solve a mystery—to find what Constance wanted her to find and stop the visions once and for all. Now here she was, choosing an outfit to impress a boy who, by all accounts, was nothing but trouble. Yet when Haven imagined seeing Iain Morrow later that night, she found herself out of breath. Somehow a single grain of hope had sprouted and strangled her common sense.

She tried to be rational. Iain Morrow was a notorious womanizer—and if the Jeremy Johns rumors were true, he might soon be in jail for the rest of his life. But Haven's logic was of little use. Haven knew she still hoped for nothing more than to find Ethan Evans walking down the red carpet at the Apollo Theater.

The slim salesgirl arrived with a silver box in her hands and knelt to pull the shoes out of their tissue. A wisp of blonde hair was sticking out from under the girl's slick black bob, and Haven realized she was wearing a wig. Haven slipped on the heels and adjusted the straps. As she took a turn around the shop, she happened to glance out the windows. Across the street, in another store, a man was watching her. He was casually flipping through a rack of men's shirts, but his eyes never left Haven. It wasn't the man from the train, though they shared an uncanny resemblance. Perhaps it was the cut of his gray suit or the razor-sharp part in his hair. Haven put the shoes in their box.

"I'll take them," she said. "By the way, is there an exit at the back of the store?" Haven asked as the salesgirl started to ring her up.

"Why?" the girl responded suspiciously. "What exactly are you planning to do?"

"There's a man across the street. I think he's been following me."

"Really?" The girl looked out the window. "You mean the guy who looks like he's with the FBI?"

"That's the one."

"*Is* he with the FBI?" the girl asked. "Is this one of those 'If you see something, say something' moments?"

"What?" Haven blurted out. "Of course not!"

"You're not a terrorist or anything?"

"Are you kidding? I'm from Tennessee."

"The Unabomber was from Chicago. Timothy McVeigh grew up in Pendleton, New York. The Weathermen—"

"Okay!" Haven stopped her. "I get it. I'm not a terrorist."

"Well, in that case, yeah, we share a courtyard with a lighting store on Bowery. Tell them Janine said to let you through."

"Thanks," Haven said.

"No problem. Listen, you sure you don't you want me to call the police or something?"

"What would we tell them? They can't do anything unless he does something. I'm not sure I want to find out what he has in mind."

"Good point," said the girl. "Follow me."

Haven grabbed her shopping bag and let the shopgirl lead her to a door at the back of the store. Two minutes later, she hailed a cab on Bowery and sailed back uptown.

STILL A LITTLE anxious from the near encounter with the mysterious man on Elizabeth Street, Haven rushed through the lobby of the Windemere, eager to get upstairs to her room. She almost failed to notice the man from the train lounging in one of the leather chairs. Once again, he was pretending not to see her, though she could tell that his eyes weren't reading the magazine he held in his hands. The surge of panic left her a little dizzy, but she managed to make her way to the reception desk. It wasn't until she'd already started speaking that she realized she was addressing the same unfriendly woman from the night before.

"That man has been following me," she gasped.

"Which man?" the clerk inquired without a trace of concern.

"The one in the chair by the palm tree. He has short brown hair and he's wearing a navy suit."

As she spoke, the man in question was joined by another man wearing an identical suit. They looked enough alike to belong to the same family or cult. The two men spoke for a few seconds, then exited the building together without so much as a glance at Haven.

"I'm sorry, *which* man did you say was following you?" the clerk asked rudely.

"Never mind," Haven spat back.

* * *

BY SEVEN THIRTY, Haven was sitting on the bed in her hotel room, fully dressed and watching the clock on the bottom left corner of Channel One. At precisely eight twenty-five, she stood and checked her reflection in the mirror. She'd done her best with her hair, and the black dress that she and Beau had made tricked the eye into believing she was shapelier than she had any right to appear. Haven added a touch of cherry lip gloss and pursed her lips for the mirror. She looked good. Even the handsome bellhop who helped her avoid the lobby and leave through the hotel's service entrance flirted with her the entire way.

Outside the Apollo Theater, the crowds were writhing behind the velvet ropes that lined a crimson carpet. It took Haven fifteen minutes to slither and slide her way to the front row, and by the time she was standing with her belly pressed against the rope, the guests were already arriving. Beau would have loved the parade of movie stars and socialites, but none of them were of any great interest to Haven. She watched the end of the line as they glided past, searching for the face she'd come to see. All she wanted was one quick look at Iain Morrow.

As nine o'clock approached, Iain Morrow had yet to make his appearance, and Haven's feet had begun to ache. The line of luminaries was thinning, and the star power had dimmed. At last, a black Mercedes with tinted windows arrived at the end of the carpet. A door swung open, and a stunning girl in a short silver skirt toppled out of the car, laughing hysterically. The flash of paparazzi cameras lit up the night, and it was several minutes before three figures emerged from the blaze of blinding lights. The girl in the silver skirt wobbled on three-inch heels, and if it hadn't been for the arm around her tiny waist, she would have kissed the carpet. The arm holding her up belonged to Iain Morrow, and his other one was draped around an even prettier girl who wore a glazed expression and little else. The girls were both clearly wasted, but Iain Morrow walked a straight line down the red carpet, barely blinking in the glare. The crowd had gone wild watching the spectacle, and the black-clad bodyguards who tailed the threesome scanned the ropes for signs of danger.

For a few seconds, Haven didn't bother breathing. The world had gone quiet and still around her. Though he looked nothing like Ethan, Iain Morrow was more beautiful in person than Haven had imagined. Tall and lean, with a body that could make any outfit look fashionable. Dark brown hair worn delightfully unkempt and the sort of tan one only acquires while lying on hidden beaches in the south of France. Arched brows that hovered mischievously over bright green eyes. As he moved closer, Haven instinctively tried to take a step back, wishing she could vanish into the crowd. But she found herself pinned against the rope, unable even to turn away. Just as the trio passed by, one of the models caught her heel in the carpet and stumbled toward Haven, all whirling arms and smudged mascara. Haven reached out to catch her, and as she did, her hand brushed another that had come to the girl's rescue. A jolt shook Haven, and she felt herself totter just as the model regained her balance. Haven looked up to see Iain Morrow peering down at her, a lopsided grin on his lovely face. He turned to one of his bodyguards and pointed to Haven. His lips moved, but she couldn't hear his words.

"Her?" The bodyguard mouthed. Iain gave the man a sharp nod and continued down the red carpet with his two tipsy strumpets in tow.

Still trapped at the front of the mob of spectators, Haven could only watch them leave. She didn't notice the bodyguard ducking under the velvet rope. He lifted Haven by the waist and carried her through the crowd.

"Hey! What are you doing? Let me down!" she cried, though only a few people seemed to hear her and no one seemed to care.

The man lugged her through a service entrance at the side of the building and down a long, dark corridor. Weak fluorescent lights flickered from the ceiling and exposed pipes gurgled along the walls. Haven had given up demanding an explanation. The bodyguard remained mute no matter what threats she hurled at him. Finally, they came to a plain metal door. The man opened it, turned on a light, and set Haven down inside the empty room.

"Wait here. He'll be down soon," the man informed her brusquely before leaving.

"*Who* will?" Haven shouted at the closed door.

She paced the room, searching for a means of escape. The air was dank and musty, and she was starting to shiver when the door opened. Iain Morrow stood in the hall, looking unusually disheveled and slightly out of breath. For a moment, he didn't move. He just stared at her with wide eyes.

"There you are," was all he said before he took her in his arms, bent down, and kissed her. Once she'd managed to convince herself he was real, Haven began to kiss him back.

# CHAPTER THIRTY

"Eeeeaaaannnn. Eeeeeeeeaaann!" sang a voice in the hallway.

"Where did he go?" whined another in a English accent.

"Ooops!" There was a loud thud, followed by giggling.

"You did that on purpose!" one of the girls screeched. They were moving closer.

"Damn," Iain muttered, letting his hands fall from Haven's face. He was even better looking when annoyed.

"Are those your *dates*?"

Iain pretended to sniff at the air. "Is that . . . no wait . . . is that *jealousy* I detect? They're not my girlfriends. They're more like *props*."

Haven blushed. Somehow his words were more intimate than his kiss. Iain Morrow was *teasing* her. He knew she could be jealous—and he knew she could take a ribbing for it. She felt exposed and exhilarated, as if he'd caught a glimpse of her naked.

Taking Haven by the hand, Iain guided her into the hallway, where they found the two models clinging to each other, each struggling to keep the other upright.

"Iain!" slurred the fragile-looking blonde with raccoon eyes. "Where did you go? We've been looking all over for you!"

"The awards show is starting and they won't let us inside," the tall brunette wailed. "You *know* they're doing the tribute to Jeremy first. Why did you leave us?"

Iain shrugged. "Ladies, I have no idea what you're talking about. I haven't gone anywhere. I've been right here all along."

The two girls traded a glance, each hoping the other had understood.

"Who is *she*?" the blonde slurred.

"This is my cousin," Iain replied, bringing Haven's hand to his lips.

"*She's* your cousin?" The brunette started to snicker, but ended up looking sick.

"Now, Gwendolyn," Iain chided the brunette like a naughty child. "Is that any way to behave?"

"Who do you think you are?" Haven bristled.

"I'm an actress!" the British girl announced to Haven's amusement.

"Eeeaaannn!" moaned the American. "How are we supposed to get in without you?"

"My dear, the building is packed with men much richer and lonelier than I am. Do you really need me to spell it out for you? Now please. Excuse us," he added, and the girls began to shuffle away, still supporting each other like contestants in a three-legged race.

"They'll probably be wandering the halls for the rest of eternity," Iain noted as the two models came to a halt, bewildered by a fork at the end of the corridor. "Let's get the hell out of here."

"Where are we going?"

"You'll see," he told her.

* * *

WHEN THEY REACHED a door with a flashing EXIT sign, Iain paused and let go of Haven's hand. He peeled off his linen jacket and passed it to her. She was both touched and confused by the gesture. It was well over eighty degrees outside.

"There's a car waiting for us. Put this over your head until we're inside," Iain explained.

"You want me to put your jacket over my *head*? Did you run out of brown paper bags?" Haven snapped. He'd just kissed her, and now he didn't want to be seen with her?

"Don't be ridiculous, Constance. You're adorable as a brunette. And that accent is just about the cutest thing I've ever heard. But we can't afford to be photographed together."

Haven pretended not to notice that he'd called her Constance, but her entire body was tingling. "Why not?"

"Because I'd rather not set the paparazzi on you just yet. You'll see. After a while, they won't even let you use the bathroom alone. Plus, I doubt your latest set of parents would want you running around New York with a notorious miscreant. Do you really want them to find out about it on *Access Hollywood*?"

"No," Haven admitted.

Iain grinned, and Haven hoped he couldn't hear her heart racing. "Of course you don't," Iain said. "Some things *never* change."

"Okay, you win. But how am I supposed to get to the car if I can't see where I'm going?"

"Allow me." Iain threw the jacket over her head and scooped her up into his arms. "Try to look limp. They'll think one of my dates didn't make it through the show."

Haven leaned her head against his chest and inhaled deeply. The scent that rose from his skin made her lightheaded, almost giddy. She heard the door open and then the sound of a dozen cameras clicking.

"What happened, Iain? D'you slip her a little something?" a man shouted.

"She's not dead is she?" another yelled, and Haven kicked her feet in mute response.

"I'm merely escorting this young lady home," Iain blithely informed the paparazzi. "She had a little too much to drink."

"Which one is it?" It was the first man's voice. "The Victoria's Secret girl or that Chanel model?"

"Do I look like the sort of man who kisses and tells?" The photographers snickered. "Never mind. Don't answer that question. Good evening, gentlemen."

Haven felt herself being lowered into a car. The door slammed and suddenly there was silence.

"You can take that off now," Iain told her, and Haven peeked out from underneath the jacket. "Tinted windows. They can't see a thing. Not even the driver."

Outside, countless men with cameras dangling from their necks pressed their faces to the windows, trying to catch a glimpse of the car's occupants. With their cheeks and noses mashed against the glass, they appeared monstrous, subhuman. Iain pushed an intercom button on the armrest.

"The mews," he told the driver. "And try not to be followed." As the car screeched off, Haven nervously studied Iain's handsome profile. For a moment, he seemed troubled. His brow sank, throwing his eyes into shadow. His lips were pressed tightly together as though sealed against leaks. This was not the shallow playboy she'd been expecting. For a moment, Iain Morrow looked like a man with a terrible weight upon his shoulders.

"What's wrong?" Haven asked, suddenly acutely aware that she knew next to nothing about the person beside her.

"Don't mind me," Iain assured Haven, taking her hand. "I just didn't expect to find you so soon. There were a few things I was hoping to get out of the way first."

"I'm sorry," Haven said, afraid to ask what he meant. "My timing has never been very good."

"There's nothing for you to be sorry about. I've been waiting for this my entire life."

Iain's gloom had lifted, leaving the familiar grin in its place. Just a little bit lopsided, it was the same smile Constance had fallen in love with when she first saw it across a piazza in Rome. The face framing it might have changed, but there was no doubt it belonged to the boy she'd adored. No one else could have mastered an expression that was equal parts mischief, caution, and pluck. This is Ethan, Haven told herself. The thought left her so giddy she was glad she was already sitting down.

"You've really been waiting for me?" she asked.

"Let's see if I can prove it to you." He pushed Haven back on the plush seat of the car and kissed her once more. His hands wandered over her silk dress, but Haven didn't stop them. Every part of her body was on fire, and when she felt his hand on her bare thigh, she thought she might pass out from pleasure.

"Not yet," she told herself without realizing that she'd spoken aloud.

"I'm sorry." Iain pulled Haven upright and helped smooth her hair. "I guess I couldn't help myself. Ninety years is a long time to wait."

"Too long," Haven agreed, adjusting her dress, which had ridden up almost to her waist. There was no longer any doubt in her mind. Iain Morrow might have looked nothing like the Ethan she'd drawn as a little girl, but Haven knew she'd found the man from her dreams. That's what Constance had wanted. Now all Haven had to do was figure out *why*.

## CHAPTER THIRTY-ONE

Just before the Mercedes reached Washington Square Park, Iain's driver pulled up at one end of a cobblestone lane. Tall iron gates kept unwanted vehicles and trespassers out of a block-long passage, which was lined with houses that resembled quaint, ivy-covered cottages compared to the skyscrapers around them. Old-fashioned lanterns lit the lane, and colorful blooms dripped from window boxes. The entire scene appeared charmingly antiquated, like an illustration ripped from a fairy tale. The street sign read WASHINGTON MEWS.

Haven stepped out of the car and slipped back in time. Everything looked exactly as it always had. Aside from a shiny new motor scooter parked outside one of the buildings, there was no trace of the twenty-first century.

"We're home," Iain said, taking Haven's hand and guiding her toward a little white cottage. They were alone in the lane. Even the roar of the Fifth Avenue traffic was silenced, and all she could hear was the click of her own heels on the cobblestones. When they reached the red door, Haven stopped and peered up expectantly at the second floor. The green velvet curtains were still hanging in the windows. Her entire body began to tingle again. This was the place she was destined to find.

She turned to Iain. "I died here," she said.

"We both did." Iain reminded her as his fingers gently stroked her cheek.

"What happened?"

He shook his head. Either he didn't remember, or he didn't want to tell her.

"The house is yours now?"

"I asked my father to buy it for me for my thirteenth birthday. He thought I'd gone insane."

"You've known about me for that long?"

Iain smiled. "I've known about you so much longer than that."

INSIDE, THE HOUSE was pitch-black, and she heard Iain fumbling around in the darkness. Then, lamp by lamp, the room was revealed. Haven stood stunned as her eyes roamed the cottage. She could see her own taste in every piece of furniture, every work of art. They were exactly what she would have chosen herself, and she knew that Constance had been the decorator. The space itself was immaculately clean. It was as though the little building had been patiently waiting for her to return for almost a century.

"I thought the house burned down," Haven murmured, overcome by nostalgia.

"It did. It's taken me years to get it back into shape."

"But all the things. They're mine, aren't they?"

"They're replicas," Iain explained. "Reproductions. I re-created the house from memory."

"You remembered all of this?" Everything Haven knew about the past had come from her visions or her father's notes. Constance and

Ethan still didn't feel quite real to her. Yet here was the first undeniable proof that they both had existed.

"I remember everything. Go ahead," Iain urged her. "Have a look around."

HAVEN WANDERED the ground floor of the little house with her hands at her sides, afraid at first to touch anything. A dressmaker's dummy stood naked in one corner, next to a desk stacked with brightly colored tins. She opened one and found it filled with emerald beads. Another held mother-of-pearl buttons. Little objects cluttered every surface, and Haven reached out and picked up a palm-size sculpture of a reclining nude, which lay on the fireplace mantel. A warm, pleasant sensation rippled over her skin. Turning the object over in her hands, she knew somehow that it was an exact copy of a piece that Constance's grandmother had given her for her eighteenth birthday.

"What do you think?" Iain was sitting on the edge of the couch, waiting nervously for her reaction. His eyes hadn't once left her face. His gaze was every bit as intense as Ethan's. It felt as if he could peer inside of her.

"You did this for *me*?"

"Yes," he said. "I wanted it to be perfect when you got back. So you'd know for sure it was really me. So we could pick up where we left off."

"You knew I'd come to New York?" *He knows who you are. And he'll be looking for you,* she heard Leah Frizzell's voice say. Haven pushed the thought from her mind.

"Well, there was always the chance that you'd ended up somewhere in China, but I *hoped* you were close enough to find me again. I went to a great deal of trouble to make myself conspicuous. I used to have my assistant alert the paparazzi every time I went out for a cup of coffee. I thought that if I let them photograph me, you might see me one day. Of course, that was before the paparazzi turned against me."

"But they were the reason I found you. I saw you on TV."

"Then I guess it was worth it, after all." Iain was pleased. "Aren't you going to finish your tour?"

Haven's eyes landed briefly on the narrow stairway that led to the second floor.

"There's no lamp upstairs. I kept everything the way that it was, so you'll need a candle," he told her. "Take the one on the windowsill."

HAVEN PAUSED at the top of the stairs. The room was exactly as she remembered it. A full moon hovered above the skylight, and the white sheets below it glowed silver. Little crystal bottles half filled with perfume sparkled on the vanity. Haven caught a glimpse of her own reflection in the mirror. It was the only thing that seemed out of place. The warm wind flowed through the windows, making the curtains billow and float like ghosts.

She heard the sound of footsteps behind her, and the seconds slowed. She let Iain take the candle from her hand, and soon the only light left was that of the moon. A warm hand caressed her bare shoulder. She turned, with her eyes closed, and felt his lips meet her own.

"I've been waiting for you, Constance," Iain whispered.

The kiss began gently and grew hungrier. She felt her knees buckle, but she didn't fall. For the first time in her life, Haven was completely, impossibly, happy. Still, she managed to push him away.

"What's wrong?" Iain asked.

"Not yet," Haven told him.

"But we were married," Iain said. "Don't you remember?"

"Not yet," Haven repeated.

## CHAPTER THIRTY-TWO

Haven lay in bed, trying to count the events that had brought her back to the little room in the Washington Mews. The glimpse of Iain on the gossip show, the fire at her grandmother's house, the clumsy bimbo at the Apollo Theater. There had been too many coincidences to be anything other than fate. Haven hoped she could figure out why she'd been led there before she fell helplessly in love with the boy lying next to her.

"So what do you remember?" Iain's arms were around her, his face buried in her hair. She'd been sure he was sleeping. It was late, and the moon vanished as clouds converged, leaving the room dark.

"I remember *you*," Haven told him.

"Anyone else?" Iain asked casually.

"Dr. Strickland, a girl named Rebecca . . ." Haven searched her memories. "I remember my parents a little bit."

"That's it? No one else?"

"I don't think so," Haven said. "I don't remember as much as I should. I had visions when I was little, but I tried to stop them. They only came back a few months ago."

"You wanted to *stop* them?" Iain sounded hurt, and she was glad she couldn't see his face. "Why?"

"My family is religious," Haven tried to explain. "They didn't understand. For eight years, my grandmother thought I was possessed by a demon. But you—you remember it all, don't you? Tell me about Constance and Ethan."

"Where should I start?"

"Start with this house," Haven told him. "The first thing I remembered was this room."

"Let's see, then. This house . . ." he murmured as if conjuring the past. "Your grandmother lived in an old mansion on Washington Square Park. This house was the mansion's stable. When she died, she left them both to you. You sold the mansion and decided to live here."

"In the stable? What happened to the horses?"

Iain laughed at the thought. "It wasn't a stable at that point. All the rich families had cars. Your grandmother had used it as a studio. She was an artist, too. That was one of the reasons you two were so close. Your parents were a bit more . . . conventional."

"I remember meeting you here," Haven said. "I was nervous that someone would see you coming in."

"So you remember our secret rendezvous?" Iain's fingers dipped underneath the top of her dress and traced the edge of Haven's lace bra. "I must admit—I've thought about those a bit myself. We had to be careful back then. It wouldn't have looked right for an unmarried young lady to be welcoming a man into her home. Particularly a man who didn't occupy the same social station."

Haven pulled his hand away and held it. "You were poor, weren't you?" she asked.

"Sometimes you get lucky and sometimes you don't," Iain explained.

He didn't seem upset that his advances hadn't gotten him anywhere. "Ethan's life wasn't as easy as mine. His parents died when he was young, and he was passed around from foster family to foster family. His last set of guardians had him institutionalized. He kept talking about other lives that he'd lived, and they thought he'd lost his mind. That was just before Dr. Strickland discovered him and brought him to New York. Of course, people eventually found out that Ethan had spent a year in an institution. Even if Constance's parents had been okay with their daughter marrying a pauper, they certainly weren't going to let her marry a lunatic."

"People thought you were crazy? Is that why they accused you . . ."

Haven paused when Iain's breathing suddenly stopped. "Accused me of what?" he asked.

She hadn't meant to bring it up so soon. "I had a vision. I heard people talking about you and Dr. Strickland."

"Did they say that I killed him?" Though Iain was still beside her, he suddenly felt far away.

"Yes," Haven admitted. The pause that followed told her that the explanation might not be as simple as she'd hoped.

"August Strickland was like a father to me. I owed him everything. I would never have harmed him. And I had no reason to—I didn't even know that he'd made me his heir. I still wish he hadn't. That was how the rumors got started. There were certain people who wanted me out of the way. They saw their opportunity and they took it."

"Is that why we eloped? To get away from the rumors?"

"We eloped because I was desperate to marry you. There were a number of reasons we had to act quickly. But we would have been married in any case."

"But then we died before we could make it to Rome."

"Yes." It sounded as if he was admitting a terrible failure.

"And you don't know how the fire started?"

"No," Iain declared with a hint of exasperation. "I never did and I still don't. There were no fire alarms in those days, and the blaze got out of control very quickly."

They lay quietly together, but Haven's mind was still racing. "Iain?" she asked.

"Yes?"

"What about Jeremy Johns?"

"I was wondering when you'd ask. I'm friends with his girlfriend, but I don't know what happened to him. I went to his show the night he vanished. I said hello—and left. From what I've heard, Jeremy was in trouble with some powerful people. I had nothing to do with his disappearance. I've never killed *anyone*—not in this life or any other. Now. Is there anything else we need to get out of the way?"

There was. Haven couldn't seem to rid her mind of the vision she'd had in Dr. Tidmore's office. "One last question?" she finally blurted out.

"Go ahead."

"Who was Rebecca?"

When Iain finally responded, his voice was flat. "A girl we knew."

"She was in love with you, wasn't she?"

"Yes," he said with a sigh.

"And were you in love with her?" Haven almost whispered.

"We've had this conversation before, you know," Iain said. "And I still don't understand how you could ask such a thing. I spent years searching for you. I married you. Rebecca was nothing to me."

"I'm sorry." Haven searched for his lips in the darkness.

"I love you, Constance. Don't you understand that?"

"Haven," she whispered as she kissed him.

"What?"

"That's my name now. It's Haven."

## CHAPTER THIRTY-THREE

"Haven."

"Hmmmm?" Haven emerged from a dreamless sleep. She opened her eyes to find Iain perched on the side of her bed, wearing an open pajama top and a pair of jeans. It was the most remarkable thing she'd ever seen at eight o'clock in the morning.

"I brought you some coffee. What would you like for breakfast?"

"Sleep," she said, tucking her face back into the pillow.

"That's not on the menu. You'll need something a little heartier. It's going to be a long day. We're taking a trip."

"But I just got here!" she moaned.

"Come on. Get out of bed," Iain said with a laugh. It was a relief to see him in a lighthearted mood after the previous night's conversation. "Where are your things?"

"At the Windemere Hotel." Haven gave up hope of going back to sleep and rolled over to face him.

"I'll send someone to get them. How many bags do you have?"

"Just one," she yawned. "Most of my clothes were destroyed before I left."

"Destroyed?" Iain asked.

"Long story, not related."

"I'd love to hear it," he prodded gently.

"Maybe later," Haven said.

"Okay. In the meantime, can I take you shopping?"

"I have my own money, thanks."

"Haven." Iain caught her eyes and held them. "You know my fortune is just a fluke, don't you? It's luck, that's all. Last time you were rich. This time I'm loaded. Next time we'll probably both be broke. So don't get too worked up about it. The money is *ours* now. Some of it we'll use to do good things. Some of it we'll spend. Now get out of bed and get ready."

"Where are you taking me?" she asked.

"It's a secret." He shot her a grin on his way out of the room.

AFTER A LONG, leisurely shower, Haven padded down the stairs barefoot, wearing the same black dress she'd worn the night before. She found Iain toasting bagels in the little kitchen that was tucked in the corner of the ground floor, pulling plates from the cupboard and gathering silverware from the drawers. He hadn't heard her. Haven stopped by the front door and watched him, entranced by the movement of his long, tan arms. It was hard to believe that Iain Morrow might belong only to her. There was so much about him that seemed familiar—his crooked smile, the grace with which he moved, the way his eyes always lingered on her face. Everything else was different. Still, Haven had never felt so attracted to anyone. It took all the self-restraint she could muster to keep from bounding across the room and throwing her arms around him.

There was a rustling at the front door; then the mail slot opened with a clang and a handful of letters fell at her feet. She stooped to pick them up, and her eyes landed on a white envelope. Instead of a return address, there was only a silver snake swallowing its own tail.

"Just in time for the mail," Iain said, looking up from his work.

Haven placed the small stack of letters on the counter in front of him, the white envelope on top. "Is this from the Ouroboros Society?" she asked.

Iain kissed her forehead and glanced down at the envelope. "Looks like it."

"Are you a member again?"

"I joined a few years ago. I thought I might find you there."

"That's funny," Haven remarked. "I was going to go there today."

Iain froze for a moment. "Have you been in touch with them?"

"Not yet."

"Then don't waste your time." To Haven's ears, it sounded a little too much like an order.

"Why not?" she began to argue. "Maybe they could help me recover more of my memories."

"The OS isn't the same," Iain told her. "The people who run it now are nothing like Strickland. He wanted to help people. Now it's all about social climbing. And unless you were born with some kind of special gift, you're considered a drone."

"Really?"

"*Really*." There was a knock at the door. When Haven instinctively turned to answer it, Iain grabbed her wrist. "No," he insisted, loosening his grip when he saw Haven wince. "I'm sorry. Let me get it."

He opened the door a crack, just enough to peek into the lane. A few terse words were exchanged with a man on the other side, and then Iain took a suitcase from the visitor.

"Your things have arrived," he announced.

Haven ignored the suitcase. "Am I not allowed to answer the door?" she asked when they were alone once more.

"We just have to be careful," Iain explained. "Now have some breakfast and get ready. We've got a long day ahead of us."

AS SOON AS she'd eaten, Haven slipped into a sundress and followed Iain up the stairs to the roof of the little building.

"Is *this* where we're going?" A charming deck had been built on the roof. Two wooden lounge chairs faced west, as if to watch the sun set over the Hudson. Potted trees swayed in the wind, water droplets on the flowers sparkled in the sun, and the sound of traffic was little more than a soft whoosh in the distance. Though they could be seen by thousands of people in the tall buildings that circled the mews, it felt as though they were completely alone.

Iain took her to the edge of the roof. "Look down. Don't get too close to the drop."

"What are we looking for?" Haven asked.

"Anyone who doesn't look like he belongs here," Iain told her.

"I don't understand."

"Paparazzi," Iain explained. "They hang out in the mews sometimes. A picture of the two of us together could wind up on every blog in the country."

Haven frowned. Even she knew that Iain's love life wasn't the big story. If the tabloid photographers had been sent to the mews, it was because of Jeremy Johns. "Is that why you didn't want me to answer the door this morning? Were you worried about paparazzi?"

Iain's face was unreadable as he watched the street below. "Like I said, we just have to be careful. They're all out for my blood these days, and I don't want you getting dragged into it."

Haven scanned the surrounding area. The cobblestone lane was empty. A few NYU students loitered in front of a dorm on University Place. A man with a briefcase was hailing a cab.

"Well, I don't see anybody suspicious."

Iain was still looking. "That's the problem. Sometimes you don't. They're experts at blending in."

"How are we going to avoid people we can't even see?"

"How far can you jump?" Iain asked, pointing to the gap between his building and the one beside it.

"You're kidding."

"Not at all," Iain assured her, his mood lightening. "I promise it's not as bad as it looks."

They reached the edge and peered down at the four-foot-wide space between the two roofs.

"You're dumb as dirt if you think I'm going to jump over that," Haven said.

Iain planted a kiss on her lips. "I love all these charming Southern expressions you've picked up," he said when he released her. "But please don't tell me they turned you into a prissy little belle down there. You used to do this sort of thing just for kicks."

"I did not!" Haven insisted.

"All right, maybe not. But I don't remember hearing you complain this much. Just try it."

He took a couple of steps back, sprang forward, and sailed over the gap. Standing on the other side, he held his arms out to Haven. She shook her head in irritation and waved him to one side. Then she held her breath and jumped. A second later, she landed on her feet, completely exhilarated and ready to take another leap.

After crossing the roofs of three more buildings, Haven and Iain came to the end of the row. They scampered down a fire escape and dropped into a small courtyard with an opening to the street. A silver Mercedes picked them up on the corner of University Place and Eighth Street. They ducked inside without attracting the attention of anyone other than two NYU girls who were still fumbling for their phone cameras when Haven and Iain sped away.

* * *

FIFTEEN MINUTES LATER the car turned into the Midtown Tunnel. Racing deep beneath the waters of the East River, they were moving farther and farther away from the island of Manhattan. "You're taking me to *Queens*?" Haven asked when she saw the signs on the other side of the tunnel.

Iain pretended to pout. "You don't like Queens? I've always thought it was the most romantic borough. Now come over here." Haven slid across the seat until she was next to him. "That's better. Untie that," he said, pointing to the strip of fabric that served as the belt of her sundress.

"Excuse me?" Haven giggled.

"Take it off," Iain insisted, reaching over and untying the bow. Haven pulled the strip out from beneath her. "Now close your eyes," he ordered. When Haven complied, he wrapped the fabric around her head until the world went dark. "No peeking," he ordered, pulling her closer and kissing the top of her head. She leaned against his chest, her other senses engaged like never before. When her hand accidentally brushed against his thigh, she left it there, marveling at the fact that she could. No one had ever been *hers* before. She was dying to see how far it would go.

THE CAR CAME to a stop, and the driver opened the door. Iain untied the blindfold and helped Haven out of the car. They were standing on a runway with an airplane in front of them.

"Behold the family jet," Iain said.

Haven couldn't quite summon a smile. "Are you kidnapping me?" she asked.

Iain didn't seem to know how to respond. "I was *hoping* you'd come of your own free will."

"Are we going very far?" Haven asked.

"That depends on how you define *far*." Iain looked a bit disappointed by her lack of enthusiasm.

"Should I have brought clean underwear?" she joked nervously.

"We brought some for you just in case." The driver removed two suitcases from the trunk and loaded them onto the plane.

"What about a passport?" Haven asked.

"Don't worry about *that*," Iain assured her. "Passports are for the public. I haven't used one in years."

HAVEN CLIMBED the airplane's stairs and strapped herself into one of the plush leather seats. It wasn't until the plane took off that the terror set in. Little more than twelve hours after their very first kiss, she was flying to some unknown destination with a person suspected of murder. Not just in one life, but in two. Everything had happened too fast, Haven thought. She had jumped without looking, and now she was trapped. If something bad were to happen, she'd have no one to blame but herself.

Outside Haven's window patches of brilliant blue ocean were peeking out from between the clouds. Wherever they were going lay east, across the Atlantic Ocean.

## CHAPTER THIRTY-FOUR

*"Don't leave." The voice was soothing, hard to resist. "You belong here with me. He won't love you the way I do. Please. I can't lose you again."*

"HAVEN." She felt someone stroking her hair. "We're almost there."

"Where?"

"You'll see," Iain promised. "What were you dreaming about? You were mumbling in your sleep."

"It was a dream?" she asked, still struggling to emerge from the haze. "I could have sworn I was talking to someone."

"Who?" The question was as sharp as a slap.

"I don't know. A man." All Haven knew for sure was that the voice hadn't been Ethan's. "You can't be jealous of a dream, can you?"

"Of course not," Iain said with a smile that wasn't at all convincing.

IT WAS DARK when they landed at an airport that looked the same as any other. Even the car that met them was identical to the one that had dropped them off. Haven slid into the backseat beside Iain and let her head rest on his shoulder. Her eyes closed, and she listened to the hum of the wheels on asphalt, too tired for questions. She'd never felt so exhausted. A car horn roused her briefly. Outside, beneath the moon, a featureless landscape raced past the window.

HAVEN WOKE THE NEXT morning in the bedroom of a small but perfectly decorated apartment, with old wide-planked wooden floors, bookshelves lined with ancient, leather-bound volumes, and antique furniture that might have been rescued from a ramshackle villa. The white linen nightgown she was wearing was just the sort of thing she would have purchased herself had they sold such things in Snope City stores. But she'd never seen the garment before and couldn't recall putting it on.

Iain was sitting by a pair of open doors that led out to a sun-washed balcony, reading a book. The blue-faced demon on its cover held a wheel in its claws.

"Where am I?" Haven asked, though she already knew.

Iain closed the book and smiled mischievously. "Why don't you see for yourself?" he said, gesturing to the open doors.

The apartment looked out over a long, oval piazza with three fountains in the center. On the ground floors of the ancient buildings that circled the piazza, cafés catered to foreigners. Haven watched from the balcony as three wild blond children splashed around in one of the fountains while their frustrated parents consulted a map. Constance and Ethan had met in the very same spot ninety years earlier. Aside from the tourists in their sneakers and shorts, nothing had changed. Haven half expected to see a woman's hat tumble across the piazza.

"It's the Piazza Navona," she whispered, looking up at Iain, who had come to stand beside her on the balcony. "Does this apartment belong to you?"

"It does. Do you like it?" he asked.

"It's beautiful," she said.

"I was fifteen when I came here, and it was the first place that felt like home. My mother was living in Tuscany at the time, and I ran away from her villa. I hopped on a train to Rome, thinking I would find a way back to my friends in New York. But when I got here, I didn't want to leave. Of course, a couple of days later, one of my mother's friends spotted me at the Ritz and had her bodyguard pick me up. But as soon as I was eighteen, I bought this apartment. Now I come here whenever I can."

"Why did you run away?"

"It's not important. Let me show you something." He put one arm around her shoulders and traced the outline of the piazza with a finger. "Do you see the peculiar shape of the piazza? Does it remind you of anything?"

"I don't know," Haven admitted. The heat radiating from his hand on her shoulder made it difficult to concentrate.

"It's the shape of a racetrack. Do you know why? It's because the piazza was built on top of a stadium where the Romans came to watch the games. There were horse races here, and sometimes they would flood the arena for naval battles. Now it's just an echo of what it used to be two thousand years ago. But most of the buildings you're looking at were built with the stones from the stadium. It's all still here. In Rome, the past changes shape, but it never goes away. Every era leaves its mark. The whole city is the same. You can see thousands of years of history in one tiny church."

"It's like us," Haven whispered.

"Exactly. Though some of us are even older than Rome. Would you like to take a walk? Will you let me show you around?"

"Can you help me check my e-mail first? Or my messages? I'm pretty sure my cell phone won't work in Italy."

Iain smacked his forehead with the palm of his hand. "Damn. My phone. I knew there was something I forgot to bring. Don't worry, we'll figure something out first thing tomorrow. For now, let's just enjoy our first day together in almost a hundred years."

AS THEY STROLLED through the streets, Haven's hand tucked into his, Iain brought the ancient city to life for her. He described the lush gardens and luxurious baths that once surrounded the squat, round temple known as the Pantheon, and with an eyewitness's attention to detail, he told her of the bloody battles that had taken place at the Colosseum. With Iain as a guide, the forum became more than a jumble of ruins. Ancient marketplaces bustled with life and pagan temples echoed with the mysterious sounds of forgotten rites. He seemed to know every street and alley in the city. It was clear that he belonged there. The Italian women they passed stared at Iain as if a god had materialized on the streets of Rome, and Haven could tell from the way their eyes swept over her that they wondered how any mortal could have claimed him.

With the golden light of late afternoon gilding Rome's trees, they walked to the top of the Aventine Hill and watched the river below. A tour group caught them kissing in the garden of a monastery, and the pair ran laughing into a piazza across from a medieval church. As Haven stood back to admire the building's tall bell tower, Iain vanished beneath its portico. She found him leaning against the church's wall, beside a giant image carved into marble, which appeared to be centuries older than the building that surrounded it. The round, flat sculpture featured the bearded face of an anonymous god with empty eyes and a gaping mouth.

"It's la Bocca della Verità," Iain explained. "The mouth of truth. They say if you tell a lie while your hand is in the statue's mouth, it will bite it off. Care to try?"

"No thanks," said Haven. There was something about the image that she found unsettling. It was as if a great black void lay behind the face. She feared what her fingers might brush against inside of the toothless cavity.

"Then I'll go first," Iain said, thrusting his fingers between the statue's lips. "Anything you want to ask while my hand is at stake?"

There was. But the questions that came to Haven's lips would have destroyed a perfect day. And there was always a chance that they came with answers Haven wouldn't want to know. The truth, she'd discovered, dwelled in dark, hidden places, and sometimes it was better not to force it into the light.

"No," she told Iain, and it was true as soon as she said it. The other women—the models in the pictures and the girl who'd loved Ethan—took their cue and vanished along with Jeremy Johns from Haven's thoughts.

"See, that's what I've always loved about you. You're so sweet—and so naive." He laughed even louder when Haven punched him on the arm.

AS SOON AS the sun went down, the Romans came out, strolling through the streets with no aim but to see and be seen. Teenagers traveled in wild packs, young couples carried their infants on their hips, while old ladies conjured youth with leather miniskirts and heels. Not far from Iain's apartment, Haven and Iain slipped out of the crowd and into a tiny restaurant. There were no windows and no door—just rectangular holes cut in the side of an old building. The guests sat at one long, rustic wooden table, and the only light came from a hundred flickering candles. In the center of the floor, an ancient mosaic showed a god driving a chariot, his fingers clenching the wrist of a terrified maiden. As they were guided to their seats, Haven was careful to step over the image.

"Have we been here before?" Haven whispered once they were seated. "That mosaic . . ."

"Do you recognize it?"

Haven nodded. There was something about the image that both terrified and thrilled her.

"I thought you might," Iain said. He took her hand and began to trace the lines on her palm as if reading a story that was written on her skin. "There was another one like it in a villa on the island of Crete. The man who owned the house was rich and powerful. Some people called him a magician, though that wasn't exactly true. But his neighbors knew enough to avoid him whenever they could. They used to say that their minds went cloudy in his presence. Businesses would fail after they made him a client. Families were torn apart if he paid them a visit.

"It was on one of those visits that he met a young girl from a prominent family and fell madly in love. When he asked for her hand, her father couldn't deny him. There was no doubt that he adored the girl. She was too young to know any better, and she thought she loved him, too. But as time went by, he started to worry that her feelings might change. That she might meet someone she loved even better. The thought of losing her almost drove him insane, so he locked her away in his villa. For several years, she spent her days sewing gowns that no one would ever see and drawing the outside world on the walls of her bedroom.

"One day, while the man wasn't at home, there was a fire at the villa. It had been so long since anyone had seen the man's wife that only one of the servants remembered to save her. When he found the girl half dead, he carried her to the home of two friends and hid her there. The girl and the servant fell in love as she recovered, and once she was well enough to travel, they slipped away to Rome. Her husband spent the rest of his days searching for her."

"Is that story true?" A single image still lingered in Haven's mind. She could see a room with a mosaic floor. Flowering meadows stretched to the horizon in every direction. Only from certain angles was it clear that the swaying grass and dazzling sky were merely painted on the walls.

"In essence," Iain said. "I might have tidied it up a little bit."

"It's about us, isn't it?"

Across the table Iain watched her, his somber green eyes searching her face for the encouragement to continue. "Yes."

"How long ago did that happen?"

"Julius Caesar died shortly before we left for Rome. By today's calendar it was 44 B.C."

A million questions were bouncing around in Haven's brain. But before she let the first slip past her lips, she made sure that no one else at the table was listening. The conversation sounded strange enough to her own ears. An eavesdropper would think they had both lost their minds. "So we've known each other for *two thousand* years?"

"Maybe longer. Even my memories are a bit fuzzy before that."

"And we've been the same people all this time?"

"Not exactly. Every life changes us a little. But our essence remains the same. Like Rome—it's changed a great deal since 44 B.C., but in many ways, it's still the same city."

"Does *everyone* come back to earth over and over again?"

"I don't think so," Iain said. "Just those of us who have something that keeps us here. I don't think there are many of us."

"What's keeping *you* here?"

"You." Iain motioned to the waiter, who left and returned shortly with a carafe of red wine, which he poured into both of their glasses. Haven looked guiltily around the restaurant.

"This is Italy. You're allowed to drink here at sixteen," Iain informed her. "And when in Rome . . ."

"Are you trying to get me drunk?" Haven twirled the stem of her wineglass between her fingers.

"Of course." The tension contained in those two little words made Haven tremble. She could tell from the way Iain stared at her that he wasn't going to wait much longer.

"So how does this all work?" she asked, feeling herself blushing. "How do people find each other again?"

"All I know is that we're drawn to people we've loved before. Is there anyone in your life that you feel particularly close to? Someone you liked the moment you met?"

Haven thought of Beau and nodded.

"Then you may have known that person before."

"And do *we* find each other in every life?"

The sorrow on Iain's face gave her a sense of how little she knew. "I wish it were that easy. I look for you in every life, but I don't always find you. And sometimes I find you too late."

"Too late?" It was a possibility that Haven hadn't considered.

"In eighteen eighty-five, I found you in Paris. My father was a wealthy English merchant, and as soon as I was able, I insisted that he put me in charge of his office in France. I hadn't been in the country three days when I saw a peasant girl faint in the street as I walked to work. I managed to pick her up before she was run over by a carriage, and I took her back to my hotel. It was you. You had walked over a hundred miles to make it to Paris, and you'd caught a fever along the way. I tried everything to save you, but you died a week later in my arms. I caught the fever as well and died not long after you did."

"That's terrible!" Haven said, blinking back tears as if the pain were still fresh.

"Yes, but at least we had a few precious days together. The lifetime before that, you were already married when I met you, and your husband—"

"Married?" Haven broke in. "Why didn't I wait for you? How could there ever have been anyone else?"

"Let me see if I can explain. You were born with special gifts—you can draw and sew, can't you?"

"Yes," Haven said, wondering how the two subjects could be connected.

The waiter returned with menus, and Iain waited until the man was gone to continue.

"Those are gifts that have been passed down from one life to the next. Talents like yours are rare, but not as rare as you'd think. That's why Mozart could play the piano before he was out of diapers. Or why there's always a seven-year-old math prodigy in the news.

"I have a gift, too. I can't write operas or do calculus in my head. What I can do is remember things. Most people forget their previous lives. But for some reason, I never lose my memories. They always stay with me. So I always know that I have to find you. But sometimes you don't remember *me*. And I'm not the only one who finds you irresistible. In fact, I think that's one reason why I keep coming back."

He stopped and took a sip of wine, leaving Haven in suspense.

"Why?"

"To keep you away from the competition."

"You're joking!"

"Maybe. But I promise you this: Now that I've found you, I'll never let anything come between us."

His knee brushed against hers under the table, and she had to gulp her wine to quench the fire that was building in her belly.

On the way home, stuffed with pasta and tipsy on wine, they ducked into dark alleys and doorways for long, hungry kisses. When they reached the apartment, Iain picked her up and carried her to the bed in the dark, his mouth on hers as his hands unzipped her dress. He lay her down on the crisp, white sheets that fluttered in the breeze blowing in from the balcony. She felt her dress being slipped over her head, and she shuddered as a warm hand was laid on her bare stomach.

"I love you," Iain whispered, and Haven thought she might melt with pleasure.

## CHAPTER THIRTY-FIVE

Haven was alone. The balcony doors were open and the piazza below was still quiet. She turned her head toward the bathroom door, which stood open, and then listened for sounds from the living room. The apartment was empty. She wondered if the previous days had been just a dream. It all seemed too much to hope for, and Haven had never been known for her luck.

Then her eyes landed on the clothes Iain had worn to dinner, thrown over the back of a chair, and everything that had happened the night before returned to her at once. She was glad no one was there to see the flush that consumed every inch of her skin. She couldn't decide what was behind it—nervousness, embarrassment, or the desire for more. If what Iain had told her at dinner was true, she must have done this all before. Haven just wished she could remember how it all worked.

She slid out of bed and rummaged through her suitcase for something to wear. She'd just slipped into a pair of jeans when she heard the front door open and Iain moving about the kitchen. Tiptoeing across the living room, Haven reached the kitchen door just in time to see him locking one of the cabinets. He looked both relaxed and regal in his wrinkled white shirt, which he wore untucked and rolled up to his elbows. The memory of the firm, smooth chest beneath it made Haven feel faint.

"Good morning," he said, gliding over to the two shopping bags that he'd placed on the kitchen counter. "You're up early. We were out of supplies, so I went to the market. What would you like to eat? I make an excellent omelet these days."

"What's in the cabinet?" Haven asked, trying to keep her voice steady and light.

"I keep a few euros in a box in the cupboard for unexpected trips and emergencies." Iain grabbed her hand and pulled her body to his. "How are you?"

Haven sighed happily as he bent down to kiss her. It was impossible to think clearly when he was so close.

"I'm perfect," she said.

"Yes, you are." He laughed and released her from his embrace. "So, what would you like to do today? Anything in Rome that you've been dying to see again?"

"How about the Sistine Chapel?" she said, pulling six eggs and a wedge of cheese from one of the shopping bags. It was the first site in Rome that popped into her mind.

"I've never been there," Iain admitted. "I'm not usually one for churches."

"Great! We can see it together for the very first time."

"It will be crowded," Iain warned.

"So we wait in line for a while. I don't mind, do you?"

"It's not the wait that worries me. It's the tourists. *American* tourists."

Haven rolled her eyes. "Don't tell me you're one of those snobs who complain about other Americans."

"I don't mind Americans. I *do* mind being in their pictures. I'd prefer to keep a low profile while we're here."

"You know, if we're going to be together then sometime, somewhere, someone is going to snap a photo of us—" Haven stopped as an unpleasant thought passed through her mind. "This isn't about Jeremy Johns, is it? You're not on the run from the police, are you?"

Iain frowned. "No, I'm *not* hiding from the police, Haven. I'm just trying to protect you."

"I don't see what harm a photograph could do me." Haven couldn't have cared less about the Sistine Chapel, but there was a point to be made. "You can just wear a hat and some sunglasses. We're not going to keep hiding."

She had made it clear that Iain couldn't win. "Okay," he said uneasily. "But I refuse to pose for snapshots with tour groups."

"Fair enough."

"And afterward we're going to spend the rest of the day avoiding major tourist sites."

"Agreed."

"And there won't be any complaining."

"Absolutely none," Haven assured him.

"And you'll let me buy you something pretty."

Haven rolled her eyes again and laughed. "We'll see."

"Okay, then go have a seat on the balcony, and prepare for the best omelet you've ever had."

IT *WAS* THE BEST omelet Haven Moore had ever eaten. The coffee, the orange juice, even the toast tasted better than anything she'd consumed before. But given the company, the view, and the memory of the previous night, she might have swallowed a lump of cardboard and never known the difference.

"Did you know how to cook like this before?" she asked, trying not to talk with her mouth full.

"No. I guess you pick up something new in each life. My mother taught me how to make a few things. She was a well-known chef before she married my father."

"What is she now?"

"A drunk," he stated matter-of-factly.

"I'm sorry."

"Don't be sorry," Iain said. "You take the prize for difficult childhoods. It can't be easy being possessed by Satan for eight years."

"It wasn't as bad as it sounds," Haven joked, surprised to find herself discussing the subject so blithely. "At least I had Beau. But can you imagine growing up in a town where everyone's convinced that the devil likes to hang out in east Tennessee?"

"Ridiculous!" Iain shook his head at the notion. "Everyone knows the devil's not down South. He lives in New York City."

"That's a joke, right?" Haven finally asked.

"What else would it be? By the way—who's Beau?" Iain asked, nonchalantly poking at his food. Haven tried not to laugh. She'd never made anyone jealous before.

"He's my best friend. We had a business together, designing dresses."

"Ah, a man who's confident in his masculinity." Iain was buttering the same piece of toast for the third time. "What's he like?"

"Let's see. Tall, blond, good-looking, quarterback of the football team, funny, charming, brilliant." Haven paused to take a long, leisurely bite. "Oh, and *gay*."

"Hallelujah." Iain wiped imaginary sweat from his brow. "I was starting to get a little worried there. So does Beau have a boyfriend?"

"In Snope City, Tennessee?" Haven scoffed. "Even if there were other gay guys in town, they'd never have the guts to come out of the closet. Beau's going to lead a pretty miserable existence if he doesn't get the hell out of there."

"I wouldn't worry too much. I have a hunch he'll find someone soon," Iain said.

"You think?" Haven asked, trying to decipher the look in Iain's eyes.

"So if Beau's your best friend, why haven't I heard more about him?"

"We had a fight before I left Tennessee. I told his father a secret that I wasn't supposed to share. I was just trying to do what was best for him. . . ."

"But he didn't see it that way."

"No," Haven admitted.

"Yes, it's funny, isn't it? You try to do what's best for the people you love, and you just end up in trouble for your efforts."

Haven raised an eyebrow. "We're not back to having our picture taken, are we?"

"Now why would I steer a perfectly pleasant conversation in such a controversial direction?" Iain asked innocently.

THE QUEUES THAT led into the Sistine Chapel were shorter than they'd expected, though the twenty-minute wait in the sweltering summer sun was long enough to produce a new batch of freckles on Haven's nose. Finally they found themselves inside a large room filled with several hundred sweaty tourists staring at the ceiling and stepping on each other's feet. Just as Haven predicted, none of them paid the slightest bit of attention to the handsome young man wearing a Yankees hat and sunglasses. Even Iain's movie star looks couldn't distract from the beauty of the art.

After ten minutes of studying Michelangelo's artwork with her head tilted at an unnatural angle, Haven was finally forced to bring her gaze back to Earth. A painting along the chapel's north wall captured her attention. In the background of the picture, the artist had painted three separate scenes. The work, by Botticelli, was called *The Temptation of Christ*.

"Do you know the story?" Iain took off his sunglasses.

"Of course." Haven was happy for the chance to show off a little. "When Jesus went into the wilderness, Satan appeared to him in the disguise of an old hermit and tried to tempt him three times. He tempted Christ with food, and he took him to a pinnacle and told him that if he jumped, angels would catch him. Finally he offered Christ all the riches of the world. But Jesus never gave in to temptation."

Haven felt Iain watching her. "Do you think you could resist?" he asked. "If someone offered you everything you ever wanted, do you think you'd be able to turn it down?"

She thought for a moment. "I wonder," Haven mused. "I *hope* I'd be able to resist. Especially if the price were my soul. But I've lived a pretty sheltered life. Snope City wasn't exactly packed with temptations. I can hardly remember getting *anything* I wanted. So God knows what I'd do if someone offered me *everything*." Out of the corner of her eye, she saw a woman wearing a fanny pack and Birkenstocks poke her companion and point in Iain's direction. "Come on, let's get out of here," she whispered.

IAIN SAID LITTLE as they left the chapel and strolled toward the river. He kept his head lowered as though his thoughts were too heavy to support, and he seemed entranced by the shuffling of his feet. When they were halfway across the Ponte Sant'Angelo, Iain grabbed Haven's arm, and they slowed to a stop. Beneath them, the waters of the Tiber offered a murky mirror image of the world above. Taking her face in his hands, he bent and kissed her. It was the sort of sad, yearning kiss perfected long ago by sailors and soldiers and men who led dangerous lives.

"Haven, will you stay here with me?" he asked while Haven's eyes were still closed. It almost sounded as if he were pleading. "We could be happy in Rome. Let's not go back to New York, all right?"

Haven laughed uneasily. "But won't they kick us out at some point? I don't even speak Italian."

"That's easy to fix," Iain argued. "And it's not as if we'll need to work."

"You're serious, aren't you?" Iain's intensity was beginning to worry her.

"Whenever you're ready, we could get married again. Please. I don't want to go back."

"I don't understand. Why not?"

As she waited for his response, Haven heard the distinct mechanical click of a camera. Two girls in UNC T-shirts were standing several yards away, giggling with their mouths hidden behind their hands. Iain, who'd turned horribly pale, didn't move. Haven walked over to the girls, whose eyes grew wider the closer she came.

"You guys want a picture with him?" The two girls were too shocked to speak. "It's all right," Haven assured them. "I'm Mr. Morrow's personal assistant. Go stand next to him, and I'll take your pictures."

"You will?" whispered one of the awestruck girls, handing Haven her cell phone.

"Of course," Haven said. As the two girls inched shyly toward Iain, Haven carefully erased the photos they'd taken of her and Iain together. "Now smile!" she ordered.

"Sorry about that," she told Iain once the girls had disappeared. "I promised not to make you pose for any photos. Where should we go now?"

Iain ignored the question. "So will you?"

"Will I what?" Haven tried to buy some time.

"Stay in Rome. With me."

"I don't know. *Maybe*," she said with a sigh. She thought of Beau and her mother and wondered if she could bear to leave them both behind. "You'll have to let me think about it."

"Maybe is good enough for now." Iain's mood instantly brightened. He put his hat and glasses back on and offered Haven his arm.

"I'll give you till tomorrow to decide. Now it's my turn to lead the expedition."

HE LED HAVEN through the streets, steering her out of the path of killer Vespas and transporting her over more than one mammoth mud puddle. At last they arrived at a clearing, a square so small it was little more than a bulge in the road. Yet it was packed with antique vendors, their stands overflowing and mingling at the edges. Brass clocks and doorknobs and delicate glass ornaments sat side by side, each item a treasure just waiting for the right person to notice it.

Iain stopped in front of a wooden cart covered in dozens of centuries-old prints that flapped in the wind and immediately set to work sorting through a stack of illustrations torn from ancient books.

"What are you looking for?" Haven asked.

"I promised to buy you something pretty," he replied. "I came across an illustration the last time I was here. I didn't have any cash on me then, and I've been meaning to come back for it. Ah ha!" He pulled a picture from the pile and handed it to Haven.

The image showed a young man and woman lying together in a springtime meadow. Tall grass rose all around them, nearly hiding the couple from view. The trees that bordered the field were in full bloom. Birds soared overhead, and brightly colored flowers dotted the landscape. The white columns of a temple could be seen in the distance. Haven's finger traced the rough right edge of the page. Part of the picture had been torn away. A dark blur—a smudge or the tip of a storm cloud—was creeping into the image from the missing half.

"I noticed her before." Iain pointed to the girl. A long ribbon wrapped multiple times around her head couldn't contain the mound of black curls that broke free in every direction. "She has your hair."

"Poor girl," Haven muttered. "I don't know what I would have done if I'd been cursed with this mop and had no access to modern styling products."

"What's wrong with your hair?" Iain pulled one of her curls straight and let it bounce back to shape. "I think it's fantastic. It makes you look wild." He was either completely sincere or an excellent liar.

"*Really*?" Haven tried to imagine herself through Iain's eyes, but all she could see was the same girl she'd known for the past seventeen years. "But Constance was so beautiful."

"She was. But I've known you with dozens of faces and hairstyles. They were all different, and as long as you were there underneath them, I liked them all." Iain counted out the price of the print and gave the cash to the vendor. When the carefully wrapped package was handed over to him, he passed it directly to Haven. "This is to remind you."

"Remind me?"

"Of what's waiting for you here," he said.

BACK AT THE APARTMENT, Haven unwrapped the print and propped it up against a stack of books on the side table. Then she finally unpacked the clothes she'd brought from New York and shoved the suitcase under the bed. She had a feeling she wouldn't be going anywhere for a while.

"Looks like you could use a few things." Iain had been watching as she put her four dresses and two pairs of jeans on hangers. "We can go shopping tomorrow if you like."

"I just wish I had my sewing machine. I could have a dozen new outfits by the end of the week."

"Good idea." Iain flopped down on the bed. "We'll buy the apartment next door and turn it into a workshop for you. And then, if you like, we'll find a little shop where you can sell your designs. Isn't that what you always wanted?"

It was, Haven thought as she lay down beside Iain and let him wrap her in his arms. It was *exactly* what she always wanted.

## CHAPTER THIRTY-SIX

Haven woke up alone for the second morning in a row. By the time she'd showered and dressed, Iain still hadn't returned. She ate her breakfast on the balcony and watched the cafés below begin to open. With a strong, hot coffee in her hands and the sun inching its way up her legs, she looked across the rooftops at the city she might soon call home. This was her reward for a whole decade of difficulty. She'd lived through the cruel jokes, the sneers, and the loneliness. But now that was all in the past, and Snope City was an ocean away. She had found her way back to the fountain in the piazza—and to the person she had loved for two thousand years. This, Haven thought, was where the visions had been leading her. This was what Constance had wanted all along.

Haven left Iain a note, grabbed her handbag, and set out to wander aimlessly through the narrow, twisting streets of Rome. Without Iain at her side, they didn't seem quite as welcoming. The ancient buildings crowded too closely together, and at times they seemed to lean toward her as if to smother her in their embrace. Twice, Haven heard footsteps approaching too quickly. When she spun around, she found no one, but the feeling of being watched never went away.

She paused on the Via Giustiniani in front of a shop that seemed to specialize in plastic gladiators in bulging loincloths and considered buying one as a gag gift for Beau. Looking past the display in the window, Haven spied the elderly shopkeeper cleaning the floors. Every few seconds his sweeping slowed as his attention shifted to a tiny television set fastened to the wall. A buxom blonde anchor was delivering the morning news. The face of a young man appeared above the anchor's right shoulder, only to be quickly replaced by a picture of the Italian prime minister in an electric-blue Speedo. Haven gasped and took a step back from the window. The face had belonged to Jeremy Johns.

Haven turned away from the shop and hurried back in the direction of the apartment. Had she imagined the photo or was she losing her mind? Why would Jeremy Johns be on Italian TV? Her heart was pounding so loudly that it almost drowned out the sound of a familiar voice coming from a sidewalk café. She stopped in the street and listened. His words were inaudible, but Iain's tone was businesslike. Thinking she'd surprise him, Haven inched closer and slid behind the restaurant's outdoor service stand.

"You saw the news, I suppose?" she heard Iain say. "I'm coming back to the city. The DA says I need to be available to answer more questions. . . . I *would* have stayed, but now they know where I am. So that means the show's back on. Marta said she'd be ready for the fifteenth. I asked her to set aside any work that I haven't seen. . . . Yes, she's all right. It wasn't exactly unexpected. She's known for a while. . . . So have you talked to the *Times*? The *Observer*? Excellent. Keep working. I'll be back in touch when the plane lands this afternoon. . . . What's that? . . . The girl in the picture? The one with all the hair? She's nobody. Just someone I picked up here. I'll see you back in New York."

Haven peeked around the service station and saw Iain sitting at a table, sipping a cappuccino and tapping away at his phone. This wasn't the same person she'd slept with—the one who had asked her to stay with him in Rome. She had caught a glimpse of the real Iain Morrow—a person who thought nothing of insulting her or lying about leaving his phone in New York. Haven had always thought of herself as the kind of girl who could counter any ill treatment with a cutting remark or a hearty slap in the face. But the fury she expected never arrived. Instead, she just felt like a fool. Now the past three days would have to be reexamined—their meaning recalculated.

Haven craned her neck, trying to catch a glimpse of the phone's screen, just as Iain dropped it into his shirt pocket and began to gather his things. If he was heading back to the apartment, Haven had to beat him there. It was the only way to catch him without exposing herself as a snoop. She took off in the opposite direction and skidded around the corner into a street that ran parallel to the Via Giustiniani. Once she reached the Piazza Navona, Haven bolted up the stairs, crumpled up the note she had left behind, and was lounging on the balcony by the time Iain arrived.

"We made the papers," he said when he saw her. He looked hounded—even the mischievous glimmer in his eye was gone. Without it, Iain really did seem like a different person.

"What are you talking about?"

Iain dropped a copy of an Italian newspaper on her lap. It was folded to showcase a black-and-white picture. Though she couldn't read the caption, Haven had no trouble identifying the back of her own head. And Iain's profile couldn't have been clearer. The girls on the bridge outside the Sistine Chapel had snapped a picture of the two of them as they'd walked away.

"They sent it to an American blog yesterday afternoon. It's in all the papers this morning. Everyone wants to know who you are."

Haven tossed the paper to the floor. "What's the big deal? You can't even see my face in the picture."

"No, but now the whole world knows we're in Rome. I spoke to an associate of mine, and even *he* asked me about my mystery girl."

It was the opportunity Haven had been waiting for. "You spoke with an associate? I thought you left your phone in New York."

Iain sighed and pulled the phone out of his shirt pocket. "I guess I twisted the truth. I wanted you all to myself for a few days."

"But you could have at least let me check my e-mail. I'm sure my mother's frantic by now. She hasn't heard from me since Tuesday."

"I hadn't thought of that. Here, would you like to call her?" He held out the phone, but Haven ignored it.

"Why did you lie to me?"

"We all tell little lies," Iain said flatly. "I just wanted everything to be perfect. I should have realized—"

"What?"

"I have to go back to New York for a while."

"And what do you expect me to do?"

"Stay here," Iain said. "Enjoy yourself."

"I'm *not* staying in Italy all alone. Besides, you told me you never wanted to go back." The whole thing had been a fantasy—sweet little lies told to a stupid girl who was too eager to believe them.

"I don't *want* to go back. I *have* to. Something came up, and I need to deal with it immediately," Iain said, pulling his suitcase from the closet.

"If you go, you're taking me with you," Haven insisted.

"*No*," Iain told her.

"I . . ." Before she could continue, Haven felt her eyes roll back in her head and her legs collapse beneath her.

*Constance was peeking through a crack in the green velvet curtains. The moon was out now, shining in the puddles left by the storm. Across the street, someone shifted, and the moonlight briefly revealed a patch of pale flesh. All night, the figure had been there, watching her house from a doorway across the street. He had barely moved for hours.*

*Again she wished that Ethan could be with her. They hadn't shared a night together since the reporters started shadowing him after Dr. Strickland's death. Ethan had warned her that one of the newspapers might assign someone to watch the mews house. But somehow she knew that the man in the doorway didn't work for the press.*

*She went through her mental checklist once more. The door downstairs was locked. The windows were bolted. There was no other way into the house. She sat back in the chair that she'd pulled up to the window and waited for daylight.*

## CHAPTER THIRTY-SEVEN

For most of the flight back to New York, Haven pretended to sleep. She needed time to think—time to figure out how to deal with everything she had learned. And with the shades pulled and her face pressed into a pillow, it was easier to hide her tears.

There was little doubt now that Iain Morrow wasn't the person Haven had hoped he'd be. His lies might have started with something as simple as a phone, but who knew how far they had gone. What scared Haven most was not how easily Iain had been able to hide the truth, but how eager she had been to believe him. She knew exactly what her grandmother would have said—that Haven was turning out to be just like her mother. She had let her good judgment be clouded by lust. And in her own way, Imogene would have been right. Haven had fallen for the same girlish notions that had seduced Mae Moore—true love and soul mates and happily ever after.

The visions of Constance's life may have led her to Iain, but maybe it wasn't love she was meant to find. As the plane began its descent through the clouds, Haven resolved to keep searching for the answers she needed. She wouldn't allow a heartbreak to get in her way.

IT WAS TWO O'CLOCK in the afternoon when the plane landed, and three before they arrived at the little house near Washington Square Park. The street was blissfully empty. Iain's driver carried their bags into the house and then stayed by the door, awaiting his orders. Iain charged upstairs to the bedroom and returned moments later with a black messenger bag hanging off his shoulder.

"I have to go out for a little while," he informed Haven. "I should be back before dinner. It's probably not a good idea for you to leave while I'm gone. James will stay with you. If you need anything, just let him know, and he'll get it."

The driver, a bulky man with the face of a bulldog, nodded and stepped forward into the living room. Haven struggled to find the right words to express her horror.

"I don't need anyone looking after me," she hissed.

"Trust me," Iain replied, bending down to kiss the top of her head. "You do. This city is dangerous, and you're not well."

"Dangerous? I lived here for twenty years!" Haven argued.

"Yes, and you died here, too. We don't want that to happen again. What if you fainted while you were out on your own? Do you have any idea what sort of things might happen to you in a place like Manhattan?"

"Nothing's going to happen to me!"

"That's right," Iain said firmly. "Nothing is."

SOON AFTER THE DOOR slammed, Haven took a seat at the living room desk and cracked open the laptop that was lying there. She spent several minutes cursing softly to herself as she pretended to surf the Internet. James sat on the sofa, staring at a fixed spot in space as if he were trying to open a portal to another universe. Haven knew that she needed a plan. She had to get out. If nothing else, her sanity and self-respect demanded it.

"James," Haven drawled in her most sugary Southern accent. The man grunted as his massive torso slowly twisted in her direction. "I didn't have anything to eat on the plane, and I'm practically *dying* of hunger. Do you think you might be able to go out and pick me up a burger somewhere?"

"No problem," James replied. Using the minimum number of muscles, he pulled out a cell phone and punched a single key. "The lady wants a hamburger." He paused and pressed the phone receiver to his chest. "You want fries with that, miss?"

"Sure," said Haven, feeling utterly defeated.

"Fries, too," James barked. He flipped the phone shut and dropped it into his breast pocket.

Just as Haven turned back to the computer, she heard her own ringtone. She dove for her handbag and fished out her phone. An unfamiliar Snope City number appeared on the little screen, and Haven's heart leaped when she realized it might be Beau.

"Hello?"

"Haven Moore!" Her mother's voice always squeaked whenever she was upset. "How *dare* you not call me for three whole days. You know how worried I've been?"

"Sorry," Haven offered absentmindedly. She was hardly in the mood for a lecture. While her mother yammered away, Haven looked at the computer and randomly clicked one of the browser's bookmarks. A gossip blog now appeared on the computer screen. At the top of the page was the photo of her with Iain on the Ponte Sant'Angelo.

"Where have you been? Are you okay? Why aren't you at your hotel?" Mae Moore demanded.

"I'm staying with a friend for a few days," Haven explained. "It's cheaper that way."

"What friend? How do you have friends in New York? Is it someone from that Snake Club?"

"The Ouroboros Society. Yes, it's someone from there."

Haven's mother sighed with relief. "Well, are they helping you at all? Did you find out anything new?"

"Yeah," said Haven, now completely distracted. She had called up another gossip site, and the same picture was prominently featured. Iain hadn't been exaggerating when he said it was all over the media. It was *everywhere*. Haven's anxiety grew as she took a closer look at the photo. The caption beneath it read, *Who did Iain Morrow kill to get* this *girl?* Though the camera hadn't captured Haven's face, there were at least two people who would know that wild black hair the second they saw it. How long would it be before her grandmother figured out that she'd been in Rome?

Haven scrolled down, and a different picture appeared on the screen. She clapped a hand over her mouth so her mother couldn't hear her gasp.

"Well, like *what*, Haven?"

"I'll have to tell you about it later, Mom. Something just came up." She had to find a way to reach Beau.

"Something more important than talking to *me*?"

"You know it's not like that. I'll call you later this evening. Bye, Mom."

"Haven!" She heard Mae Moore yelp on the other end of the phone just as she hit the "off" button.

Haven stared at the computer. The new picture was blurry and poorly lit. Yet it was easy to see that it was the photo of a corpse. Jeremy Johns was dead. His body had been discovered by two teenagers cutting across an empty lot in Los Angeles, not far from where the musician had last been seen. The kids who'd found him snapped a photo and posted it online before they bothered to call the police. Though much of the body was badly decomposed, the authorities had been able to identify it by the distinctive snake tattoo on the forearm.

Every nerve in Haven's body was now set on alert. She carefully erased the page from the browser history and pushed back her chair.

"I'm going to take a quick shower," she informed the giant on the sofa as she casually climbed the stairs. "If my food comes, just leave it in the kitchen, okay?"

She turned on the faucet in the bathroom and tiptoed up to the door that led to the roof. In less than three minutes, she had climbed down the fire escape to University Place. As soon as there were several blocks between her and the mews, Haven ducked into a doorway on Mercer Street, pulled out her phone, and dialed Beau's number. Hidden in the shadows, she watched people pass by in the blazing sunshine. A black Mercedes came to a halt under a nearby streetlight, and Haven pressed herself against the wall until the car disappeared in the direction of SoHo.

Beau answered immediately. "Haven! Are you okay? I've been worried to death."

"I'm fine," Haven assured him.

"Well, thank God for that." Beau sighed with relief, and a long, awkward pause followed. "So. Tell me the truth. Are you Iain Morrow's sex slave?"

Haven almost smiled. The teasing was a sure sign she'd been forgiven. "Wow, right to the point. You don't waste time, do you?"

Beau cackled so loudly that Haven held the phone away from her ear.

"Oh my God. You *are*. I can hear it in your voice. My sweet little girl has become a woman."

"Shut *up*!" Haven squawked, hoping no one had overheard.

"It *was* you." Beau was practically gasping for breath. "You're the mystery girl in Italy! I hope you know you don't deserve it. Why can't *I* find someone who wants to whisk me off to Rome?"

"Are you aware you have to leave the state of Tennessee to get to Rome?"

"Watch yourself, Haven Moore," Beau growled. It was impressive how quickly his mood could turn. "You really made a mess of things back here. I may have to secretly hate you for the rest of your life."

"Does that mean your dad's going to make you go to Vanderbilt?"

"I *refuse* to discuss this subject with you. Where certain things are concerned, you are *not* to be trusted. Besides, why would I want to talk about my boring old future when we could be discussing your budding sex life? So how does it feel, Cinderella? Are you the happiest girl in the world?"

"Not exactly."

"Why?" Beau's laughing trailed off. "What's going on?"

"Haven't you seen the news? They found Jeremy Johns. *That's* why we're back in the States. Iain's been called in for questioning. He must be talking to the police right now."

"What do you mean, 'he must be'? Don't you know for sure?"

"All he told me was that he had to go out for a little while." Haven started to explain and then stopped. "Look, I really screwed up this time. Iain isn't the person I thought he was. We've been together for three days, and he's already lying to me. When we were in Rome, he insisted he didn't have a phone there—but I found out he did. Then we had to leave unexpectedly, and he wouldn't tell me why. So now we're back in New York, and he's assigned one of his bodyguards to babysit me. He didn't even want me to leave the house. I had to break out. Can you believe it?"

"Calm down, Haven. It sounds like Mr. Morrow is just a massive control freak." Beau always relished his role as the voice of reason. "Maybe he's trying to protect you. If all this reincarnation stuff is real, and it turns out he used to be Ethan, he probably wouldn't want to lose you again, would he?"

"Maybe . . . or maybe he took me to Rome just to get me out of New York." It was the first time Haven had put into words the feeling that had been nagging at her.

"Why would he do that?"

"Maybe there's something here that he doesn't want me to find."

"Like what?"

"Like proof that he killed Jeremy Johns?"

"Oh, come on, Haven. You really think billionaire playboys kill people and dump the bodies in empty lots? That's crazy. Besides, how can you be so quick to judge? Have you forgotten that just last week *you* were accused of a crime you had nothing to do with?"

"*That* was different," Haven argued.

"Oh, yeah? Different how? I—"

"Shhh!" Haven whispered. "Wait a second."

Two men had turned the corner onto Mercer Street. Dressed in dark suits and sunglasses, they walked with purpose, their heads slowly swiveling as though they were patrolling both sides of the street. As they passed Haven's hiding spot, the shorter of the pair smiled straight at her. There was something about the man's tacky, colorful tie that told her he wasn't a threat. But even after he and his friend had disappeared, she found herself unable to relax. The fear Haven had felt on her first day in New York had returned.

"Haven? You okay?"

"Sorry," she told Beau. "False alarm. I guess I *have* been a bit paranoid lately. When I got to the city, I was sure I was being followed, but it turned out my stalker was just some guy who was staying at my hotel. I could have died of embarrassment."

"Nobody can blame you for being a little jumpy. You know they've officially labeled the fire at your grandma's arson? The sheriff might have had a chance to catch the guy who did it if he'd listened to you in the first place."

"Yeah. Like *that* was ever going to happen." Haven let out a bitter laugh. "Half of Snope City probably thinks the devil himself started the fire."

"Naw, the latest theory is that you personally opened a portal to hell."

"In that case, it's too bad it didn't swallow the whole freaking town. Dr. Tidmore come up with that by himself?"

"Dunno. I've been boycotting church since you left. Not that it makes a difference. Dad said Tidmore's off on vacation. But we're getting off the subject here. What are you going to do about Mr. Morrow, anyway?"

"Nothing, I guess," Haven said.

"*Nothing*? You've spent the last few minutes trying to convince me that he's a pathological liar who murdered a musician, but you're still going to keep hanging out with him?"

"I don't have much of a choice right now, Beau. I have to figure out why I'm here. Maybe I'm not supposed to ride off into the sunset with Iain Morrow. But Constance wanted me in New York for some reason. And she wanted me to find Ethan. I can't just go running back to Snope City when things get a little weird."

"Spoken like someone who's been driven insane by good sex."

"Beau! Shut *up*!"

"Sorry," the boy said, trying to control his laughter. "I can't help myself. But seriously . . . did you find out anything from the people at the Ouroboros Society?"

"I haven't been there yet."

"*What*?" Beau practically yelled. "That's one of the reasons you went to New York in the first place. Why haven't you gone to see them?"

"I *told you* I just got back from Rome."

"Well, get your butt over there right now. Maybe they can help you figure out whether lover boy is really dangerous."

"You're right," Haven said.

"Of *course* I'm right. Just let me know if there's anything else I can do to help. And promise me you'll try to be careful, okay?"

"I promise." She was about to put the phone away when she heard a tiny voice shouting back at her.

"Hey, Haven!"

"What?"

"I almost forgot. Leah Frizzell stopped by the house yesterday."

"Yeah?"

"She said to tell you that there's someone like you up there. Someone else who has visions. Leah wants you to keep an eye out for her. She says the girl will show you the truth."

"What does *that* mean?"

"Who the hell knows?" Beau said. "I never said I spoke crazy. Look, my dad's hollering for me. I gotta go. Call me when you get back from the OS."

"Hey Beau!" Haven yelled before he could hang up.

"What now?"

"I really wish you were here," Haven told him.

# CHAPTER THIRTY-EIGHT

Haven found herself in a quiet, leafy square a block away from bustling Park Avenue South. In the center of the square, a tall, wrought-iron fence enclosed a lush and lovely park. The statue of a melancholy man with his head bowed in thought seemed to hover above the greenery. Two people strolled the gravel paths beneath the statue, speaking in hushed tones. Haven watched as a small boy tried to push the park's gate open, only to find it locked. He stood for a moment with his fingers wrapped around iron bars, gazing into the secret world in the center of Manhattan.

Among the mansions that lined the south side of the square stood an old brownstone with a wide balcony that faced the park. Thick green vines crawled up the front of the building, clinging to the balcony, creeping across windowsills and dangling over the front door. The house seemed abandoned—like the scene of a grisly crime, now inhabited only by ghosts. Haven knew at once that it was the mansion from her visions—formerly the Strickland family home and currently the headquarters of the Ouroboros Society. As she climbed the stoop to the entrance, memories of meetings, celebrations—even funerals—flashed like a slide show in her head. The images stopped as soon as she opened the door. The interior of the building had been completely renovated. It was now airy and modern—nothing at all like the wood-paneled mansion she remembered. Haven instantly felt cold. She would have sworn that she'd never been there before. The mansion was as sterile and lifeless as a computer-chip factory, and a voice in Haven's head was begging her to leave.

A few yards from the door, a receptionist sat at a steel and glass desk. The beige leather chairs in the waiting area were crammed with little children and their parents. The adults were filling out questionnaires as the children read books or played video games. Haven noticed one small girl with a copy of Dante's *Divine Comedy* lying open on her lap.

"May I help you?" the young man at the front desk asked politely. With his perfectly combed hair, black glasses, and white shirt, he looked as though he'd been sculpted out of plastic.

"Hi there." Haven couldn't pull her eyes away from the crowd of visitors in the lobby. "Are *all* of these people members of the Society?" she asked softly.

"Certainly not," the receptionist replied with all the emotion of an automated recording. "Parents bring their offspring in for past-life analysis. But most of these children merely watch too much television. Only a tiny percentage will ever be offered a membership. Now. May I help you?"

"Yes," Haven said, recalling her task. "I'd like to make an appointment with Ms. Singh, the president of your Society."

The receptionist looked caught off guard, as if Haven had asked for an audience with the queen. "And you are?"

"My name is Haven Moore."

The receptionist blinked twice. "Ms. Singh is out of the office," he informed her. "But I expect her back at any minute. If you would like to take a seat, she may be able to see you when she returns."

"That's okay," Haven said, eager to make her escape. "I'll come back later."

"Oh no, I *insist*," the young man said, pointing to the one empty seat in the reception area.

AN OS EMPLOYEE called out a pair of names, and two identical little boys hopped out of their seats next to Haven in the waiting room. The boys' mother was too engrossed in her book to notice that her sons had disappeared or that they'd left three empty juice boxes behind on the floor.

"Is this seat taken?" A young man in jeans and a crisp blue shirt pointed at one of the newly empty chairs. He was older than Haven, though by how much she couldn't say. And he was handsome—like a catalog model or an actor in a TV ad. Still, his features left little impression. If she had closed her eyes, she might have remembered his dark hair and eyes, but she doubted she'd be able to conjure his face.

"No." She smiled. "It's all yours."

He sat down and she offered him her hand, which he held for perhaps a beat too long. "I'm Adam Rosier." The young man had the deep, resonant voice of a newscaster. She suspected his accent wasn't American, but Haven could detect no actual trace of its origins.

"Haven Moore."

"Haven." It was as if he were committing the name to memory. "Would this be your first visit to the OS?"

"Yes," she confirmed. "Is it yours?"

Adam's smile was slow and indulgent. "No, I've been a member for quite a while. It's a wonderful organization. Are you here for an evaluation?"

"Actually, I'm waiting to speak with Ms. Singh," Haven explained.

"The receptionist said she might have time to meet with me today."

"I see. Then I assume you've remembered a previous existence." He made a brief show of looking her over. "You were someone quite interesting," he concluded. "I can always tell."

Haven leaned toward him and dropped her voice a little. "I think I may have been a member of the Ouroboros Society in its early days. I was hoping Ms. Singh might be able to help me fill in some of the gaps in my memory."

"How fascinating. I've always been interested in the history of the Society. Do you remember any of the people you might have known back then?"

"A few," she said.

"So is that what brought you all the way from Tennessee? Are you searching for someone special from your past?"

Haven leaned back, and her fingers dug into the arms of her chair. "Did I mention I'm from Tennessee?"

Adam laughed, and Haven's anxiety vanished. "No, I'm just good at placing accents. It's a talent. Everyone around here has an unusual gift or two. You grew up in the mountains, am I correct?"

"You're right," Haven marveled. "I'm impressed!"

"Have you been in the city for long?"

"No, I just got here."

"You just got here," Adam repeated, as though trying to make sense of the phrase. "And where are you staying—if you don't mind my asking?"

"With a friend." Haven didn't feel comfortable revealing much more.

"I see." Adam smiled again. "Well, if you wear out your welcome, the Society has rooms for rent. They're quite tasteful and remarkably affordable."

"Thank you. I'll keep that—"

"Miss Moore?" The receptionist was hovering above her. "I'm

afraid Ms. Singh just called in. She won't be back until tomorrow morning. Would you care to make an appointment?"

Haven was relieved she wouldn't need to stay any longer. The building's frigid atmosphere was already beginning to seep into her bones, and she longed to be back outside beneath the summer sun. "I guess so."

"How about Monday at eleven? Unfortunately, that's the earliest time I have. As you can see, we're rather busy."

"Monday's perfect."

"Thank you, Miss Moore." The receptionist closed his old-fashioned appointment book and offered a patronizing smile. "We'll see you next week."

Haven stood up, and Adam Rosier rose with her. "It was nice to meet you," she told him.

"A pleasure," he confirmed. "You know, Haven, if you're interested in doing a little research on your own, the Gramercy Park Historical Society is only two buildings away. They have quite a few documents from the early days of the OS. You might be able find some of the information you're looking for there."

"Thank you. I'll check it out," Haven said, unsettled by the way his eyes never moved from her face. It was both flattering and frightening to be the object of such scrutiny.

"I hope to see you on your next visit to the Society," Adam told her. "I'm often here. Perhaps we can have a cup of coffee? I could tell you more about us. I might even be able to convince you to join the OS."

He had the cool confidence of someone whom others rarely refused. There was an unexpected air of power about him as if he were a prince disguised as a commoner or a god masquerading as a mortal.

"Sure," Haven was surprised to hear herself say. "Next time."

# CHAPTER THIRTY-NINE

Outside the Ouroboros Society, the sidewalks were empty. A bright glint of light directed Haven's eyes toward the windows of an apartment across the park. She thought she detected the outline of a figure standing in a dark room, surveying the square below. Haven quickened her stride, and within seconds she was bounding up the stairs of a redbrick mansion just steps from the OS. Inside the building's front parlor was the office of the Gramercy Park Historical Society. Haven approached a tiny woman with horn-rimmed glasses who was attacking the room's surfaces with a feather duster, stirring up clouds of motes that settled as soon as her back was turned. All around her the walls were crowded with nineteenth-century photos of the buildings that surrounded the park. Blurry figures swept along the sidewalks—the ghosts of pedestrians moving too quickly to be captured by the cameras of the day.

The woman in the office froze when she spied her guest, her duster poised inches from a bust of Stanford White. "Are you Haven Moore?" the woman inquired.

"I am."

"I'm the librarian. The OS just called and asked me to set that aside for you." The woman pointed to a large box on a nearby chair. "It's everything we have on the early years of the organization."

"But I only left there a minute ago." Haven was taken aback. "How did you find it all so quickly?"

"You're not the first person sent over by the OS," the woman noted, setting down her duster. Her movements were precise, economical. "I keep all the materials together so they're ready when needed. The reading room is on the second floor. Come along, I'll show you."

Haven followed the woman up a single set of stairs. A red velvet rope on the landing blocked access to the mansion's upper floors while a door opened into an enormous reading room. Inside, the shades were pulled and the space was dimly lit by four small lamps clustered in the center of a long, ornate table. The air was cool and smelled of dust and decay. Shelves of books circled the room, and several small statues stood atop them. The faces of men long dead and forgotten stared down at the girl who had invaded their domain. If the building wasn't haunted, it was missing a good opportunity, Haven thought.

"Is it usually so empty this time of day?" she asked the woman as she slid the box onto a table in a corner.

"Empty?" The woman glanced around the room. "Yes, I suppose it is, isn't it? I'm sure you'll have company soon enough. Let me know if there's anything else I can get for you," she added as she bustled toward the stairs.

Haven opened the box to find a few books and a half-dozen document cases. But the first item she pulled out was an old scrapbook, its black cover brittle and crumbling. Yellowing newspaper articles had been affixed to the book's pages. Most appeared to be from either the *New York Daily News* or the *New York Daily Mirror.* To Haven's astonishment, the articles focused on Ethan Evans, and all the photos that accompanied them had managed to capture him scowling or sneering. Haven skimmed the headlines.

August Strickland Dead at 65, Protégé Named Heir
Evidence Points to Murder in Strickland Case
Evans Questioned in Philanthropist's Death
Evans Love Triangle May Have Led to Murder
Suspect in Strickland Murder Perishes in Fire
New Leadership at Strickland's OS
Evans's Mistress Collapses at Funeral

She paused at the last article. The grainy picture beneath the headline showed a young woman with dark hair being supported by a figure whose head had been severed when the photo was cropped. Though the girl wore a veil, Haven could see her tear-soaked face well enough to identify her. It was Rebecca. The surge of hatred and jealousy that coursed through Haven's system came as a complete surprise.

*Grief-stricken Rebecca Underwood collapsed at the funeral of Ethan Evans yesterday, further fueling rumors that the two had been lovers. Although Evans secretly married heiress Constance Whitman in the hours before their deaths, sources report that the relationship was little more than a financial arrangement, and that Rebecca Underwood remained his mistress.*

*Earlier this year, Evans was suspected by many of murdering his wealthy mentor, Dr. August Strickland. Now some are claiming that the fire at the Washington Mews was an attempt to add millions to Evans's newfound fortune. Did Evans accidentally perish in the act of murdering his rich bride? Our source has confirmed these suspicions. But with Evans dead, there is little now that can be done. . . .*

Haven recognized cheap gossip when she saw it, but the cruel speculation still stung. She tore through the rest of the scrapbook, past more chatty columns and a few serious police reports from the *New York Herald Tribune*. While it had taken months for New York's gossips to grow tired of the sordid story, the official investigation into Strickland's death appeared to have stopped with Ethan Evans's demise. But Haven found the most interesting piece of information glued to the very last page of the scrapbook. *Donated to the New York Historical Society by Frances Whitman. 1995*, read a small, typewritten strip of paper. This was a possibility that she had never considered: Constance might still have family in New York.

Haven suddenly felt a presence and peered up from the scrapbook to find a drab little woman watching her from the entrance. She offered Haven a quick, humorless nod before heading for a seat at the far end of the long reading room table, her shapeless gray skirt swishing about her calves. Moments later, a man in khaki Dockers strolled past the table and continued toward one of the chairs facing the room's fireplace. Once settled, he tucked his nose into a book that had no title on its spine.

Haven had hoped for some company, but the other visitors only added to the eerie atmosphere of the room, so she focused her attention to the other materials that had been packed in the box. A yellowing pamphlet written by August Strickland outlined the mission of the Ouroboros Society. The organization, he wrote, "welcomes individuals of both sexes and all races or religions who commit to using their God-given talents for the betterment of the world." Then Haven spent several minutes scrutinizing an official photo from the early days of the club. Strickland stood in the center of the picture, surrounded by a dozen smiling followers. He was not a tall man, but his bushy white hair added inches to his height. His fond gaze was focused on the younger man by his side. Ethan Evans grinned at the camera, his expression completely carefree.

Haven laid the photo beside one of the newspaper clippings in the scrapbook. Which was the real Ethan Evans—the carefree young man or the scowling suspect? Even her visions of Ethan offered few clues. Constance had yet to reveal her whole story. And unless Haven could find some way to see more of the past, she might never uncover the truth about Ethan.

AS HAVEN LEFT the Historical Society, she saw the gate to Gramercy Park swing open, and she bolted to catch it before it could close. The middle-aged woman who had emerged shot Haven a nasty look, which did nothing to stop the girl from entering. After taking a stroll around the empty enclosure, Haven found a wooden bench opposite the Ouroboros Society and sat down to watch the front of the mansion. She'd hoped the sight would summon a vision, but at first nothing came to her. All she knew was that the experience at the Historical Society had left her feeling chilled and lonely. Had Constance been murdered by the man she loved? Was that what she wanted Haven to discover?

*"He's not good enough for you."*

The man's voice was close, only a few feet away. Haven jumped from the bench, expecting to find that someone was sneaking up behind her. But the park was deserted, and the light was fading fast.

*"Your grandmother was a fool to leave you that money," her mother said. They were having tea on a terrace, surrounded by the sky. Far below, Central Park Lake glistened in the early autumn sun. "You'll end up a target for every ne'er-do-well in the city."*

*"Grandmother wanted me to use the money to live my own life. To marry for love. Or not marry at all, if that's what I choose."*

*A breeze ruffled the tablecloth, and Elizabeth Whitman smoothed down her hair, which was carefully twisted and tucked into a golden bun at the nape of her neck.*

*"Silly old woman. Now the only way you'll know you've found true*

*love is if you marry someone with more money than you have."*

*"I'm perfectly happy to trust my own instincts where love is concerned, Mother."*

*"I hope you're not alluding to that young man you met in Rome. I hate to be the bearer of bad news, my dear, but everyone in town says he's only after your fortune. And I have it on very good authority that he spent a part of his childhood locked away in an asylum."*

*Constance shrugged. "Let them say what they like."*

*"I don't care what August Strickland tells you, young lady. Your fortune and upbringing set you apart. Why, just the other day, I met a young man who would be perfect. His name is—"*

*"Don't bother, Mother. I'm not interested." She could tell by her mother's pursed lips that the conversation would soon take a turn for the serious.*

*"I was hoping it wouldn't come to this, Constance. But I'm afraid your father and I simply can't allow you to continue seeing Ethan Evans while you are living under our roof."*

*"Then I suppose I should inform you that I don't intend to be living under your roof much longer. I'm moving downtown next week."*

*Her mother laughed at the ridiculous suggestion. "Nonsense! Your grandmother's house is far too large for a girl your age."*

*"I don't plan to live in her house."*

*"Then where?" Elizabeth Whitman gasped. "Oh, Constance, no! The stable?"*

HAVEN FELT GRASS beneath her fingers. Somewhere above her, a man spoke.

"What do you think happened to her?"

"I don't know," replied another voice.

"Should we call an ambulance?"

"I don't know."

Haven opened her eyes. Two men were squatting by her side. The first, dressed in a navy suit, was the man she'd seen in the store on Elizabeth Street. The other was the khaki-clad man from the reading room.

"Who are you?" Haven demanded as she stood up and brushed the leaves from her clothing. The last orange rays of daylight glowed like a fire burning somewhere in the west, and chandeliers blazed in the mansions surrounding the park. Only the shuttered windows of the Ouroboros Society remained dark.

"We were passing by the park, and we saw you faint. Are you sick? Can we help get you home?"

"Do you live here?" Haven asked.

The man in Dockers shot his companion a quick look. "No," he admitted.

"Thanks for your help, but I'm fine now. I've really got to go," Haven said. Her legs were stiff, but she limped as quickly as possible toward the park's exit. Something was wrong. How had the two men gotten into the locked park when only residents of the square were given a key?

"Wait!" One of the men caught up with her. "Where are you staying?"

"Brooklyn," Haven lied as she opened the park's gate and rushed to grab an idling cab. As the taxi sped off, Haven peeked out the rear window and saw the two men standing on the sidewalk, watching her disappear down Twentieth Street.

WHEN THE CAB came to a halt at the Washington Mews, Haven checked the lane for paparazzi before sprinting to the little white cottage and banging on its red door. Heavy footsteps stomped across the living room floor.

Staring down at her from the doorstep, Iain seemed taller, his body more powerful than she had remembered. His eyes were bloodshot, and their irises were a startling green. He was both beautiful and terrifying—exactly like the pictures of Ethan Evans in the scrapbook.

"Where have you been?" Iain demanded. "I've had everyone out looking for you."

"You first," Haven snipped. As she brushed past, she was surprised to find herself fighting the urge to throw her arms around him. He seemed so worried. It was hard to believe it might all be an act.

"Where did *you* go today?" she asked, attempting to turn the tables.

"I'm not the one who's sick."

"For your information," Haven said, "I've been taking a walk."

He followed her across the living room. "I thought I told you to stay here this afternoon."

"And be babysat by your overgrown goon? I had things to do." She couldn't trust herself to look at him. She couldn't let her anger fade.

"Did you go to the Ouroboros Society?"

Haven paused. "Yes, I did," she admitted. "But I didn't stay very long. The person I wanted to see wasn't there."

"Are you going to go back?"

Haven shrugged. "I doubt it. The place gave me the creeps. It wasn't anything like I remembered it."

"I *told* you."

"Yes, but some things I have to find out for myself. I didn't come to New York to be treated like a five-year-old. I don't want to feel like I'm being watched all the time. I can leave, you know."

The threat hit home, and the anger seemed to drain from Iain's body. He reached out for Haven's hand. "I'm just worried. You passed out in Rome, and you haven't even seen a doctor yet."

"Nothing bad is going to happen to me," Haven said, jerking her hand away.

"There are terrible people here," Iain said softly. "You have to be careful. Sometimes it's hard to tell them apart from—"

"There are terrible people everywhere, Iain. And I'm finally learning how to recognize them."

Haven felt the cell phone in her pocket vibrate. She pulled it out and flipped it open. A text message had just arrived from Beau.

*Still think he's dangerous?*

"What is it?" Iain asked.

"Nothing," Haven said, quickly erasing the message.

# CHAPTER FORTY

The house was filled with the scent of flowers. Every available surface held a vase of beautiful blooms. Never before had Haven seen so many flowers outside of a garden center or a graveyard. She'd asked Iain to sleep on the couch downstairs, but he hadn't been able to keep his distance. In the morning she had discovered an envelope with her name on it leaning against a lamp on her bedside table. A key fell out onto the sheets when she opened it.

*I'm sorry,* the card read. *I don't ever want to lock you away. This is the key to the front door. Come and go as you like. But please avoid being photographed. I will see you this evening. Love, Iain.*

Haven grabbed a pale pink rose from one of the vases and tossed it out the open window. Satisfied by the gesture, she rooted through her things for a pair of jeans and a T-shirt. Beneath a layer of underwear at the bottom of the suitcase she'd yet to unpack lay the print Iain had bought for her in Rome. Haven felt an unexpected twinge of jealousy as she stared at the blissful couple lying hidden in the grass.

It wasn't the young woman in the illustration she envied—it was the naive girl that Haven had been back in Italy.

She laid the print facedown next to Iain's note and got dressed. After checking to see if the house was empty, she made coffee and carried a cup up to the roof. Settling down in one of the wooden lounge chairs, she phoned Beau.

"'Lo," Ben Decker answered.

She felt better just hearing his familiar voice. "Hey Mr. Decker, it's Haven. How are you?" She lowered her voice to a whisper. "Beau ready to move out of town yet?"

Ben laughed. "I just made him paint the house, and now I reckon it's about time to reshingle the roof. They say it's gonna be ninety degrees today. Just the right sort of weather for working with hot tar."

"You're a cruel, cruel man, Mr. Decker."

"I'm glad I still have it in me," Ben confessed. "By the way, I saw your mama in town yesterday. Sounds like you got her in quite a tizzy."

"Oh God." Haven groaned. "I completely forgot to call her back. Imogene's probably put a price on my head by now."

"I wouldn't be surprised," Ben said with a chuckle. "Well, I don't suppose you called to talk to me. Let me wake up Prince Charming for you."

"Haven! It's seven o'clock in the morning," Beau protested when he picked up the phone.

"Sorry," Haven said. "I must have a hellish case of jet lag. I didn't even notice the time."

"So, d'you go see the reincarnation people yesterday?" Beau asked through a yawn.

"I did. But the woman I wanted to talk to was out of the office."

"Then you have to go back," Beau insisted.

"I don't know if I should. The place was a little creepy. And I'm not sure if I need to now. I met an interesting guy while I was waiting at the OS, and he suggested I visit the Historical Society next door.

They had a box filled with stuff on the Society, and I found a scrapbook with a bunch of old articles about Ethan Evans."

"And?"

Haven took a deep breath. "Let's just say the stories weren't all that flattering. A lot of people seemed to think that Ethan was a pretty bad guy. They say he murdered Dr. Strickland for his fortune. There were even rumors that he set the fire that killed Constance."

"That's crazy! Why would he kill *Constance*?"

"So he'd inherit all her money and live happily ever after with the other woman he'd been bonking—a girl Constance knew named Rebecca Underwood. The girl I saw with Ethan the day I trashed Tidmore's office."

Haven heard Beau spring out of bed, his bare feet hitting the floor with a slap.

"Whoa—do you really believe Ethan did all that?" He was wide awake now.

"I don't know *what* to believe. Some of the articles in that scrapbook made the *National Enquirer* look like the *New York Times*. But it would explain a lot, wouldn't it? Think about it, Beau. Maybe that's why I had to come here. If I find proof that Ethan was a killer, I could end up solving three murders at once."

"Three? I know about Constance and the Strickland guy," Beau said. "Who's the third?"

"Jeremy Johns."

Beau whistled softly. "Damn, Haven. This is getting pretty serious. You're not talking about something that happened ninety years ago. Jeremy Johns has only been dead for a few months!"

"I know! But I can't leave the city until I find out what's going on. I'd never be able to live with myself."

"I see what you mean." Beau paused to think. "But isn't there anywhere else you could stay? You'd be an idiot to keep sleeping at some psycho's house."

"I guess I could take a room at the Ouroboros Society. But how am I supposed to solve this if I'm hiding from my only suspect?"

"Are you sure you can solve this, Haven? I mean, sounds like all you've found so far are a bunch of old newspaper clippings. Do you have any real clues?"

"Not real—" Haven started to say. "Wait a second. I did find out that Constance has a relative who may still be alive. Someone named Frances Whitman. She was the one who donated the scrapbook to the Historical Society—in 1995."

"Well, there you go—that's a clue! You gotta go see her."

"How? She could live in Tibet for all I know."

"Did you look her up on the Internet?"

"No," Haven admitted sheepishly.

"Good God, Haven. A person who didn't know you so well might think you were scared or something. Hold on." He laid down the phone, and Haven heard him start up his computer. A few minutes later, Beau reappeared on the other end of the line. "That couldn't have been easier. Her address is 150 Central Park West. She held a fund-raiser there last month for some park renovation project."

Haven could see the building in her mind, its twin towers reflected in Central Park Lake. The Andorra apartments. Constance Whitman had once lived on the seventeenth floor, and even the thought of returning made Haven squirm.

"I don't know," she said, her courage faltering. "Constance's parents had an apartment there. I don't think I'd feel comfortable—"

"Dammit, Haven!" Beau bellowed, and Haven jumped. "Sometimes we gotta do things we don't want to do. You have no problem waking me up at seven o'clock in the morning, but you're not willing to do anything that makes you *uncomfortable*?"

"You're one to talk," Haven pointed out. "You can't even leave Tennessee."

"Don't you *dare* change the subject. I *told* you we are not going there. Now grow some balls and go see Ms. Whitman. Otherwise I'm not going to help your sorry ass anymore."

"All right." Haven sighed.

"And call me when you're done!"

"Bossy, bossy, bossy," Haven mumbled as she hung up the phone.

EVEN FROM A DISTANCE, the Andorra was intimidating. Big enough to house everyone in Snope City, it was renowned for the two towers that rose so far into the sky that the neighboring buildings seemed stunted. The towers had always reminded Constance of horns, Haven recalled as she reluctantly made her way north along Central Park West. When she finally arrived, she found herself looking at two identical entrances and instinctively chose the one to the south. Even as she stepped through the door, Haven felt her body tense up, as if she were revisiting the scene of a terrible dream. If the elderly doorman hadn't greeted her with a friendly smile, she might not have found the courage to speak.

"I'm here to see Frances Whitman," Haven announced.

"Is she expecting you?" the man asked as Haven stared at his epaulets. The doormen's uniforms hadn't changed since the days when Constance's parents had lived in the building.

"No."

"Your name?

"Haven Moore." She waited as the doorman rang the Whitman apartment and relayed the information. After a moment he turned back to Haven.

"Ms. Whitman would like to know the purpose of your visit."

"Please tell her I have a few questions about Constance," Haven said, taking a chance.

The woman on the other end of the intercom must have been listening. "Okay, miss," the doorman told Haven after a short pause.

"You can go up. She's on the seventeenth floor."

"Apartment D," Haven added.

"Have you been here before?" asked the doorman.

"Not for a very long time," Haven told him truthfully.

A HUSKY MAID in an old-fashioned blue-and-white uniform answered the door just seconds after Haven buzzed.

"This way," the maid announced, leading Haven through a maze of museumlike rooms, each more lovely than the next. As they passed the living room, Haven caught a glimpse of a prim blonde woman with an angry expression sitting on the edge of a velvet-covered sofa. A man wearing old-fashioned spectacles sat beside her with his arms folded across his chest. Haven blinked, and Constance's parents disappeared.

At last Haven arrived at a door. When the maid opened it, Haven at first saw nothing but sky. Squinting in the sunlight, she followed the woman out onto an enormous terrace that overlooked Central Park Lake—the same terrace she had seen in her vision. With the city smog beneath them, the air smelled sweet and clean. Rosebushes scaled the building's brick wall, their crimson flowers dangling from trellis holes like the heads of criminals left to suffer in stocks. In each corner of the terrace, topiary trees trimmed in perfect spheres sneered down at their cousins in the park below. Haven expected to find some aristocratic dowager pruning the roses, but sitting at a table with the paper and a pot of tea was a woman in her midthirties, wearing jeans and flip-flops.

"I'm Frances," the woman said, rising to shake Haven's hand, then gesturing to the seat across from her at the table. With her short blonde hair and willowy figure, she looked far more like Constance than Haven ever would.

"Haven."

"I'm just having some tea. Would you like a cup?"

"Yes. Thank you," Haven said.

"I must admit I'm intrigued," Frances said as the maid set down another cup and saucer. Haven instantly recognized the china's red and gold pattern. The dishes belonged to a set Constance's mother had inherited from an aunt. "I was expecting someone quite a bit older. How on earth do you know about Constance?"

Haven had her answer ready. "I'm researching the history of the Ouroboros Society for school. I came across an article about Constance's death, and I wanted to find out more."

"I see. An intrepid girl reporter," Frances said. "What school do you go to? I graduated from Spence about a million years ago."

It was the one question for which Haven hadn't prepped. "Blue Mountain."

"Blue Mountain? Where is *that*?"

"Tennessee," Haven admitted.

"And you've come all the way from Tennessee to interview *me*?" Frances Whitman didn't buy it for a second.

"I have a few other things planned while I'm here," Haven said, wishing she could lie as easily as Iain."This apartment belonged to Constance's parents, didn't it?"

Frances smiled knowingly. "Yes. Constance was their only child. When they died, their nephew—my father—inherited the place. I'm the last of the Whitmans, so I got it when my parents passed away a few years ago."

"Did your mom and dad ever meet Constance?"

"Oh God, no. Constance died *at least* twenty years before my father was born, and the family didn't like to talk about what had happened. I doubt I would even have known her name if I hadn't come across her obituary when I was about your age. It said that she'd died along with her lover in a tragic fire, which of course I found terribly romantic. And it mentioned that they had both been members of an organization called the Ouroboros Society that was devoted to the study of reincarnation. After that I was hooked. I visited the OS and started reading all the old articles I could find at the Historical Society. And then I remembered the basement."

"The basement?" Haven asked.

"Every apartment in this building has its own storage facility in the basement. When my parents moved in, we tried to put some boxes down there, but our space was jammed full. I guess we just forgot about it. But after I started reading about Constance, I went back down there." Frances paused to taste her tea. "And I hit the jackpot."

"What did you find?" Haven asked eagerly.

"All of Constance's things. Her parents must have packed up everything that wasn't destroyed in the fire and put it in storage. There were boxes and boxes of these crazy flapper dresses with the most beautiful beading I'd ever seen. I think she may have made them herself. And there were photos of her with her boyfriend and different people from the OS. I even found some old love letters."

"From Ethan?"

Frances's eyes glimmered. She had gossip to share. "I don't think so. None of the letters were signed. Whoever wrote them was trying to win her over. As far as I can tell, Ethan never had to try that hard."

"Do you think I could see the letters?" Haven asked.

"Sure—if I still had them."

"Where are they?" Haven asked.

"Gone. A couple of months after I found the stuff, the building's storage facility was robbed. Our next-door neighbors lost a fortune in furniture. They took all of Constance's boxes, too."

"Why would anybody want to take a bunch of old letters and dresses?"

Frances shook off a flip-flop and propped her bare foot up on a nearby planter. "I imagine the thieves knew what they were doing. Those dresses were probably worth a mint. The guys showed up on the security tapes. I watched them myself. Two professional-looking types loaded all the stuff into a truck parked out back. They left fingerprints and everything. You'd think the cops could have caught them, but we never heard a thing."

"What about the scrapbook you donated to the Gramercy Park Historical Society?" Haven asked. "How did that get left behind?"

"The Gramercy Park Historical Society? I've never heard of it. You must mean the New York Historical Society. Anyway, the thieves didn't leave the scrapbook behind," Frances said. "As far as I know, it never belonged to Constance. I found it at the Sixth Avenue flea market back in the nineties. The guy who sold it to me said it had come from the estate of some rich old spinster—his word, not mine. He didn't know her name. He thought she must have followed the case back in the day."

Haven let the information sink in. "And what did you think of the articles in the scrapbook?" she finally asked. "Do you think Ethan Evans could have murdered Constance?"

"Absolutely not," Frances said with a vigorous shake of her head. "I think he and Constance were madly in love. I'm thirty-six years old, Haven, and I've already been married three times. And even though all my husbands turned out to be jerks, I'd still like to believe I know real love when I see it. Maybe you'll say I'm just a hopeless romantic. But I read the police report. Constance and Ethan died in each other's arms. In fact, the firemen found the bodies still locked in an embrace. Does that sound like murder to you?"

"No," Haven had to admit. There was something stirring inside of her that she had thought was dead. "I guess it doesn't."

"Exactly," Frances said with a satisfied smile. "So. Now that I've told you everything I know, why don't you tell me why you're *really* here, Miss Moore."

The question took Haven by surprise. "Excuse me?"

"Oh, come *on*," Frances replied with a comic huff. "Blue Mountain High School? Are you kidding?"

"I don't understand," Haven stammered as she started to rise.

"Please, sit down," Frances urged. "There's no need to get upset. You can trust me. I've been expecting Constance to show up again since I first read about her. Now a girl from Tennessee comes to see me with questions about my cousin who died in 1925? It can't be a coincidence." She raised one eyebrow in expectation. "So. Give me the scoop."

"I . . . I really don't know what to tell you, Ms. Whitman. I think you may have read too many books on reincarnation. Thank you for your help, but I have another appointment this morning."

"Such a shame," Frances pretended to pout. "All right then. Just promise you'll come back to see me when you've finished your 'research.'"

"I promise," Haven lied. She was beginning to feel light-headed. A vision was on the way, and she had to force herself to remain upright and alert.

ONCE SHE HAD FLED the Andorra, Haven crossed the street in a daze and stumbled into Central Park, hoping she could reach a safe place before she was overcome by the vision. Haven plopped down on the grass by the lake—just as Constance must have done a hundred times before—and the world faded into darkness.

*She felt her seat rocking beneath her and realized she was sitting on a boat in the lake. The sky above was black and starless. A whizzing, whistling noise filled the air, and then lights exploded above. All around her, the fireworks glittered against the dark water.*

*In the week since her ship had returned to New York from Europe, Constance had spent every spare moment in Ethan's company. She had finally found the life she'd been missing. She believed him when he told her they were meant to be together. Yet one nagging doubt still remained.*

*"How long have you known Rebecca?" she asked. She had seen how Rebecca's beautiful face glowed whenever Ethan entered a room.*

*"A little over a year, I suppose."*

*"She's in love with you, isn't she?"*

*"She thinks she is," Ethan said.*

*"What does that mean?"*

*"It means she has me confused with someone else from her past."*

*"Does that happen often?" Constance asked, a note of concern creeping into her voice.*

*"It happens," he said. "But never to us."*

*Ethan rowed the boat out to the center of the lake and gave her his lopsided grin before he blew out the flame in the one lantern they'd brought.*

*"Come here, Constance," he insisted.*

*"It's dark," she said.*

*"Why do you think I brought you here?"*

*She felt fingers encircling her wrists, and strong arms pulling her toward the middle of the boat. Water splashed against the sides when she fell into his lap. The boat could capsize. She'd seen it happen before. A girl had drowned doing the very same thing. But Constance still couldn't resist.*

WHEN SHE WOKE, Haven could hear the oars of rowboats dipping into the water. A girl laughed in the distance, and Haven imagined Constance and Ethan skimming across the surface of the lake, their ghostly silhouettes glimmering in the moonlight. She sat up with a jolt when she felt something prodding her side. A beagle was sniffing at her.

"You okay?" its teenage owner inquired. "I was about to call an ambulance."

"I'm fine, thanks," Haven said, making use of the kid's outstretched hand to pull herself to her feet. She had to find a way to stop fainting in public. And yet she couldn't have been happier that the last vision had come. Along with her meeting with Frances Whitman, it was the perfect antidote to the suspicions that had been eating away at her like poison. Frances was right. Ethan would never have murdered Constance. The boy on the boat had been crazy in love. Haven had felt it in the way he'd pulled Constance into his arms. That kind of passion was impossible to fake. When he had kissed her that night on the water, Constance had believed that nothing—least of all another woman—could ever come between them.

HAVEN HURRIED BACK to the mews house to find Iain lounging on the sofa, reading the *New York Times*. He peered over the paper at her, smiled, and didn't ask any questions. He was trying hard to live up to his promise to give Haven her freedom. All of the feelings she'd had for him in Italy rushed back to her at once, and she knelt down on the floor beside the couch and kissed him.

"Don't you want to know where I've been?" she asked playfully, hoping their argument had been forgotten.

"Only if you want to tell me," Iain said. "Otherwise, your comings and goings are no longer my business."

"I guess that must mean you're having me followed?" Haven joked.

"Very amusing. But since you're in a better mood, I'll go ahead and ask. What *have* you been doing today?"

She was going to tell him everything. "I went up to Central Park Lake and watched people row boats like we used to."

"Ah, I was so romantic back then."

"You still are. Thanks for all the flowers this morning." She thought of the rose she'd tossed from the window and felt a sharp pang of regret.

"My pleasure." He kissed her. "I'm sorry I was so hard on you yesterday. I can only imagine how confused you must be. I have to remind myself that you don't remember everything the way I do. I hope you'll remember more someday, but in the meantime, will you please *try* to trust me?"

"I will," Haven promised.

"Good. I just wish I could take you to dinner and seduce you with more stories of our past. But I have plans tonight that I can't cancel."

"Anything exciting?" she asked, closing her eyes and resting her head on his chest.

"If you call dinner with your nine-hundred-year-old attorney exciting."

Haven's eyes popped open. He was lying again. She didn't know how, but she knew it.

"What time are you leaving?" she asked. "Maybe I'll go see a movie."

## CHAPTER FORTY-ONE

Haven slumped down in the back of the taxi and kept one eye on the red door. It was ten past eight. Iain was running late, and the cab's meter was ticking away. The black Mercedes sat idling at the end of the cobblestone street, spewing a thick cloud of exhaust as it waited for its passenger. Haven was beginning to wonder if she'd missed him—if he'd decided to walk or catch a taxi—when the red door opened and Iain emerged, wearing jeans and a black jacket. Without so much as a glance at the taxi, he ducked into his Mercedes. When it pulled onto Fifth Avenue, Haven's cab slipped out behind it.

With the sun sinking in the west and lamps across the city illuminating, countless scenes played out behind New York's windows. People cried and fought and danced in their underwear, all unaware that the world could see them. Anticipating a long ride to the upper reaches of Manhattan, Haven settled back and watched them pass by. But the trip was surprisingly short. The Mercedes turned west on Twenty-first Street and came to a stop in front of a converted auto repair shop, its street front now a single sheet of glass. Haven's heart plunged. Inside the building, hundreds of people had gathered for a party. They milled about behind the window like creatures in a bizarre zoo exhibition. And not one of them matched the description of a nine-hundred-year-old attorney.

Haven paid her cab driver and watched from the shadows on the other side of the street as Iain wove through the crowd. Each person he passed planted a kiss on his cheek, patted him on the back, or whispered in his ear. Haven realized, her heart hitting the ground with a thud, that this was *his* party. And she hadn't been invited. With anger driving her on, Haven joined a group of girls flirting with the two men handling the guest list and followed them inside the party.

The building housed an art gallery, and its stark white walls were dotted with paintings. Haven stopped in front of one of the works. The brushstrokes were broad and wild and the colors so vivid they seemed alive. The image showed the ancient city of Rome ablaze. Temples crumbled in the background as tiny citizens fled for their lives. In the foreground, far from the action taking place elsewhere on the canvas, a shadowy figure in black rested casually on one of the hills overlooking the city, watching the chaos in the distance. The figure was no more in height than an inch or two—easy to miss among all the swirling colors.

Slightly shaken, Haven moved along to the next painting. The same man watched from a lifeboat as a passenger ship slipped beneath the ocean's murky waves. A third showed a grief-stricken blonde eavesdropping on her husband and another woman. She, too, was being observed. There were dozens more paintings. Disasters and tragedies. Scenes of anarchy and upheaval. And hidden in each, somewhere in the foreground, the dark figure was setting it all in motion, like the conductor of a sinister symphony.

"WELCOME LADIES AND GENTLEMEN, critics and freeloaders." Obscured by the crowd, Haven spotted Iain standing on a low stage in the center of the gallery. One of his arms was wrapped around a thin young woman in a black dress shaped like a belted garbage bag. Her eyes, ringed with black liner, peeked out from beneath long, dark bangs. Under the harsh gallery lights, her skin was whiter than the walls, and she looked like the victim of an old-fashioned wasting disease. Haven was surprised the girl was able to stand—and even more surprised to see her bright red mouth stretch into a Joker-like smile.

"Thank you for coming to the opening of Marta Vega's new show, 'Agent of Entropy,'" Iain continued. "As you all know, I'm a big fan of Marta's work, and I'm honored to have the opportunity to give these remarkable paintings a temporary home in my late father's gallery. Eventually, I hope that some of them will find a permanent place in my living room. That is, if my pockets prove deep enough." The crowd tittered knowingly. "So enjoy yourselves, enjoy the art, and most of all, enjoy the free booze. Thank you."

Iain left the stage with his arm around Marta Vega and made a beeline for the bar. Haven slipped out of their path and around a corner where she watched them ordering drinks and whispering to each other for all to see. Haven could imagine what the other guests were saying. Jeremy Johns's body had been discovered only two days earlier. Now here they were—the suspect and the motive. The pair had no shame being seen together while Jeremy Johns was still lying on the coroner's slab.

Haven glared at Iain's hand as it brushed across the girl's pale skin, left bare by a deep scoop in the back of her dress. It was hard to believe the same hand belonged to the person she'd known in Rome. But Haven knew the truth had a way of slithering out when it thought she wasn't watching. Once again she was seeing the real Iain Morrow. And the real Iain Morrow—the one who graced the gossip columns and posed for paparazzi—was a liar and a womanizer.

"WHAT DO YOU THINK?" Haven was startled by the sound of the woman's voice. Just to her right, with little more than a column between them and Haven, a couple stood studying one of Marta Vega's paintings. The photo on the OS Website hadn't captured Padma Singh's beauty. In person, the Society's president was stunning, with violet eyes, thick black hair that cascaded around her shoulders, and the body of a succubus. While most of the males in the room ogled Padma, Haven's eyes were drawn to the woman's companion—a dapper young man in a perfectly cut suit. With a pair of chunky black glasses resting on the bridge of his nose, Adam Rosier was barely recognizable. Before the two had a chance to see her, Haven slid behind the column and out of view.

"The quality of her art has eroded," she heard Adam confide in his newscaster voice. "The brushwork is sloppy, the colors are nauseating, and everything else is depressingly primitive."

"And the subject matter?" Padma inquired with a hint of nervousness in her voice.

"The subject matter is the only interesting part of the whole mess," Rosier stated. "But her choice makes it abundantly clear that the drugs are eating away at her mind."

"Yes, Marta's work has grown quite *provocative*, hasn't it?" Padma agreed. "Perhaps we should ask her to explain her inspiration."

"I don't think that will be necessary. I'm not even certain she knows. But this show must close before it becomes an embarrassment. Whatever money is being spent on the gallery can be put to better use."

Adam had the power to close down Marta Vega's show? Haven's heart raced. Her instincts had been right for once—Adam was someone important. Her curiosity craved another glimpse of his face, but Haven knew she shouldn't take the risk.

"It's Iain Morrow's money," Haven heard Padma inform Adam. "The Society didn't pay for any of this."

"Then perhaps we should consider cutting ties with Mr. Morrow as well," Adam replied bluntly. "I'm afraid he's made quite a mess of things."

"He has—but do we need to be so hard on him, Adam?" Padma's tone was suddenly sugary. "I still consider Iain an asset to the Society."

Haven couldn't resist any longer. She peeked around the column and saw Rosier turn on the woman with a smile that was almost cruel.

"You've always been a sucker for a pretty face, haven't you, Padma?"

Padma flinched. "It's not like that this time. I'd just rather not act too hastily where Iain is concerned. I know he's responsible for sponsoring this show, but don't you think we should give him a chance to clean up the mess he's made?" She posed the question carefully, as if frightened of what the response might be. "He's always asking for ways to earn more points."

Rosier appeared to ponder the suggestion. "Do you really think Iain would go to such lengths to remain a part of the OS?"

"Yes," Padma confirmed, looking relieved. "I'm sure that he would."

"Then let's not waste any time," Rosier said.

"I'll talk to him tomorrow," Padma promised.

As the duo glided along to the next painting, Haven hung back. Iain had emerged from the crowd to greet Padma. Haven couldn't hear what he was saying over the chatter of the other guests, but she saw him offer his arm to the president of the OS. Haven ducked behind the column just as the two began to saunter back in her direction. She looked around and found she was trapped in a corner of the gallery. The only possibility of escape was a fire exit with a high-tech alarm above the door. It would make a terrible racket, and perhaps even draw the fire department, but it was Haven's only chance. She barged her way through the crowd and pushed at the door, bracing her ears for the alarm. It swung open silently and closed with a thump as Haven stumbled out into an alley.

"Hey, did you let that shut all the way?" The question came from a cloud of smoke to the left of the fire exit. A girl stepped out of it, her pale skin glowing unnaturally beneath the security lights. It was

Marta Vega. "I had it propped open so I could get back inside."

"Sorry." Haven checked to see if the door had locked. The last thing she needed was to be stuck in an alley with Iain's other girlfriend.

"It's all right," Marta told her when the door wouldn't budge. "They'll probably come find me. If not, I'll just climb the fence. Do you need a cigarette?"

"I don't smoke," Haven said.

"Then why are you out here?" Marta asked.

"I'm avoiding my boyfriend. He's here with another girl." Haven couldn't summon the spite to say any more.

"Ah," said Marta. "That sucks."

"No joke," Haven agreed. "Why are *you* outside? Isn't this supposed to be your party?"

"Yep. Wasn't my idea, though. I'd rather not be here at all. The whole show's going to flop."

"Why do you say that? *I* like your work," Haven said.

"You do?" The girl looked up, curious. "Really?" She seemed so genuinely surprised that Haven felt a stab of pity.

"Sure. I'm a big fan of dark and disturbing. I noticed the man hidden in all of them. The one who's making everything go down. Who is he supposed to be?"

"You noticed him?" Again, the ruby red mouth stretched into an unhinged smile. The sleeve of Marta's dress fell past her elbow as she took a long puff from her cigarette. Beneath a silver armlet in the shape of a snake, the girl's emaciated arm was covered with bruises and track marks.

"Of course."

"You must be special. Most people don't. They look right past him. Anyway, he's not really a man. He's more like a force of nature. Chaos. Entropy. It doesn't matter what you call him, 'cause he doesn't have a name. He's the reason that things fall apart."

"How fascinating."

"Not fascinating enough."

"What do you mean?" Haven asked.

"Nothing. It's just that this was my last chance, and I screwed it up. But I have to paint whatever is in my head, you know. These were the visions that were sent to me. They wouldn't go away until I put them on canvas. It's a shame they're so hard for other people to look at."

"You have visions?" Haven asked, her heart pounding. Was this was the girl Leah had mentioned? The one who could show her "the truth"?

"That's where I get my ideas. When I first started painting, they were beautiful. But they've been getting darker for the past few years. They keep me awake at night now. It all started when I joined."

"Joined what?"

Marta took a long drag on her cigarette. "Forget it. You seem like a nice little Southern girl. Believe it or not, a couple of years ago, I was a nice girl from Nebraska. Now my boyfriend's dead and everything's gone to hell. New York's a dangerous place. You don't want to start messing around with the wrong types. Look what happened to me." She held both arms in the air, and the sleeves of her dress plunged to her shoulders. When seen in the light, the track marks were terrifying.

"But Marta," Haven started as the door swung open. She stepped back to avoid being hit and found herself hidden from view.

"I've been looking all over for you." It was Iain's voice. His whisper was harsh and insistent. "Come back inside. There are people who want to talk to the artist."

"Do I have to?" Marta protested. "Nobody likes the paintings anyway."

"How do you know that when you haven't spoken to anyone all night?" Iain snapped. "Do I need to remind you how much is at stake here?"

"*You* were the one who wanted the show," Marta complained, though Haven heard her moving toward the door. She peeked around at Haven. "You coming in?" she asked. Haven shook her head silently. "Then it was nice to meet you. If you really like the stuff, you can probably find it sitting next to the Dumpster later tonight." Then she disappeared.

"Who are you talking to?" Iain demanded.

"Just some girl I met in the alley." Marta's voice was already mixing into the party chatter. "Don't worry, it's no one from the Society."

When the door closed, Iain remained outside.

"Hello?" he called. "Someone there?"

Haven peeked out from her new hiding place behind the gallery's Dumpster and saw Iain's frazzled eyes roaming over every inch of the alley. His head snapped toward a rustling sound that came from the trash, and he watched a large rat sprint across the pavement. Once he was satisfied that Marta's new friend must have been nothing more than a drug-induced fantasy, he rapped at the gallery door. It opened immediately and he vanished inside.

# CHAPTER FORTY-TWO

Haven was livid.

As soon as she arrived back at the mews house, she spent some quality time scrubbing the toilet bowl with Iain's toothbrush and spiking his shampoo with cooking oil. Then Haven cursed fate and Frances Whitman as she crammed her belongings into her suitcase. Somehow the woman had stumbled across the very words Haven's heart had been desperate to hear. The moment Frances had insisted that Ethan loved Constance, Haven's defenses had dropped, and she'd returned to Iain exposed and vulnerable. Now she would suffer for being so foolish.

But Haven didn't leave once her suitcase was packed. She sat and stared at it instead. As much as it hurt to stay, she couldn't go home. Constance had guided her to New York. Haven was there for a reason, and she couldn't go anywhere until she knew what it was.

Still, the pain was worse than she'd ever expected—and she hadn't been prepared for the blow. For the first time, Haven understood how her mother must have felt when she had discovered the truth about

Veronica Cabe. If this was the damage love could do, Haven wanted no part of it.

At three o'clock in the morning, she passed out with the television blaring. It was a restless sleep, filled with dark images from Marta Vega's show. But in Haven's dream, she was inside the paintings, powerless to stop what had been set in motion—unable to bring order to the chaos.

Iain woke her with a kiss.

"Where have you been?" she croaked, praying he would tell her the truth.

"Out with my lawyer." Iain scooped her off the couch and carried her up to the bedroom. Despite his performance at the party, he seemed remarkably sober.

"What time is it?"

"Late."

"You've been out with some old lawyer all this time?"

"We had a lot to talk about," Iain said.

"Like what?"

"Aren't you nosy? What do you mean, 'like what'? You really want to hear about my legal troubles?"

"I want to hear the truth," Haven said. Somewhere inside, she still expected him to have an explanation for everything.

"And that's what I'm telling you." He lied so easily that it crushed her. She wanted to scream at him, to tell him she'd seen him at the party with his hands on Marta Vega. She wanted to make him admit that he wasn't who he claimed to be. That the person she'd dreamed of her entire life was nothing more than a fraud and a liar.

But she knew an angry confrontation would ruin everything. She had no choice but to stay close to Iain Morrow if she wanted to solve Constance's mystery.

"I'm sorry," he whispered when she started to sob with frustration and rage. "It's almost over."

She could taste her own tears when Iain's lips met hers. Though she knew she should resist, she was just too weak. As Haven forced Marta Vega out of her head, she briefly wondered if Constance had ever done the same to Rebecca. Then the pain vanished, as if Iain's kiss was the only cure for the wounds he had inflicted. One last time wouldn't kill anyone, Haven decided.

## CHAPTER FORTY-THREE

"Hello?"

"Haven? Where the hell are you?"

"I'm in the bathtub." Haven groaned and lay back with the washcloth over her eyes. She wanted nothing more than to scrub the events of the previous evening out of her brain.

"In the bathtub *where*?" Beau demanded.

"The mews house," Haven admitted wearily.

"Haven! Jesus! What were you thinking? I thought you weren't going back there! As I recall, your exact words were that you'd be an idiot to keep sleeping at some psycho's house."

"Those were *your* exact words, not mine. But I guess I am an idiot. A big idiot." Her voice cracked on the last "*idiot*."

"What happened?" Beau asked softly. "You okay?"

Haven pulled herself together before she spoke. "I had a little setback. Frances Whitman led me down a wrong path. She had me all convinced that I was living some big love story. But I've figured it all out now. I'm going to find out why Constance wanted me to come here, and then I'm going home."

"Home? To Snope City?"

"Why not? *You're* down there, and there's nothing in New York for me anymore," Haven said. "But listen, can we talk about this later when I'm out of the bath?"

"You forgot, didn't you?"

"Forgot *what*?"

"You sent me an 'urgent' text at two A.M. You know, if you're going to treat me like your personal secretary, the least you can do is remember in the morning."

"Sorry." Haven didn't have it in her to play along with Beau's attempts to cheer her up. "What did I send you?"

"A couple of names. Marta Vega and Adam Rosier. You asked me to see what I could find out about them."

Haven sat up, splashing bathwater all over the floor. "What did you find out?"

"The Rosier guy seems pretty clean. His name doesn't show up anywhere."

"Really? Not even in connection with the Ouroboros Society? I'm sure he's someone important."

"Nope," Beau said. "But don't despair. I've got plenty of dirt on Marta Vega."

"Perfect. Give me a minute to dry off and make some coffee," Haven said, though the news already had her on edge. "By the way, have I ever told you you're a wonderful snoop?"

"Gee, I don't know whether to be flattered or offended."

"Try flattered for once." Haven threw on a shirt she'd taken from Iain's closet to use as a robe. "If I want to offend you, I'll ask about school."

Downstairs, she searched the first floor of the house. There was no sign of Iain. His side of the bed had been empty when Haven woke, and she hadn't seen a trace of him since. "Okay, shoot," she told Beau as she filled the kettle with water.

"Marta Vega. Born Trisha Taylor in Coon Rapids, Nebraska. Won a big art competition when she was sixteen years old. Moved to New York City when she was seventeen and shacked up with Jeremy Johns."

"And when did she start cheating on him?" Haven snipped as she set the kettle down on the stove and lit the gas.

"That's just gossip, Haven. I'm trying to stick to the facts for now."

"Whatever."

"Anyway, I found out a couple of interesting things about Marta. First off, she's a member of the Ouroboros Society."

"I figured she must be," Haven said. "I heard the president of the Society talking about her."

"And a drug addict."

"Knew that, too. Did you find anything out about Marta and Iain?"

"Nothing that would stand up in court. But they do seem to be pretty friendly."

"I wonder—" Haven started to say.

"What?"

"Well, remember I told you that Ethan cheated on Constance with someone named Rebecca Underwood?"

"Yeah."

"I wonder if there might be some connection between Rebecca and Marta. Iain told me that people have a way of finding each other across lifetimes."

"So you're positive that Ethan was unfaithful?"

Just the thought made Haven wince. "I don't know for sure about Ethan, but I *do* know in this life Iain Morrow is a big, fat, cheating liar."

"*Really*? Do tell."

The kettle began to whistle, and Haven yanked it away from the flame. "Try not to sound so excited, Beau. This is my life. It's not some celebrity gossip show."

"Sorry."

"Apology accepted." Haven took a deep breath and finished preparing her coffee. "So I followed Iain last night. He said he was going to have dinner with his lawyer, but he went to an art gallery instead. I saw him there with Marta. He had his hands all over her."

"*No*! The slut!"

"She's not a slut." Haven was surprised to discover she couldn't muster any hatred for Marta. "She's actually kind of cool."

"I was talking about Iain."

"Oh. *Right*. Anyway, the weirdest part of the whole evening was that I ended up running into Marta outside the gallery. And get this, Beau: She said that the ideas for her paintings come to her in visions. I didn't have a chance to ask her much about it, but I think she might be the one that Leah Frizzell was talking about—the girl who's supposed to show me the truth."

"Well, that's *awkward*," Beau said. "Are you going to suck it up and go talk to her? You want to know where she lives? I've got the address right here."

Haven wished there was another way. "Just what I wanted to do today—spend some quality time with my boyfriend's lover."

"You don't have to go, Haven," Beau reminded her. "I know I gave you a hard time about going to see Frances Whitman and the Ouroboros people. But this is something else all together. You don't have to do it. You can come home whenever you're ready."

"Sure—and spend the next sixty or seventy years hating myself for being such a wuss?" Haven scoffed. "No thanks. I have to figure out what's going on here before I go back. And if that means paying a friendly visit to Marta Vega, then so be it."

"What if she doesn't want to talk to *you*?" Beau asked.

Haven remembered the sad, lonely girl in the alley. "Marta will talk to me," Haven assured him. "I'm pretty sure she'd talk to *anybody*."

THE BUILDING NEAR the corner of White and West Broadway was a century-old tool factory that had been renovated to suit the sort of people who never got their hands dirty. It was six stories high and almost the length of a city block, yet the intercom listed only six names. Each apartment took up an entire floor of the building. Haven rang the buzzer labeled VEGA and waited. A minute later, she pressed the button again, and a voice came over the speaker.

"Go away," it growled.

"Marta?" Haven spoke hurriedly into the microphone. "My name is Haven Moore."

"I said go away," the voice repeated. Its owner sounded exhausted.

"Marta, please. I met you last night at the gallery. I need to ask you about your visions. It's a matter of—"

Haven heard an electronic buzzing. She pushed at the door to the building and let herself inside.

The old freight elevator was a turn-of-the-century antique. Inside its steel cage, Haven watched the floors pass by within fingers' reach until she made a rough landing on the fifth floor. The elevator released her into a tiny room with a single door. Haven hesitated—then knocked.

Seconds later, she heard the sound of multiple locks turning inside. Finally, the door opened a crack. A bloodshot eyeball examined Haven, then disappeared. The door swung open wider, offering a view of a vast, dimly lit loft. Every surface in sight was coated with a spongy layer of dust and soot. The books on the shelves no longer had names. Objects abandoned on a coffee table had formed shapeless stalagmites. What must have been a bicycle propped against the wall was now a shaggy, two-horned beast. Judging by its thickness, the dust had begun collecting for months.

"Shut the door," ordered the voice, which suddenly sounded far away. "And be sure to lock it."

Once she had secured the loft, Haven traced the voice to another door at the far end of the hall. A weak strip of light at the bottom of a pair of curtains lit a once-luxurious bathroom. Now the claw-foot tub was filled with pillows and dirty bed linens. A stack of books teetered on top of a laundry basket, and hypodermic needles cluttered both sides of the porcelain sink. An easel stood near the window, displaying a half-finished painting. Perched on top of the closed toilet lid, with its arms wrapped around its knees, was a ghost dressed in a man's undershirt. It smiled at the horror on Haven's face, its skin stretched tight across its bones.

"So what kind of name is Haven, anyway?" Marta rasped.

"Hillbilly," said Haven, taking a seat on the edge of the bathtub. "Are you okay? You don't look so good."

Marta's laugh sounded life-threatening. "I'm fine. I just don't sleep much anymore. Sorry about all the security. Did you see them?"

"Who?"

"The gray men. They've been watching the house since early this morning. Not a good sign."

"I didn't see anyone." Haven wondered if Marta was already high.

"You need to look harder," Marta insisted, sounding quite lucid. "They blend in. That's their job."

Haven pushed the door closed. The bathroom may have looked dingy and smelled worse, but it suddenly felt cozy and safe. At least you could be certain that no one was watching.

"Is that why you've been living in your bathroom?" Haven asked. "Because you think people are spying on you?"

"No," Marta said with a defeated shrug. "I don't really give a damn if they get me. I've been living in this room since Jeremy died. It hurts too much to look at all of his stuff out there."

"I'm sorry," Haven said. "I know they just found his body. It must have been a horrible shock for you."

"It was only a body," Marta replied. "And it wasn't a shock. I knew he was dead the night he disappeared."

"How did you know?" Haven probed carefully.

"Jeremy and I hadn't spent a day apart since we met. He would never have left me. We didn't work without each other. You'll know what it's like when *you* meet the right person."

The last sentence hit Haven like a punch. "How long were you two together?" she followed up quickly. She didn't want Marta to see she'd been rattled.

"Since we were thirteen years old."

"*Thirteen*? Wow. So young."

"It's not really that young if you've known each other for as long as we have. Then when we were seventeen we moved to New York together to join the Society."

"The Ouroboros Society?"

"That's the one." Marta's spine stiffened. "You know about it?"

"I've heard of it," Haven told her. "When did you and Jeremy become members?"

"A few years ago. We got the call right after the Omaha paper interviewed us for a story they did on child prodigies. The OS paid for us to come to New York, helped us divorce our parents, and loaned us the money for this apartment."

"That must have been a pretty big loan."

Marta pulled her legs even closer to her chest. "Yeah. It took us forever to pay it back. Good thing Jeremy's skills were in such high demand. I have expensive habits to maintain, remember?" She showed Haven one of her track mark-covered arms, and then quickly pulled it inside her filthy undershirt. "So who are you, anyway? What were you doing at the gallery last night?"

"Like I said, my name is Haven Moore. And I was pretty sure I was Iain Morrow's girlfriend until I saw you two together last night."

"Oh my God!" Marta managed to exclaim before she burst into maniacal laughter. "I can't imagine what you must have thought."

Haven couldn't force herself to laugh along. "Actually, I think you can."

"No, no, no," Marta's wheezing was beginning to make Haven nervous. She tried to remember the CPR training she'd gotten in gym class freshman year. "There's nothing going on between us. Iain just likes to put on a show. He's *way* too goody-goody for my taste."

"We are talking about Iain *Morrow*, aren't we?" Haven asked with a raised eyebrow. "The guy who makes the gossip columns three times a week?"

"Iain's not as wild as he pretends to be. Jeremy used to say that the stick up his butt had a stick up *its* butt. Wouldn't touch drugs. Never really dated anyone. Spent all his time sucking up to Padma."

The statement chilled Haven before she understood what it meant. "Wait. Padma Singh? The president of the OS?"

"Didn't Iain tell you he's one of the favorites over there? Padma doesn't deal with the drones. She only has time for the special ones. Or the rich ones like Iain. You know, if he really is your boyfriend, you guys should probably spend some time getting to know each other a little better."

Haven couldn't have agreed more. "Do you know the guy that Padma was with at the gallery last night? Adam Rosier?"

Marta shook her head. "Don't think so, and I'm usually pretty good at remembering names. But there are a lot of people at the top I don't know. Anyway, I thought Padma came alone. I doubt she'd bring a date if she knew she was going to see Iain. She's always hitting on him. Jeremy used to give Iain shit about it all the time. Actually, he gave Iain shit about almost everything. He was always jealous that we were friends."

"So they didn't get along?"

"They *hated* each other."

"Did Iain hate Jeremy enough to kill him?" Haven asked, relieved to get the big question out of the way.

Marta scowled. "Those rumors are bullshit. Iain couldn't kill anyone. Look, I'll be totally honest with you. Jeremy had a pretty serious drug problem. He'd try *anything* you put in front of him. The OS wasn't too happy with him, so they probably had somebody put the wrong thing in front of him. Hopefully, I'll be with Jeremy again soon. The way things are going, I doubt I have more than a few months left in me."

"Wait," Haven said. "Back up a second. You think the *Ouroboros Society* had something to do with Jeremy's death?"

"People connected to the OS disappear all the time."

Haven thought of all the innocent children she'd seen waiting in the Society's lobby. "Can you prove it?" she asked Marta. "Do you know where Jeremy could have gotten the drugs that killed him?"

Marta shook her head. "They could have come from anywhere. Half the people in the Society deal drugs."

"The OS allows drug dealing, too!"

"It's a little more complicated than that." Marta shifted her weight nervously. "You remember the Greek myth with Hades and Persephone? The one where the lord of the underworld kidnaps a girl and drags her down to hell?" Haven nodded. "While she's down there, he puts this amazing feast in front of her. Every delicious thing you could possibly imagine. She knows she shouldn't touch anything, but the girl's starving, and after a while she can't resist. So when nobody's looking, she takes a few measly pomegranate seeds and pops them in her mouth. And that one little weakness dooms her. She's stuck in Hades."

Marta paused, as if exhausted from talking. She swept her bangs away with the back of her hand, revealing eyelids as purple as plums.

"That's what the Ouroboros Society does. They put everything in front of you, but if you show an ounce of weakness, you're hooked for good. You start asking for things you can't afford. And when the bill comes, you find out that they own you."

"I'm not sure I understand."

Marta turned her gaze to the light slipping under the bathroom curtain. "Why am I telling you all of this? I'm really not supposed to talk about these things. Society secrets, you know. I'm in enough trouble already."

"I'm just trying to find out what my boyfriend's been up to," Haven reminded Marta, choosing her words carefully, as if defusing a bomb. "Besides, who's going to listen to any gossip *I've* got? You and Iain are the only people I've met in New York," Haven said, though that wasn't strictly true.

"All right. I guess I don't have much to lose at this point. I'll tell you how the Society works. But if anyone asks—including Iain—you didn't hear it from me." Marta began arranging the hypodermic needles on the side of the sink. "The OS accepts three kinds of members. People who've brought talents from previous lives. They're kind of like gods. Then there are the people who just remember things. They're the rank and file. And then there are the gray men."

"Gray men?"

Marta looked up. "People call them that because they're so bland. They're the drones—the lowliest members of the OS—the wannabes. They weren't born with any memories or talents. They're just willing to do the Society's bidding. Keep everyone else in line."

"Why do they need to keep people in line?"

"Because of the system. Padma likes to say that the OS is the greatest networking organization in the world. The members are supposed to help each other. They'll get you into the right schools or loan you money or get you a gorgeous girlfriend. But then you have to pay the favor back."

"What's wrong with that?" Haven asked. "It all sounds pretty good to me."

"Sure. It sounds good to everyone at first. But paying favors back can be tough for members like Iain who don't have skills to trade. At least *he's* got money. He can buy his way up the ranks. But a lot of members have to do whatever they can to keep their accounts in good standing. Some sell drugs. Some sell other things, if you know what I mean. And if you can't—or won't—take care of your debts, well, that's when the gray men show up."

The corner of a magazine was poking out from under the mildew-covered bathmat. Using the toe of her shoe, Haven slid the bath mat to one side. Beneath it was a music magazine with Jeremy Johns on the cover. "Is that what happened to Jeremy?" she asked. "Did the gray men take him?"

"No, Jeremy's debts were paid a long time ago. All he had to do was perform at some big-shot member's fortieth birthday party, and he'd make a fortune in points. Jeremy just wanted out. He thought the whole system was sick. But my account is low. That's why the gray men are outside right now. I needed to sell some paintings last night, but there weren't any takers. And I'm not going to sleep with some nasty old guy for a few lousy points."

"So why don't you just leave?"

"You don't *quit* the OS." Marta started to fidget. "Hey, Haven. Do you mind if we talk about something else now?"

"Can we talk about your visions?" Haven asked, hoping they could return to the subject of the Society once Marta felt comfortable again.

"Sure. I guess. What do you want to know?"

"How did they start? What sort of things do you see?"

"I've had them for years," Marta said. "But they started to get really disturbing just after I moved to New York. I pass out for a few minutes and see something terrible happen. The same guy is always there, but I've never gotten a good look at his face. Afterward, I have to paint what I saw just to get it out of my head. I never thought a gallery would show the work. It's not exactly something most people would want to hang on their walls. But when Iain saw the paintings, he insisted. He wouldn't take no for an answer."

"Do you have any idea what the visions mean?" Haven asked.

Marta stole a peek at the unfinished painting that was propped up on an easel in the corner of the bathroom. All Haven could see was a chaos of colors. "I think they're things that have already happened. Some people get to look into the future. I'm only able to see the past. Just my luck."

"Maybe they're trying to tell you something," Haven suggested.

"Well, if they are, I sure as hell haven't been able to figure it out. You want to take a look at the rest of my work? Maybe you can solve the puzzle."

"You have more paintings here? They're not all at the gallery?"

Marta grinned. "Come on," she said.

The girl rose from the toilet seat and padded barefoot across the apartment, leaving a trail of footprints in the dust. She opened a door and motioned to Haven to follow her. Inside a storeroom, painted canvases were piled three feet high. A narrow path wound around multiple stacks.

Haven gasped. "How many are there?"

"All together? Around three hundred. Sometimes I do three or four a week. I can't seem to stop."

"And they're all different?"

"Yep."

Haven pulled a canvas from the top of one of the stacks. It showed a group of ruffians gathered around a large hole in the ground. Inside the pit, a single snarling dog faced a fearsome army of rats. It was clear that real beasts in the painting weren't the animals about to fight for their lives but the men eager to witness the bloodshed. At the far edge of the crowd a faceless man was enjoying the spectacle.

"You said Iain talked you into displaying your work?" Haven asked, wondering why anyone would want to exhibit Marta's terrifying tributes to the dark side of humanity.

"Yeah, he dropped by to see me a few weeks before Jeremy died to give me shit about using drugs. Then he saw a painting I was working on, and I swear, I thought he was going to pass out. After that he wouldn't stop pestering me to show at his gallery. Jeremy was totally against the idea. He said the paintings were dangerous. If he were still alive, there would never have been a show at all."

"Where's the painting that Iain liked?"

"Here," said Marta. "Funny thing is, Iain didn't even want it at the gallery." She disappeared behind one of the stacks and returned moments later holding a poster-size painting in front of her. In the center of the work was a voluptuous, dark-haired girl. A fox stole clung to her shoulders, the poor creature's mouth clamped around its own lifeless tail. The girl's hands pressed against the chest of a young man with auburn hair, and her eyes pleaded silently. Beyond them, halfway down a hall that led to the room, a petite blonde watched the scene, her face contorted in horror. Constance. Behind her, at the end of the hall, stood the now familiar dark figure.

Just as Haven's knees began to buckle, she was brought to her senses by the sound of the door buzzer.

"How about that. Two visitors in one day. I haven't been this popular in months," Marta deadpanned. "Have a look around. I'll be right back."

"Hello?" Haven heard her shout into the intercom.

"It's me," came the answer. It was Iain.

Haven rushed to Marta's side. "Don't let him in!" she whispered.

"I can't talk now," Marta told Iain, an unmistakable note of anxiety in her voice. "I'm busy. Come back later."

"It can't wait, Marta. Let me in, or I'll let myself in."

"Where's your fire escape?" Haven asked as Marta pressed the buzzer that unlocked the front door.

"There," Marta said, pointing back at the room with the paintings. "But be careful or they'll see you go out that way. Don't let yourself be followed."

"Who's going to see me? Iain's driver?"

"No, the gray men," Marta said. "I know you think I'm crazy, but believe me, they're real."

## CHAPTER FORTY-FOUR

At the bottom of the fire escape, Haven crouched and jumped down to the street below. She inched toward the end of the alley and peered out at the street. A man waited patiently while his dog relieved itself on the hubcap of a black Hummer. Taxis cruised past with bankers in their backseats. A class of day-care students in matching yellow T-shirts waddled behind a teacher like a group of tiny ducklings. It was nothing more than an ordinary New York City scene, until one by one Haven started to see them. The two shadowy figures in a gray sedan parked across the street from Marta's building. The woman standing in the window of the Laundromat. A neatly coiffed hot-dog vendor. Marta had been right. There was no way to leave the alley without being spotted.

Haven remembered the man on the train from Johnson City. The men who had found her in Gramercy Park after she fainted. All the bland, unremarkable people who faded into the background and went unnoticed. Were they gray men, too? If they were after her, they'd had countless opportunities to grab her. Why hadn't they taken them?

Then, as she watched the watchers, Haven saw the gray men's heads shift in unison. From where she stood, Haven couldn't see the action that had drawn their attention. Whatever it was didn't last long, and within moments, the sedan departed, the man in the Laundromat was heading down the street, and the hot-dog stand stood deserted.

Just as Haven stepped out onto the sidewalk, a woman in a figure-hugging charcoal gray dress emerged empty-handed from a boutique. Haven needed only to see the mane of dark hair swishing across the woman's back to identify the president of the Ouroboros Society. Keeping a safe distance, she followed Padma Singh as she began to walk east. It meant something to see her there—Haven knew that much. It couldn't have been a coincidence.

Hanging half a block back, Haven watched groups of tourists part for Padma. Men dropped their girlfriends' hands as she approached. Women snuck peeks at her over their shoulders. Mixing among the average people, Padma appeared more than human. Even her businesslike stride seemed impossibly sexy.

Past City Hall, on the edge of the financial district, Padma crossed Pearl Street, heading toward the East River. The surrounding buildings shrank and aged, and cobblestones emerged out of the asphalt. A few blocks away lay all that was left of the city's old seaport. The streets in the area had once been some of the most dangerous in the world, crowded with rambunctious sailors from around the globe and the hardened New Yorkers who preyed on them.

Padma took a left on Water Street and stopped in front of an old brick house that sat in the shadow of the Brooklyn Bridge overpass. Barely three stories tall, with two sweet dormers peeking out of its pitched roof, the structure was dwarfed by the larger buildings that squeezed it on either side. Padma rang the bell and waited impatiently on the sidewalk until a door opened and she vanished inside.

Haven crept closer. With each step the sun seemed to dim. She could hear the sounds of men laughing, glasses clinking, horses' hooves clopping. Standing in front of the little brick house, she knew she had seen it before. A plaque was bolted to the building's brick wall.

*The Rose House. The third-oldest building in Manhattan, it was built in 1781 by Captain Joseph Rose, a wealthy trader. Over the course of its history, this building has been a boarding house, a brothel, a tavern, a speakeasy, and home to the so-called Wickedest Man in New York.*

Haven peered up at the Rose House. It was so small, so unremarkable. Yet she sensed there was something hidden inside. Something watching her from the windows, waiting to pounce. The door was still open, she noticed. Its lock hadn't caught. But she felt that if she dared set one foot inside, she might never come out. Haven stood mesmerized, like a mouse waiting for a snake to make the first move, until the sound of footsteps on cobblestones drew her attention away. A figure stopped and stood halfway down the street. She slumped to the ground before she could get a good look at its face.

*Constance would have recognized the fur stole from a mile away. Everyone had one these days, but Rebecca's seemed more gruesome than most. Perhaps it was the bloodred rubies where the fox's eyes had once been. Now that she thought of it, there had been a number of recent additions to Rebecca's wardrobe. Someone had to be paying her bills.*

*It was late to be out alone, especially in this part of town. And her feet hurt. She had followed Rebecca all the way from Washington Square. She'd been on her way home when she had spotted the girl cutting through the park. Rebecca's hurried pace and furtive glances told her the girl was on a mission. Constance was certain Rebecca was on her way to a rendezvous.*

*Now they were down by the docks, where girls from good families never set foot. Rebecca stopped at a building on Water Street. Though it looked as if it might collapse into rubble, it wasn't completely deserted. Light squeezed between the boards that barricaded the windows. Could this be where Ethan had chosen to hide?*

*Rebecca knocked once and then stepped inside.*

## CHAPTER FORTY-FIVE

Haven was lying on a couch, staring up at a speckled white ceiling. A head suddenly appeared in her line of vision. The woman who was bending over her wore her hair in a style popular among the men in Snope City's barbershop, and there wasn't a trace of makeup on her face.

"You're in the staff lounge at the Ouroboros Society, Miss Moore. Now that you're feeling a bit better, maybe you would like to take a seat in the waiting room? You have a little more than ten minutes before your eleven o'clock appointment."

"My *what*?" Haven said as she pulled herself upright.

"It's Monday, Miss Moore. You have an eleven o'clock appointment with Ms. Singh."

"Wait a second. How did I get here?" Haven demanded.

"I'm not authorized to answer these questions," the woman said pleasantly. "You'll have to ask Ms. Singh."

* * *

HAVEN'S STOMACH SOURED as she sat in the waiting room, observing the latest batch of children who had come to the Ouroboros Society for past-life analysis. Beside her, a little blonde cherub with pigtails was busy kicking her heels against the legs of a leather chair. The girl's mother sat on her other side, filling out an endless form. Every few minutes, she leaned over to whisper questions to her hyperactive offspring. Haven wondered if the girl might one day find herself at the top of the Society's ladder. Or maybe she would end up a drone. It was impossible to tell. Haven wished she could warn her, but she couldn't imagine the child's mother would listen.

Young OS workers dressed in identical white-and-black outfits picked out individual kids from the crowd. With the same blank smiles on their faces, the employees led the little boys and girls down the hall, away from their proud parents.

"Hello." Haven turned to see the little girl staring at her intently. "What's your name?"

"Haven. What's yours?"

"Flora." She resumed kicking the chair before another thought occurred to her. "Did you used to be someone else?"

"Yes," said Haven. "And you?"

"Yep." The girl's head bobbed up and down. "My name was Josephine. I lived in Africa, and I was a scientist."

Given Flora's childish lisp, it wasn't the most convincing announcement.

"Really?" Haven said. "What kind of scientist were you?"

"I was an epidemiologist. I studied diseases."

"That's nice," Haven told her. The child had clearly been coached. She could barely *pronounce* "epidemiologist."

"Excuse me, miss," the girl's mother interrupted. "I just need to ask my daughter one quick question. Flora, what was it that you called Ebola the other day? It sounded a little like hemorrhoids."

The little girl glanced over at Haven and rolled her eyes.

"Hemorrhagic fever, Mommy. That's what I died of," she told Haven. "And I was *this close* to finding a cure."

"Miss Moore?" The receptionist was hovering over them. His uniform—comprised of a white, shortsleeved shirt, crisp black trousers, and thick-framed black glasses—gave him the appearance of a cartoon scientist. "Ms. Singh can see you now."

With a clipboard clutched protectively to his chest, the receptionist guided Haven down a long beige hall. Along the way, they passed a half-dozen rooms with observation windows set into the doors. Inside each room, an adult dressed in the Society's colorless uniform appeared to be examining a child. Just before she was deposited in an enormous office, Haven saw a young redheaded boy burst into tears.

"Have a seat," Haven was instructed. "Ms. Singh will be back in a moment."

The room, like the Society's lobby, looked as though it had been decorated by robots. The floor was the glossy white of an ice-skating rink and the sofa upholstered in snowy suede that had never been sullied by human skin. There were no knickknacks, no paintings, no artifacts from the past. Only vases filled with white flowers. The place was as promising and as terrifying as a blank canvas.

Haven recalled the vision that had brought her there—Rebecca entering the same old building that Padma had visited. Why hadn't she realized that they were one and the same? Now, after ninety years, Haven was about to meet her rival face-to-face. She was almost looking forward to it.

"I'D SAY IT WAS quite a coincidence—finding you on the street like that—if I believed in coincidences." Padma had entered the room. Up close, there seemed to be too much of her. Too much hair, too much hip, too much cleavage straining against the neckline of her dress. She reminded Haven of an overripe fruit, plump and delicious but just short of rotten. "Would you care for a cup of coffee?" the president of the OS inquired, gesturing to a silver coffee service on a console table near the door.

"No," Haven said through clenched teeth. If she were any more wired, she might act on her urge to leap up and strangle the woman. Never before had she felt such an intense hatred for another human being.

Padma poured herself a cup of thick dark liquid and carried it with no noticeable caution across the white expanse. She placed it on a fragile-looking table and settled into a plush chair across from her guest. Haven stared at the cup, its contents capable of staining everything around it. All it would take would be one tiny tremor.

"You're Constance Whitman." Padma kept her violet eyes trained on Haven as she sipped her coffee. She didn't disguise her dislike for the girl. "I found you in the street and had my people bring you back here. They told me you spoke while you were unconscious. You should really try to work on that. Goodness knows what you might give away."

"And you're Rebecca Underwood."

Padma smirked. The statement hadn't surprised her. It was almost as if she'd been expecting it. "What on earth were you doing at the seaport?"

"I saw you downtown," Haven said. "I followed you to the river." She began to sift through the long list of questions she wanted to ask. Why had Padma and Rebecca been down at the docks? Had Rebecca and Ethan been lovers? Why did so many OS members disappear? But Padma spoke first.

"Are you back to avenge Constance's death?" She seemed to enjoy the shock that registered on Haven's face. "I always knew she'd fight back. I just didn't expect her to return quite so soon."

"You know the truth about what happened to Constance?" Haven asked.

Padma regarded her coolly. "You don't?"

"That's why I came to New York. To find out."

Padma hesitated. "Are you sure you want to know? Sometimes it's best not to delve too deeply into the past. We've all had lives that would best be forgotten."

"I'm sure," Haven confirmed. "And don't bother pretending that you give a damn about my feelings."

"Fine. Constance was murdered," Padma stated bluntly. "By Ethan Evans."

Haven had tried to prepare herself, but the answer still stung. "But *why*?"

"Because she got in the way."

"Got in the way of what? Your affair?"

Everything in the room was still. Haven could hear someone admonishing a crying child outside in the hallway. A smirk began growing on Padma's face.

"What do you know about reincarnation?" she asked, ignoring Haven's question. "Why do you think we keep coming back?"

"Dr. Strickland believed that we've come back to help mankind," Haven said.

Padma dismissed the idea with a jaded roll of her eyes. "Strickland was a sweet man, but he was also a terrible fool. The truth is, we keep coming back because we're too attached to earthly things. It could be money or power or sex or drugs. Each lifetime we're given the chance to overcome our addictions. Some of us do. Most of us don't.

"Strickland thought we could conquer our weaknesses by serving others. He wanted us all to take vows of poverty and devote our lives to performing good deeds. But human beings are greedy by nature. And human nature is too powerful to overcome."

"What does all this have to do with Ethan?" Haven asked.

"Of all the people in the Society, Ethan was the most talented. Strickland never had much time for those who weren't born with gifts they'd brought from other lives. Even my skills never really impressed him. But Ethan remembered *everything*. He'd lived dozens of lives and he remembered them all. The old man treated Ethan like a son. Strickland never realized that it was all just a game. Ethan's real gift was making people trust him and then using their trust to destroy them. He did it to Strickland. And he did the same thing to you."

"To me?"

Judging by Padma's smug expression when she settled back in her chair, Haven knew she was going in for the kill. "All Ethan ever wanted was your money. Everyone knew it but you. Even after he killed Strickland. Even after you caught him with me, you refused to believe the worst of him. You thought the two of you were going to run away together, but the whole time he was plotting to kill you. He was the one who set the fire downtown. It's a shame he didn't get out in time. We could have been so happy together."

"You're making this up," Haven snarled. Padma seemed to be savoring the story a little too much.

"Am I?" Padma paused to moisten her lips. "Then here's something to think about. Do you remember that you and Ethan were meant to leave for Rome the night you died?"

"Yes, but how do you know that? It was a secret."

"How else would I know? Ethan *told* me. But then he postponed your trip at the very last minute. Don't you see? It was all part of his plan. He used the promise of Rome to win you back and convince you to marry him. He never booked passage on any ship. He planned to kill you as soon as he was in a position to inherit your fortune."

Padma's version accounted for everything Haven had seen in her visions. "How could Constance have been so stupid?" she muttered.

"It has nothing to do with stupidity." Padma gazed at Haven with something like pity. "Isn't it obvious? Ethan Evans is *your* addiction. He's the reason you keep coming back. He could sweet-talk Constance into believing just about anything. I saw him do it a million times."

Haven held her tongue.

"You don't think it's possible to be addicted to another person?" Padma added. "Believe me, it's not that uncommon. How else would you explain love at first sight?"

"I suppose it makes sense," Haven admitted reluctantly. She thought of the previous night. Iain had lied to her, abused her trust, yet she still hadn't been able to say no to him.

"I'm sorry," Padma said, though her smile suggested otherwise. "This must all be terribly painful for you. But now you can go back to Kentucky or West Virginia or wherever it is that you're from and move on with your life."

But there was still one thing that Haven couldn't figure out. "If everything you say is true, why did the Society allow him to become a member again?"

"Who?" Padma demanded, lurching forward and spilling her coffee on the pristine white rug. Haven instantly knew she had said too much. "Are you telling me that Ethan Evans is back?"

Haven watched the coffee seep into the rug's fibers. How could Padma not know that Iain was Ethan?

"If you have any information about Ethan, I insist that you give it to me!" The woman was on her feet and moving toward Haven's chair. "Has Adam heard about this?"

"I don't know what you're talking about," the girl insisted, leaping up before Padma had a chance to reach her.

"You do! I can see it. You're lying! You know where he is!"

"Go to hell." Haven was out of the snowy white office and on her way down the hall.

"You can't leave!" Padma insisted. Her composure vanished as she chased Haven through the lobby and toward the exit, where she grabbed for the girl's elbow. "Weren't you listening to *a word* I just said?"

With her fists clenched, Haven wheeled around to face Padma.

"You better take your hand off of me. I'd love an excuse to teach you a lesson. You sure you want to give me one?"

The waiting room went silent. Even the smallest pair of eyes was trained on them. Padma released her grip, straightened her posture, and smoothed her hair. "I'll be watching you," she whispered to Haven. "If Ethan's somewhere on this planet, you can be sure that I'll find him." Then she spun on her heels and stormed down the hall.

HAVEN TOOK TWO TRAINS, a bus, and a cab just to make sure that she wasn't being followed. All she wanted to do was grab her suitcase and get out of town. She had come to New York for answers, and she'd found them. Constance Whitman had fallen in love with the wrong man. And that man had killed her. Haven wondered if her visions would stop now that she'd learned the truth about Ethan. Or would she always be tormented by images of the person who'd betrayed Constance and broken her heart?

Haven already knew the answer. The attraction—the need to be with him—was as strong as it had ever been. She would have to fight the addiction for the rest of her life—maybe longer.

As she walked south on University Place, Haven's dark thoughts were interrupted by the honking of horns and the murmur of a crowd in the distance. She soon found dozens of men with cameras swarming the entrance to the Washington Mews, some pressed against the gates and others spilling into the street. The crowd parted as a black Mercedes pushed through. Two daredevil photographers leaped in front of the moving car, snapping pictures through its windshield. It wasn't Iain's Mercedes, but they didn't seem to know that.

"Did you do it, Iain?" a paparazzo shouted.

"Where's Marta Vega?"

"Have you talked to the cops?"

"Did you murder her like you murdered her boyfriend?"

As the Mercedes drove away, the crowd began to thin. A portly man with a camera stomped past Haven, heading for a car he'd left double-parked down the street.

"What's going on?" she asked.

"If Iain Morrow keeps killing people, he's going to make me a very rich man," the man called back over his shoulder.

## CHAPTER FORTY-SIX

Haven snatched the ringing cell phone off the café table. A Snope City number appeared on the caller ID. Her mother had left three messages in a row, and her pleas had grown increasingly colorful. Haven needed to come home, Mae Moore insisted—before Imogene ended up doing something they'd all come to regret.

Each message tortured Haven a little more than the last, and she wished she could set her mother's mind at ease. But such a feat would require a mammoth lie. And after all she'd been through, Haven preferred to be an outlaw rather than a liar.

"Anything else?" A waitress came to hover over Haven's table. She was young, with Crayola-colored hair swept back into an elegant chignon. "Another cappuccino?"

"Sure," Haven said, buying another half hour at the dingy café a few blocks from Washington Square Park. She didn't dare move until Beau answered her calls. Something terrible had happened to Marta Vega.

"By the way," the waitress said under her breath as she leaned in to clear away Haven's old cup, "have you noticed you have an admirer?"

"A what?" Haven blurted.

"Shhh. He's over by the espresso machine. No! Don't look now," the girl hissed when Haven craned her neck. "Wait until I'm gone if you want to see him."

"Can you at least tell me what he looks like?" Haven pleaded.

"An accountant, maybe?" the girl suggested. "Or maybe an undertaker? Anyway, he came in right after you, and he's been stealing looks at you all this time. At first I thought it might be a coincidence, but you've been here for a while now, and he still hasn't left."

"Crap!" Haven whispered.

The waitress nodded as if her sickest suspicions had been confirmed. "He's stalking you, isn't he?" she asked.

"Probably," Haven admitted.

"Okay, don't panic," the girl said, keeping up appearances by wiping the table with a smelly rag. "Just go to the ladies' room. There's a window that opens up on the alley. People use it all the time when they want to skip out on the bill."

"What about all the coffee I've had? How am I supposed to pay for it?"

"Coffee's on me," the girl said. "I know what it's like to be some creepy dude's fantasy girl. Believe me, with this hair you attract them like flies."

"Thanks," Haven told her. "I really appreciate this." As she stood up and made her move toward the restroom, she caught sight of the man sitting by the espresso machine, dressed in the drab uniform of the gray men. When he glanced up at Haven, a jolt of terror left her shaking. She'd taken so many precautions, and still they'd managed to find her.

"Good luck," the waitress whispered.

The state of the café bathroom made Haven happy she hadn't ordered food. Even the EMPLOYEES MUST WASH HANDS sign was covered in a layer of grime and muck. But the window above the toilet opened just as the waitress had promised. Haven left a hunk of hair behind on a rusty nail sticking out of the sill, but she landed safely on her feet in the alley and took off running.

When she finally stopped to catch her breath, she found herself in the center of Greenwich Village, surrounded by tiny brick buildings that would have looked ancient even to Constance's eyes. The narrow, winding streets were empty and the sidewalks deserted. It felt as if she'd wandered into a ghost town in the middle of Manhattan. For the twentieth time in two hours, Haven dialed Beau's number.

This time he answered with a lazy "Yup?"

"It's three P.M.! Where have you been? Didn't you get all my messages?" She could hear the hysteria in her own voice.

"Excuse me? I've been *working*. Dad decided we needed to plant a crop of corn in the backyard. I'm really starting to wonder if the old man might be losing his mind—"

"I've been trying to reach you for *hours*." Haven cut him off.

"I didn't realize I was on call," Beau snapped. "What's going on with you, anyway?"

"Aside from running away from all the weird men who've been following me? I'm trying to figure out why there are paparazzi swarming the mews house," Haven said. "I went back to get my suitcase, and there were fifty guys with cameras lurking outside. I can't go home, and I don't have Internet access, and I have no idea what's happening."

"D'you ever consider going to a library? Or a computer store? Or a copy shop? There must be about forty places within a block of you that have Internet access."

Haven wasn't amused. "I don't have time to hunt down a computer right now. I just had to climb out a bathroom window and run halfway across town to escape from some creep who was watching me. So do you think you could take a teensy peek at the Internet and tell me what's going on?"

"Since you asked so sweetly. Let's see what I can find." She heard the sound of the computer starting and Beau scratching himself. "Hmmm."

"What?"

"Hold on, I'm reading!" The minute-long pause was excruciating. "Marta Vega is missing."

"That's what I thought! But how? I talked to her this morning."

"You talked to her *this* morning?" Beau asked.

"I told you I was going to see her."

"Well, you must have been one of the last people who *did* see her. They say she's been kidnapped. A neighbor saw Marta being dragged out of her apartment around nine thirty and called the police."

"Oh my God," Haven whispered. She listened to the clicking of Beau's mouse in the background and tried to remember what time she'd left Marta's house.

"Damn . . ." Beau murmured.

"What?"

"Haven?" Beau asked cautiously. "I got something important to ask you. I want you to think real careful."

"Okay."

"Do you know where your boyfriend was today?"

"Why?" Haven asked, already bracing for the answer she knew was on the way.

"Marta's neighbor described the kidnapper, and he sounds just like Iain. Haven?" Beau asked when he heard the gasp on the other end of the line.

"I knew it! He was there," Haven whispered in horror. "He took her."

"Don't joke like that."

"I was at Marta's house when Iain showed up. I had to leave through the fire escape. I think he's going to kill her."

"*What*?"

"I'm serious, Beau. Iain's dangerous. There's no doubt now. Padma Singh told me that Ethan really did kill Constance and August Strickland for their money—"

"Wait. You talked to Padma Singh?"

"It's a long story," Haven said, "but I found out that she used to be Rebecca Underwood. She said that Ethan set the fire in the mews house."

"You gotta tell the police!"

"Tell them what? That my boyfriend killed two people in his last life? They'll lock *me* away."

"Tell them about Jeremy Johns, then," Beau urged her.

"Tell them what? I don't know anything about what happened to Jeremy Johns! And from what you just told me, I don't know any more about the Marta Vega case than the tabloids!"

"You're right, you're right." Beau tried to calm her. "I just don't get it. Why would Iain want to kill Marta Vega? I thought they were having an affair."

"I was wrong. Marta swore they're just friends. She also told me people disappear from the OS all the time. They've got some system where people do favors for each other. If you can't repay all the favors you've received, then they have someone take you out. Marta's account was getting low. So maybe the Society had Iain deal with her."

"Hold up. You're saying the *Ouroboros Society* has people killed?"

"Marta claims it's totally corrupt. They even have people called 'gray men' to make sure everyone stays in line."

"And you've been *dating* a member of this organization?" Beau marveled.

"That's one of the weirdest parts. Iain's a member of the OS, but Padma has no idea who he was in his last life. He's been hiding his real identity."

"Why would he do that?"

"I don't know!"

"Well, I know one thing. I don't want you going anywhere near Iain Morrow if you think he might be a part of all this."

"*You* don't want me?" Haven asked.

"Come *on*," Beau groaned. "You were taking a bath at his house when I talked to you this morning. We both know what that means. So if Iain Morrow asks you to vouch for his whereabouts, you just tell him *no*. I don't care how good the nookie is. I don't want you doing time for some serial killer."

"I wouldn't help Iain Morrow right now if my life depended on it. But somebody has to save Marta."

"That's what the police are for. Jesus, Haven. Is *any* of this sinking into your thick skull? You gotta be careful. Promise me you'll be careful."

"I will," was all Haven was willing to say. She finally understood why Constance had wanted her to find Ethan. She wanted Haven to stop him from killing again.

## CHAPTER FORTY-SEVEN

Haven's cell phone rang the moment she dropped it back into her bag.

"Hi there. Where are you?"

Murderer or not, Iain's voice could still send her heart racing. Haven battled to keep her emotions under control. What was wrong with her? Haven wondered. After everything she'd learned, how could she still be in love with Iain Morrow?

"Greenwich Village," she told him. "Shopping," she added.

"Have you been home this afternoon?" He made it sound like nothing more than an ordinary question.

"Yeah," Haven said. "There are paparazzi all over the place. One of them said Marta Vega has disappeared. Everyone seems to think you're responsible. Are you?"

There was a slight pause. "I'd rather explain in person," Iain said. "I'm sending a car now. It will meet you on the corner of Christopher Street and Seventh Avenue. Can you get there in fifteen minutes?"

"That depends. Where exactly am I going?"

"Sixty-fifth Street. Don't worry—the driver knows the address. I'll see you soon."

Haven knew Beau would never approve of what she was about to do, but someone had to try to save Marta. And Haven was starting to suspect she was the girl's last hope.

THIRTY MINUTES LATER, the car pulled up in front of an understated apartment building on one of the most exclusive streets in the city. A doorman ushered Haven to the elevator lobby and inserted a key above the buttons. Trapped inside the shiny, elegant box, Haven rode silently to the twenty-fifth-floor penthouse, staring at her image in the elevator's polished brass. It was only four o'clock, but her clothes were already wrinkled, her mascara was smudged, and her hair—as usual—was shooting in every direction. But Haven couldn't have cared less about her appearance. She knew she was on a mission that might well prove deadly.

The elevator doors opened, and Iain met her with a kiss.

"What is this place?" Haven asked, pulling away from him. They were standing in a marble foyer decorated with ornate furniture and statues of naked Greek goddesses.

"My father's old apartment," Iain explained. "He liked to call this his Donald Trump room. I've been trying to sell the place, but Dad's taste in home decor seems to scare off potential buyers. Do you think you can stand it for a few days? We'll have to stay here until the paparazzi calm down."

"I'll stay if you tell me where to find Marta Vega."

Iain laughed as though he hadn't understood. He seemed awfully relaxed for a killer. "Pardon me?"

"You kidnapped her. So where is she?"

"I did not *kidnap* Marta," Iain said. "She's probably on a beach somewhere by now. God knows she needed to clean up and get some color."

"But—"

"Forget about Marta. I have something for you. Something that should keep you busy until we have a chance to get back to Rome. It's in the house, but you're going to have to find it."

Haven opened her mouth to argue, then shut it just as quickly. The grin on Iain's face was so lighthearted that she couldn't bear to confront him. She'd never encountered such an excellent actor.

"It's somewhere in this apartment?" she finally muttered. "You want to give me a hint?"

"Have a look around," Iain insisted. "You'll know it when you see it."

Haven wandered through a dozen dreary rooms, most decorated with a herd's worth of leather upholstery, a painting of a naked lady, and at least two mounted animal heads. Thick curtains blocked out the sunlight, and the air still bore a hint of cigar smoke. In Jerome Morrow's wood-paneled study, Haven discovered a series of black-and-white photographs hanging on the wall. Each showed Iain at a different age, and all appeared to have been taken when the boy wasn't looking. There was Iain reading a leather-bound copy of *Faust*. Iain poised to dive into an alpine lake. Iain looking wistfully out a window at the rain. But the photos appeared to stop before Iain reached his teenage years. It was as if the boy in them had suddenly died.

Not far from the study, Haven came upon a bedroom that might have belonged to the Iain in the pictures. It appeared oddly empty, as if it were being slowly dismantled. There were a few bright patches on the blue walls where pictures had been recently removed, and there were large gaps between the few books that were left in the bookcase. Even the bureau drawers were bare. Whatever clues Haven might have been able to find had been carefully spirited away.

At the far end of the hall, Haven came to a larger bedroom set in the corner of the building. The curtains were open, and two walls of windows looked out over New York City. With sunshine pouring in, Haven could tell that the room had recently been dusted and cleaned. The white bedspread looked new and even the paint smelled fresh. Her suitcase rested on a luggage rack near the closet. Iain's black messenger bag was hanging on the back of a chair. On the desk was his mobile phone.

Haven froze momentarily as her fingers gripped the device. Finally, she had access to some answers she could trust. She listened for the sound of footsteps in the hall. Somewhere in the distance, she heard Iain moving about. She tapped the phone with one finger and the screen lit up. On the bottom right corner was a familiar icon. As breathless as a tomb raider cracking the lock on an underground vault, Haven clicked the spinning silver snake. It expanded to take over the entire screen. When it stopped rotating, eight options appeared on the screen.

*Rules and Regulations*
*Communicate with Members*
*Society News*
*Suggestions*
*Your Account*
*Report New Charges*
*Dispute Charges*
*Inbox*

Haven tapped *Your Account* and found herself staring at what looked like a bank statement. She gasped as she began to read. At the top of the page, in bold letters, was written, *Iain Morrow, member since 2007*. Beneath that, two columns listed *Deposits* and *Withdrawals*. Beside most were names and short descriptions.

Haven stared at the statement, her eyes passing over the long list of escorts until she reached the item at the bottom: a deposit made to Iain's account the day before. Who had made it? What was it for? And what had been deposited? It couldn't be money, Haven decided. The numbers made that impossible. She paged through previous statements. Most of the withdrawals were for girls, though there were quite a few deposits labeled *Cash donation* or *Business loan.* Iain had been using his fortune to keep his Ouroboros Society account in good standing. And he was using his credit to buy sex. Haven knew this was the system Marta had mentioned—the one that Jeremy Johns had found so disgusting.

| *Date* | *Member* | *Description* | *Deposit* | *Withdrawal* | *Balance* |
|---|---|---|---|---|---|
| *4/2* | *G. Stewart* | *Escort: Oksana* | | *15* | *110* |
| *4/6* | *G. Stewart* | *Escort: Jaqueline* | | *15* | *95* |
| *4/15* | *G. Stewart* | *Escort: Heidi* | | *15* | *80* |
| *4/22* | *G. Stewart* | *Escort: Vivienne* | | *15* | *65* |
| *4/27* | *G. Stewart* | *Escort: Oksana* | | *15* | *50* |
| *4/30* | *Administrative* | *Cash donation* | *25* | | *75* |
| *5/4* | *G. Stewart* | *Escort: Gwendolyn* | | *15* | *60* |
| *5/10* | *M. Vega* | *Gallery loan* | *10* | | *70* |
| *5/26* | *G. Stewart* | *Escort: Oksana* | | *15* | *55* |
| *5/26* | *G. Stewart* | *Escort: Natalie* | | *15* | *40* |
| *6/15* | *Administrative* | *Confidential* | *75* | | *115* |

On the upper-right corner of the screen, a red envelope logo flashed three times then disappeared. Haven left the *Your Account* page and navigated to *Inbox*. A message labeled *Urgent* had just been sent by Padma Singh. It opened automatically.

*I just picked up your voice mail. I have meetings tomorrow. How about Wednesday? Café Marat on Nineteenth Street at 8?*

Haven made a mental note of the message before she closed it and opened the next. It was from Marta Vega, and it had been written only two days earlier:

*They're outside the house. I need to get out while I still can.*

The third was a note to all members from Padma:

*Dear All,*

*I shouldn't need to remind members of the importance of keeping one's account in good standing. However, a spate of recent bankruptcies has convinced me that there are many in the Ouroboros Society who could benefit from a refresher.*

*It is your personal duty to ensure that your account maintains a minimum balance of fifteen points at all times. Should your balance dip below this level, your account will be frozen and you will face disciplinary action. If it drops to zero, you will be immediately expelled from the Society. Necessary steps will then be taken to prevent you from revealing critical information to the public or the press. Those who attempt to betray the Society will be severely punished.*

*There is no excuse for any member to ever face expulsion. Points are easy to earn, even for those of inferior rank. If your balance is low, I recommend contacting Mr. Gordon Stewart or Ms. Theda Devine to ask about employment opportunities. They can help you find ways to provide essential services to high-ranking members—while allowing you to earn the points you'll need to recover your standing within the community.*

*We are the Eternal Ones, and the Ouroboros Society was created to help us maintain our rightful roles in this world. But the system will not work unless everyone plays his or her part. All we ask is that you keep a suitable account balance.*

*Padma Singh, President*

Just as Haven closed the message she realized she was no longer alone.

"Did you find it?" Iain's face fell when he saw the phone in her hands. He said nothing as he turned and left the room.

When Haven started to charge after him, she finally saw what she'd been meant to find. A small sign tacked to a door on the far side of the bedroom read FOR HAVEN. With Iain's phone still clenched in one hand, she turned the knob and stepped into an adjoining chamber. A brand-new sewing machine sat on a table, and the shelves that lined the walls were filled with rolls and rolls of the most beautiful fabrics that Haven had ever seen.

Haven's eyes explored the little room, her feelings shifting every second. She couldn't land on a single emotion. Beneath the anger, guilt, heartbreak, and fear, she even sensed a little hope struggling to break through. Haven was careful to leave it behind when she left to look for Iain.

## CHAPTER FORTY-EIGHT

Haven found Iain in the apartment's kitchen. Big enough for a crew of chefs, the cavernous room seemed a lonely place for a single cook. Iain had been preparing dinner when she arrived, and one small section of the granite countertop was littered with onion peels and carrot tops. Now he stood amid the makings of his meal with a knife in one hand and a tomato in the other, as if he could barely summon the will to move. If Haven hadn't been so angry, her heart might have broken at the sight.

"I didn't know you were such an *active* member of the Ouroboros Society," she said, launching her attack.

At first Iain refused to look at her. "I don't recall saying I wasn't. You knew I was a member. I never hid it from you."

It was true, she had to admit. "I saw the list of girls in your account. How long have you been hiring prostitutes?"

The question got his attention, but the disgust on Iain's face made Haven question her line of attack. "Did it *say* they were prostitutes?" he asked.

"It said they were escorts."

"Exactly. And that's what they did. They *escorted* me. Anything else would have cost a lot more."

"But why hire escorts in the first place?"

Iain turned to face her. With his chin up and arms crossed, he looked ready to withstand all assaults on his character. "I was waiting for you. But I had to keep up appearances, and for that I needed dates for the parties I went to. I didn't want to take anyone who might think I was actually interested. So I hired models as escorts. It worked out rather well until now, I'd say."

"And you never—"

"Never. If you don't believe me, you can log back into my account. Send a message to Gordon Stewart. He's the guy who makes the dates. See what *he* says."

Haven was beginning to feel foolish. She'd never imagined there could be an innocent explanation for what she'd seen. Still, she refused to stop. "What about Marta? What happened to her?"

"That's another thing. How do you know about Marta anyway?"

"I saw you guys together at your father's gallery. I thought you two might be involved, but then I went to see her—"

Iain's left eyebrow rose. "Wait a second. You were at the gallery?"

"I followed you," Haven said.

"Do you know how dangerous that was? You came very close to getting yourself in a great deal of trouble." Clearly horrified by the thought, Iain didn't linger on the subject. "So what did Marta tell you when you went to see her?"

"She said you guys were just friends."

"Then I guess I've been proved innocent once more. When should I expect an apology?"

"Not yet. I was there this morning when you showed up at her apartment right before she disappeared. Did you take her?"

"Yes," Iain admitted.

Haven took a stumbling step backward as if she'd been punched. "You did?"

"Marta was in trouble. I had to help her leave town. That's one of the reasons I came back to New York when I did. But I had to keep my plans a secret. Even Marta didn't know anything until I went to get her. She landed in Mexico three hours ago. Now there are *two* people who know that. Let's try and keep it that way. Anything else?"

Haven was no longer feeling so confident. She was in danger of hurting someone whose actions and motives might have been nothing but noble. "I spoke with Padma Singh after I went to see Marta."

"Oh *God*, Haven!" Iain picked up his knife and slammed its tip into the wooden cutting board. "I thought I warned you to stay away from the Ouroboros Society."

"Well, why didn't you *tell* me what was going on there with the drug dealing and the gray men? Why did *Marta* have to explain it to me?"

"So Marta told you about the OS? How high *was* she when you talked to her? Do you have any idea how much danger she put herself in? How much danger she put *you* in?"

Haven had never thought of it that way.

"And what did you and *Padma* discuss?" Iain demanded.

"Padma Singh was Rebecca Underwood."

"I *know*, Haven. Does she know who you were?"

"Yes."

"What did you tell her? It's important that I know. Did you tell her who I am?"

Haven ignored the question. "She said Ethan murdered Constance and Dr. Strickland."

Iain nodded stoically, as if his worst fears were being realized. "You see? This is *exactly* why I didn't want you to go there. Padma would say anything to come between us. And I bet she can be quite persuasive, can't she?"

"So Ethan didn't kill anyone?"

"Not a single person. Ever. I swear. I *hope* you didn't tell Padma that I was Ethan. Did you?"

"No," Haven said. "But she has a hunch that Ethan is back."

"Damn it! Do you have any idea how hard it's been to hide my identity from her? I've had to invent an entire past life!" Iain took a deep breath to cool his temper. "We'll need to get out of New York before they figure it all out. Now do you understand why we can't be photographed together?" he asked, and Haven nodded. "Is there anything else you want to ask me? Has anyone else been whispering lies in your ear?"

"No."

"Are you *sure*?"

"Positive."

"When did all this girl-detective business start, anyway? What did I ever do to make you mistrust me?"

"You lied about the phone in Rome. You lied about having dinner with your lawyer. You lied about—"

"Okay," Iain stopped her, his anger fading. "Those were fibs. I'll admit it. But my intentions were good."

"You know what they say about good intentions," Haven said.

"You have no idea how true that really is," Iain replied, picking up the last tomato and chopping it into fine chunks.

"Iain?" Haven said once he'd finished.

"Yes?"

"I'm sorry. I got carried away. I just have one more question."

"Yes?"

"If you're innocent, why are you putting up with all of this from me?" Haven asked.

"Because I love you," Iain said simply. "I always have. I love your bad temper. I love your jealous streak. I love your strength and pigheadedness. And I know you love me. And sometimes love makes people go a little crazy. The insanity won't last forever . . . I hope."

"But if we're really meant to be together, shouldn't this be a lot easier?" Haven asked. "Why has it all been so hard?"

Iain threw the chopped tomato into the pot and wiped his hands on a dish towel. "Come here," he ordered. When Haven was close, he wrapped his arms around her and kissed the top of her head. "Don't expect me to be perfect. Despite all my lives, I'm still only human. I can't deliver perfection, and I'll only disappoint you. But I want you to remember that you're the most important thing in the world to me. I'm trying to protect you," he said. "Do you understand?"

Haven nodded.

"Sometimes I'm going to screw things up. I may even tell a white lie now and then. But you have to give me the benefit of the doubt, okay?"

"I will." Thankfully, only Haven seemed to notice the slight hesitation in her voice.

"And do you promise to never go near the OS again?"

"I promise."

"Good. Dinner's going to take a while to cook. Can you think of anything we can do to pass the time?"

Haven giggled. "Nope," she said.

"How about a guided tour of the house?" Iain offered, picking her up and tossing her over his shoulder. "We'll start with the bedrooms."

LATER THAT NIGHT, Haven woke from a vivid dream. The world she'd visited with her eyes closed was an ancient, mysterious place that bore no resemblance to the one Haven had seen in her visions. She'd been greeted by a voluptuous woman, her body clothed in shimmering golden robes. The woman held both hands over her head, and in each fist writhed a poisonous snake. Three more serpents twisted about the woman's torso. As the woman opened her mouth to speak, Haven sat upright.

Her eyes adjusted to the darkness, and she saw Iain beside her, lying facedown on the bed. His back was bare, and she let her fingers trace the length of his spine. When she reached the base, he moaned softly and the sheet shifted, exposing a small tattoo of a silver serpent swallowing its tail.

## CHAPTER FORTY-NINE

"Haven," Iain whispered in her ear.

Haven opened one eye. "Where are you going?" she asked when she saw he was dressed.

"Something's come up. I have to meet with my lawyers," he said, forcing a smile. "And this time I'm telling the *truth*." His attempt at a joke fell flat. Haven could see he was worried.

"Is everything okay?" she asked.

"It will be." Iain bent down and kissed her. "I forgot to stock up on coffee for you, but there's a café a couple of blocks down Lexington if you need some. I'll be back in a few hours."

When she heard the elevator doors open and shut, Haven propped herself up in bed and stared out the bedroom window. Across Central Park stood the Andorra, its two towers reflected in the lake below. Frances Whitman's terrace was just a speck of green on the hulking beige facade. Yet that one patch of color taunted Haven. She had arrived in New York a week earlier and was still no closer to finding the truth about what had happened back in 1925 to the girl from the other side of the park. If Ethan hadn't killed Constance—who had?

The cell phone in Haven's handbag rang, and she leaped out of bed trying to get to it in time. She saw that it wasn't Iain or Beau just before the call went to voice mail.

"Haven, this is your mother." It wasn't a particularly friendly way to start a message. "Imogene was looking through a magazine this morning, and you would not *believe* what she came across. A picture of her very own granddaughter. With a boy. In *Rome*. As you might imagine, she was on the phone to Dr. Tidmore the second she saw it. Hunted him down on vacation to tell him that your demon has finally taken control.

"I *warned* you, Haven Moore. I told you it was time to come home. Now, if you aren't on your way to Tennessee by this evening, Imogene is going to report you as a runaway, and we'll have the New York City police find you and haul your bottom to the train station. I'm sorry it's come to this, but you've really left us no choice."

Haven stared at the phone. So Imogene the hypocrite liked to read a little gossip now and then, did she? It figured. Haven erased the message and pulled on some clothes. She needed coffee to deal with this unfortunate turn of events.

The café on Lexington was packed, and the line snaked out the door and onto the sidewalk. Haven dialed Beau as she began walking south, looking for a less crowded option.

"Haven?" Beau didn't wait for her to respond. "Are you safe? You had me so worried that I barely got an hour of sleep."

"I did?" Haven asked before she recalled her last conversation with Beau. It felt like an eternity had passed. "Oh, yeah. It was a false alarm. Iain didn't kidnap Marta."

"A false alarm?" Beau scoffed. "How the hell . . . Hold on. I can't wait to hear all about this, but you'll have to let me call you back in a minute. I'm on the other line."

Haven kept walking. None of the cafés in Midtown seemed to suit her. She was already across from Grand Central Station, beneath the giant steel gargoyles of the Chrysler Building when she finally heard her phone ring.

"That was a lot longer than a minute," Haven pointed out. "It's been at least half an hour."

"Don't get all snippy with me. For your information, I was talking to Leah Frizzell. Why she doesn't just call you directly is anyone's guess."

"She told me she thinks someone might be eavesdropping on my conversations," Haven explained.

"Yeah, but how does she figure I get the information to you? Telepathy? Anyway, she's dusted off her crystal ball again, and she wants you to know that you're being watched."

"Right now?" Haven couldn't help but take a peek over her shoulder.

"She didn't say. See, that's the problem with Leah's visions. She's got a blind spot the size of an eighteen-wheeler."

"There you go again," Haven said. "How many things does Leah need to get right before you start to believe her?"

"What do you mean, 'how many things'? Right now, her success rate's somewhere between a telephone psychic and a Magic Eight-Ball. What's all this about a false alarm, anyway?"

"Iain didn't kidnap Marta. He just helped her get out of town. I guess she was in trouble with the OS."

"And what about all the things Padma Singh told you?"

"Lies," Haven said. "She'd do just about anything to keep Constance and Ethan apart. That's why Iain had to keep his real identity a secret from the Society."

"And you believe all this?"

"Of course!"

"Well, I sure hope this is the end of the roller-coaster ride, Haven."

Beau still sounded skeptical. "I was starting to get kind of nauseous. So what are you going to do now? Live happily ever after with your billionaire boyfriend?"

"I don't know. Iain had to get up early this morning to go see his lawyers. I have a feeling something's happened with the Jeremy Johns case," Haven began to explain before she recalled her own troubles. "But listen—I didn't call to talk about all of this. I need you to do me a favor."

"Okay. What is it this time?"

"Imogene saw that picture of me in Rome, and now my mom says she's going to report me as a runaway. Will you go talk to Mom and work your magic? Try to calm her down?"

"Why can't *you* call your mother?"

"'Cause if I talk to her, she'll expect me to tell her everything, and I don't want to be forced to lie. But if you let her know that the picture is just a big misunderstanding, that might be enough to convince her to call off the dogs for a while."

"So you're saying you're too big a wuss to call your own mother."

"Yeah," Haven admitted.

"I appreciate the honesty," Beau said. "But at some point I'm going to have to take some time off from being your slave so I can start living my own life."

"Spending all your free time trawling the Internet for juicy gossip doesn't count as a life."

"You're hilarious."

"It's a gift. So will you do it?"

"I'll try to drop by there later," Beau said. "But I still say this would be an excellent day to start doing your own dirty work."

"Why bother when you're so good at it?"

"Funny. *Goodbye*, Haven."

"*Goodbye*, Beau."

* * *

HAVEN STEPPED INTO a patch of morning sun as she crossed the street. She felt her pale skin start to sizzle before she stepped back into the shadows cast by the buildings of Lexington Avenue. She hurried through two more patches before she suddenly found herself facing a dead end. The avenue no longer stretched out before her. A pair of wrought-iron gates blocked her path. Beyond the fence, Gramercy Park was empty and in bloom. Pink flowers lined the paths like garlands at a wedding. The air bore the scents of freshly cut grass and freesia, and tree branches framed the row of beautiful mansions on the other side of the park. Haven tried to recall the route she'd taken through Midtown. How had she walked so far without noticing?

"Hello, Haven."

A young man was approaching the gates from inside the park. Tall and lean, he strolled at a confident, leisurely pace, with his hands tucked into the pockets of his jeans. Everything he was wearing—from his black T-shirt to his shoes—looked new, never worn. He was very handsome, Haven thought, though it was difficult to see his features clearly beneath the bright morning sun. She might not have recognized him if it hadn't been for the chunky black glasses that sat on his nose. Haven suspected they were more of a fashion statement than a necessity.

"Hello, Adam," she replied.

He was now standing less than two feet away, with only a row of iron bars between them. "How lucky to run into you. I was just taking my morning constitutional. Would you like to get that cup of coffee we spoke about?"

Haven knew she should turn around and leave. She'd promised Iain she'd never return to the Ouroboros Society. And after everything she'd learned, she couldn't understand what might have drawn her back to Gramercy Park. Had some part of herself wanted to return? "I'm not sure I have time," she told Adam. "I'll need to head back soon."

"What's the rush?" Adam's resonant voice was hard to resist. "Wouldn't you like to take a quick stroll through the park? It's lovely this time of year, and I've been looking forward to seeing you again."

It was flattering to be admired by someone so sure of himself. With his good looks and confidence, Adam could have had anyone. Haven was curious to know why he seemed to have settled on her. So when Adam unlocked the gate, she took a quick look behind her and stepped inside. There was no harm in joining him for a walk, she thought.

"How have you been?" he asked as they ambled side by side. A breeze whipped around them, blending the park's aromas with less pleasant odors from outside the gates. Once or twice Haven caught a whiff of something old and musty—like a mausoleum opened for the first time in a century. "Have you enjoyed your time in New York so far?"

"It's been a little crazy," Haven confided, glancing up at her companion. His long pale face with its prominent cheekbones and strong jaw seemed too perfectly formed to be real.

"I can only imagine," Adam said. "Have you had a chance to think about joining the Ouroboros Society?"

"Yes," Haven told him. "I don't think it's for me."

"That's a shame." Though he seemed to have anticipated her answer, Haven could tell that he wasn't prepared to accept it. "I hope your conversation with Padma hasn't turned you against the Society. She may have gone a little too far, I'm afraid. I wouldn't want you to go back to Tennessee with the wrong ideas about us."

Haven stopped in the shadow of a spruce tree. The wind sent her curls flying, and she had to hold her hair back out of her eyes. She looked for the gate, but it was no longer visible. The little park seemed to have swallowed them. "I'm sorry, Adam, but who *are* you?" she asked. "What exactly do you do at the OS?"

"I make sure everything runs properly." He wasn't accustomed to answering questions. Haven could tell he was humoring her.

"But Padma is president. And aren't you a little young to be running anything? What are you—twenty-two?"

Adam looked amused. "I'm older than I look. Padma is the public face of the Society. She oversees the day-to-day affairs. That's all. We're not sure how long we'll allow her to hold that position."

"We?" Haven asked. "Who are 'we'?"

"I can't give you names. But think of the most powerful businessman in America today. Or the best-known actress. Or the most successful artist. The OS has never made its membership rolls public, so few people realize just how influential we really are."

"You forgot to mention the drug dealers and prostitutes."

"I'm sorry?"

"Your accounting system seems to have a few flaws. I've heard that when members get into debt they have to sell their souls—or their bodies—to get out again."

Adam Rosier smiled once more, this time unconvincingly. "May I ask how you know about these 'flaws' in our system?"

"Does it matter?" Haven asked.

"Oh, I would say it matters a great deal to me," Adam replied, his cool never cracking. "Our members are bound by a strict confidentiality agreement. No one is allowed to speak of our system. The fact that you know about it represents a serious security breach. Who told you?"

"No one *told* me. I remembered the system from my last life," Haven lied.

Rosier removed his glasses. For a moment his eyes seemed as flat and lusterless as pebbles. "I see where you're going, Haven. There have always been members who choose to misuse the OS. But the Society wasn't set up to act as anyone's nanny. Until now we have always maintained that what members did with their accounts was their own business. That may have to change. Padma appears to be letting the corruption get out of control. We can't allow the abuses to prevent people like you from joining."

"Why do you care if I join?" Haven asked. "I'm nobody."

Adam looked appalled by the suggestion. "That's not true, Haven. You have remarkable gifts—talents you've never been able to use properly. I've seen what you can do. There's no doubt in my mind that with our help, you could become one of the most famous designers in the world."

"How do you know about my 'gifts'?"

"To tell you the truth, I've known you for quite some time," Adam confessed, looking pleased that the truth was finallly out. "In fact I was here in 1925 when you first joined the Society. We were friends."

"We were?" Haven searched her few memories for anyone who might have fit the bill.

"I'm not surprised you don't remember me. I've always been rather forgettable," Adam explained with a touch of sadness in his voice. "But I'm afraid this all brings up a slightly unsavory subject that I must discuss with you."

"Ethan Evans?"

"Yes," Adam said. It was impossible to surprise him. "You see, I knew you both back then. Ethan was very charming and highly intelligent. But never once did I detect any evidence of a conscience within him. He used people for his own pleasure—without any regard for their feelings or their safety.

"No one could ever connect Dr. Strickland's death to Ethan, but I am not the only person who believes Ethan was responsible. He was very dangerous back then, Haven. And he's just as dangerous today. The essence of a person doesn't change from one life to the next. If anything, some people get worse with time."

Rosier paused before deciding to continue. "I'll be honest with you, Haven. I know that Ethan has returned to earth. I know who he is in this life."

"Who?" Haven challenged him.

"Iain Morrow."

Haven gasped. She'd been sure he was bluffing. "How do you—"

"A picture of the two of you together was recently brought to my attention. I'm well aware of the connection you possess. I know you're drawn to him. But I feel I must warn you, Haven. You're being drawn to the wrong person. He's just as dangerous for you as he is for everyone else. *He* set the fire that killed Constance. And he'll kill you too if you give him the chance."

"I don't believe it," Haven said.

Adam gazed down at her as though she were something he cherished and hated to hurt. "Will you believe me when he's in jail?" he asked.

"Jail?" Haven almost choked on the word.

"A woman in Los Angeles stepped forward yesterday. She witnessed Iain Morrow and Jeremy Johns fighting on the night Jeremy disappeared. She claims she saw Iain knock Jeremy down, and she didn't see Jeremy get up again."

"The woman's lying. Jeremy died of a drug overdose."

"No, Haven. The autopsy results came in yesterday, too. He died of blunt-force trauma. Someone hit him in the head with a rock."

"How do you know all of this?"

"I told you. The Society has very powerful connections. We're always called first whenever there's news about any of our members."

Haven was too stunned to speak. She slumped down onto a park bench and stared off into the distance. A tempest was building inside of her. Disappointment and rage were combining to form a terrible force that Haven feared she couldn't control.

"You're upset," Rosier observed as he sat down beside her. "I'm sorry. I didn't want to be the one to tell you."

"Then why did you?"

"Because I care. Much more than you realize. You deserve better, and I don't want to see anything happen to you. It's time you were allowed to live long enough to reach your potential. I can help make that happen if you'll let me."

"How? How can you help me?" Haven asked, though she already suspected there were few limits to what Adam could do. Had she somehow picked the wrong man to love?

"The Ouroboros Society was designed for people with gifts like yours," Adam replied. Haven had been searching for solace. Instead she was getting a sales pitch. "You could be rich and famous, with the most interesting and successful people on the planet as your friends."

"As long as my account balance stays above fifteen points," Haven muttered. She wasn't interested in fame or fortune.

Adam frowned. "We can fix the problems with the accounting system. You needn't worry about that anyway. Only the lowest orders of the Society are forced to comply."

"It's a tempting offer, Adam, but no thanks."

Rosier refused to give in. "Our members aren't *all* bad, Haven. Why don't you come to the little party we're having tomorrow evening? You can meet some of the others. You might be surprised to learn what kind of company we keep at the OS."

"Let me think about it," Haven said without enthusiasm. She was eager to bring the conversation to a close. "I'm sorry, Adam, but I'm not in the mood to talk anymore. Do you mind if I just sit here alone for a while?"

Adam hesitated before he rose from the bench. "Of course not," he said. "But promise me one thing. If you need help for any reason, you'll come find me. I'll be waiting for you."

"Thanks," Haven said, wishing he'd leave.

"And I hope you'll come to the party tomorrow," Adam added.

"We'll see," Haven told him.

She closed her eyes and felt the rage seething inside of her. She kept it pent up, waiting to hear the sound of Adam's footsteps heading toward the park's gates. He lingered too long, and Haven could feel his steady gaze on her face. When at last he was finally gone, she opened her eyes and discovered she was still being observed.

## CHAPTER FIFTY

There was a man standing just outside the northern gate of Gramercy Park, his face half hidden behind sunglasses. His outfit—navy sweatpants, polo shirt, New Balance sneakers—was that of a gray man. He was staring straight at Haven when his mouth began to move, as if he were talking to himself. Haven saw a flash of light bounce off a gadget in the man's right ear, and she realized he was wearing a headset.

Remembering Leah's warning, Haven moved quickly. She crossed the park and left through the southern gate. She walked briskly down Irving Place to Nineteenth Street and ducked around a corner. Standing with her back to the rough brick wall of an apartment building, she took a compact out of her purse and used its mirror to peer back toward Gramercy Park. She waited for two long minutes, but the man didn't appear. When Haven snapped her compact closed, she saw the patrons of an outdoor café across the street watching her. A few began to snicker as she bolted for Park Avenue South.

It was lunchtime, and all the taxis that passed were already filled. Joining the stream of people heading north on the avenue, Haven studied the reflection in every shop window she passed, searching the crowd behind her for signs of the man with the headset. Near the corner of Twenty-fourth Street she slowed to take advantage of a row of windows that belonged to a bank branch. Inside, a few patrons leaned over a long table that stood against the glass. Most were endorsing checks or filling out deposit forms. But one of them was watching the street. His eyes met Haven's for the briefest moment. Later, the only thing that Haven would recall about him was the headset he'd been wearing.

The traffic light turned green just as Haven began to weave around idling cars, through the traffic, frantically trying to reach the opposite side of the street. Stranded on the avenue's landscaped median, ankle-deep in a juniper shrub, she kept her eyes trained on the bank, watching to see when the man made his exit. The white glare of the sun on its windows burned dark spots on her eyes, and the blur of cars whizzing by less than two feet away left her dizzy and nauseous. When the light turned red again, Haven hopped off the median and sprinted west.

A little more than a block away, she found herself inside flat, grassy Madison Square Park, which offered few places to hide. When Haven stopped to catch her breath, she realized just how exposed she was. At that time of the afternoon, even the benches were empty. Most of the park's visitors were gathered at the dog run, where two German shepherds were engaged in a vicious brawl.

A man in shorts and a polo shirt jogged past her. He stopped at a fountain and propped a foot up on the edge. When he bent down to tighten the laces, Haven recognized his gray New Balance sneakers and saw the headset in his ear. It was the man from Gramercy Park, and he was waiting for her to make her next move. Haven spun around and raced in the direction from which she'd come, barely avoiding a stream of taxis speeding up Madison Avenue. She followed a woman in a business suit through the doors of an office building and found herself inside a magnificent lobby the size of a train station, its vaulted ceiling trimmed with glimmering gold. She ran all the way across the block-long lobby, exiting through a revolving door that deposited her on Park Avenue South. There she turned right and ducked into a drugstore on the corner of Twenty-third and Park. Peeking over one of the shelves, she saw the jogger race past, heading south. Finally safe, she slumped down on the floor of the shampoo aisle and tried not to vomit.

The gray men had been waiting for her the moment she left Gramercy Park. What were they after? Had Padma sent them? For the next fifteen minutes, Haven loitered in the drugstore, browsing through floppy hats and cheap sunglasses as the salespeople watched her warily. Before she left, she stripped out of her T-shirt, wearing only the tank top she'd had on underneath. She tucked her hair beneath a denim hat and donned a pair of faux-tortoiseshell sunglasses. Trying not to appear too cautious, she stepped out into the street and held out her hand to hail a cab. Relief washed over her when a taxi stopped to let out a fare half a block from where she stood. As she waited for the businessman inside to hunt for his wallet, a black car pulled up to the curb beside her. The passenger door opened, and a bulky man in a black suit picked Haven up and crammed her into the backseat like a piece of cheap luggage.

The door slammed shut, and Haven scrambled to open it, only to find that the handles wouldn't budge. She beat on the glass partition that separated her from the front seat and screamed for help. The driver ignored her, and the people passing by on the sidewalk outside didn't pause. The tinted windows were thick, and no one outside could hear Haven's cries. As the car took off down the avenue, Haven rummaged through her purse for anything she could use as a weapon. She thought of breaking her mirror into razor-sharp shards or blinding her kidnappers with hair-relaxing spray. At last she opted for a ballpoint pen, which she grasped in her fist like a dagger.

Soon they were traveling west toward the Hudson River. Warehouses lined the streets and few pedestrians strolled the sidewalks. On Twenty-first Street, just past Tenth Avenue, the car came to a stop beneath an ancient railway overpass. When the driver got out, Haven clenched her weapon and started to pray. One of the backseat doors opened, and she pressed herself against the opposite side of the car, waiting for the man to reach in and grab her. Instead, someone else slid in beside her.

Iain stared at Haven, her hair spilling out from under the tacky denim hat, her skirt bunched up around her thighs, and a ballpoint pen in her fist.

"Didn't you promise me you wouldn't go back?" he demanded.

## CHAPTER FIFTY-ONE

"How *dare* you have me followed?" Haven snarled. "Were those gray men working for *you*? Did you make some sort of deal with Padma Singh? Let me out of the car, you psycho! Let me out this second!" She hurled herself toward the door, but Iain caught her by the wrist and pulled her back.

"Not yet." He kept his composure, but Haven could see Iain was furious. "I want you to explain why you went back to the Society after I told you to give the detective work a rest."

"My apologies, Mr. Morrow," Haven spit, wishing she had the guts to punch him in his pretty nose. "I guess I'm not very good at taking orders from liars. What are you going to do now? Make me disappear? Kill me like you killed Jeremy Johns?"

Iain snorted and shook his head. "My God, Haven, you have *no idea* what you're talking about. Do you know how long those gray men have been watching you? Have you seen them before?"

Haven stopped trying to break free and stared at him. "What are you talking about? Weren't they working for you? Didn't Padma loan you her drones?"

"You really think I have gray men working for me? That shows how much *you* know."

"Well, I know about Jeremy Johns," Haven hissed. "How could you kill someone with a *rock*?"

"Where did you hear that?"

"I have my sources," Haven said, borrowing Adam's words.

"Did you speak with someone this morning?" Iain asked, watching her closely through narrowed eyes.

"Why don't you just ask your thugs? You must have had *someone* tailing me if you knew where to find me."

"Answer my question, Haven."

"You first," Haven insisted. "How did you find me?"

"I asked James to look after you. He followed you to the park, and he saw you leave with a gray man behind you. The gray men aren't after *you*, Haven. They want to see if you'll lead them to Ethan. "

Haven still couldn't get past the first part of Iain's statement. "I can't believe you told James to watch me! What's the point, anyway? Why bother to keep me safe if you're just going to kill me yourself?" she sneered. "The same way you killed Constance."

The anger left Iain's face, and his head seemed to droop with exhaustion. "What's wrong with you, Haven?" he asked. "What could have changed since I left the apartment this morning? Everything was so wonderful last night, and now you're convinced that I killed the person I love most in the world?"

"If I'm wrong, why don't you prove it? Tell me what's really going on," Haven pushed him. "Why are so many people following me?

"I can't tell you that."

"You *can't tell me*?" The full force of Haven's anger finally broke loose. "What the hell kind of answer is that? I've been an idiot to trust you. You've done nothing but lie to me and hurt me. I came all the way to New York, thinking I was supposed to be with you, and you turn out to be a lying, cheating, kidnapping murderer!"

Iain lifted a hand to stroke Haven's face. "I'm sorry—"

"Stay away from me!" Haven shouted, slapping his hand away. "I'm going to make you pay for what you did to Constance. And I'm not going to let you kill any more people."

"This is pointless," Iain muttered hopelessly. He pressed the intercom button in the backseat. "Stop the car," he ordered.

The Mercedes rolled to a halt, and the driver jumped out to open Iain's door.

"Take Miss Moore wherever she wants to go." Iain climbed out of the car without looking back at Haven. "If she wants me alive, she won't go back to the Ouroboros Society."

"Iain!" The door slammed in her face, and Haven felt her mind drifting into the darkness.

"Where to, miss?" the driver asked over the intercom. "Miss?"

*She nervously toyed with the golden band on her finger. It had been there for only a few hours, and yet it already seemed to be part of her. A tower of luggage waited in the corner. The sun was setting. He should have arrived hours earlier. The ship might leave without them.*

*Outside in the lane, a boy in a dirty cap paused long enough at her door to drop a note through the mail slot. She rushed down the stairs to find it waiting for her on the mat. She knew when she saw it that the news was not good.*

*The trip to Rome was postponed, Ethan had written. He would be there soon to explain.*

## CHAPTER FIFTY-TWO

"I am such an idiot." Haven was hiding out in the cleaning-fluids aisle of a grocery store on University Place. As far as she could tell, the only potential eavesdropper was a stock boy rocking out to death metal on his iPod while several cases of antibacterial toilet cleaner waited to be shelved. Haven felt a bit safer in his company. There was no way a kid with so many tattoos and eyebrow piercings could possibly be a gray man.

"So I guess you've heard?" Beau asked on the other end of the phone.

"About the eyewitness?" Haven sighed. "Yeah, I've heard."

"I just saw it on the news. I was about to call to break it to you. So what do you think? You think the lady's lying? Do you think she saw Iain kill Jeremy?"

"Why are you asking *me*?" Haven said. "I've been wrong about everything since I got to New York. Which is why I may be forced to spend the rest of the day hiding in aisle number three of the

Greenwich Village Food Emporium."

"You're where? What the hell happened?"

"I went out to get some coffee, and somehow I ended up walking all the way to Gramercy Park. Then I ran into a guy I know from the Ouroboros Society. He told me about Jeremy. He also claims he knew Ethan and Constance back in 1925 and that everything Padma told me about Ethan was true. He did kill Strickland. And he started the fire that killed me, too."

"Hold on. Who's this guy you're talking about?"

"His name is Adam Rosier. He's some sort of big shot at the Society."

"I remember the name," Beau said. "You asked me to look for information about him, and I couldn't find a thing. But why are you hanging out with *anyone* from the Society? Didn't you tell me that the OS is totally corrupt? Don't they go around killing people?"

"Yeah, but Adam says Padma is to blame for all the corruption, and that he's trying to clean it up."

"Still." Beau didn't sound impressed. "Don't you think it's a little naive to trust some random guy from the OS when you can't even trust the person you've been in love with for two thousand years?"

"Why would *Adam* lie? Anyway, I might have given Iain the benefit of the doubt if he hadn't decided to kidnap me."

"*What*?" Beau exclaimed. "Are you serious?"

"Totally serious," Haven said. "Turns out he's been having me followed. After I left Gramercy Park, a guy grabbed me off the sidewalk, threw me into a car, and took me to see Iain."

"Damn. How'd you get free?"

"They let me go. I had them drop me off at Union Square."

"They let you go? That's not really much of a kidnapping then, is it? What did Iain say when you saw him?"

"He was mad that I went near the OS again. He said if I wanted him alive, I wouldn't go back. He claims gray men have been following me to see if I'd lead them to him."

"Now you've got *my* head spinning," Beau said. "I thought it was one of *his* guys who grabbed you off the street."

"Exactly! How many people have been following me? And why does Iain want me to stay away from the OS if he's there all the time himself? I saw on his phone that he's having breakfast with Padma Singh tomorrow morning."

"The woman who used to be Rebecca Underwood? The one who's supposedly responsible for all the corruption at the OS?" Beau paused. "Look, I don't want to be the one to make things worse, but—"

"But what?"

"I just got back from talking to your mom like you asked me, but there wasn't much I could do. Your grandmother called Dr. Tidmore. I guess he's up north somewhere visiting friends. He's agreed to come to New York and escort you back to Tennessee. They want you to phone him ASAP."

"You're kidding!" Haven shouted, causing an old lady at the end of the supermarket aisle to jump and drop a pack of mothballs.

"'Fraid not. Imogene thinks you've gone totally wanton. Apparently, your soul is in peril, and drastic measures must be taken. Your mom just thinks you're too young to be vacationing in Europe with some boy she's never met. She said it's either Tidmore or the police."

"Then they've both gone completely insane. Let them call the police, 'cause there is no way in hell—"

"All things considered, Haven," Beau interrupted, "it might not be such a bad idea. You know I don't like Tidmore any more than you do, but it sounds like you've gotten yourself in an awfully big mess."

"You too? Crazy must be contagious. I am *not* going to call Dr. Tidmore."

"Fine. Then I'm going to come up there myself and get you."

"No, you aren't. I don't need anyone to save me, Beau. Besides, if you're here it'll just complicate things."

"You're going to get yourself killed."

"I am *not* going to get myself killed. I've got a plan," Haven insisted.

"Your plan better not involve playing kissy-kissy with your kidnapper."

"Do you think I'm stupid? I'm not going to play kissy-kissy with anybody ever again. Iain's staying at his dad's apartment uptown. So I'm going to sleep at *my* house tonight."

"*What* house?" Beau asked.

"I gotta go," Haven told him. "I've got grocery shopping to do."

## CHAPTER FIFTY-THREE

"Miss! Miss!" As soon as she pulled her key out of her pocket, the paparazzi waiting outside the mews began to shout. They were a motley bunch—potbellied pros with cameras that cost more than their houses stood alongside greasy, muscular punks dressed like New Jersey frat boys. A few in the crowd could have doubled as ax murderers or serial killers. After a night spent staking out the mews, most of the men were unkempt, some downright filthy. And each of them wore a layer of stubble and dark bags beneath his eyes. They looked as though they'd seen everything there was to see—all in the past twenty-four hours.

Haven set her bucket full of cleaning supplies down on the cobblestones and pulled out her keys. "What do you want?" she asked them in an accent that belonged to no particular country.

"Who are *you*?" one of the men called out. None of the photographers had recognized Haven with her unruly hair pulled back in a bun.

"Who do you *think* I am?" Haven pulled a mop out of the bucket and shook it at him. "I am the maid." A murmur of disappointment passed through the mob.

"Where's Iain Morrow?" another asked.

"How should I know? You think he asks maid's permission whenever he wants to leave town?"

"A thousand dollars if you tell me where to find him."

"Two thousand!" someone else shouted.

A few of the bolder men broke out of the crowd and ventured past the gate toward Haven. They walked slowly, almost sideways, as if approaching a wild beast. One of them took his wallet from his pocket and waved it in front of him, hoping Haven understood the international sign for bribery.

Haven slipped inside before they could reach her. She stood for a moment with her back to the door, feeling the wood vibrate as the paparazzi pounded on the other side. The rank odor of rotting vegetation was turning her stomach. She counted a dozen glass vases filled with dead, drooping blooms floating in murky liquid. In just a few short days, the fragrant flowers that Iain had given her on their first morning back in New York had turned foul and disgusting.

After the paparazzi gave up and returned to their posts, Haven toured the house with a garbage bag, dumping the contents of the vases inside it. Yet the horrible stench still lingered. Upstairs she opened the windows and collapsed on the unmade bed. She could hear the men chatting below in the lane as they waited for her to emerge. The paparazzi would figure out that she wasn't a maid when she didn't leave before dark. But they'd never be able to catch her when she exited via the roof in the morning. The trick wouldn't work twice, but Haven hoped she'd only need to spend a single night at the mews house before she returned to Snope City. She prayed she'd find the proof she needed to send Iain to jail the very next morning—at his breakfast meeting with the corrupt president of the Ouroboros Society.

Exhausted, Haven let her head roll to the side, and her eyes landed on the print from Rome that was sitting on the bedside table. Once it had meant so much. Now, like everything else in the little house, it seemed like an artifact from another life.

Her cell phone rang, and Iain's number flashed on the screen. Haven let the call go to voice mail. She sensed Iain would start searching for her soon. But he'd never think to look at the mews house. As long as the paparazzi were standing guard outside, it was the safest place in all of Manhattan. With that one thought to comfort her, Haven closed her eyes.

*Someone sat down on the edge of her bed. A hand clapped over her mouth before she could scream.*

*"It's me," Ethan whispered. The moon was missing, and she could barely see him in the darkness.*

*"What are you doing here?"*

*"Keep your voice down. There are people outside. We need to get out of New York. I've booked passage on the* St. Michele. *It leaves for Italy in a week."*

*"And Rebecca? Is she coming, too?"*

*"Rebecca?"*

*"There's no point in lying, Ethan. I saw you with her. I heard her say that you're meant to be together."*

*"Did you hear my response?"*

*"I didn't have the stomach to listen."*

*"I told her that I'm going to marry you."*

*"You did?"*

*"I did. In fact, I intend to marry you before we leave New York. If you'll have me, that is."*

*"But I saw Rebecca go to meet you last night. I followed her all the way to that house on Water Street."*

*"The house on Water Street?"*

*"It was late. Who else would she have been meeting?"*

*Ethan's eyes widened just as they heard a loud pounding on the door below. He jumped up from the bed and looked out on the lane.*

*"It's the police. I can't stay here. It's not safe for you, either. Go to your parents' house as soon as you can. I'll meet you at City Hall on Monday morning at nine. We'll leave for Italy that evening."*

*"But—"*

*"You have to trust me, Constance."*

The ringing of her cell phone dragged Haven out of the vision. It was quiet by the time she found it hidden among the sheets. There were ten missed calls from Iain. But there was no time to check messages. It was seven thirty in the morning, and Haven had half an hour to make it to breakfast with Padma and Iain. Thankfully, she'd fallen asleep with her clothes and shoes on. All there was left to do was splash her face, brush her teeth, and take the stairs to the roof.

SET IN A CORNER building one block south of Gramercy Park, Café Marat featured a wall of tall windows along Nineteenth Street. They all stood open, letting the cool morning air flow through the premises. Outside on the sidewalk, little tables hugged the wall of the building, their white tablecloths fluttering like giant moths. Haven watched from across the street as Padma arrived and chose a seat near the open windows. A few minutes later, Iain showed up. Padma greeted him a little too fondly with kisses on both cheeks. Haven wished she could strangle them both.

She scurried across to the café and slid into a chair at a sidewalk table just to the left of Iain and Padma's window. With her back to the building's wall, she was all but invisible to them. And as long as the streets remained clear of traffic, she could listen to every word they uttered.

"You don't look very well," she heard Padma remark. "Is all the attention beginning to get to you?"

"Have you seen the paparazzi camped outside my house?" Iain

replied. "It's like they expect me to show up with Marta in a body bag. But they're just a nuisance. It's the police that are really giving me trouble. They're hounding me about Jeremy Johns."

"Still?" Padma was surprised. "I thought we made all that go away. I saw to it myself."

"I was called in for more questioning yesterday. There's an eyewitness now. Though I can't imagine what she could have seen. Are you sure the Society didn't have a hand in her coming forward?"

"Why would we do something like that? I'll call our contact in the LAPD. Don't worry, we'll be able to fix this."

"I don't want anything to happen to the woman," Iain insisted. "I just want her to stop making things up."

"Oh, she'll stop," Padma assured him. "I'm sorry this Jeremy issue has dragged on for so long—particularly since you had nothing to do with it. But how are you feeling otherwise? I know you were close to Marta. These last few days must have been terribly difficult for you." Padma's voice almost sounded sincere.

"It wasn't easy," Iain admitted. "But now you know how far I'm willing to go for the Society."

"Your efforts have been appreciated," Padma replied. "You'll be promoted into our upper ranks soon. That's quite an impressive feat for someone who brought only the most basic skills from his previous lives."

"And I know I have you to thank," Iain said with a laugh. "Without your recommendation, I would never have gotten the job."

"We can discuss how you plan to repay me later." Padma was flirting shamelessly. "What did you do with her, anyway?"

"Are you sure you want me to tell you?" Iain asked. "I was under the impression you guys like to know as little as possible."

"You're right, of course. I shouldn't let my curiosity get the best of me. . . ."

The sound of footsteps pulled Haven's attention away from the conversation. Nineteenth Street's sidewalk was empty but for a single young man wearing a crisp white shirt and black pants. His eyes were blank and his posture robotic. A black briefcase hung from his right hand. It was the receptionist from the Ouroboros Society on his way to work. Haven spun around and planted her face in the café's menu, praying she hadn't been spotted. She was certain he couldn't have missed her, but his footsteps never missed a beat, and he passed by without pausing. As soon as the Society drone turned the corner, Haven returned to eavesdropping.

" . . . appreciate it if you would set up a meeting with him," Iain said.

"Is that what this is all about?" Padma pouted. "I was *hoping* you'd asked me to breakfast for the pleasure of my company."

"I did," Iain assured her. "But I didn't think you'd mind a *little* business mixed in with our pleasure."

"As long as it's just a *little* business and a lot of pleasure. Why do you need a meeting?"

"I want more work. I think I've proved that I'm dependable."

"Not to mention ambitious. We like that. But I'm in charge of these things," Padma insisted. "And there's not much to do at the moment now that Marta's gone. Except—"

"Except what?"

"I have a private matter to deal with. I would need someone discreet—and I'd have to pay in points from my personal account. . . ."

As a tattooed waitress approached her table, Haven was pounded by a wave of panic. If she spoke, Iain might hear her. But she wouldn't be allowed to sit at the café without placing an order. Digging through her handbag, she found a slip of paper.

Before the girl could speak, Haven scribbled, *Coffee and the bill, thanks.*

"No problem," chirped the waitress, who was obviously accustomed to dealing with eccentric New Yorkers.

Crisis averted, but her nerves still jangling, Haven picked back up on the conversation.

" . . . who is she?"

"Just a little problem from the past," Padma said dismissively. "I knew she'd turn up someday, but I didn't expect her so soon."

"And you want me take care of her?"

"Eventually. For the moment I'm waiting to see if she might prove useful."

"Useful?" Iain asked.

"There's someone else I need to find. She might know where he is. . . ."

A shadow darkened Haven's table, and she jumped, almost ready to shriek. The two men standing over her table wore gray suits and sunglasses.

"Come with us," one said, reaching for her arm.

"Quietly," said the other.

"Keep your hands off me!" Haven snarled.

"We're here to protect you," the first man insisted.

"Don't make a scene," said the second.

"Let go of me!" Haven wrenched her arm free, knocking over a water glass, which shattered on the concrete.

"What's going on?" Padma was standing at the open window, watching the confusion outside on the sidewalk.

"Too late," the first man murmured.

"That's the girl I was talking about!" Padma looked as if she'd been caught red-handed.

"Nothing to worry about, Ms. Singh," said one of the OS men with an unctuous smile. "You just enjoy your breakfast. We'll take care of this."

Iain pushed Padma out of the way. "Get away from her!" he shouted at the men as he prepared to leap from the window.

Before Iain could reach the sidewalk, the waitress arrived with the coffee, and Haven sprang from her chair and shoved the girl's tray at the gray men. They were still wiping the scalding hot liquid from their faces when Haven tore off down the sidewalk toward a cab that was stopped on the corner of Eighteenth Street. She dove inside just as the two men began closing in on her.

"Drive, drive, drive!" she screamed. The taxi jolted forward through a red light, and Haven was soon making her escape down Second Avenue.

"Oh my God oh my God oh my God!"

"Haven?" Beau answered his phone. "Is that you?"

"Beau! I got it! I can't believe I really got it!"

"Got *what*, Haven?"

"Proof! I just followed Iain to a café, and I overheard him talking to Padma. They murdered Marta Vega."

"Slow down!" Beau ordered. "Who did what?"

"Iain really did kill Marta Vega! He did it just for Society points. I heard him say so himself. Then they started talking about me. I'm next on their list. Padma wants me dead!"

"This isn't good, Haven. What are you going to do?"

"I'm going to call the police and tell them what I know. Hopefully they'll send that bastard to jail for the rest of his life!"

"Yeah, but what are you going to do when you get off the phone?"

Haven hadn't thought that far ahead. "I'll need to hide for a while. They'll have gray men looking everywhere for me," she said, feeling her adrenaline high fading and her nerve slowly draining away. "Now that I think of it, I guess I'm in some serious trouble."

"I figured as much. What you gotta do is find Dr. Tidmore. I've got his number right—"

"What? That's your answer? Have you lost your damn mind?"

"Okay, then find somewhere safe to hide out. A library or a church, maybe. I'm getting in my truck right now. I'll be there before dawn."

## CHAPTER FIFTY-FOUR

Haven was squatting next to an overflowing restaurant trash can, listening to Muzak, and wondering if she'd ever hear the sound of a human voice. She'd been on hold for at least ten minutes when the classical rendition of "I Want a New Drug" cut off mid chorus.

"Detective Flynn."

"Are you the detective in charge of the Marta Vega case?"

"I am. Who's this?"

"A concerned citizen."

The man laughed. "Never heard that one before."

"Marta Vega is dead. I know who killed her."

"Let me guess," Flynn said, his voice swimming in sarcasm. "Iain Morrow."

"You know?"

"Everybody in New York knows that Iain Morrow killed Marta Vega. You're the twenty-third person to call today. Too bad nobody seems to have any proof. What about you, miss? You got any proof?"

"I overheard him talking to a woman named Padma Singh. He—"

"Who is this?" Detective Flynn demanded as if he suddenly suspected he was the butt of a practical joke.

Haven ignored the question. "Iain and Padma are both members of an organization called the Ouroboros Society. So was Marta Vega. I don't know exactly how, but Iain is responsible for her death."

"Who *is* this?" Flynn was angry now.

"Why do you keep asking that? I'm *trying* to help you."

"Listen, whoever you are—you've got your facts wrong."

"I don't! I swear! Iain Morrow and Padma Singh are dangerous."

"You can't go around accusing innocent people of murder. If you call again, I will personally hunt you down and arrest you."

"But Marta—"

"The Ouroboros Society is a respected institution in this town. So stay away from Padma Singh and stop wasting my time."

The line went dead. Haven stared at the phone in her hand, shocked by the conversation that had just transpired. For the first time since she'd escaped from Iain, she began to register just how dire her situation had become. She'd spent the day skulking through the stacks of the Jefferson Market Library, trying to get through to Detective Flynn on the phone. Now it was getting dark, and the library had closed. Haven was hiding in a filthy, rat-infested alley, and she had nowhere left to go. Even the police had turned against her.

On the other side of the street, a hunched-up woman disappeared through the doors of a Catholic church. After a quick search for men in suits or gray sedans with tinted windows, Haven scampered in behind her.

Lit only by the weak evening sunlight that filtered through the stained-glass windows and the candles that flickered in the nave, the church was cool and dark. Five bodies peopled the pews, each of them female and all of them old. Haven chose a seat in the deepest shadows and lowered her head in prayer. Haven's grandmother never missed a chance to bad-mouth a Catholic, and had she seen the girl praying among the ancient Italian ladies, she would have disowned her in a heartbeat. But Haven doubted God shared many of Imogene's opinions. As far as Haven was concerned, there was too much evil in the world to take issue with anyone who was trying to do the right thing.

When Haven lifted her head again, her eyes landed on a stained-glass window that showed Saint Michael battling a winged Satan. She recalled Leah Frizzell's first warning, and she knew the girl had been right. The devil *was* in New York. August Strickland's Society had been transformed into a den of drug dealers and murderers. And there was no longer any doubt that Iain was involved. Haven wished it weren't true. Deep down, she still wanted nothing more than to wake up one morning in the little apartment overlooking the Piazza Navona. But now there was no more hope of that happening. After what she'd heard at the Café Marat, returning to Iain would not only be wrong, it would probably cost her her life.

But Haven knew her heartbreak was nothing compared to what Marta Vega had suffered. The poor girl—murdered by someone she had once considered her friend. Now only the paparazzi seemed interested in finding the killer. How many other disappearances had gone uninvestigated? How many murders had Padma Singh ordered? Dozens? Hundreds? There seemed to be no one able to stop her. Except—

A tall, dark figure emerged from the back of Haven's mind as if he'd been waiting there all along. Adam Rosier. He'd told her to find him if she needed help. Haven had never expected to take him up on the offer, but now she knew that she must. Adam was the only person with the power to stop the killings—and the only person in New York that Haven had no reason to mistrust. If Adam promised to clean up the OS, Haven could give him all the evidence he needed to finally get rid of Padma Singh and send Iain Morrow to prison for good. Adam would do whatever she asked, Haven thought. She knew that he cared, even if she couldn't remember why.

Relieved to have finally arrived at a plan, Haven slid out of her pew and hurried through the church's doors and into the darkness.

HAVEN FOUND THE Ouroboros Society headquarters lit up like a Chinese lantern. Slim silhouettes clutching wineglasses and champagne flutes posed in the windows. She had forgotten the Society was hosting a party. On the top step of the mansion's stoop stood a worker in one of the Society's black-and-white uniforms. As Haven watched from the shadows, the drone opened the doors for a succession of elegant guests, many of whom looked uncannily familiar. They were all too perfectly polished or undoubtedly distinguished to be ordinary mortals. When one of the women stopped on the stairs to greet an acquaintance, Haven recognized her as the peppy host of Mae Moore's favorite afternoon talk show. The woman's acquaintance looked a great deal like a former secretary of state.

Haven decided to stay in the shadows. She couldn't search for Adam while the party was on. Padma was certain to be there. Haven would have to wait in the park until it was over. It wasn't the most appealing prospect. In the dark, it was impossible to tell what the trees might be hiding in between their branches, and the statue in the center of the park seemed more plotting than pensive. The sky rumbled, and Haven prayed that the weather would continue to hold.

As soon as the street was quiet once more, Haven studied the fence around Gramercy Park, searching for the best place to climb in. She settled on a spot next to a low-hanging tree, grasped one of the metal bars, and began to pull herself up.

"Haven Moore? Is that you?"

Haven lost her grip and tumbled to the sidewalk. She looked up to find a tall silver-haired man peering down at her through wire-framed glasses.

"Dr. Tidmore? What are you doing here?"

"Your mother asked me to come. She said the Ouroboros Society might be the best place to find you."

## CHAPTER FIFTY-FIVE

A fat drop of rain hit Haven on the nose. When she glanced up at the sky, a second drop landed in the middle of her forehead. The trees in Gramercy Park swayed and shook as the wind rushed into the square from every direction. A bolt of lightning illuminated the preacher's pale face, and the thunder that followed closely behind told Haven the storm was quickly approaching.

Two elegant ladies dressed in full-length gowns glided past at top speed, their silk garments already speckled with raindrops. Haven knew both of their faces from her mother's gossip magazines, and she wished Beau were there to supply the names.

"What do you say? This looks like a good enough place for a chat," Dr. Tidmore remarked, pointing up at the brightly lit windows of the Gramercy Park Historical Society. "It's probably nice and quiet this time of night."

Haven's eyes passed from the preacher to the building and back again. "It's open?"

Dr. Tidmore climbed the stairs and twisted the knob on the front door. "The sign here says it's open till ten." He stopped with his body half in and half out of the building. Haven hadn't budged. "Are you coming or not?" he inquired impatiently.

As the rain began to fall harder and faster, Haven charged up the stoop. As little as she fancied Dr. Tidmore's company, she needed a place to take shelter from the storm.

INSIDE THE HISTORICAL SOCIETY, the same woman wearing horn-rimmed glasses was dusting again, and Haven wondered why she would choose to do chores in such an expensive-looking dress. She greeted her guests with a curt nod as they walked past her and took the stairs to the second floor. When Haven reached the reading room, she was glad to find it lit by a raging fire. It might have been a warm summer night outside, but the atmosphere in the room felt chilly and damp.

"Why don't we sit here for a moment?" Dr. Tidmore suggested, pointing toward the pair of chairs planted a few feet from the fireplace. Haven gazed into the flames. "The fire won't bring back bad memories, will it?" Dr. Tidmore asked.

"No," Haven told him. She settled into the chair and felt the fatigue wash over her.

Dr. Tidmore sat and leaned forward with his elbows on his knees, trying to make the chat seem informal. Instead it felt even more awkward. "Your grandmother is very upset that you've run away."

Haven shook her head wearily. "You know how Imogene exaggerates. If I'd really run away, I wouldn't have been so easy to find."

"Point taken." The preacher exposed too many teeth when he smiled. "She and your mother say they saw a picture of you in a magazine. With a boy."

Haven stared at Dr. Tidmore as her scalp started to tingle.

"So you think you've found him?" the man asked a little too eagerly.

"Found who?"

"Ethan. Isn't he the young man in the photograph? I believe his new name is Iain Morrow? Isn't that what the magazine said?"

"I thought you didn't believe in reincarnation, Dr. Tidmore." Haven tried to keep her temper in check but didn't succeed. Her voice rose with each word. "I thought the whole idea was the devil's work. Isn't that what you preached in your sermon?"

The force of Haven's fury pushed Tidmore back in his chair. "There's no need to be hostile, Haven. Can't you see that I'm trying to help you?"

"The way you helped me back in Tennessee? By turning the whole town against me? Why *are* you here, anyway?"

"I was visiting some friends outside the city." A log in the fireplace collapsed, drawing Dr. Tidmore's eye with a shower of embers. "Your grandmother called and asked me to bring you home. She's afraid that your virtue might no longer be intact."

"My virtue is none of her damn business, and it's *certainly* none of yours!" Haven spit. "And I'm not going back with you. Beau Decker is coming to get me. He'll be here by tomorrow morning."

"And then you'll be leaving?"

"Yes, and then I'll be leaving."

Dr. Tidmore faked another smile and tried a different approach. "So have you spent much time with the folks at the Ouroboros Society while you've been in New York?"

"Not really."

"No? I read up on it a little after I heard about it. Sounds like a fascinating organization. They might be the perfect people to help a young girl get settled in the city. I could talk to your grandmother, if you'd like."

Haven didn't know what to make of the offer. "No offense, Dr. Tidmore, but I've already made up my mind. And I'd rather not have you doing me any more favors."

Tidmore laughed. "I can't say that I blame you. But I'm afraid I won't let you go back to Tennessee with Beau. Now that you're finally here, Adam would like you to stay in New York."

"Adam?" Haven asked. The heat from the fire had grown far too intense. It was as if her feet had been set directly on the coals.

"Adam Rosier," Tidmore said. "I believe you two have met."

*Below in the darkness, the paths of Central Park were outlined with tiny, glowing orbs. Constance leaned against the terrace railing, tracing the paths' twists and turns with her eyes. In three days their ship would sail for Italy. Until then, she was stuck at the Andorra with the loathsome Elizabeth and Bernard Whitman. Her parents had wasted no time in presenting her with a replacement for Ethan. He was rich, handsome, and impeccably turned out. They didn't even seem to mind that he'd recently been appointed president of the Ouroboros Society. Throughout dinner he had flattered her mother and charmed her father—all without taking his eyes off Constance. Before she had met Ethan, she might have fallen for him. Now she just wanted him to leave.*

*"Are you cold, Constance? Would you like my jacket?" He had discovered her out on the terrace.*

*She smiled but didn't turn to face him. "No, thank you."*

*"Your thoughts are elsewhere tonight."*

*"I'm sorry. . . ."*

*"Don't be. I know these past weeks have been difficult for you. It must be painful to learn that the person you love isn't quite the man you expected him to be."*

*She said nothing. It was best to let them all believe.*

*"If you'll give me a chance, I would like nothing better than to help you forget."*

*"That's kind of you, but I don't know how much longer I'll be in New York," Constance said.*

*He wasn't pleased by her answer. "Oh? Are you planning a trip?" he asked curtly.*

*"More than a trip." It would have been cruel to encourage his hopes.*

*"With him?"*

*She let the silence speak for itself.*

*"Don't leave." His voice was soothing, hard to resist. "You belong here with me. Please, Constance. I can't lose you again."*

*She turned to face him. "How can you say that? You barely know me." As soon as the words left her lips, she knew they weren't true. The dark eyes and hair were suddenly familiar, as if they had just come into focus.*

*"I've loved you for centuries. I've followed you across oceans and continents. Whatever you want, you can have it if you'll only agree to be mine."*

*"I can't, Adam. You know I love someone else."*

*"Even after everything that's happened ?"*

*"Yes."*

*"He's not good enough for you, Constance. He'll never love you the way I do."*

HAVEN EMERGED FROM the vision with her heart pounding. She knew the man Constance had been speaking to on the terrace. Adam Rosier hadn't aged a day in ninety years. She pulled herself up and discovered she was on a couch in a deserted room. Her feet were bare, and she searched for her shoes. They were missing, along with her handbag. As the panic set in, she rushed for the door. The knob wouldn't turn. She yanked open the curtains to find the windows sealed shut. The sky was dark, and the moon hadn't risen. Black clouds loomed overhead, rumbling as they pelted the city with rain. She recognized the park below. She was on the top floor of the Gramercy Park Historical Society.

She needed to find a way to call for help. With panic building inside of her, Haven grabbed a silver picture frame from a nearby desk and hurled it, hoping to break a window. Instead, the frame bounced off the shatterproof glass and landed faceup on the floor. The photo inside showed Constance sitting on a bench inside Gramercy Park, an uneasy smile on her face. The features of the man beside her were a blur.

Spinning around, Haven searched for something—anything—that might help set her free. Then she stopped. What she saw made it perfectly clear that there would be no way out. Two of the room's walls were decorated with ancient, hand-painted frescoes of flowering meadows. Three wooden wardrobes showcased rows of beautiful gowns. Some were Constance's dresses—most likely the ones stolen from Frances Whitman. Others appeared to belong to earlier eras. To her horror, Haven realized she knew all of them. She'd sewn each gown with her very own fingers, and she had worn them in lives she had yet to remember. Haven reached out to touch the sleeve of a green velvet dress that had to be at least five hundred years old, but it crumbled the moment her fingers brushed against it. A fine powder drifted down to the floor.

Much of Adam Rosier's bizarre museum appeared to be suffering a similar fate. Little piles of dust had gathered wherever Haven looked, and on the shelves of a large cabinet at the far end of the room, half-burned items from Constance's home were displayed like treasure. Upon closer inspection, nothing in the room had made it to the twenty-first century in pristine condition. Everything was falling apart.

A morbid fascination took the place of terror as Haven toured Adam's collection. She examined every item but touched nothing until she found herself standing in front of the cabinet. The six drawers on the bottom were wide and deep. It took all her strength to pull the first one open. When she examined the contents, she wished she'd resisted the temptation. Inside lay a skeleton in a moth-eaten gown. The five remaining drawers were similarly filled, though some of the bodies looked fresher than others. Haven didn't need to be told who they were. The bodies belonged to the women who had worn the dresses Adam had collected. This was how Haven had ended at least six of her lives.

## CHAPTER FIFTY-SIX

Haven stared at the door as she waited. Inside the sealed room, the silence was absolute. It felt as if the world had stopped. Discarded objects formed a small pile beside her on the sofa. There was a slightly charred statue of a reclining nude, an empty perfume bottle, and a T-strap shoe. Haven had considered using each as a weapon before abandoning her escape plans altogether. The person who had imprisoned her had conquered time. She doubted if a shoe could do him much damage. In fact, she was beginning to doubt that he was a person at all.

A key scraped inside the lock, and Haven bravely rose to greet her captor. But her guest wasn't Adam Rosier. A woman in a stunning white gown floated through the door and closed it gently behind her. Padma's regal nose was swollen, and her mascara dripped down her cheeks. The arrogant president of the Ouroboros Society had disintegrated into a terrified, sniveling mess.

"Shh!" she implored. "No one knows I'm here. I need to talk to you before Adam has a chance to leave the party."

"You have to let me out," Haven insisted.

"I can't do that," Padma said. "There are gray men everywhere tonight. You wouldn't get very far."

"Then tell the woman who works here to call the police. Tell her I'm being held against my will."

"The woman who works here?" Padma repeated as if she hadn't understood. "You're talking about Belinda? The one with the glasses? My dear, she's a drone. She takes her orders from Adam."

"But this is the Gramercy Park Historical Society. I came here—"

"There's no such thing as the *Gramercy Park Historical Society.*" Even in her frazzled state, Padma couldn't help but sneer. "This building is owned by the Ouroboros Society. Adam uses it to meet with some of our more prominent members—the ones who'd rather not sit in a waiting room with a bunch of screaming brats."

"He invented the Historical Society just to trick me?"

"Yes," Padma confirmed. "He's used the same scam before, but believe me—that's just the beginning of what he can do."

"Who is he? *What* is he?"

"I don't know what he is," Padma said. "Adam's been around as long as I can remember. I've known him in several lives. He never ages, he never changes, and he never stops looking for you."

"Me? Why *me*?" Haven asked.

Padma gave her a brisk once-over. "I've wondered the same thing myself. I can't quite understand the attraction. Adam could have anyone. Perhaps that's it. Perhaps you're the only thing he can't control. If he knew I was here . . ."

Haven had tired of Padma's veiled insults. "Why *are* you here?" she demanded.

"You were at Café Marat this morning. Were you eavesdropping on my conversation?"

"I know you hired Iain to kill Marta Vega. Is that what you're asking?"

"No, Adam ordered *that* himself," Padma said dismissively. "You're surprised?" she added when she saw Haven's face. "How can you *possibly* be surprised?"

"Why would Adam want Marta dead?"

"Her *art*," Padma said as if it should have been obvious to all but a simpleton. "Adam doesn't like having his portrait painted."

"That was *Adam* in all of Marta's paintings? The little man making all the terrible things happen?"

"He gets around, doesn't he? What else did you hear this morning?"

"I know you were going to ask Iain to kill me as well. Do you really want me out of the way that badly?"

Padma's expression suddenly sweetened. She reached out her hand to touch Haven's arm, but the girl shook it off. "You of all people should understand," Padma said. "When I discovered Ethan was back, I went a little crazy. The thought of spending another century alone . . . it was simply too painful. But I doubt I would have gone through with the plan. I'm many things, but I'm not a killer."

"You sounded pretty cold-blooded to me," Haven said. "There's no doubt in my mind you were completely serious."

The sweetness soured, and Padma grimaced. "Don't tell Adam," she begged. "Please. He was furious that I even suggested you leave New York. If he had any idea . . ."

"What about Iain?" Haven demanded. "They know who he is, don't they? What have they done with him?"

"It's too late for Iain." Padma paced the length of the room, wringing her hands. "I should have realized that Adam was trying to get rid of him. That woman in Los Angeles who said she saw Iain kill Jeremy Johns was clearly a drone. Adam was using her to get your boyfriend out of the way. If only you'd told me who Iain was when you had the chance, I might have been able to protect him. But now I've lost him for another lifetime."

Haven felt her knees begin to buckle. "He's dead?" she managed to ask.

"Not yet, but they have him. The gray men took Iain right after you ran away from the café. Even if it weren't for you, Adam couldn't allow him to live. Iain knows too much. He's a danger to the Society. And other than you, the Society is the only thing Adam cares about."

"So you're just going to sit back and let Adam Rosier kill the person you love."

"What else can I do?" Padma wailed miserably. "Everything I have I owe to Adam, and if I betray him, he'll take it all away. You're lucky you only remember one of your past lives. I've been poor and miserable so many times. I can't go back to living like that again."

"Then you never loved Ethan," Haven said. "If you had, the money would mean nothing to you."

"You're judging *me*?" Padma's lip curled into a snarl. "It's not my fault that Iain's going to die. If you hadn't been so selfish, he could have lived happily with me. And you could have been a queen. Adam would have given you anything you wanted. Now you're going to stay locked up in this room for the next sixty years. Then you'll die, too, and it's just going to start all over again."

"Iain's not going to die," Haven told her.

"And how do *you* plan to save him?"

"I'm not. You are. As soon as you leave here, you're going to make the phone call that saves Iain's life."

"I hope you aren't expecting me to call the police," Padma said. "Adam has men at the top. They're everywhere. Not just in the NYPD—in the mayor's office, the governor's cabinet, D.C. No one is going to interfere with the Society."

Haven took an old eyeliner pencil from Adam's collection and scribbled ten digits on a white silk handkerchief that bore Constance's initials. "If you want me to keep your secret, then call this number. Tell the person who answers where to find me."

## CHAPTER FIFTY-SEVEN

It was late in the evening when he finally arrived. Darkly handsome and debonair in a perfectly cut tuxedo, he could have been a character in a Jazz Age silent film. The slight blurriness of his features only added to the effect. He almost seemed to flicker, Haven observed, as if he were composed of pixels instead of flesh and blood.

"Hello, Haven." He was always so polite, so perfectly proper.

"Adam."

"May I have a seat?"

Haven shrugged. "Go ahead. It's your building. I'm just trapped here for the rest of my life. I see it's not the first time, either." She gestured toward the skeleton-filled drawers.

Adam sat beside her on the sofa, and Haven felt a chill penetrate her skin. "I *am* sorry," he said. "I was hoping it wouldn't come to this. But if locking you in here is the only way to keep you near me, then I have no other choice. It's been too long. And I've been so lonely."

"Locking me away didn't work before," Haven pointed out. She almost felt sorry for him. She knew the misery love could bring. "Isn't that what started all of this?"

"You remember our life on Crete?" Adam's voice was wistful. "It was all so perfect then, wasn't it? I didn't want anything to change. I tried to protect what we had, but, as you know, I failed horribly."

"Yet you're willing to try the same thing again? Imprisoning me and hoping I'll love you?"

Adam's dark eyes circled the room before they returned to rest on Haven's face. "This isn't what I had in mind. I hoped only to win you over and convince you to be mine. I adore you, Haven, and I don't enjoy holding you against your will. When I do, it's an act of sheer desperation. Sometimes the need to be near you grows too strong, and I'm unable to resist it.

"I was looking forward to spending decades together with you. I came so close to breaking the cycle with Constance, and I was certain we would have this life together. Yet my plans have fallen apart once more. You know too much to ever care for me this time around. But now that I have you, I'd rather not let you go."

"What do you mean, you were close to 'breaking the cycle' with Constance?" Haven asked.

"If I can make you stop loving him in just one lifetime, you'll never find him again. The connection will be broken, and you'll belong only to me."

"Is it really that easy?" Haven wondered.

Adam's laugh was bitter. "On the contrary, it hasn't been easy at all. I took great pains to frame Ethan Evans for August Strickland's death. It was terribly complicated, you know. I had to kill the old man, forge his will, start the rumors. Do you see how far I'm willing to go for you? And it almost worked. Particularly after I recruited Rebecca. I almost turned you against him for good."

Adam spoke as if it were all just a game. The pity Haven had started to feel for him withered and died.

"You killed Dr. Strickland?"

"He would have died eventually, anyway," Adam said as if stating a simple fact. "A few extra years are nothing in the scheme of things. I'm sure he's back by now, starting his own little utopia in France or Rwanda."

"Did you kill Constance, too?"

"Absolutely not!" Rosier was aghast. "Your lives may be short by my standards, but even a week away from you makes me suffer. Can't you see that? Can't you see that I'm dedicated to protecting you? In this life, I've been watching over you since you were nine years old—since I found you!"

Haven shuddered. "You've been watching me for the past *eight* years?" Even the notion made her feel polluted.

"Watching *over* you," Adam corrected Haven as he slid toward her on the sofa. "I've had people keeping you safe since the day your father first contacted the Ouroboros Society. Of course, I couldn't always be by your side, but I did visit a number of times. When your sixth-grade science teacher had a nervous breakdown, I was your substitute teacher for three days. I was at your father's store the day he hired Veronica Cabe. I helped your grandmother choose the books to be banned at the Snope City library. But mostly I relied on the reports filed by Tidmore."

"Tidmore works for you, then?" It was starting to make sense.

"Tidmore volunteers his services. He's been a loyal member of the Society for quite a few years now. I sent him to Snope City shortly after we received your father's letter. He was supposed to help you forget the past. Of course, we had to deal with your father before that could happen. He kept recording every word that came out of your sweet little mouth. I thought you deserved a fresh start, Haven. No one should be saddled with centuries of memories. I know too well what that's like. Once you were old enough, you would have come to New York, and I would have given you the life you've always dreamed of."

Adam reached out a long, pale hand and let it brush Haven's thigh. Haven flinched and moved out of reach.

"You had to *deal* with my father? What did you do to him?"

Adam's expression was empty. "*I* didn't do anything. I simply gave Tidmore permission to do what he felt was necessary. He recruited Veronica Cabe to break your parents apart, hoping your father would leave. But when your father didn't take the bait, Tidmore was forced to arrange the accident. Placing Veronica's body in the passenger's seat was a particularly nice touch, I thought."

"The accident was staged? My father never cheated on my mother?" Haven thought of the suffering her mother had endured. Haven's father might have been the one who died, but Mae Moore had been tortured for eight long years.

"No, though it would have been easier for everyone if he had. I wanted you to have a perfect childhood. I'm sorry it turned out to be less than ideal." Adam's hand was inching across the sofa toward Haven again. The skin beneath his perfectly manicured nails was a lifeless blue.

"Less than ideal? You killed my father and let me be raised by an evil old woman who told everyone that I was possessed. You call that *less than ideal*?"

"It was all for your own good, don't you see?" Adam seemed incapable of understanding what he had done wrong. "And for a while everything went almost exactly as planned. But then your visions returned, and I knew you were being drawn to Ethan as you are in each lifetime. Tidmore and I did everything possible to keep you safe in Snope City until we could find him. But Tidmore could tell you were determined to leave. That's when he suggested the fire. Though if I had known how dangerous it would be, I never would have approved. I want you to know, Haven, that the drone responsible has been severely reprimanded. He should never have left you alone in a burning building." Adam was creeping toward her again. Haven caught a whiff of dampness and decay.

"You set the fire in my grandmother's house?" Even after everything she'd heard, the information still took Haven by surprise.

"We had to do *something* to keep you in Tennessee," Adam explained. "Tidmore thought you'd be safest if you spent a few months under lock and key. We would have secured your freedom once we'd dealt with Ethan. But then you ran away from Snope City, and we lost track of you once you reached New York. I was worried I'd never find you again until you showed up in the waiting room of Ouroboros Society. I had no idea where you'd been before I saw the photo of you and Iain Morrow together in Rome."

"So you've known about Iain for days then? You've murdered at least three people to get to me. Why didn't you just kill *him* when you found out who he was?"

"What good would killing Iain have done?" Adam asked. "The cycle would merely have started all over again. It was better to convince you that he wasn't worth loving and have him sent to jail."

"So you invented the Gramercy Park Historical Society to make Ethan look like a murderer and tried to frame Iain for Jeremy Johns's death? Did you really think tricking me would win me over?"

Haven felt Adam's icy fingers finally make contact with her thigh, and she jumped up from the sofa to escape them.

"I did what I had to do! He's not good enough for you!" Adam insisted, his frustration growing. "I'm the only one you can truly trust! He was my *servant* in Crete and he betrayed me. I couldn't bear to see him do the same to you. I always suspected he wasn't the white knight he pretends to be. Now at last I have the proof I needed, but it's come too late for this lifetime."

"What *proof*? You framed him for Jeremy's death."

"Yes, but I didn't frame him for Marta Vega's. He took the initiative himself. He said he wanted to improve his standing in the Society. Perhaps he thought it might erase any suspicions I might have had about his identity. Whatever the case, he practically begged for the job."

"A job you ordered."

"A job he chose to take."

It was true. Haven couldn't deny it. "So none of this would have happened if my father hadn't sent that e-mail to the OS?" she asked as she circled the room. It was still hard to believe that everything had started with one simple act. "My grandmother's house would never have burned? My father and Veronica would still be alive?"

"Perhaps. It's impossible to know," Rosier told her. "But one thing's for certain. You would have made it to New York one way or another. This is your destiny. That's why I stayed at the Society. I knew it would draw you back to the city, and I planned to be here when it did. Of course, the past ninety years haven't been a complete waste. I understood the Society's potential the first moment I heard of it. Strickland brought together the country's best and brightest. People who, through some great accident, had been born with knowledge and skills they'd accumulated over the course of many lifetimes. Strickland saw the good that such people could do for the world. I, of course, saw something quite different."

Adam rose from the sofa and walked over to where Haven stood. He was slowly chasing her, Haven thought with a shudder. She didn't want to think about what would happen when he caught her.

"So you're the one who destroyed Dr. Strickland's Society? Not Padma?"

"Padma let things get a little out of control. I'm not terribly interested in the drug dealers or prostitutes, Haven. They're merely necessary evils. In the past nine decades, I've taken people who could be enriching the world or saving lives and trained them to focus on their own petty needs. Doctors who could be finding cures for terrible diseases now earn fortunes crafting noses for Hollywood actresses. Photographers who could be documenting injustices instead sell pretty pictures to tasteless moguls. I teach promising politicians how to line their own pockets. I encourage talented writers to spin out trite bestsellers."

Rosier was almost glowing with excitement. He seemed to have momentarily forgotten his pursuit of Haven.

"The secret of the system is to keep people focused on a number," he continued with pride. "Members watch their account balances rise and they watch them fall, and soon even the most charitable refuse to do anything for free. Everyone wants to know what he or she will get in return. It's chaos. Anarchy. Every man for himself."

"Why?" Haven asked. "Why take an organization that was meant to help people and destroy it?"

"That's what I *do*," Rosier said as if no other explanation were necessary.

"Marta Vega said you make things fall apart."

"She was right. But I don't think she understood. I'm a critical part of the system. Imagine that the world was allowed to reach perfection. One day you wake up and everyone on earth is content. Do you know what that would be like?"

"Wonderful?" Haven offered.

"*Terrible*," Adam corrected her, moving closer. "The world would be static. Nothing would ever change. Happiness is dull, Haven. All the most powerful emotions come from chaos—fear, anger, love—especially love. Love is chaos itself. Think about it! Love makes no sense. It shakes you up and spins you around. And then, eventually, it falls apart."

"I don't believe that," Haven said. "I don't believe it always falls apart."

"That's hope speaking," Adam said. He was near her now. Close enough to kiss. "I've suffered from it myself. I spent centuries hoping that one day I could convince you to stay with me forever. Even though there was no reason to believe that I would. But everyone has a weakness. I know, because it's my job to find them. Apparently, you're mine." His hands gripped Haven's shoulders and pulled her to him. She could feel his icy breath on the nape of her neck. "Don't you see?" he whispered. "I'm the only one you can trust. One day his love would have dimmed or died. Mine is eternal."

Haven's mind was growing hazier. She wouldn't be able to resist him for long. She used her last ounce of will power to lean back, away from his kiss. "Adam?"

"Yes?" he replied.

"Are you the devil?"

Adam smiled placidly. "Do you see any horns or a tail?"

"That's not an answer. We both know the horns are a myth."

"I'm afraid the answer isn't as simple as you'd like it to be," Adam said. "I've been called many things. But I suppose 'the devil' is as good a name as any."

## CHAPTER FIFTY-EIGHT

There was a knock from the hallway, and Adam Rosier scowled. It was the first time Haven had seen any hint of surprise on his face. He released Haven from his embrace and unlocked the door.

"What are you doing?" he snapped at the person on the other side. "I thought I told you to never set foot on this floor."

"I'm so sorry!" The trembling voice belonged to the woman from downstairs. "There are men outside, and one of them said there would be trouble if I didn't bring him to you."

"Bring *who*, Belinda?"

"Me," replied someone with a thick Southern drawl.

"Ah, yes," Adam said with a resigned sigh. "The wild card. I should have known. As long as you're here, you might as well come in."

"Do we know each other?" Beau asked as Adam stood aside to let him enter.

"Unfortunately," Adam said.

"Beau!" Haven ran to the sopping wet boy in a John Deere hat and jeans and threw her arms around his neck. "Thank God you're here."

"Apparently Tidmore wasn't as successful as he thought," Adam grumbled.

Haven let go of Beau and turned to confront Rosier. "Successful at what?"

"Keeping this nuisance out of my hair. Why didn't you listen to your preacher and stay in Tennessee, Mr. Decker?"

"Beau?" Haven asked. "What's he talking about?"

Beau was too stunned to answer. "Who *is* this guy?" he asked Haven.

"We were just discussing that very question," Rosier said. "You can call me the devil if you like. Didn't Tidmore tell you we'd meet if you left safe little Snope City? Now here I am, waiting to drag you down to hell, just like he promised."

"Beau?" Haven tried again.

Beau glared at the man in the tuxedo. "Dr. Tidmore told me that God wouldn't punish me for being gay as long as I never acted on it. He said it was my cross to bear, and that as long as I kept myself away from temptation, I'd be fine. There wasn't any temptation in Snope City, so that's why I thought it might be best to stay put."

"You listened to Dr. Tidmore?" Haven cried. "You hated him!"

"That didn't make him any less convincing," Beau said.

"God isn't interested in your pathetic love life, Mr. Decker," Rosier said. "But believe it or not, Tidmore was doing you a favor by keeping you in Snope City. Now that you're here, you'll have to deal with *me*."

Beau ignored him. "Wait a second. Is this joker really the *devil*?" he asked Haven.

"I think so," Haven told him.

"Belinda!" Adam called out to the woman waiting on the landing. "Will you send someone up to get Mr. Decker? He's beginning to bore me."

"Hold on, Beelzebub," Beau told him. "Maybe you should take a look outside."

Adam and Haven walked to the windows. Beneath the streetlights, a crowd of men in yellow rain ponchos had swarmed the sidewalk.

"Who are they?" Haven wondered.

"Paparazzi," Beau explained. "I was searching for you at the Washington Mews when that woman called. She said not to bother with the police, so I figured these guys were the best backup available."

"What difference can a bunch of photographers make?" Rosier sneered. "Most of them look as though they're a hamburger away from a heart attack."

"Well, let's see," Beau said. "I told my new friends downstairs that Iain Morrow's girlfriend was locked up inside here. I said I was going to go get her, and that if anything happened to either of us, they'd have the story of a lifetime. They're down there waiting for us to come out. They'll wait forever if they need to. And they'll probably take lots of pictures once they sense something's up. I don't suppose you want the publicity, do you?"

It seemed like forever before anyone spoke.

"It's me or the Society, Adam," Haven finally said. "Take your pick."

"Don't be ridiculous, my love. I don't have to *choose*." Adam Rosier sat down on the sofa and motioned toward the exit. "You're both free to leave."

Beau and Haven shared a glance. Neither had expected their escape to be quite so easy.

"Go ahead," Adam urged Haven. "Take this opportunity to say goodbye to your friends and family. Find Iain if you're able. I don't mind. Now that Marta's dead, you'll discover it's over between you. So enjoy yourself. When I'm ready, I'll find you. I promise. I have men all over the city—all over the *world*. There's no place you can hide. I'll miss you terribly while you're gone. But I've waited this long to have you—I can wait a little longer."

"I got an idea. Why don't you try holding your breath while you wait?" Beau suggested.

"My dear Mr. Decker, I think you underestimate just how long I can hold my breath," Adam replied.

"Come on," Beau said as he grabbed Haven's hand. "It's time to take Lucifer up on his offer." Together they flew down the stairs, past the woman in the horn-rimmed glasses, who stood like a statue on the landing. When they reached the front door of the mansion, Beau paused with his fingers clutching the doorknob.

"I parked my truck on Lexington Avenue," he said. "We're going to have to make a run for it unless you want to stick around and make small talk with the paparazzi. By the way, you got any ideas about where you want to go? I'm guessing home is out of the question for the moment. But we should probably get you some shoes."

Haven looked down at her bare feet. "We have to save Iain before we go anywhere."

"The same Iain who killed Marta Vega and was thinking about killing you?" Beau stared at her as if she'd lost her mind. "You want to tell me how that makes any sense?"

"It doesn't," Haven admitted. All she knew was that she couldn't bear to live in a world without Iain. The need to be near him hadn't disappeared. "But I have to do it, anyway."

"Well, if you insist." Beau turned the doorknob. "I've already come face-to-face with the devil today. How much worse could it get? You ready for a little run?"

"Ready."

Haven and Beau burst out of the building, and the sky lit up with the flash of cameras. They tore through the crowd and around the park. Some of the paparazzi gave chase, holding their cameras out in front of them and snapping pictures as they ran.

"Stop!" someone yelled.

"Is that the *maid*?"

"You lying hillbilly!" another shouted.

"Where's your boyfriend?" screamed a third.

One by one, the men in yellow ponchos fell out of the race until the only people behind Haven and Beau were two men in gray summer-weight suits. A truck crossing Lexington Avenue pulled out in front of their pursuers, and Haven and Beau ducked into the only open business on the block. The basement shop was filled with tall baskets of brightly colored Indian spices. A teenage girl behind the counter looked up to find a giant boy and a barefoot girl, their clothes dripping and their hair plastered to their heads.

"There are men after us," Haven panted.

The girl asked no questions. "Here." She lifted a panel of sari fabric that decorated the wall behind the counter. Haven and Beau hurried into the small, concealed storage space and waited inside with their knees tucked to their chests.

The chimes over the door rang.

"Yes, can I help you?" they heard the shopgirl ask.

"Have you seen a girl? Seventeen years old? Barefoot?"

"Barefoot?" the shopgirl scoffed. "This is a food store. Shoes and shirts are required. Are you trying to trick me, sir? Are you with the health department?"

"Yes. The health department. I'm going to need to take a look around."

"Be my guest. But you will find no health-code violations here. My parents run a very clean shop." The girl was trailing behind the man as he stomped around the store. "The bathroom is cleaned twice a day. The floors are mopped every evening at seven. If you're sniffing around for mouse feces, you will not find any, sir. And you will find no bugs crawling our walls. This store has been open for twenty-two years, and we have never had a single cockroach. In fact, we do not welcome animals of any variety, sir. No dogs, no cats, no birds, no monkeys, no—"

"Okay, okay," the man growled impatiently. "Inspection over. You pass."

Haven and Beau heard the door chimes and waited a few seconds before sliding out of their hiding space.

"That was amazing," Beau told the girl. "You saved us."

"My parents say I was an actress in my last life," the girl said. "That man was from the Ouroboros Society, wasn't he?"

"What? You know—" Haven sputtered.

"Not now. Come back when you have time to talk." The girl smiled and handed Haven a pair of cheap plastic flip-flops. "These are compliments of the house. Is there anything else I can do for you this evening?"

"You wouldn't happen to have an umbrella, would you?" asked Beau.

## CHAPTER FIFTY-NINE

A single streetlight stood beneath the Brooklyn Bridge overpass, casting a sickly yellow glow over the little brick building at the end of Water Street. The rain had turned into a downpour, and the city was deserted. Even the rats had given up and gone home for the night. Haven and Beau stood across the street from the house and silently watched. Inside, there were no signs of life.

"That's the one," Haven said. She knew Iain was in there. She could feel his presence the way she could feel her own heart beating inside her chest.

"Are you sure?" Beau whispered. "It looks totally abandoned."

"I'm sure," Haven confirmed. "I followed Padma here once. Rebecca, too. That's Adam's building."

She led the charge across the cobblestones. A clogged gutter had created a swirling moat along the curb, and at the corner a whirlpool churned a mixture of cigarette butts and plastic grocery bags. Haven trudged through the fetid water in her flip-flops. When she reached the front door, she found it unlocked.

"Great security," Beau remarked as they stepped inside, out of the rain.

"I don't think he needs it," Haven pointed out. "Nobody's going to steal from Adam. Besides, what's there to take?"

The bottom floor of the house was completely empty. There was no furniture—not even a single appliance. A saloon-style bar had once run the length of the room, but it had been ripped out and removed. All that was left behind were the scars in the plaster. The rain tapped on the windows, and a cool draft stirred the scraps of trash and leaves that had collected in every corner.

A piece of paper caught Beau's eye, and he bent down to grab it off the floor. He straightened out the scrap and showed it to Haven. It was a newspaper clipping from 1963 describing the assassination of Lee Harvey Oswald. "I think we've got the wrong house," Beau announced. "Nobody's lived here for ages."

"No, this is the place," Haven insisted. "Let's try upstairs."

The second floor was equally barren. Beau flung open every door and searched every closet, but there was still no sign of Iain. When they climbed the stairs to the third floor, they found the first sign of habitation—a large room furnished with a single black lounge chair. Paintings covered every inch of the walls. They were crooked, overlapping, on top of each other, as if hung in a hurry by a madman. Christians were shown being fed to the lions, atom bombs detonated, gangs fought, and children were snatched away from their parents. And all of the works featured the same small figure watching in the distance.

"Now that's pretty damn creepy," Beau marveled.

"These are Marta Vega's paintings. Adam must have stolen them after her show. He's in all of them, you know." Haven pointed to the little man in one of the scenes. He was standing in the middle of a rowdy crowd, watching a public hanging. "I guess Adam likes to admire his own handiwork."

"There's no accounting for taste, now is there?" Beau said in a failed attempt at humor. Despite his bravado there was an unexpected tremor in his voice. It was finally sinking in that he'd come terribly close to leaving a handsome young corpse. "Well, that's it, Haven. We've looked everywhere, and right about now I'm thinking we should get the hell out of this place while we still have a chance."

"No." Haven refused. "Iain's here. I'm sure of it. It doesn't look like there's an attic, so there must be a cellar or a basement in the building."

Haven hurried back down the stairs. She could feel time slipping away. An army of gray men might arrive at any moment. Then Iain and Beau would die, and she'd end up a permanent exhibit in Rosier's museum. Haven rushed from room to room on the main floor, searching them more thoroughly than before. Around the corner from where the bar had once been, Haven found a door leading to a set of wooden stairs that descended into darkness.

"You didn't bring a flashlight, did you?" Beau asked.

"Nope."

"And you're still sure you want to do all this for someone who was willing to kill you?"

"Yep." There wasn't a doubt in Haven's mind.

"All right, then," Beau said, as if he had no option but to follow her. "Let's do it."

When the stairs came to an end, Haven felt around her in the darkness. To her left and right were walls. Walking forward slowly, she trailed her hand across the ragged bricks until her fingertips began to lose all sensation. Something crunched as her flip-flops met the floor.

"How long *is* this tunnel?" Beau whispered after they'd been walking through the darkness for the longest five minutes of their lives. "I'm pretty sure we've gone halfway to hell."

"Shhh," Haven replied. One of the walls had come to a sudden end, and another tunnel branched off to the right. At the end, a rectangle of light appeared etched in the wall.

Beyond the door, they entered what looked like a theater. In the center, a giant pit had been carved out of the Manhattan bedrock. Stands of wooden seats circled the hole. Haven sensed that terrible things had once taken place there, but now the pit was filled with a strange assortment of objects that had all been tossed inside. Staring up at Haven was the face of a wooden saint, which must have been ripped from the walls of a demolished church. She spotted an airplane life jacket, a gnarled car fender, and a skeletal hand. Rats dove and surfaced in the sea of junk, and the smell in the room suggested that there was plenty of food for them in the pit. A few were gnawing at a figure on top of the pile, rolled in a rug and wrapped with ropes.

Haven knew in an instant what they'd found. The pit was filled with Adam's trophies, keepsakes he'd collected from the scenes of his triumphs. And sitting in the stands above the hole was Dr. Tidmore, reading a book, its pages illuminated by a clip-on book light. His gray hair was gone, replaced by its original red, and his clothes were stylish and youthful. The glasses he now wore featured the same chunky frames that Adam preferred. He looked ten years younger than the man she'd known in Snope City.

"What in *the* hell?" Beau's eyes bounced back and forth between the preacher and the pit.

"Good afternoon, Haven. Hello, Beau." Tidmore looked up from his book with an amused expression on his face. He didn't appear at all perturbed by the interruption.

"What *is* this place?" Beau asked no one in particular as he continued to take in the scenery.

"It's a rat-baiting pit, Mr. Decker," Dr. Tidmore explained. "In the good old days it would have been coated in blood. Every evening men brought their prize dogs here so they could do battle with armies of rodents. Adam invented the sport. When it went out of fashion in New York, he found another use for the room."

"Skip the history lessons," Haven demanded, getting right to business. "Where's Iain?"

"Enjoying some good company." Tidmore gestured toward the figure in the pit, which had attracted a few more rats. "I told Adam I'd babysit him until he stopped struggling. Looks like my job may be over. Oops! Maybe not. I just saw a twitch."

"You were just going to let him die?" Haven asked, her voice dripping with hatred.

"I would have killed him myself if that's what Adam wanted." Tidmore took off his glasses and wiped them on his shirttails. He seemed perfectly calm and reasonable. "Don't you think you're being a little bit precious about this, Haven? Your silly boyfriend will be back soon enough. So will your father, for that matter."

"How could you murder other people just for points?" Haven snarled. "Didn't you learn *anything* in church?"

Tidmore chuckled at her naiveté. "They aren't *just* points, Haven. After this, I'll have earned enough to reach to the highest level of the OS. It's another realm entirely. There are no worries there, no unpleasantness. You live like a god. I will miss Snope City, though. It was nice having my own flock. Being important. Shaping people's opinions . . ."

"Burning down houses. Destroying lives . . ." Haven added.

"Those were just bonuses," Beau quipped.

"Well, you're just going to have to wait a bit longer to move up in the world," Haven told Tidmore. "We're here to take Iain."

"Be my guest." Tidmore opened his book once more.

"Why are you—" Haven started to ask.

"As much as I would enjoy it, I'm forbidden to hurt you," Tidmore explained without looking up. "You're Adam's queen. And you wouldn't be here unless he allowed you to be here."

Haven didn't bother to question Tidmore's story. Once she knew he could do nothing to stop her, she clambered down into the pit. As her legs sank into the muck, she tore off the ropes wrapped around the figure and rolled it out of the rug. Both of Iain's wrists were tied, and a strip of black tape covered his mouth. But his eyes were open and aware. Haven gently unsealed his mouth.

"Iain, are you okay?" she asked. A tear fell before she remembered to hate him. "Have they hurt you?"

"No, but the last few hours haven't been a whole lot of fun," Iain said as she freed his limbs.

"Then let's get out of here," Haven said. Once she had finished untying him, she turned away and reached up for Beau's hand.

"Hello, Beau," Iain said after he, too, had been pulled to the surface.

"Why does everyone in New York seem to know me?" Beau demanded.

"Not the time. Not the place," Haven told them. "Come on, you two."

"You won't make it very far," Tidmore trilled, looking up from his book. "All you're doing is delaying your destiny," he added as Haven passed by him on the way out the door. "Even your nasty old grandma knew you'd end up in bed with the devil one day."

Haven turned around, walked back to Tidmore, and punched him in the face. She bruised her knuckles in the process, but the pain felt good.

"You don't really think this is the end?" Tidmore sniggered as blood dripped from his nose. "You'll never be able to stop the Society. You have no idea how powerful Adam is or how many people he controls. There are gray men everywhere. You'll never be able to escape."

"Why don't you just sit back and watch us?" Beau said.

# CHAPTER SIXTY

Outside Rosier's house, the rain had finally stopped. Haven had expected to be greeted by at least a gray man or two, but there was no one around to prevent them from fleeing.

"Follow me," said Iain, sprinting west along Fulton Street. He didn't stop until he'd reached the front of City Hall. There, a lush garden hid the city from view. The water in the garden's fountain was dancing in the darkness, even though no one had been there to watch it.

"Is this safe?" Beau asked.

"Nothing's safe," Iain answered. "But I have a plan."

"No." Haven was finished.

"No?" Iain asked.

"Beau and I are leaving. I love you. I can't help it. That's why I saved your life, but now it's over. There's absolutely no way I could be with you after what you've done."

Iain looked crushed. "What have I done?"

"You let them corrupt you. You killed Marta Vega for points. And if you ever hurt anyone again, I will personally hand you over to Adam Rosier and let him do what he wants with you."

"I don't know what you're talking about, Haven. Marta Vega is in Mexico like I told you. I spoke with her this morning. She was on her way to a yoga class. Beau, do you have a cell phone I could borrow? We'll give her a call right now."

"No international service," Beau apologized.

"Then you'll just have to take my word for it," Iain told Haven. "Please."

"No," Haven said, beginning to walk away. She could feel the strange pull he exerted on her, and she knew if she stayed there for long, she would never be able to withstand it. "Come on, Beau."

"Stop!" Iain rushed after Haven and grabbed her arm. "Don't you see? This is what Rosier wants. That's why Tidmore let us go. Rosier thinks he's already won. But he's made a huge mistake. Please—just give me a chance to explain."

Haven turned mutely to face him.

"Hey, you know what?" Beau said awkwardly. "I'm gonna go sit over there and let you guys have your little chat." He pointed at a park bench on the other side of the fountain. "You just let me know when it's over."

Neither Haven nor Iain bothered to respond.

"Well, okay then," Beau muttered to himself.

"Do you remember when Constance told Ethan that she'd seen Rebecca at the Water Street house?" Iain asked. Haven nodded. "After that, he went down to the docks to check it out. Rosier can be hard to recognize, but when Ethan saw the house and the pit, he finally realized who was framing him for murder. With Ethan in jail, Rosier could have Constance *and* the OS. I wasn't going to let him have you—and I knew I couldn't let him destroy Strickland's Society. But we both died before I could stop him.

"For the last few years, I've been trying to finish what Ethan started. I hid my identity and got close to Padma. I was hoping to find proof of some corruption so I could expose the OS, but they do a pretty good job of keeping it under wraps. Then I saw Marta's paintings, and I knew I had the perfect opportunity. If Rosier saw her work, he'd want her to disappear. And I could offer myself for the job and get the proof I was after.

"That's when you showed up. I almost chucked the whole plan. But then that picture of us made the papers, and I knew it was only a matter of time before someone at the OS saw it. So I had to come back and see my plan through to the end."

"If that's true, why didn't you tell me?"

"I didn't even tell Marta!" Iain protested. "I had her dragged kicking and screaming out of her apartment. That was the only way it would look real enough to convince Padma—and the only way Marta could escape from the OS for good."

"But why didn't you tell *me*, Iain?"

"Because Ethan told Constance who Rosier was and he killed them both. I couldn't let that happen again. You were safer knowing as little as possible."

"Rosier didn't kill Constance and Ethan," Haven said. "He told me he would never have hurt her. I believe him."

"Then who killed them?" Iain asked with a convincing show of confusion. "Was the fire really just an accident?"

"No. It wasn't an accident. And at this point there's still only one suspect," Haven said.

"Ethan?"

"Who else?"

Iain sighed. "I can't prove Ethan's innocence. But I can prove that I was trying to trap Padma. I recorded all of our conversations with my phone. Adam's men took it when they grabbed me, but I have most of the files downloaded onto my computer. Unfortunately, it's still at the mews house, and it's too dangerous to go back to get it."

"It doesn't matter," Haven said. She didn't care if it killed her. She had to know the truth. "We're going."

## CHAPTER SIXTY-ONE

When they drove past in the taxi, Washington Mews was quiet. The rain had stopped, and nothing seemed to move. Even the flowers in the window boxes remained perfectly still. Something was wrong, but Haven couldn't put a finger on it. It felt staged—like a movie set constructed from painted plywood with nothing behind the buildings' facades but the scaffolding that held them in place.

"That place is exactly how you described it, Haven" Beau marveled. "It's like something out of a fairy tale. Where are we going, anyway?"

"Here," Iain said, and the driver pulled to the curb. They were now three blocks away from the mews. "There's no telling who's watching the house, so we'll have to go in the back way."

The first rays of light had already begun to slink down the streets. The three of them walked with their backs to the rising sun. When they reached the corner of Eighth Street and University Place, Iain pointed to the courtyard with the fire escape that led to the roof.

"This is where Haven and I part ways with you," he told Beau.

"Would you mind hanging out by the entrance to the mews and keeping an eye out for anyone unusual? At this time of day that includes pretty much everyone."

"I'm thinking I should go with you guys," Beau said. "I'm not sure it's a good idea to leave Haven alone with you yet."

"He's a little overprotective," Haven explained to Iain. She looked up at Beau. "I'll be fine," she promised.

"He's always been that way," Iain remarked. "I wouldn't expect it to change anytime soon."

"How do you know what I've *always* been like?" Beau was annoyed. "We've known each other for half an hour."

"We've known each other for at least five hundred years," Iain corrected him. "You were her brother when we first met. It took you a while to warm up to me back then, too."

"Beau was my *brother*?" Haven said.

"I've never heard anything that made more sense," Beau drawled. "Nobody but family would treat me as badly as she does."

"How do I treat you badly?" Haven started to argue.

"Perhaps you two could finish this later?" Iain broke in. "Beau, will you please watch the entrance for us?"

"What should I do if I see anyone suspicious?"

"Kick a car," Iain said.

"Kick a car?"

"To set off the alarm."

"Gotcha," Beau said. "Good thinking."

HAVEN AND IAIN were up the fire escape, over the roofs, and into the house in no time. On the first floor, they found Iain's laptop sitting on the living room desk.

"This is it," Iain said. "Let's go."

"No. I want to hear it." Haven's whole life depended on what Iain had recorded. She couldn't wait any longer.

"Haven, it's not safe," Iain argued. "We can listen to it somewhere else."

"Go ahead and leave," she told him, cracking open the computer. "But I'm not going anywhere until I hear the files."

An alarm went off in the distance. Then another and another. The sound of a motor grew louder. Haven ran to the windows and tore open the curtains. Outside in the lane were two men on a motorcycle, their faces hidden behind dark helmets. The one on the back took a bottle from his backpack, lit a wick made from a scrap of fabric, and tossed it. Haven heard glass shatter, and she fell to the ground.

*She ran to the window when she smelled the smoke. Somewhere nearby a building was on fire. Someone was standing below her window. With her face turned to the sky, the girl looked radiant. When Rebecca smiled, Constance understood. It was her own house that was burning. By the time she turned from the window, the flames were already getting closer. Soon she could smell her hair beginning to singe. She crashed through the room, knocking over furniture, searching through the smoke.*

*"Ethan!" she heard herself scream. The panic took over. She couldn't get enough air. "Ethan!"*

Haven woke with arms wrapped around her. Iain had carried her to the bedroom upstairs. The smoke was getting thicker, and she heard the wail of a fire engine in the distance. "We have to get to the roof," she said coughing.

"It's too late," Iain told her. "The stairs are on fire."

"There has to be another way out," Haven insisted.

"You need to jump," Iain said. With smoke billowing around his head, he seemed to be disappearing. Haven had traveled ninety years and a thousand miles to die in the same spot as Constance Whitman.

"I'm so sorry," she whispered. "I should have trusted you."

"It's okay, Haven." Iain kissed her and pulled her to her feet. "Whatever happens, we'll be together again soon. I'll find you. I promise."

"I love you," she told him.

"And that's all that matters," he said. "Stand back." The smoke was growing so thick they could barely see. He took the chair from the vanity and used it to smash the bedroom window. Then Iain helped her out onto the windowsill. Beau was waiting below, trying to position himself to catch her. "Take this," Iain told Haven, shoving a folded piece of paper into her pocket.

"You'll jump next?" she asked.

"Of course," Iain assured her with his crazy, lopsided grin.

For a moment, Haven hesitated. Then she heard a crash behind her. When she tried to look back into the house, she slipped and fell, not feet-first but on her side. A few seconds of excruciating pain followed. She heard the sound of a fire truck in the distance, and then the world went dark.

## CHAPTER SIXTY-TWO

*She was still sitting on her steamer trunk when he finally arrived.*

*"We missed our boat," Constance said without turning around to greet him. "Where have you been?"*

*"I went to see Rebecca," he said.*

*"You did?" Her heart sank.*

*"I needed to confirm a hunch," Ethan told her. "And I did. He's back. I can't believe I didn't recognize Rosier, but it's him, Constance."*

*"I know."*

*"You know? And you didn't tell me?"*

*"We were already planning to leave, and I didn't want you to worry," Constance said. "Why did you have to talk to Rebecca?"*

*"I needed her to confess. They've been working together to break us apart. After you told me you'd followed her to that house on Water Street, I paid it a visit. That's where he lives. There's a pit in the basement. . . ."*

*"Then why did you make us miss the boat? Shouldn't we be running as far as possible?"*

*"We can't go anywhere, yet. We can't let Rosier take control of the Society. Do you have any idea what he could do with it?"*

*Constance remained quiet.*

*"He killed Strickland. Rebecca says she'll testify. We have to keep him away from the OS."*

"OH GOOD. YOU'RE awake."

Haven instantly knew something was wrong. Her hand brushed against her right leg. It felt rigid and rough. "Where am I?" she asked.

"Saint Vincent's hospital. You've had an accident."

As her eyes adjusted, Haven began to make out the silhouette of a nurse. The curtains were closed, and the room was lit by the flashing buttons and screens of a dozen machines. "Where's Iain?" Haven demanded.

"I'm sorry?" The lights came on.

"My boyfriend. Iain Morrow."

The nurse lost all color in her face, and Haven saw her press the intercom button and speak into the microphone. "Can I get the doctor in here, please?"

"What are you doing?" Haven asked, struggling to sit up before the dread could drown her. "What happened to Iain? Where are my clothes?"

"They're in the closet, but you won't be able to wear them," the nurse warned her. "They had to cut them off you when you got to the hospital. Your leg was badly broken."

"Where is my friend Beau?" Haven demanded. "I want to see him!"

"He's just outside, Miss Moore." The nurse was using a tone of voice usually reserved for children and the insane. "I'll find him right after you have a talk with the doctor."

"I don't want to see the damn doctor!" Haven yelled. "Go get Beau!"

A young man in scrubs and a white lab coat appeared in the doorway.

"Good afternoon, Haven." At the sound of the voice, goose bumps erupted on Haven's flesh. Adam Rosier pulled a chair over to her bed-side. With his carefully groomed appearance and shiny stethoscope, he looked like the star of a hospital-themed soap opera. His name tag read DR. DENTON.

"Don't leave me here with him!" Haven screamed at the nurse. "Get Beau!"

"Please," Adam said as the nurse left the room and closed the door behind her. "Don't make me give you a sedative. I'm only here to apologize."

"Your men nearly killed me!"

"I'm so sorry, Haven. They've both been punished. They can be a little reckless sometimes. But in their defense, they did think the house was empty."

"I'm sure Rebecca thought the house was empty when you had *her* burn it down, too."

"Rebecca?" Adam blinked.

"I had a vision. I saw her do it," Haven said. "Rebecca killed Constance and Ethan."

"You must be mistaken," Adam insisted. "I assure you that I had nothing to do with your last death. And Rebecca would never have acted on her own."

"Never? You're so sure? She wanted to stop Constance and Ethan from leaving the city. So she convinced Ethan that she had evidence that you killed Strickland. But instead of delivering it, she set my house on fire. She only meant to kill me, of course, but she ended up getting two for the price of one."

"That's impossible," Adam repeated. "Rebecca was specifically instructed not to hurt you."

"I guess she's not so good at obeying orders then," Haven said, "because yesterday Padma was trying to hire Iain to kill me again."

Rosier remained as calm as ever, but Haven knew Padma was as good as dead. "If what you say is true, I swear she'll pay dearly for it." He took Haven's hand and her flesh crawled. "But you must believe that *I've* never tried to harm you. The only reason I destroyed your house was to get rid of the link to your past. Now there will be one less place to look for him when he's back. Not that it should matter, of course. The cycle has finally been broken. But I do like to be careful."

"When he's back?" Haven asked.

"Hey!" someone bellowed. "Get the hell out of here." Beau was standing at the door.

"Mr. Decker," Adam greeted him. "You are quickly becoming the bane of my existence. Shall I call hospital security and have you thrown out on the street?"

"Be my guest." The way Beau's fists were clenched Haven could see he was itching for a fight. "But I'd think twice if I were you. See, I happen to be in possession of some recordings that my friend Iain Morrow made. I had a listen this morning, and it seems to me like your little club might be in a whole lot of trouble if the *New York Times* gets a hold of them. He's got the president of your club ordering up a murder in no uncertain terms. And it seems she gave him a membership list, too. A lot of famous people are going to be *pretty* embarrassed if I decide to make trouble for you."

"What do you want?" Rosier snarled.

"I want you to leave Haven alone," Beau demanded. "And if I catch one of your creepy-looking friends snooping around, I promise you and he both'll regret it. Now get the hell out of here."

Rosier stood and smiled adoringly at Haven. He wasn't giving up the war—he was merely conceding the battle.

"I hate to leave you, my darling, but perhaps it's better this way. I'll never win your heart in this life, but now that I no longer have a rival to lure you away, you'll soon come to me of your own free will. We'll be together for the rest of eternity. So until then," he said, lifting Haven's hand and planting a cold kiss on it. "I'll be waiting for you as always."

"Did you hear what I just told you?" Beau barked.

"WHY DID YOU make a deal with him?" Haven asked once Rosier was gone. "We've got to get those recordings to the newspaper. We have to expose the OS."

"There are no recordings," Beau whispered. "The computer was destroyed in the fire."

"And the membership list?"

"I just made up that part. But I did find one thing after you fell." Beau reached into his back pocket and pulled out the folded piece of paper that Iain had given Haven only moments before she'd jumped.

Haven opened it up and found a picture of a couple embracing, surrounded by tall grass that hid them from view. It was the print Iain had bought her in Rome.

Suddenly, the desire to see Iain nearly dragged her out of bed, broken leg and all. She had to hold him, kiss him, apologize a thousand times for the things she had done. He had continued to love her while her faith in him had been shaken. That was all the proof she needed that Iain Morrow was whom Constance had meant for her to find.

"Where's Iain?" Haven asked Beau. She tried to keep the question casual despite the emotions that were raging inside of her. "Did you tell him about the computer?"

"Umm." Beau couldn't look up from his hands.

"What?" Haven demanded. "Is Iain hurt? Is he in this hospital?"

"Umm," Beau repeated. "Haven, I really hate to have to tell you this. Iain never made it out of the fire."

## CHAPTER SIXTY-THREE

The renovated Snively house peered down at Snope City like a diva in a fancy new gown. Its second story was even grander than it had been before the fire, with two fairy-tale turrets instead of one. The paint was a fresh, blinding white, and the crimson azaleas that circled the building were still in full bloom. Imogene's contractors had worked wonders in the three months that Haven had been gone.

As Beau's truck began the climb up the hill to her grandmother's house, Haven smoothed her skirt and flexed her right leg. Maybe they should have waited longer to travel, she thought. Her leg had been free of its cast for a couple of days, and it still felt stiff and unfamiliar. But Beau had to report to Vanderbilt soon, and Haven had no reason to complain. She knew how unjust it was that her body could mend itself in a few months while Iain's would never recover at all.

THE DAY SHE'D been discharged from the hospital, Haven had returned to the mews house. There was nothing more than a black hole where the building had once been. The neighboring dwellings, however, had scarcely been touched. It looked as though the house had been rooted out with surgical precision, like a tumor or a rotten tooth.

Haven had stayed for over an hour, standing in the lane and staring at the ruins—accepting the searing pain in her broken leg as a punishment for her starring role in Iain's death. It was her lack of trust, her faithlessness that had killed him. If Haven had only believed Iain's story, they would never have returned to the mews house. Haven closed her eyes, but she couldn't feel Iain's presence among the charred chunks of wood and plaster. She feared the cycle had finally been broken—that this time around she'd lost him for good.

THE NEXT MORNING, Beau drove her to Iain's funeral, but they didn't go inside. Instead, they sat outside Grace Church and watched Iain's rich relatives console one another with prim kisses and pats on the back. Police had corralled a hundred young women behind blue barriers, where they screamed and moaned for someone they'd never known. Haven's eyes remained dry. The pain and guilt were far too intense for tears.

A blonde in a sleeveless black dress and sunglasses crossed the street in front of Beau's truck. When her head turned in their direction, Haven saw her do a double take and hurry over to the passenger window.

"I read about it in the paper," Frances Whitman told Haven. "It happened again, didn't it?"

Haven simply nodded.

"I'm very, very sorry, Constance," Frances said. "Maybe next time—"

Haven stopped her. "There might not be a next time," she said.

FOR THE FIRST WEEK after the funeral, Beau and Haven stayed at the Windemere Hotel. Haven never left the room. She spent most of the day staring down at the street below. Once in a while, Haven would imagine she'd spotted a gray man lurking in the crowd. But then the man would greet a child fondly or hand a dollar bill to a homeless person, and Haven would exhale with relief. Adam Rosier appeared to be keeping his promise. And according to the local news, Padma Singh had disappeared. The police suspected foul play.

Later, on one of her few trips to the other side of the street, Haven was cornered by a man in a suit. With her savings running low, she and Beau were living on energy bars and coffee from the deli across from the Windemere. The man found her in the soda aisle and greeted her by name. Haven was about to bean him with her crutches when he handed her his card. He worked for a law firm in Midtown, and he'd been looking for her. Haven Moore had inherited the Morrow family fortune.

MAE MOORE RAN out of the house at the first sound of a truck making its way up the long, steep driveway. Before Beau could turn off the engine, she opened Haven's door and scooped her daughter out of the passenger seat and into a hug.

"You're so skinny," she said, holding Haven back to take a look at her. "You look like you haven't eaten anything in months."

"That's why I brought her down here," Beau said. "I figured you'd be the perfect person to fatten her up."

"You want to come in, Beau?" Mae asked him. "I just made some chicken."

"No, thank you, ma'am," Beau said. "I'm looking forward to seeing my dad again."

"He must be awfully proud of you," Mae beamed. "Going to Vanderbilt on a scholarship and all. I guess he's going to have to learn how to make do without you."

Beau gave Haven a secret smile. Only the two of them knew that Haven would be the one footing the Vanderbilt bill—with the money she'd inherited from Iain. It seemed fitting, Haven thought. They were related, after all.

"Oh, I suspect my dad will manage pretty well," Beau said, starting the engine up. He seemed eager to get away. "Haven, I'll stop by the house tomorrow. Good luck."

Haven couldn't help but grin when she followed Beau's eyes to the front door where a little old lady stood in a prim flowered dress buttoned all the way to her chin. To Haven's surprise, she seemed nervous. Dr. Tidmore's unexplained disappearance had clearly shaken her.

"Hello, Imogene. Like what you've done to the house." The dusty air had cleared, and the dark antiques had been replaced by furniture more suited to the twenty-first century.

"Good thing I always kept up on those insurance payments," her grandmother said. "You can have the same room if you want it. I was going to turn it into a hobby center, but your mama was convinced you'd be coming back."

"Don't worry, Imogene," Haven told her. "I may be back, but I'm not staying for long. You'll have your hobby center before you know it."

Haven left her grandmother in the foyer and took the stairs two at a time. On the second floor, at the end of the hall, her bedroom door stood open. The new furniture was stunning—dark mahogany wood accented by rich blue fabrics. She pulled her Rome print out of her handbag and propped it up on the desk.

"I forgot to tell you, Haven." Mae Moore was standing in the doorway. "Some girl stopped by the house before you got here. I wrote her name down in the living room."

"Leah Frizzell?"

"That's the one. I told her you were on your way to Snope City, and she invited you up to her church tomorrow. She said you two could hike down to the falls afterward. Of course, your grandmother would like it if you'd come to church with us in the morning. The new preacher's giving his first sermon."

"You've *got* to be kidding me."

"Well, I told her it was a long shot, but I said I'd give it a try," Mae Moore said. "So what do you think? Do you like your new room?"

"You did a good job picking everything out," Haven told her. "The room's beautiful."

"I didn't do a thing," Mae confessed. "You know I don't have any talent for decorating. Your grandmother chose everything in here herself."

"But I thought she said she wanted to turn it into a hobby center."

"Now you don't believe that, do you?" Mae chuckled. "When did Imogene Snively ever have a hobby other than getting her hair done? She did this for *you*. She cares about you, Haven."

"Humph," Haven said to disguise the fact that she felt a little touched. "She's sure got a funny way of showing it."

"Well," Mae said in a hushed voice, "don't quote me, but I suspect she's just a little bit jealous. You know she was only about a year older than you are when she had me, don't you?"

"Sure," Haven said. "But didn't most people have kids a lot earlier back then?"

"I don't think Imogene has ever considered herself 'most people,' do you?"

Haven laughed.

"She was supposed to go off to college," Mae continued. "She didn't think accidentally getting pregnant could change all that. But your grandfather found out and conspired with her parents to keep her in Snope City. They locked her in one of the rooms here until she agreed to marry Jimmy Snively. I don't think she ever got over it."

"Grandpa held Imogene prisoner until she married him?" It all sounded a little too familiar. "Why didn't she go to the police?"

"Snope City was different back then. Families could get away with that kind of thing. Your grandmother's parents thought she was wild, so they decided to break her. And they did." Mae paused to straighten a tiny wrinkle in the bedspread. "Mama's always been the kind of lady that needed a lot of fire and passion in her life. She didn't get it from love, so she found it in the church. But I think there are certain times when she gets a bit jealous. Like when I met Ernest—or when you were about to go off to school."

Tears began to well in Haven's eyes at the mention of her father's name. She needed to find a way to tell her mother what she had learned. She'd thought about it the whole drive home, but she hadn't found a solution. "What's that?" she asked instead, pointing to a large cardboard box that was sitting under the window.

"That? Oh, that's what was left after the disaster. The fire department wouldn't let me back into the house, so I snuck in early one morning after they'd moved all the furniture out and picked up anything that could be saved."

"Was it the day I left for New York?" Haven asked.

"Yes, I suppose it was. Why do you ask?"

"I think I saw you." Haven smiled.

"Well, thank goodness nobody else did! And here I was thinking I'd been so discreet." Mae Moore hauled the cardboard box to the center of the room and opened the top. The acrid smell of smoke rose from within. "I tried airing this stuff out, but it didn't do any good."

Haven peeked inside, half afraid to be confronted by the last remaining mementos of her first seventeen years. There were various knickknacks—Haven's favorite hair clip from the fourth grade, a homemade Christmas ornament, a bow from a dress she'd sewn when she was twelve. Haven picked out a small photo album, many of its plastic sheets melted together by the heat of the fire. She reached inside one of the sleeves and pulled out a folded sheet of wrapping paper and a picture of her mother and father posing in Imogene's yard with their brand-new daughter. Haven opened the paper and found her father's handwriting.

*This morning at four o'clock, I heard someone walking through the house. I grabbed my rifle and went downstairs, thinking it might be a burglar. Just when I got to the living room, I saw a tiny figure leaving through the front door. I put the gun aside and ran out on the front lawn just in time to see Haven start walking down the road. She had her little suitcase with her and one of her dolls.*

*When I caught up with her, she looked up at me like there was nothing unusual about what she was doing. "Hi, Daddy," she said.*

*"Well, hey there, Haven," I said. "Where you off to?"*

*"New York."*

*"That's an awful long way," I said. "And it's pretty cold outside."*

*"I know, but I can't wait anymore. I need to find Ethan. He's waiting for me."*

*"Don't you suppose you ought to wait till you're older?"*

*She thought about the question. "How much older?"*

*"Oh, I don't know. Eighteen, maybe?"*

*"What should I do until then?"*

*"I guess you could spend that time getting ready. You don't want to go up there and not be prepared, do you?"*

*"You're right," she told me with the most serious expression on her face. "I need to be prepared this time."*

*Then she let me pick her up and carry her back into the house. Within five minutes, she was back asleep.*

HAVEN STARED at the sheet of paper as her heart broke once more.

"It gets easier," Mae Moore tried to assure her. "It's best to keep yourself occupied for a little while."

"Mama, I've got something to tell you," Haven said. "I can't give you any proof that what I say is true. I can't even tell you how I found out."

"This is sounding pretty ominous, Haven!" Mae Moore joked nervously.

"Daddy never had an affair with Veronica Cabe."

"Now, Haven . . ." her mother started.

"No, hear me out," Haven insisted. "Veronica Cabe was brought to Snope City to tempt him. It didn't work. He loved you so much that he barely even knew that woman *existed*."

Mae Moore couldn't seem to figure out whether she should be shocked, offended, or both. "What are you *talking* about? *Who* brought Veronica here? How do you know all of this?"

"I told you I couldn't tell you," Haven said. "But Daddy sent a letter to the wrong people, and they made it all happen. The rumors about Veronica—even the accident—they were behind it all. Dr. Tidmore was the one who did the dirty work."

"Haven, that's just ridiculous!" Mae exclaimed.

"Why do you think he didn't come back to Snope City?" Haven said. "Preachers don't just up and quit like that. Believe me, Mama. *Please*. When I was in New York, I met the man who ordered it all. He told me everything. He told me Tidmore fixed the accident so it looked like Daddy and Veronica had been together."

"Why would someone do such a thing?" Mae whispered.

"Because he could," Haven said sadly.

## CHAPTER SIXTY-FOUR

*She was sitting on top of a hill, looking down at Rome. The afternoon sun had turned the city's structures to gold.*

*"I never thought we could get here," she said.*

*"And I had faith that we would." He took her hand and planted a kiss on it.*

*"Is it over?"*

*"For now," he said.*

## CHAPTER SIXTY-FIVE

Outside the little white church in the middle of the mountains, Haven could hear the band tuning its instruments. She felt no fear as she pushed open the doors. Leah was talking to two ladies seated in the very first pew, and Earl was lugging his box of snakes onto the platform at the front of the church. When he saw Haven making her way up the aisle, he jumped down to greet her.

"Look who we got here. Miss Haven Moore, all the way from the big city."

"Hey there, Mr. Frizzell. Leah invited me up. I hope you don't mind."

"You hope I don't mind?" The old man cackled. "This is the Lord's house, not mine. Anyone he brings up that road is welcome to stop in."

"Well, thank you, anyway, Mr. Frizzell."

"We heard you had some trouble up there in New York City, that right?"

"Yes, sir," Haven confirmed.

Earl looked Haven over. "I don't see any battle scars. Looks like you came away in pretty good shape."

"Looks can be deceiving, Mr. Frizzell."

"So they can," he agreed. "Wounded on the inside, are you? We'll see if we can't do something about that today."

"I wish you could, Mr. Frizzell, but I'm afraid it's hopeless."

"Now don't let me hear you saying things like that, Haven Moore. Nothin's ever *hopeless*. Leah!" he called out to his niece. "Come on over here and see to your friend. Haven, if you'll excuse me, I'm going to get started with the sermon."

"Hi, Haven," Leah said, sounding unusually chipper. "You got your things for after the service?"

"Yeah. But I thought y'all weren't supposed to go swimming and stuff on the Sabbath."

"This is different," Leah promised.

"MORNIN'." EARL FRIZZELL took the microphone, and the church went quiet. "Y'all probably recognize our guest today. Her name's Haven Moore. She visited with us a few months ago back when everybody in town thought she'd come down with a demon. Since then she's been away, and she's battled far worse than demons. She may look okay on the outside, but from what she tells me, sounds like her faith is running low. So I figure the best way we can help is to teach Haven Moore a few of the things we know about the subject."

He reached into the wooden box that sat by his feet and pulled out a three-foot snake. Its tail shook so fast, it was only a blur, and the sound of rattling filled the room. It coiled around Earl's hands, but it did not strike.

"It says in the Bible, '*In my name shall they cast out devils; they shall speak with new tongues. They shall take up serpents; and if they drink any deadly thing, it shall not hurt them.*'"

He transferred the snake to one hand and held it over his head. "*This* is faith. And it don't make a lick of sense to most people. You go to the library, and every book you find about rattlesnakes will tell you that this creature should've given me a nasty bite by now. But I *believe* it won't. At least not until the good Lord decides it's my time to go.

"You see, faith means listening to your heart, not just your head. It's not about ignoring facts; it's about being willing to see around them sometimes. The *fact* is, this snake could kill me. There is *no* disputing that. But I have faith that the Lord will protect me. And as y'all see, I'm still standing here.

"There are some people out there who think you can understand everything. They think that if you read a whole bunch of books or go to church every Sunday you'll know exactly how the world works. But not a single one of them could tell me how come this snake hasn't killed me. Or how Leah can give prophecy. Or why Haven Moore has visions of places she's never seen. They may *think* they understand how God works, but if we were able to understand how God works, we wouldn't need faith, now would we?"

Earl gently returned the snake to its box. "The problems come when it's time to put our faith in things other than the Lord. There's no doubt that other people can be tricky. But once again, it's all about listening to your heart. That don't mean you should ignore what your head's telling you. But your heart will do a much better job of helping you figure out who's good and who ain't. Who deserves your faith, and who doesn't. If you judge solely by evidence, you could wind up making some big mistakes.

"Love and faith go hand in hand. You can't have one without the other. And as we all know, taking that leap ain't always safe. Sometimes you judge poorly, and you land right on your face. But unless you make the jump, you'll never know what's on the other side. You just gotta find the guts to do it.

"Now let's turn it over to the band and see what the Lord has to tell us today." As a fast-paced gospel tune began to play, he stepped down off the platform and walked over to Haven. "That mean anything to you?" he asked.

"It did," Haven told him. "Thank you."

"Think you might be up for giving one of our snakes a spin now?"

Haven racked her brain, trying to come up with a polite excuse.

Earl Frizzell's smile grew wider, and Haven's face turned red. "Don't you know when somebody's fooling with you?" he cackled.

## CHAPTER SIXTY-SIX

"Careful," Leah warned. "These hills are full of copperheads, you know."

They were inching down the side of the mountain, their sneakers slipping on the slick, muddy trail and weeds slapping against their thighs.

"So I guess you're off to Duke in a couple of days," said Haven, just to make conversation. "Beau's going to Vanderbilt, you know. I can't tell you how jealous I am of you two. I'll probably be stuck here in Snope City for the rest of my life."

"I doubt it," Leah told her. "You've got a few adventures to finish."

"You sound like you know what you're talking about."

"I've seen some things," Leah said. Haven waited for the girl to elaborate, but she didn't.

"So what are you going to be studying at Duke?"

"Physics. It's been my favorite subject since I was little. It kind of comes naturally to me. Sometimes I think I might have been a physicist in another life."

"*You* think? But I thought Christianity and reincarnation weren't compatible."

Leah smiled at Haven over her shoulder. "My faith is big enough to accept all of God's wonders."

They walked in silence, and neither spoke until they reached the stream that led to the falls.

"You met him, didn't you?" Leah asked.

"Who?"

"The one I told you about."

"Yes," Haven said. "He ruined my life."

"You were tested," Leah said.

"And I failed," Haven told her.

"You couldn't have failed. You're here, aren't you?"

"I lost the only thing that mattered to me."

"You're sure about that?" Leah asked.

"Yeah," Haven said sadly.

At the end of the stream, the woods opened and revealed the granite pool. Haven kicked off her sneakers and peeled off her shorts and T-shirt. She laid her towel out on the rock and dived into the dark, cool water. She pulled herself out by the waterfall and watched the vapor rising from the bottom. Then she lay down on her towel and closed her eyes. She tried to ignore a rustling in the woods.

"What is that?" she asked Leah, but there was no answer.

Haven opened her eyes and propped herself up on one arm.

"Leah?" she called. The girl was gone. "Hello?"

A figure emerged at the edge of the woods. Haven blinked. Iain looked tired and thinner than he had in New York, and there was a scar on his temple where a wound had healed. Dressed in jeans and a simple white T-shirt, he was the most beautiful sight Haven had ever seen. She ran across the edge of the pool, only inches from where the water spilled over the side, hoping she wouldn't discover he was just a mirage. When Iain caught her, she felt every nerve in her body explode with pleasure.

## EPILOGUE

Haven opened the door to find an older woman standing in the hallway of the apartment building, proudly holding out a bank envelope.

"We sold four more today, Miss Haven!"

"It's just *Haven*, Lucetta. Four more of the blue dress?"

"And a black strapless and an emerald."

"You're kidding!"

"I don't joke about money," replied the Italian woman, fingering the multiple gold chains she always wore around her neck.

"Well, either I'm one hell of a designer or you're one hell of a saleswoman," Haven said.

"I think both," Lucetta said smugly, turning to leave.

AFTER SPENDING SIX MONTHS hiding out at the Decker farmhouse, Iain and Haven had moved to Rome one week after Haven turned eighteen. Just past midnight on her first night in the city, Iain blindfolded Haven and led her through the streets. When they stopped, and the blindfold was lifted, Haven had found herself in front of a tiny boutique that bore her own name. Iain had even hired Lucetta, Haven's first employee. They'd hit it off the moment they met.

Of course, Haven's decision to move to Rome had not been warmly received by Mae Moore. She made Haven swear that she'd enroll in college before she turned twenty. And Imogene was certain that her granddaughter would fall under the influence of Catholics. But it was Haven's money that was going to pay for the plane tickets, and eventually they both had to accept the inevitable.

HAVEN PASSED THROUGH the kitchen on her way to the balcony, where Iain was reading an Italian newspaper.

"I checked on dinner," she told him. "It looks like it's done."

"Come here," he said, dropping the paper and pulling her down on his lap. "It's done when *I* say it's done." She giggled as he kissed her.

They hadn't spoken of Constance or Ethan since the day Iain had materialized at Eden Falls. Nor had they discussed any of their other lives. With the past behind them, there was nothing left to haunt their relationship. Everyone believed Iain Morrow was dead—and by all rights he should have been. If he had been two feet to the left when the roof of the mews house collapsed, it would have crushed him rather than providing him with a means of escape.

Iain couldn't make contact with Haven while she remained in New York. The Society might have been watching, and the police still considered him the lead suspect in the death of Jeremy Johns. So he hid out in Mexico with Marta Vega before helping her get settled in Paris. At last, using funds he'd carefully stashed away some years before, he traveled to Snope City, where the first person to greet him had been an unusual girl with red hair. She told him she'd known he was coming.

Marta was now living drug-free in an apartment not far from the

Louvre. But being clean and sober hadn't brought much cheer to Marta's art. Her housewarming present to Iain had been another dark and twisted work that showed two people surrounded by an angry mob. As always, a tiny figure in black stood watching from a distance. Iain kept the painting in a closet in the hallway.

Neither Iain nor Haven had uttered the name of the man in black for months. Haven focused on her designs, while Iain played dead. Beau called regularly from Vanderbilt, but there had been next to no news of Adam Rosier or Padma Singh. In the best moments, it felt as if they were both gone for good.

"GO FINISH DINNER," Haven ordered. "The table's set, and I'm starving to death."

"In a second. Take a look at the light." With the sun setting, the roofs of Rome were golden. Iain put his arm around Haven and pulled her to him.

"I'm glad we're back," Haven told him.

When Iain stepped inside the apartment, the wind caught the paper he'd left on the balcony. It whipped the pages apart and sent them flying in every direction. Haven gathered as many as she could, crumpling them to her chest. The front page fluttered off the balcony before she could reach it. She watched it drift down to the cobblestones, where it landed at the feet of a figure strolling through the Piazza Navona. Tall, trim, and dressed in black, the man quickly passed below the balcony. Just as he turned down the Via Giustiniani, he stopped in a shadow and smiled up at Haven. It was growing dark, and the young man's features were blurry. But Haven couldn't quite shake the feeling that she'd seen him before.

"Haven," Iain called out to her. She turned to see him standing in the warm light of the apartment. "Come inside."

Thank you to all those who helped make this book possible:

Ben Schrank and Anne Heltzel at Razorbill

The incomparable Suzanne Gluck

Sarah Ceglarski

Jin Ai Yap

Katherine and Albert Miller

Darcy Devine

Steven and Georgia Daly